W9-CDY-122

THE EMPEROR'S KNIFE

THE EMPEROR'S KNIFE

BOOK ONE OF THE TOWER AND KNIFE TRILOGY

MAZARKIS WILLIAMS

NIGHT SHADE BOOKS
SAN FRANCISCO

First Edition

ISBN: 978-1-59780-384-7

Night Shade Books
http://www.nightshadebooks.com

For Phil and Shyrley

MYTHYCK

TO
YRKMIR

THE JAGGED
SEA

EASTERN
PROVINCE

A

OVINCE

D·S '11

PROLOGUE

Hands found Sarmin through the confusion of his dreams and the tangle of his sheets. Large hands, rough, closing around his arm, his leg, encompassing him, lifting. In confusion he saw the world move around him, night shades sliding over sleep-blurred eyes. He saw the trail of his bedding, a palace guard bending over Pelar's bed, Asham's bed, a man lifting little Fadil, another with baby Kashim in the crook of his arm. And Beyon, his eldest brother, led away, barefoot, wide-eyed.

A palace guard carried Sarmin on a broad shoulder. Two more walked behind, and more ahead. He almost fell asleep again. He yawned and tried to snuggle, but something kept him awake, something grim behind the men's blank faces. They took him up a long, winding stair, so many steps he thought it must reach to heaven—but it ended at a single door and the small room beyond. Without speaking, the man who carried Sarmin set him upon the bed, wide enough for him and all his brothers, though when he looked, his brothers were not there.

"Why?" Five years had not armed Sarmin with enough words for his questions.

The guardsmen left and shut the door. He heard the lock turn.

Sarmin would have slept, even then, even there in that strange room, but for a high and distant wailing. *Kashim!* His smallest brother cried, and no nurse came to quiet him.

He left the bed and pulled on the iron door handle. "Release me!" A small anger woke within him. He shook the door again and shouted, using the words Beyon would say when crossed: "I am a prince! My father is the light of heaven"

Silence. Only the thin wail of the baby reaching out, reaching up.

Sarmin looked about the room. Beside the bed they had left him a chair, set beneath a slender window. He clambered up onto the seat, stood on tiptoes, and pressed his nose to the window's alabaster pane. Nothing, just a faint blur of light offered through the translucence of the stone. Kashim's cries came clearer, though. He was outside, far below.

The hand Sarmin put to the window trembled. He wanted to break it open, to see clear, but fear held him, as though it were fire he thought to push his fingers through. Another screech and anger swallowed fear. "I am a prince! My father is the light of heaven!"

The thin pane fractured before his blow, falling in pieces onto the sill beyond. He saw only the night sky, bright with stars, until he hauled with all his strength and drew himself higher.

Torches burned in the courtyard beneath the tower, a dozen points of dancing light in the stone acres below. Figures lay on the flagstones, dark shapes in the circle of firelight, small figures, smaller than the guards who held the torches. A man stepped into the circle, picking his way over those still forms. He held a baby, white against the blackness of his cloak, naked against the night. Kashim, howling for his bed, for kindness, for arms that loved him.

"Kashim...'

The man moved his hand over Sarmin's brother. Over his neck. Something glittered in his grip. And Kashim fell silent, in the middle of his cry, just as when Mother Siri would stopper his little mouth with her breast.

The man glanced once at the tower, at the window, his look unreadable. It would be unreadable at any distance. *One more?* Did the knife-man perhaps think his work unfinished? He set Kashim on the ground, among his brothers, and Sarmin fell back into the darkness of his room.

CHAPTER ONE

Twenty paces to the north, fifteen to the west. Enough to bound a room, but few to encompass a man's world. Sarmin knew every color and touch of his soft prison. When he extended his fingers they found no iron bars or cold dungeon stone. Only the curving scrollwork along the walls, the gods fixed upon the ceiling, and the flowers carved into the door marked his barriers. Nevertheless he could not leave. He paced, his bare feet deep in silken carpet.

Only silk can bind a royal.

But other things bound him too. His memories. His dreams. His mother, sitting now on a low bench, waiting for his acknowledgement. These threads caught him so tightly that sometimes he couldn't breathe.

He paced, and his mother said nothing. She only fingered the blue gem around her neck. After sundown it would burn like blue fire in the lantern light. He remembered it dangling before his childhood eyes when she pulled the soft covers around his chin at bedtime.

But that was two lifetimes gone, and other things occupied her now. She came seldom, even in the day.

Sarmin settled on the edge of his bed and reaccustomed himself to his mother's face. Save for some spidery lines about her mouth, she could be as young as he. Hair dark as calligraphy fell around her bare breasts. They proclaimed her two sons, born alive. Even if Sarmin had perished with the others, she would have the right to show where he once suckled.

The idea of such intimacy seemed absurd to him now. Her eyes wrote a story of ruthless choices, her pupils the quill-tips. Yet she spoke humbly, as befitted a woman. "I am concerned for the emperor."

The emperor. There was something yet unbound within Sarmin after all. He felt it stir beneath his ribs. "What ails my brother?"

A flicker at the edge of her mouth. "None of his wives has quickened. We have prayed and sacrificed, and yet there is no heir." A wrinkle of her kohl-thickened eyebrows. "I am frightened for him."

Sarmin imagined Beyon's wives scurrying through the palace with both breasts covered, the scorn of the Old Wives heaped upon them. The free thing inside him twisted again.

"Then I am concerned as well, but I know nothing of medicine." Sarmin spoke the truth. He knew only this room and the five books it contained. Those books held everything he would need to know if his brother died: the histories, the gods, how to eat roast pimicons with a tiny spoon. But that was not the reason for his reply. His soft room didn't fool him into thinking the palace had no sharp edges.

She watched him. He laid his hands on the cool fabric of his sheets and waited.

"I have found you a wife," she said.

His hands curled around the silk.

To everything there is a season. A time to be born, and a time to lie still in the courtyard with your blood draining through a slit throat. A time to pace. Fifteen by twenty, fifteen by twenty. Time enough to pace, to walk off youth, to count away a hidden lifetime. A time to marry.

"My son?"

My son.

"If it is time, then I will marry. Emperor willing." The last he said with emphasis.

It made no difference to her. "I will make the arrangements." She stood, whip-thin, one eye reproving him. "Do you not stand when the Empire Mother stands?"

Sarmin hastened to his feet. *Etiquette.* It was a small title for a most heavy book, the largest of his five. He even knew the page, four hundred and eleven, two hundred and six pages beyond the eating of pimicons: "Rarely is it seemly for a noble man to notice a woman at court, but when a woman ranks sufficiently high above one, even the nobly born must offer courtesies."

She turned from him and went to the door. There had once been warmth at partings, in a time before the world shrank to this single room. He remembered softness and enfolding arms as one remembers a taste or scent. Maybe it had never been so. In many empty hours he named everything "before" a false dream, the delusion of a sick mind. But now…

"Mother?"

Her gaze fell upon him like hard words. No softness there. Young Sarmin had died with his brothers. A ghost inhabited this room.

He dipped one shoulder to her. "Never mind."

For the slightest moment something tugged at her face. She was, after all, the one who had saved him. "I will send a new book," she said.

A knock, the creak of hinges, and she was gone.

Alone again as always, Sarmin paced the worn track of his days. He walked beneath the impassive gaze of the gods. He knew better than to ask them what would come, though the question fluttered behind his lips. The gods never answered. The others watched him, hidden, but he would wait for the privacy of full night to summon them forth.

As the window's glow faded, his slaves arrived: one pale as paper, the other dark as ink, and though ink and paper spoke together in books there was never a word between these two. They were stories untold, tantalising and mysterious.

Paper kept his eyes lowered to his tasks and obeisances. His arms were thin and looked translucent as the alabaster window. Ink's arms were stronger, and he met Sarmin's eyes with his own, dark brown and intelligent. Usually it made Sarmin's breath catch, but tonight he felt immune to such minimal contact.

The slaves carried lanterns.

Sarmin looked to Ink. "No light," he said.

The two left as quietly as they came, bowing their way backwards to the door. Sarmin noticed how Paper hesitated, letting Ink exit before him. The low voices of the guards in the hallway wafted towards Sarmin like exotic scents. The door closed and the lock turned.

All fell quiet.

The jewelled colors of Sarmin's room faded into the night, his window lit with moon-glow. Once, this room had been salvation. He had punched through that window and seen his brothers sprawled upon the courtyard stone. They died, and he had been saved, a loose thread held against an unknown future.

"Your father is dead." She had come at last, days later, and with those words his mother had changed his world.

He thought he had been saved. But he had only exchanged a quick death for a slow one.

Sarmin missed the high laughter of his brothers, the wild chases, the fights: all of it. One night took them all. Five given to the assassin's knife and one transformed. Beyon, whom he'd worshipped as an eldest brother, now elevated to the Petal Throne. Truly a living god, though surely none adored him as Sarmin had before their father died. How would he seem now, after the slow passage of fifteen years? Sarmin tried to imagine Beyon's smile on an emperor's face, but could see only the grim mask their father wore. Even now the memory made him tremble, but with fear or rage he could not tell.

No matter what his mother said, whatever memory of love flickered over her face, his solitude held the truth of it. The old bitterness soothed his mind and he nursed it, letting it sink its fangs deep.

In the dark, the free thing inside him beat stunted, heavy wings. He rolled to his side and searched for the hidden ones. They might answer his questions.

But a noise distracted him. At first, he thought he imagined it. He lay on his side a while longer, studying the scrollwork, but it came again. Below the distant wind-wail of the Tower-wizards, a soft scratching. And again, too deliberate for any mouse, a scrape of steel on stone.

He knew every crack and seam in these walls. How many days had he spent searching for an escape? Would they total a year? Two? He'd have found a trigger the size of a hair by now; of this he felt sure. But when he raised himself on an elbow, eyes searching the gloom, he discerned a quill's width of flickering light, growing impossibly larger.

An opening.

A man, silhouetted by torchlight, came through the wall. In one hand he held a dacarba; Sarmin recognised the long knife from a picture in his *Book of War.* It had a narrow blade, sharp enough to slide between the ribs and pierce a man's heart, made three-sided for extra harm.

Sarmin sat up and slid from the bed to the soft floor. His turn had come around at last. A squeal of a laugh escaped his lips, though part of him despaired. Perhaps he would finally be free.

The assassin leaned against the wall, closing the secret door with his back. *A time to die.*

The man must have seen something in Sarmin's expression, for he grimaced and sheathed his knife. "Please excuse the weapon, Your Highness," he said. "The door trigger is on the inside, a shaft the length of a dacarba's blade."

Your Highness. He was Prince Sarmin, next in line to the throne, and he bent knee to no one but the emperor. If he knew nothing else, held no other power, there was that.

"Who addresses me?" Sarmin summoned the authority he remembered from his father's voice and made his eyes like his mother's.

"Tuvaini, my lord. I am Lord High Vizier." Tuvaini stepped forwards, his face shadowed and indistinct. "I have come to discuss a matter of empire."

Sarmin laughed again. "Empire? This is my empire." He swept the room's span with one arm.

"You remain here because that may not always be true, my lord." Tuvaini held himself motionless, his face bland.

Sarmin was a spare, a replacement, a contingency plan for other men. He'd known it for years, but to hear the words out loud in this silent place… He looked at his hands, balled into fists, hands that had never touched a real blade.

"Two visitors in a day," Sarmin said. "There have been months when I had not so many." He crossed the room to face Tuvaini. The man stood an inch or two taller, and the planes of his face caught the moonlight.

An acid thrill burned Sarmin's spine. He reached towards the dacarba's sheath, but Tuvaini put a protective hand over the leather. "Give me your weapon," Sarmin said.

"My lord, I cannot." The vizier shook his head. "We have important matters—"

"You walk through my wall. You pass in secret," Sarmin cut across him. "Would you have me tell my mother of this visit? Would you have me call the guards who sit outside my door?"

"My lord, I come on a mission of great delicacy. What I have to say concerns you deeply. Your future hangs in a balance that I can sway."

They stared at one another. The moonlight made tiny pearls of the sweat on Tuvaini's brow. Another second, and he raised his hand from the knife's sheath.

Sarmin reached for the dacarba and held the triangular blade before his eyes. With the right edge, any tie might be cut, any bond broken. "But what if I pray for death?"

"My lord, please…" A tremble replaced the surety in Tuvaini's voice.

Sarmin's skin tingled. The courtier had come to trade in politics, but found a man who dealt in alien currencies. "The dacarba is mine. Your gift to me. A token of the—the *bond*—between us," Sarmin said. He set the knife upon his bed. "So, I've been remembered? My brother cannot sow the seed of dynasty no matter how fertile the fields, or how many?" Sarmin marvelled at the words flooding from him. The eaters of hashish, the men who drew opium from their hookahs, did they feel like this? And what drug had lit freedom for Sarmin? He glanced once more at the vizier and in that instant knew the answer. For so long he'd lived at the sufferance of others, under the will of silent men. And here in one glorious blaze of circumstance he held power, for the first time ever.

But he knew from the *Book of Statehood* that there would be a price.

"Why do you seek me out, Tuvaini, and at such risk? If my brother thinks you move against him, it will be the end of you."

The vizier hesitated, as if gathering strength. "It is not only to please heaven and win an heir that the emperor burns the Patterned." The certainty entered his voice again. "Your brother carries the marks now. I had it from the executioner who slew the royal body-slaves. The sands run swiftly. The time may come when it is you, and not Beyon or his son, who sits upon the Petal Throne."

Beyon. Sunlight and wood, laughter and punches; the lost joys came to him unbidden. That price was too high.

Treachery. He'd been frightened to see it in his mother's eyes, but the vizier didn't scare him. He moved in close and looked up at the man's thin nose and heavy brow. "You speak of replacing the emperor," he hissed. "Do you think I have no love for my brother?"

"Of course you love him, my lord, as do I," whispered Tuvaini, dark eyes flicking to the door. The real door. The guards outside carried heavy swords, hachirahs that could cut a man in two.

"I love our empire, and our beautiful city. Your brother is the embodiment of all that I love."

"Then why come to me? Find a doctor." Sarmin took a half-step towards the exit, towards the guards, and the vizier drew a harsh breath.

"Please, my lord, there is no cure for the patterning!"

Sarmin turned to face him again. "If I am to be emperor, you don't need to come in the night and tell me so. Why are you really here?"

Tuvaini took another breath. "Your Highness… has your mother been to see you?"

Sarmin felt it best not to share. "Why do you ask?"

Tuvaini's words tumbled out like hair from an overstuffed pillow. "It was my lord's mother who saved you. Glory be to her name, she foresaw this day. But she is a woman, my lord, and for a woman she has too many ideas. She thinks of the Felting folk to the north, and an unclean daughter there. My lord, these men are savage. They eat from besna trees and drink the milk from the mare's nipple. Your brother is marked… This cannot be the right woman for you. We cannot risk another curse."

Sarmin waited, but the man had finished. Sarmin wondered if he spoke true. He knew nothing about these men to the north. He examined the vizier's face. Tuvaini was like a book in himself. He knew of the court and of the many tribes surrounding the city. He knew about power.

And so could Sarmin. A forgotten Settu tile can set the whole game in motion. Sarmin knew the rules from the Book of War. Though he had only ever played against himself, he knew with the right alignment, one tile could clear the board.

Tuvaini glanced behind him as the secret door eased open. Someone waited beyond.

"My mother has no way to approach these people," Sarmin said. He remembered. Wives could not leave the palace, even the Old Wives.

"This is not true, my lord. Forgive me for correcting you," said Tuvaini with an unrepentant look. "Your mother is very close to one of our generals,

Arigu. It is he who carries out her wishes."

Sarmin met Tuvaini's eyes. A struggle, then, between his mother, this general, and the vizier, with Sarmin in the middle.

"You will come back next week and give me your impressions of General Arigu." Tuvaini would have to obey him; that was in the *Etiquette* book.

Tuvaini's eyes narrowed before he pressed his knees and head to the carpet. "As you wish, Your Highness," he murmured into the silk. He stood, took three steps back, and ended on the other side of the stone door. He pushed it to.

Sarmin looked with longing to the passageway, but instead he turned to the guards' door and knocked. "I wish for light." Silence answered him, but he knew the slaves would be called back, the fire would be fetched. He stood in the centre of the room. His eyes focused on the scroll-worked walls, finding the deeper pictures in the pattern, the spirits watching from complex depths. There for those with eyes to see, and time to hunt.

He unfurled before them, a new Sarmin, strong and free.

CHAPTER TWO

"Pray for an heir." Beneath the vizier's dry humour, Eyul could hear the disappointment.

Eyul pressed himself to the stonework as the vizier squeezed past. He took his lamp from the niche by the door and fell in behind. "Prince Sarmin was not as compliant as you'd hoped?"

"He is the emperor's brother, no mistaking that." Tuvaini hurried down the steep, narrow stair cut into the thickness of the tower wall. Ten turns brought them into the natural rock, the base of the oldest palace. They reached the chasm, and the vizier strode across the bridging stone without pause. Eyul's lamp made no impression on the darkness to either side of the narrow span, but he knew the hidden drop fell a good twenty yards. Tuvaini opened a lead. He was familiar with the passages and seemed spurred to haste by his anger. The distance between them grew as Eyul picked his way.

"So he told you his own plan?" That was what the emperor would have done. Eyul took a certain satisfaction in seeing Tuvaini vexed. The vizier prided himself on his composure.

"If that's what you call stealing my knife and praying for death." Tuvaini waved a hand over the empty sheath at his belt.

Eyul had noted the missing dacarba. It was his business to know where weapons were, and where they were not. With the bridge behind him, he picked up the pace.

Tuvaini slid through the maze of unlit corridors, making sudden turns, left, right, and left again, with a whisper of swirled silk.

"Few men who wish for death hold that desire to the very end." Eyul came to a halt behind Tuvaini at the Red Door. He heard the jingle of keys as the vizier fished in his robes for the required hook-twist.

"You didn't see his eyes." Tuvaini turned and pushed. The door swung inwards on noiseless hinges. He lowered his voice and repeated, "Pray for an heir."

The prince would not long survive the birth of another heir. Eyul felt the old chill reaching across his back. It was bad luck to kill the mad, but then, Eyul had never depended on luck.

"I serve the empire," he said. He stepped quickly through the doorway, into the light.

Tuvaini closed the secret door and brushed the scrolled fabric of the wall coverings to obscure the hairline cracks that remained. "The prince has bid me return to him soon. I will have to go—I can't trust in his sanity to hold him silent." He paced the circumference of the room. With each lamp he passed, his shadow leaped towards the fountain at the centre. Finally he slowed, and Eyul knew he'd found the voice he liked best to use, full of charm and regret. "It saddens me that the Empire Mother schemes against the empire. Your Knife may be forced into use, Eyul."

Eyul's hand strayed to the ancient blade at his hip. *It is not my Knife, it is a thing older and more cruel than I.* He recalled the day the old emperor had handed the weapon to him. He'd thought it an ugly thing, poorly made.

Emperor Tahal had been a delicate man, thin where Beyon was muscular, understanding where Beyon used force. He had folded Eyul's fingers about the twisted hilt and pressed his own hand against the razored edge. "Only with this holy weapon may royal blood be spilled without sin," he told him. "You enter into a divine covenant, Knife of Heaven. You are the Hand of Justice. Serve only the empire, and damnation will not befall you."

Would that were true. The young princes visited Eyul in his dreams. Every night they watched him. Every night their blood ran through his fingers. He felt their lifeless gazes upon him even now.

Eyul shook the memory from his mind. "And if the marks are true? We could have a Carrier on the petal throne."

"If the marks are true the pattern will carry Beyon from the throne." Tuvaini sat on the edge of the fountain and ran his fingers across the slick tiles. "One way or another." His voice sounded heavy, but with sadness or anticipation, Eyul couldn't tell.

Eyul listened to the play of the waters. He liked this room at the heart of the palace. During the day the fountain belonged to the women. They hung their firm, glossy legs over the sides and murmured together as they enjoyed the relief from the midday sun. The men gathered around the fountain in the evening, smoking their pipes and discussing matters of empire. All of them were mere ghosts at the time of midnight bells. In this dark hour, the fountain took on the stony feel of a tomb and offered a rare peace.

The Old Emperor had laid on Eyul a burden; the future of the empire might rest on the twisted Knife at his side. The pattern-marks had threatened the empire since the time of Beyon's grandfather. They spread from person to person, silently, imperceptibly, until hundreds died at once, the agony in their final moments surpassing any torturer's skill. By the time those blue shapes appeared on a person's skin, only two possibilities remained. The marked person either died, or changed for ever, abandoning his family and all that he loved to answer the call of the pattern. They murdered and thieved in unison, but to what end, no one could tell. Blank of face and eye, Carriers were mere shadows of their former selves, walking imitations of life. The emperor's Blue Shields endeavoured to burn all victims, purge the sickness, and leave no trace of the pattern. Fires burned throughout the city, achieving nothing but smoke and the stench of burning flesh. The marks continued to appear, coloring their way even to the emperor.

"The emperor—" Tuvaini began to speak.

A shadow passed, a flicker at the edge of Eyul's vision.

Ambush!

Tuvaini saw it too, a heartbeat later. He lifted his feet and spun into the fountain. "Treachery!" he cried. A knife blurred through the space where his head had been.

Eyul turned right, blade at the ready. Three shadows, two spreading to flank him, one advancing. Eyul danced aside from the lunge of a dagger and caught the black-clad arm behind the thrust. The emperor's Knife slid home, deep, steel in meat. *Two more.*

One circled Tuvaini, who struggled to his feet in dripping silk. The other—where had he gone? Instinct made Eyul dive forwards and the knife seeking his heart bit only his calf as he rolled clear.

The assassin loomed over him, his blade a flicker in his closed fist. Eyul spun on the floor, grabbed the man's sandal, and rose quickly, yanking up the captured foot. His foe toppled, arms flailing, head cracking when it hit the tiles. Eyul held only the shoe now, lost as the man fell. Without pause Eyul threw himself onto the prone figure, pinning knife-hand to floor, holding the man down with his whole body.

The Carrier made no move other than to open his eyes, and Eyul almost rolled clear at the sight of his fixed and unfocused pupils. Those eyes belonged on a corpse, but the body below him continued to struggle, lifting a free arm towards Eyul's face—an arm twined with blue lines, half-moons and circles. Plague marks. Eyul pushed it back. They lay leg to leg, arm to arm, intimate as lovers.

"Who sent you?" he asked, fighting the bile in his mouth. No answer. He rolled away, drawing his Knife over the Carrier's throat. So sharp neither of them really felt it.

Eyul struggled to his feet. Hot blood ran down his leg. He slipped across the marble floor towards the last attacker, who circled the fountain, wolf to Tuvaini's fox. He glanced at Eyul with those same vacant eyes and fled. Eyul shuddered and let him run, through the great archway to the Red Hall beyond.

Tuvaini glanced to his left and right and struggled to pull his wet robes over the lip of the fountain. It might have been funny, another time. "Carriers," he said, "in the game, and placing their tiles." He squeezed water from his robe. Blue dye joined with the blood upon the floor to make a royal purple.

"We need to know more. We'll put our hopes in the old hermit."

"Yes," Eyul said. Certainty overtook him. "We will."

"There's an old man who lives in the caves to the south," Dahla said. Her mouth was as busy as her needle-hand. Dahla sewed so fast, Mesema couldn't even count the stitches.

"Listen," said Dahla, though all the women were already listening. "Listen. The Cerani go to him with questions, silly questions that only a god could answer, such as, "Will I have a boy or a girl come summer?" or, "Will it rain tomorrow?" And the old man, he'll answer them. But first he'll say, "Give me your goat," and tear it apart and read the insides. But sometimes'—now she leaned forwards, her hand at rest against the fine fabric in her lap, her eyes white enough to match—

"listen. Sometimes he asks for children!"

The women bent over the bride-clothes, giggling and shaking their heads.

"Dahla," Mesema's mother scolded from the oven table, "how can you be so cruel? Dirini will barely sleep tonight."

Dirini herself only stared into the fire, one of her boys clutched to her chest. She couldn't take her sons to meet her new husband, and Mesema knew it broke her heart.

"It's only a night's tale, Mamma," said Mesema, her mirth fading.

"Is it? Who knows, with these Cerani? Mad hares, they are." The older woman glanced up through strands of grey, but her eyes saw something distant. Her hands kneaded the bread with a slow intensity. Mesema thought her mother's heart must be breaking. Dirini was the first daughter to marry outside the clan. Outside the People, even. She was meant for a Cerani royal.

Mesema couldn't bear to see all this grief; she looked away and pushed her own sorrow aside. The clothes had to be finished before Dirini's departure at summer's end.

A prick! Mesema quickly dropped her work before blood ruined the fine wool. She licked the wound with annoyance. She couldn't sew now, not until her finger stopped bleeding. She rose and laid the dress on the wooden bench with her uninjured hand. "Look, Mamma," she said, holding out her finger as a baby might.

Before her mother could look, a herder stuck his head through the door flap. "Chief wants Mesema."

"Lucky for you she's not working," Mamma said. She looked at Mesema and shrugged. Rarely were women called into the men's longhouse. It was their place, to drink and sing without the distractions a female might offer. The herder's face disappeared as quickly as it had come, and Mamma pointed at Mesema's trousers.

"Do I have to wear the seat felt? I'm only going—" But Mesema stopped; she could see this was not the time to argue. She stuffed the wool into her trousers, blushing. The felt would bring every rider's eye to her figure, and what man did not prize a full behind?

Outside she heard the bleating of sheep combined with the muffled sound of men's laughter. Mesema took her time at first, enjoying the night air.

A Red Hoof, one of ten captives from the last war, hurried by with a pail of water for the horse-pen. His eyes met hers, threatening the dark future when he would be free. She quickened her pace. She hadn't forgotten the sight of her brother Jakar, grey and lifeless over his horse, a broken Red Hoof spear sprouting from his chest. She hadn't forgotten the pain and sorrow of watching the enemy's riders fly away from the longhouses like ravens from a tree.

The Red Hoof passed her, too closely. She darted under the flap of the men's house and breathed a sigh of relief, though the herbs smoking in the fire pit filled her eyes with tears. Besna leaves thrown on the coals were meant to block the smell of horses and sweat, but they ruined her vision as well.

Mesema knew her father sat in the centre, on a raised platform covered with furs, but she could only move her feet and hope they brought her there.

"No wonder Cerani can't breed," he was saying. "The fools don't know how to choose a woman."

"We shouldn't complain," another man said. "Now this deal might cost us almost nothing."

Mesema heard her cousin's voice. "Dirini can marry into the Black Horse Clan now. We need to make a firm alliance there." Mesema stumbled over a row of muscular legs. The wool stuffed into her riding trousers scratched her bottom and wiggled dangerously with every step. She rubbed at her eyes and saw her father's long hair only an arm's length away.

"Father," she called, "you sent for me?" She fought to stay in the same spot as men twice her size moved around her.

"Ah, yes." He beckoned her closer and motioned to Lame Banreh at his right. "Banreh, tell this general that this is my unproven daughter." Next to Banreh sat a man with black hair and a metal breastplate. She recognised the crest: the Cerani had sold the same armour to the Red Hooves last year.

Banreh nodded and leaned towards the stranger. His lips moved and strange staccato noises came forth.

Years ago, Banreh had fallen off his horse and shattered his leg. Useless for work or war, he'd learned how to make pictures with ink and to speak some of the trade languages. Instead of scorning Banreh as her grandfather would have done, Mesema's father kept him at his side. They were as one, the chief and his voice-and-hands. Banreh communicated with visitors from other lands and scratched their agreements on dried lambskin. He was especially good with Cerani.

The stranger's black eyes veered Mesema's way. He murmured something to Lame Banreh.

Banreh avoided Mesema's gaze as he spoke. "He says she looks pretty, but she's too fat. Her posterior…'

Mesema's cheeks grew hot, but her father only laughed and slapped the Cerani's shoulder. "This man is indeed a fool," he said to Banreh. "Tell him this is the only daughter I have who is untouched by a man. If he doesn't like her, tell him again that Dirini is a strong mother with good hips." As the men around him began to laugh, he added, "I'm only trying to help."

Banreh spoke to the Cerani man once more, punching the air in a downwards motion. Mesema could tell he wasn't translating her father's exact words. Instead, he was revealing why all the Felting women had big behinds.

"Papa," she said, using the affectionate tone, "why do you bring me here while the men are drinking?"

"Because," her father said, taking a swig from his skin, "you've not proven to be a good breeder."

The heat from the fire burned her cheeks. "I haven't failed! I have one more season before I am even tried."

"I know." Her father laughed again.

The merriment escaped her. "Please let me go, Father."

At that moment Banreh looked up and said, "Mesema—wait." His kind expression and tone soothed her. But then he turned to her father, and with eleven words took her world apart.

"Chief, General Arigu agrees to take Mesema as the royal bride."

CHAPTER THREE

Summoned to the Petal Throne, Eyul came, and waited. The Blue Shields on either side of the royal doors stared ahead without acknowledging him, and the gods carved into the wood looked only at one another, from right to left and back again. It was always so; Eyul did the work that nobody wished to see, not even the gods.

So it came as a surprise when Donato, the Grand Master of the Treasury, approached in his curl-toed slippers and raised his pale gaze to meet Eyul's, and even more of a surprise when he spoke in a polite, questioning tone. "Are you waiting to see the emperor, heaven bless him?"

Eyul nodded.

This clearly presented a dilemma for Donato, who pursed his lips and glanced towards the doors. He'd reached the highest position possible for a man of tribute, yet their respective rankings remained unclear. Eyul, plucked from the dark alleys of the Maze and given to a life of blood, might yet outrank a slave of scale or quill, as long as he had the emperor's favor.

The doors swung open, the wooden gods turning to smile upon the throne. Eyul did not have the emperor's favor, would never have it, but nevertheless took a quick step forwards, solving Donato's problem with his feet. He had no desire to wait through a presentation of coin; the throne weighed heavy on his mind, even more so since last night's attack. He needed to see the emperor himself, to know whether Beyon's mind was still his own. Eyul walked towards the dais, his soft shoes quiet on the mosaic tile that sparkled in the lantern light.

He took care not to let his feet sully the purple runner, a silk road laid to return the emperor from the hunt to the throne. Eyul, a hunter himself, let his eyes follow the emperor's tracks, writ large in the regular bunching of the silk and the scatter of sand from the folds of his tunic. He was reminded of the old proverb, *The Cerani emperor brings the desert with him.* It held true; Emperor Beyon kept the vast room dry and empty. Eyul remembered the cushions that once had been scattered over the cold floor and the wine that had flowed for every visitor, and felt a twinge for the court of Emperor Tahal. He'd been a young man then, and Beyon just a happy boy playing with his brothers. The palace had been lively, full of courtiers and lords from the provinces. These days, the halls held only a scattering of slaves, wives, and soldiers, and everyone spoke in whispers.

Beyon, Son of Heaven, waited on the dais in his hunting clothes, a skinning dagger tucked in his belt. He saw Eyul and widened his stance, squaring his shoulders. The throne loomed behind him, its metal roses gleaming in the morning light. Eyul drew close, avoiding the emperor's glare; he dreaded Beyon's eyes, wide and dark, like those of his young brothers. Tuvaini stood at the emperor's shoulder, his pose relaxed, no warning on his face.

At either side, bodyguards waited. Their hachirahs would take long seconds to draw; their formal high, stiff boots hindered movement. If the pattern claimed Beyon, his body-guards could not protect him from Eyul's Knife. He hoped it would not come to that.

A slave hurried past Eyul, his arms full of fresh silk. The sandy mess was whisked away and a new path set. At its start, where the fringe brushed up against the steps of the dais, Eyul made his obeisance.

The emperor let him wait. Eyul stared at these intricate tiles a few minutes longer each time he came. His knees weren't what they once had been, and his leg smarted from last night's wound, but he held his position.

"I'd like to see Donato first," Beyon said to the vizier.

Eyul cursed himself. Now he would listen to the presentation of coin after all, with his faced turned to the stone. He waited through a long silence, ended by the whisper of silk as Donato fell to his own obeisance.

"Rise, Donato, and tell me," Beyon said, "about my tomb."

His tomb. Eyul felt a cramp tighten in his leg and willed himself to remain still. Did the emperor make ready for his death? Building a tomb at twenty-six would only encourage the rumours that fluttered along the hallways at night. The vizier needed time to groom the younger brother to the throne, time he wouldn't have if Beyon exposed himself.

And yet Eyul felt comforted. *He hopes to die, rather than become a Carrier.* His mind remained his own, so far. Perhaps he would call upon the Knife before the pattern changed him—perhaps by then Beyon would welcome it. There would be no struggle, no betrayal.

Donato spoke of marble, tesserae, and gold. Beyon asked questions, his voice low and friendly. His tomb would join with that of Satreth the Reclaimer, the last emperor to reign before the pattern-marks came to the city of Nooria. Side by side the emperors would take their eternal sleep, one who never saw the marks, and one whom the marks had taken.

Eyul's hands felt cold upon the floor. It seemed the end of something.

"The emperor is now ready to receive you, Eyul." Tuvaini's voice fell soft against his ears, cool comfort.

Eyul stood and bowed, head lowered.

"Dead bodies by the fountain, Eyul." The emperor sounded amused. "I thought you liked to kill with a bit more ceremony." The reference burned, even as it reassured. As long as Beyon kept the same hatreds, the same resentments, he had not been taken.

Eyul waited a moment before answering. He raised his eyes to the emperor's face, careful not to glance towards the neck or wide sleeves of his tunic, where the pattern-marks might be glimpsed. Something in him didn't want to see the future written on the emperor's skin. "Circumstances demanded that I protect the vizier, Your Majesty. We were attacked—"

"You did well."

Eyul had no choice but to pretend he didn't hear the mocking tone. "One did get away, Your Majesty."

The emperor pivoted to face the vizier. Though the two were of a height, Tuvaini looked small as he met the emperor's gaze. Beyon's shoulders crowded Tuvaini, his arms twice as thick. Tuvaini dipped his head, calm and measured, while Beyon rocked forwards on his feet.

Beyon took a step closer. "How did they get into the fountain room, Tuvaini?"

"I don't know," Tuvaini said with a frown.

Between the streets and the fountain stood dozens of guards who would need to be bribed or killed in order for three Carriers to pass so deep into the palace. Eyul knew the guards. He overheard their conversations as he passed unnoticed through the halls. He knew their ailments and complaints, their gambling debts and smoking habits. They could be bribed, but not by Carriers. And yet there had been no deaths. Something was missing.

Eyul felt the emperor's gaze on him and met it with his own.

The emperor said, "What do you think, Eyul?"

Eyul bowed. "I apologise, Your Majesty; I would call it magic if I could."

"Did you see, at least, where they came from?"

"One from either side of me and another through the fountain. I expect they were hiding behind the tapestries. How they got there—" Eyul's shoulders drooped at the memory of being taken off guard.

"Waiting for you." Beyon stopped, and stood for a moment without speaking. "Someone attacked the royal vizier," he said at last. "Many will die for this. Start with the Red Hall guards. See what they have to say before their throats are cut." His shadow flickered as he moved towards the steps. The royal bodyguards turned, weapons rattling, to follow him off the back of the dais.

Eyul straightened and fingered the hilt of his Knife. The decision should not surprise him; Eyul had taught the emperor himself, that brutal morning, the value of killing. He wished daily that it could have been a different lesson.

Tuvaini stood alone beside Beyon's great chair, twisting the ring on his finger. "All of them, Your Magnificence?"

"What?" Beyon turned to look at Tuvaini, the fresh silk twisting under his boot. A slave inched forwards, a new runner in his hands.

"All of the Red Hall guards, Your Magnificence, or just the ones on duty that night?" Tuvaini's face held no particular expression.

"Find who's responsible, Tuvaini." The emperor turned to Eyul, standing so close now that Eyul could have cut his throat with the sacred Knife before the bodyguards had time to run between them. His lips were pressed tight, his eyes shining.

"It's been too long since you last fed your Knife well, hasn't it, assassin? How many guards in the Red Room? Six? Twelve? That should keep you for some time."

Eyul cleared his throat. "There will be a great deal of blood, Your Majesty."

"Your Majesty," Tuvaini interjected, "I don't think the guards—none of them is marked—"

The emperor swung about as his bodyguards elbowed Eyul out of the way.

Eyul was shocked by Tuvaini's audacity in mentioning the marks. He couldn't see the emperor's expression, but the stiffness of his stance, the way he balled his hands into fists over and again, told him that the next words would be sharp.

"If you know something, then come out with it."

Tuvaini lowered his chin. "We will question the guards, Your Majesty."

Eyul crumpled into his obeisance as the emperor turned towards the doorway. A second later Tuvaini's forehead banged against the dais. *So he did scare you, Vizier.* Eyul held his position for twenty breaths. The emperor was light on his feet; only the rustling of the slaves, busy placing another runner, finally signalled to Eyul that he might rise.

Tuvaini knelt beside the throne. "I will take care of the guards."

"But the emperor—"

"Told me to deal with it. He only assumed I'd use you. I need you to go to the Cliffs of Sight."

"The hermit." Eyul shook out his cramped leg.

"We must learn more about the Carriers." Tuvaini stood and brushed sand from the sleeve of his robe. Rubbing the grains between his fingers with a disgusted look, he said, "My cousin is marked. Go to the hermit. Ask him."

Distant cousin. Eyul held his tongue on that point. "Shall I ask the hermit how to fight the sickness?"

"Have you been paying no attention, fool?" Tuvaini came down the steps and walked towards Eyul. He smelled of coffee and black cardamom. His face was narrow where Beyon's was wide, his lips thinner, his eyes surrounded by more lines. Still, the family resemblance was there, and the look on the vizier's face sent a shiver down Eyul's spine.

"Fool," Tuvaini repeated. "Ask him what it means for the curse to gain an emperor." The vizier placed a hand over Eyul's Knife. He spoke the rest in a voice so low that Eyul had to lean close to hear him, close enough to feel the heat of Tuvaini's breath against his cheek. "If he has an answer, learn it; then kill him."

Let them chase me! Mesema knew her steed, better than she knew any human, man or woman, kith or kin. Tumble didn't have the height of the Rider horses, but he had their stamina, and more besides. He could turn in an arm-span. In the gullies where the Hair Streams cut through the high grass she could lose even the best of her father's Riders, no matter how many he sent.

Mesema watched the horseman crest the ridge and ride down the windward slope. At first her anger blinded her: anger at her father, at the Cerani, at their damned prince who couldn't take a bride from among his own people, anger at the fact they'd sent only one Rider to catch her. But she wiped it from her eyes and looked more closely. She knew few outside the Felt would see it, but this was no Rider; the man and the horse moved separately.

"Dung!" Mesema spat into the wind. She cursed her father's cleverness.

Banreh couldn't ride as a Felt. He couldn't talk to the horse as a man should; his shattered leg left him dumb. To outride Banreh held no honour. To leave him struggling in the gullies would only shame her.

Mesema rode to the West Ridge. She kept Tumble to a walk, allowing Banreh to close the gap. Even so she reached the ridge before him.

From the crest Mesema could see a vast swathe of her father's lands. From mountain to distant mountain the grasslands rolled, green and empty.

Banreh came alongside her, slow and easy, as if they were inspecting the herd.

"From the West Ridge your grandfather's grandfather would watch the grass in the season of winds," Banreh said. "The Hidden God would show him pictures in the ripples."

"I know this." Mesema directed her anger at him, but trying to be angry with Banreh was like trying to light wet kindling. Even so, she kept her eyes from him and studied the grass.

"What do you see there? What does the wind paint for you?"

Mesema narrowed her eyes. "Ripples chasing ripples." That's all there had ever been for her. She turned from the vista and faced him.

Banreh looked pale, blond hair coiled in sweat-darkened ringlets above his brow. The chase, such as it was, had taken its toll on him.

A momentary guilt clutched at Mesema's heart, but she remembered the Cerani prince and thrust all concern for Banreh aside. "There's nothing to see but grass. No mysteries, no magic. Just like this marriage. There'll be no Rider racing to my longhouse in the moon-dark. It's just salt and silver, trade deals."

"Look again," Banreh said.

Mesema looked. She always found it hard to deny Banreh. His eyes held a promise and a trust.

"What do you see?" he asked.

"I... I don't know." The wind blew harder, and Mesema felt suddenly cold. "A—A strange patterning. Now waves, huge waves with a man riding across them. A cliff. A prison. I don't know! Nothing."

"You see more than you know," Banreh said. He brought his horse around to stand before Tumble. Though he'd never be a Rider, her father gave his voice-and-hands a fine steed; it helped Banreh keep alongside him during hunts and ride-outs. But the Chief spared Banreh now to bring back the Cerani's prize.

Mesema was meant to leave with Arigu at autumn's turning. She remembered how Arigu had stood at the edge of the horse-pen, watching her ride away. His expressions were unfamiliar to her, his language incomprehensible. She might as well step off the edge of the world as go to Nooria.

"Why didn't the prince take Dirini?" The question burst from Mesema without permission. "She's proven. She has her children to speak for her."

"The Cerani have strange ways," Banreh said. "Dirini's children would always be considered a danger."

"Are they mad?"

"Different." Banreh rubbed at the golden stubble on his chin and looked out over the grass. "The prince has no younger brothers—they were all killed when the eldest took the throne. Why he was spared, I don't know. The Cerani general has reasons, but he doesn't tell me the truth."

"I should ride away from here," Mesema said. "I should ride and join the clanless. Chasing deer on the brown-land would be better than going to Cerana." Banreh started to reply, but she spoke over him. "Don't talk to me of duty. The Felt won't suffer if one daughter rides away."

Banreh shrugged. "When the horse fell on me I thought my life was over. I heard my leg break and I knew all my dreams broke with it."

Mesema watched him. He had a faraway look. His eyes held the green of the spring.

"I would have made a middling Rider," Banreh said. "I was never a natural, not like your father or your brother. I would have got by, but I'd always have been third-best in any group of four. Maybe I'd be dead by now, killed last summer when we fought the Red Hooves.

"Instead I found a new world, a world of strange tongues and the stories they conceal. I found writing, and in it a trail to a dozen lands beyond our own—whole new worlds, Mesema, places no Felt has ever been. Places your father could never conquer though he had ten times the Riders."

"What are you saying?" Mesema asked. "That this Cerani prince is my broken leg?"

Banreh turned to face her. "Your horse has fallen. How you get up again is a matter for you."

"Don't think to instruct me, Banreh." Mesema found her anger again. "I am not a child and you are no Elder." She met his gaze and challenged it. "Is there nothing you regret, not being a real man?"

Banreh met the challenge. "Had I been a Rider, I would have ridden to your longhouse and set my spear. But I am not, and even if I had been, the Cerani prince would still have beaten me to your bower. We are the Felt, Mesema. We carry on."

Banreh turned his horse and rode slowly towards the camp. Mesema looked once more towards the setting of the sun and the distant marches of the clanless, then she too began the ride back.

We are the Felt. We carry on.

Tuvaini passed through the royal corridors. On his right, a recess held a mosaic, bright in purple and white. He had hidden there as a young boy, hoping his uncle wouldn't find him and force him back into his lessons. He recalled the feel of the cool agate against his bare legs, the way he had held his breath, sure that the slightest sound would betray him. *He is lazy*, he prayed they would say. *A poor student. Not promising.* Then they would send

him home to the seaside. That desire faded once he came to know Emperor
Tahal.

Tuvaini passed under the carving of the god Keleb. Here, just outside the
imperial suite, he used to place the Robes of Office around the shoulders of
the late emperor. They had walked to the throne room together, Tahal and
Tuvaini, thousands of times. Tahal had spent more time with him than with
his own sons. He had known all save one would die.

All save two, as it turned out.

Tuvaini turned a corner and left the royal chambers behind. Here lay
the doors to the treasuries and scriptoria. In between them all, handsome
tapestries concealed plain tiled walls. The officers of the quill and coin were
mere men of tribute, chosen from the villages and farms of vassal lands
and trained for a lifetime of shifting papers. It was better to fill such rooms
with men of limited ambitions, men like Donato who took joy in building
monuments to failures.

Tuvaini walked on. As he neared the servants' chambers, he yawned.
Sometimes Lapella made him sleepy. It wasn't her fault; she relaxed him.
He found her door and turned the key in the lock. Whenever he entered
her quarters, he had the sensation of stepping into his home province. He
hadn't been there in more than ten years, but Lapella held for him all the
voices and scents that he missed. He even, somehow, smelled the sea about
her.

Tuvaini used to wake to the calls of the fishmongers and seabirds, the
ringing of the ships' bells and the sound of waves cresting upon the rocky
shore. The gardens under his window bloomed jasmine and rose, and his
mother used to trim them as she sang.

She had been the granddaughter of Satreth II, known as the Drunk,
the laughing stock of the empire in his day. Still, cut off from Nooria
by mountains and a desert, huddled against the shore of the gulf, they
were almost as deities through his blood. The shipbuilders and merchants
knew little of palace gossip; to them, blood was everything. Little did they
know how thin it ran. Tuvaini's people were unlikely ever to rise to the
Petal Throne. A female connection was near to meaningless when it came
to the succession.

Tuvaini put the sting of that aside. "Lapella," he called softly, dangling
the key from one finger. He found her prostrate before her altar, offering

incense to Mirra. Her fingers showed white against the soapstone base; she held hard to her prayers. Lapella never tired of Mirra. Perhaps she dreamed that one day Mirra would remove the scars from her pox-sickness, even fix her ruined womb. Tuvaini's belief was that no god should improve the lot of humans. Only the Mogyrk god had ever promised that, leaving his Yrk-men followers to practise vengeance and cruelty in his stead. The invaders burned through the empire, even raping and plundering their way through the palace itself. When Satreth the Reclaimer fell upon them at last, they learned the weakness of their god.

Tuvaini didn't interrupt Lapella; he liked indulging her sometimes. He took a seat by the window and studied the moon. He'd paid off three Red Hall guards and set them running. He had to show them how their actions were a form of loyalty, show them the wider tapestry. He was good at explaining such things. With any luck, they could make it to his home province in five days. They could work for his family there, in obscurity. Nobody would ever learn they'd allowed the Carriers to pass through the secret ways to the fountain, and by his order.

The others, who knew nothing, would be questioned and killed. Backwards as it was to reward the treacherous guards and kill the honest ones, Beyon had left him no choice. The emperor had, quite unexpectedly, advanced from cutting throats to asking questions—and then cutting throats.

Tuvaini felt some regret for the deaths. The guards had served him well, on the whole.

Lapella stood now and straightened her robes. She looked at him in her shy way, chin tucked in. "Are you thinking about the emperor?" Her meek-ness stirred him. Once, she had been bold, the tigress of the province by the sea.

He smiled. "Not any more." She came closer.

He looked at her amber eyes, the pocked scars on her cheeks.

"Are you sorry you let them use you?" she asked.

"A little." Tuvaini had seen Eyul's hair turning steel-grey, had noticed his stiffness going in and out of obeisances, but he hadn't expected the assassin to get hurt. Eyul still had his uses.

Lapella stood before him now, chasing his regrets away. "But you got what you wanted?"

"I will." He smiled again and opened his arms. She leaned into him, rose-scented and soft.

"What did you do today?" he asked.

"The same." Not much of an answer. He had no idea how she spent her days. She insisted a servant's life was better than living in the women's halls. Back home, noblewomen moved about more freely. Here, they depended on the double luck of having sons and outliving their husbands, as Empire Mother Nessaket had.

Nessaket had nearly the freedom of a man, and more cunning. He'd seen her today in the royal gardens. Not one to linger over blossoms, she'd used the flower walk to hurry from the east wing to the west. Tuvaini stood by the yellow roses and watched her disappear through the Sunset Arch, her silken train shimmering behind her. His mind filled with images of Nessaket. In every one of them, pride sculpted her features. She stood, or sat, or lay clothed in wisps, but always distant as mountain ice.

I will see her sweat and cry, see that perfect hair tangled, wild, watch those pale limbs strain.

"I see you're ready for me," commented Lapella, stroking him through his robe. He'd nearly forgotten about her, but she didn't mind. She didn't mind anything. She was his now. Before the pox-sickness came, it was said that only an emperor deserved Lapella, and only an emperor could master her. After it came, her family couldn't marry her to anyone at all. They were relieved when Tuvaini paid a small sum for her permanent service, and they didn't ask why. When he came to claim her, her spirit was still strong; her acid tongue had burned him. But he was honest and kind, and that broke her.

Tahal had taught him that one does not rule well by force alone.

Tuvaini pulled her robes from her shoulders and let them fall.

She smiled, happy for any attention he could give her. With Lapella, there was never a complaint or an unexpected demand.

Tuvaini loved certainty, hated uncertainty. Prince Sarmin's madness vexed him, and this female from the Wastes would only complicate his plans. And yet, Tuvaini had his training to fall back on; of all the men in the palace, only he had sat at the feet of the great Tahal. Only he knew when to submit, when to charm and when to break a person like an egg.

Like Lapella. He laid her across the bed and spread her legs with his knees. "You are very precious to me," he whispered.

"So you say," she said with a chuckle. A hint of her old sense of humour, but she went no further with it. Next, she would apologise. And she did. "I'm sorry I'm so ugly for you."

He could have said that the scars had faded so much that one could still see her old beauty. That her body was as firm and plump as it had ever been. These statements would have been true, but they would not serve him. Instead he said, "I don't love you for your looks." That, too, was true.

She made a little sound as he entered her. All conversation had ended. It was all right if he thought of Nessaket instead, as he pinned Lapella's arms against the cushions. Lapella didn't mind anything he did. It was a certainty.

CHAPTER FOUR

Eyul rode through the narrow streets of the Maze. He kept his camel to a slow pace along the central path, making it tread around the channel where the sewage ran, or rather where it lingered, stagnant and polluting the night. Despite the camel's protests, he held it from the easier ground to either side.

Long ago, in this place, Eyul first learned to kill, his mentor Halim guiding his hand. In the darkness of the alleyways, whose black mouths yawned to the left and to the right, he had sliced lives from their owners. The Maze made him feel old. In the forty years since he ran here as a boy, nothing had changed: same stench, same murmured night-song, distant laughter, muffled violence, quick feet.

Eyul didn't fear an attack, but why risk one? Take the path of least resistance. His camel resisted, as camels always do, giving out a loud snort of protest. He kicked it with both heels, hard, and kept the centreline.

His thoughts returned to the palace whilst his eyes remained on the alleyways. Who would employ Carriers as assassins? Who wanted the vizier dead? Eyul goaded his camel on, cursing at the throbbing in his leg where the Carrier's knife had caught him.

Getting slow, old man, getting slow.

A movement in the moonlight shadow, liquid and threatening.

"Do you really want to die here, my friend?" Eyul addressed the darkness.

He heard the whisper of retreating footsteps. When robbed of surprise, most inhabitants of the Maze were apt to withdraw.

The Carrier had also run. Eyul had not given chase; that wouldn't have been wise, not with a bleeding leg. Besides, anyone who could get into the Red Room would have had help; they would have been hidden long before he'd limped along their trail. Odd. Most odd. The patterning might not always take the life from a Carrier, but it took his fear of death. Why would a Carrier run?

Eyul followed the snaking path of the Old Way, passing a pyre tended by a lone Blue Shield. The royal guardsman wore a scarf around his mouth and nose to block the acrid smoke. The Carriers inside had fallen to nothing more than blackened bits of bone, yet he continued to stoke the flames. He didn't look up; he didn't notice Eyul leaving Nooria by the Low Door, where any man, even the emperor's assassin, might escape the snare of the city walls without undue attention.

"Who goes? And on what business?" Another soldier, gap-toothed and limping, emerged from the gatehouse. His concern was only for show; he shone his lantern on the camel, not the rider.

"My name is Rinn, and I go to count the sand." Eyul gave the old reply, a nod to legend and custom. He leaned from the saddle and placed three jade coins in the soldier's hand. The man's breath stank, fouler even than the sewers of the Maze.

"Go in peace, Rinn." The soldier turned to raise the gate-bar.

Eyul's leg throbbed, and he wondered if the patterning would enter him through the cut. Perhaps Tuvaini had more than one reason for sending him away. Eyul remembered struggling with the Carrier, held close, eye to eye, before he slid the emperor's Knife over that unclean throat. *The hermit will help me. For a price.* Eyul shuddered. The hermit always had his price.

It would be twenty days across the sands to the Cliffs of Sight. He had his water and his parasol, his blankets and his tent. And a good bow and his Knife, always those. But he wouldn't need them yet; outside the city wall, marketers waited to sell fermented juice, roasted goat, leg of dog, pickled eyes, and a thousand other delicacies. Even at this hour, when honest men lay abed, Eyul's passage stirred the vendors into action. They stepped from tent to stall, sing-songing their wares, lifting the lids on blackened pots.

Eyul twitched his nose, searching through the scents. The oily barks of duggan tree and sand-birch smoked on low fires, flavouring the meats above. His mouth watered. An old man dusted strips of dry-roasted camel-hump with pollen. Eyul caught the scent of desert-rose and his stomach growled. He had long since learned to tolerate the bland foods of the palace, but he had never begun to like them.

The old man looked up as Eyul passed. "Two jade. Best rose-camel. Two jade only."

Two jade? The man must have heard Eyul's stomach, too.

"For two jade I would want your tent as well." Eyul kept his eyes on the road.

"One! One jade, noble traveller. One jade, two strips!" the old man called from behind him now.

Eyul's camel greeted the offer with a long and undulating belch.

"On my way back, friend. If I become rich in the desert." He kicked his beast on past the souk, the common traders' tents, and the last well.

The moon made white crests of the dunes, marching across a black sea. Eyul marked his way by the Scorpion, the seven stars beneath which his mother had birthed him. In no time at all the clamour of Nooria lay in memory. Even his unruly camel felt the new peace and stopped its complaining. Soon only the sigh of the wind rippled the silence.

So. The hermit will not be pleased to see me again. A man seeks solitude in the vastness of the desert, and what happens? Men travel mile upon mile to plague him with visitations. A boy-prince seeks only love and company, and his family entombs him alone in the teeming palace.

At first Eyul thought he saw a sandcat perched atop a dune; then, as the moonlight revealed more detail, he saw it was a camel, half-hidden behind the crest. He made out a saddle and reached for his quiver as he scoured the sands for a rider. He spotted a white-robed figure, almost lost in the darkness at the base of the dune, motionless, facing him.

Eyul stopped his camel at a hundred paces and nocked an arrow to his bow. He took reassurance in the creak as the recurved horn bent to his pull. Power in his hands.

"What business have you in the White Sea?" he called out.

A woman's voice answered him. "I wait for you, Eyul of Nooria, son of

Klemet, Fifty-third Knife-Sworn."

A pause. "Come closer, then."

The wind billowed her robes as she stepped across the sand. Her hood fluttered, then fell free, allowing dark curls to twist in the air. She came within twenty paces. Skin like roasted butter-nuts, eyes darker still: from the Islands.

She held his gaze.

He pointed his bow to her right, but kept it drawn. "You have used my name, but have not offered your own; that is a rudeness in the desert."

She bent her knee slightly, but the curve of her mouth did not suggest humility. "Apologies. Amalya. Of the Tower."

A wizard. He returned his aim to her throat. "Amalya. Go back to your Tower. Tell your masters that my business is not theirs to supervise."

"You will deny the Tower?" She was brave to smile so in the face of his arrow, and braver still to step forwards, holding out one hand. A hand that held a Star of Cerana, sparkling in the moonlight. "Will you deny the one who gave me this?"

Eyul relaxed the grip on his bow, feeling the ache in his arm for the first time. Who had given her that Star? Beyon? His mother? Tuvaini? He felt old once more.

"You are as brave and obedient as I have been told," she said. "I am glad to have such a companion on my journey to the hermit's lair."

He took a moment to secure his bow, his surprise hidden in the practised movement. He spurred his camel towards the dune. "And what can I expect from my own companion?"

Amalya raised her face to the moon, eyes closed, her feet finding their own way. "Well, I can cook."

The scents of the marketplace lingered on Eyul's robes. He took a deep breath. "This is good," he said, "but surely you haven't been sent to fix my meals."

She laughed at that, a velvet noise, and tucked the Star in a pocket.

Eyul turned his eyes to the sands, looking for more surprises.

"We are safe here," she said, as if reading his mind.

A cold wave swept over him. "And if I ask who sent you?"

"I would not answer." She opened her eyes as if waking. "I am not here to hurt you, Eyul."

Before he had time to linger on those words, she spoke again, in a conversational tone. "My camel's not very cooperative. I fear I may have to walk across the desert."

"I'll help you." Eyul pulled the half-staff from his saddle-pack. "I speak fluent camel."

The debate, punctuated by staff-blows to the beast's flanks, proved short and productive. The camel agreed to bear Amalya as directed and keep its complaints to the traditional spitting and passing of wind.

Eyul took the lead. He had crossed to the Cliffs of Sight before, but that had been ten years ago, and no trail lasts long in the desert. He found his bearings by the stars; in the hot season the Scorpion's tail pointed the way.

They rode in silence. Eyul liked it quiet, but the wizard took the comfort from desert's calm. Each mile added to Eyul's unease until he longed to speak, and he had never been one to make talk for its own sake.

Eyul followed the line of the dunes where he could, but as the night wore thin their course took them from crest to crest, labouring up from the dips with the sand slipping around the camels' pads, sapping energy.

"Dawn," Eyul said, the first word to pass between them since their journey started.

The eastern mountains glowed gold and orange: the full heat of day would be upon them soon. Eyul slid from his camel with a groan. Months in the palace had left him soft, and his wound smarted. He watched Amalya climb down and took quiet satisfaction in the stiffness she tried to hide.

"Show me how they cook in the Islands," he said.

Amalya smiled and turned to unbind the roll of her belongings. Wizard or no, Eyul could see she had a magic to her. Her robes fell against her as she moved, showing her to be long in the leg and generous in hip and breast.

Maybe not such an old man after all. Eyul's lips twitched at his own foolishness.

Amalya brought out pans, small jars filled with spices, strips of dried meat, a bag of grain, and slices of dried apricots on a string. Eyul placed his own contribution on the sand in front of her: five cakes of camel dung, dried and pressed.

Amalya gathered the dung between two fire-stones and blew on it, softly, as a musician might blow upon a singing stick. Flames licked at the fuel.

She was flame-sworn, Eyul realised, like Govnan the high mage. He had met Govnan once, by chance, in the dark halls beneath the throne room. Govnan had lit a flame in his bare hand and asked to see Eyul's Knife. Neither had queried the other's purpose in the secret ways; it hadn't seemed polite. That same sense of etiquette kept him from asking too many questions of Amalya, but he knew that within them all mages carried an elemental, air, water, earth or fire.

Amalya wrinkled her nose as she brought her pot to sit across the stones. "In the Islands we don't cook on dung," she said. A gentle humour softened her words.

Eyul reached for a handful of sand and let it trickle through his fingers. "We could burn the dune instead, if you've the magic for it?"

Amalya did not rise to his bait. She poured water from her skin into the pot, careful, spilling none. "I'll save my magic for the sauce." She sprinkled cornflour from a small bag. "Some things are best left to simmer."

Eyul smiled. He yawned and leaned back against his pack. The sky shone with a faint shade of pearl, and as he watched it brighten he wondered who had sent Amalya, and why. *Get across the desert first. Then we will see.* He closed his eyes and breathed in the smell of her cooking…

He must have drifted off, because he opened his eyes to low sunshine and a bowl of stew. He accepted the dish, and Amalya crouched in the sand to eat her own meal.

"This is very good," he said, rolling the mint and pepper together on his tongue. He remembered the foods he'd passed up outside the city wall; this tasted better than rose-camel.

"Island cooking," she said with a smile.

"I should move to the Islands." He took another bite.

Amalya blew on a small morsel of meat on her spoon. "I couldn't tell you what it's like there now."

He nodded, understanding. "How long have you served?"

"Oh…" She tilted her head, fingers drumming a beat on the wooden bowl. "Fifteen years, just about. They told me I would protect the Boy Emperor. He and I are the same age, you know. I had romantic notions—Not that kind," she said when Eyul smiled. "But the idea of children ruling and defending the empire—it appealed to me. It made it easier to leave."

"They took you."

She nodded. "They came for the tribute-children when I was eleven."

Eyul scraped the last of the stew from his bowl. He remembered the terror of being taken by the guard, rough hands on his shirt collar, tears on his face. How old had he been? Seven? Eight? "You must have been frightened."

"Not for long. Govnan saw me—he wasn't the high mage then; it was before his great journey through the desert, before Kobar chose him as the Second. Govnan pulled me out of the line and claimed me for the Tower."

"And now you carry the Star of Cerana. You've come a long way. To think that Lord High Vizier Tuvaini himself would design a mission for you—"

Amalya put her bowl down in the sand and chuckled. "Nice try, Knife-Sworn. But I won't tell you who gave me the Star, or who didn't."

"But you will give me your leftover stew?"

She raised an eyebrow. "Only if you tell me how you became an assassin."

She meant it as banter, but the words cut, unexpectedly. How many years since he had thought of it? The cold stone floor, the stink of urine, his own voice, pleading... the pain. That broken boy reached out to him through the decades. *No.* "I... I can't."

Amalya handed him her bowl without speaking, no doubt regretting her question.

Eyul took a few bites in the silence and she watched him, kindness in her eyes. It made him uncomfortable. "Why don't you get some rest?" he asked. "I'll clean the bowls."

"All right," she said. Was that relief in her voice? "I'll see you at sundown."

"Sundown," he agreed.

After she crawled into her tent, Eyul scrubbed the bowls clean with sand. His eyes felt dry and tired; his head ached. The memories were as fresh to him as his ride across these dunes, but the emotion felt ancient, rooted in him. The farther he travelled from the past, the more he lived in it, each day an inexorable step, closing the circle, bringing him back to what he'd left behind.

His work done, Eyul crawled into his tent. He dreamed of blood in a courtyard and a young emperor with dead eyes.

CHAPTER FIVE

Sarmin sat and watched the wall, listening for the telltale scrape within it. In the courtyard the Blue Shields made their first round of the evening, and beneath the regular tramp of boots on flagstones, Sarmin could hear the distant cries of moorhens on the river. He stilled his breath and opened himself to all the soft noises of the night: the creak of waggon wheels in the souk, tent poles straining under a sudden breeze, shouts and cries muffled and muted into an unintelligible hubbub. The Sayakarva noises, he named them, because he heard them through the window, where the name Sayakarva was engraved in a tiny, block-like script—the craftsman's mark, no doubt.

He stared at the alabaster pane: a window that let in light, but no meaning. He had broken that window once and been rewarded with a view of his brothers dead and dying. He let them keep him blind now. He looked away.

Sarmin watched the wall, following the scrollwork, tracing a single line through the complexity. In a strange way the hidden door felt as much a betrayal as an opportunity—a greater betrayal, perhaps, than even his mother's abandonment. The walls of his room had held him longer than ever she did. For nearly two decades, these four walls had been the certainty in his life—but now? Sarmin wondered where his certainty lay; not in painted stone, nor in those who hid inside it. He traced the line to its end and looked to the next wall. That hook, that flourish—had they been there before? He struggled to see the face that belonged to those brush-strokes.

A scrape, a scratch, and then a grinding of stone on stone. The door opened by feather-widths. Lamplight fingered then flooded through the crack as Tuvaini slipped through into the room.

Sarmin noted the careful way he scanned the chamber and found some assurance in the vizier's uncertainty. "Sit." Sarmin gestured to the bed. He had pushed his small table close to it, and now he took his place in the single chair.

"Prince Sarmin." Tuvaini gave a quick bow. He crossed to the bed with quick steps, took a last glance at the main door, and seated himself.

Sarmin inclined his head. He rested his arms upon the table and laced his fingers. He held his hands tight against one another, to keep them from wandering and betraying his own nervousness. "So, tell me of the general."

"He is a passionate man, Your Highness, and a brave one. In military matters Arigu's prowess has been demonstrated on both the personal level and on the larger scale." Tuvaini kept his voice low. His eyes strayed to the moon-glow of the alabaster window.

"You speak as if you know him, Vizier."

"We knew each other as boys, Highness. We both come from Ghara, in Vehinni Province. Our fathers were friends."

"And now your friend schemes with my mother to find me a bride from among the Felt?" Sarmin said. "Tell me, Vizier, why does such an alliance frighten you? Don't speak to me of cleanliness or besna nuts. These are not matters of state, and I am no child."

Do I care that they drink sheep's milk? I know where I suckled my milk, and the bitter taste is with me still.

"He is no friend of mine, my prince."

The edge in Tuvaini's voice convinced Sarmin.

"The general sets his sights too high." A pause. "To broker a royal marriage and pick a bloodline for the empire's heir…"

He sets his sights too high for your liking, Tuvaini. He looks upon my mother. Sarmin stared at the vizier and felt the stirrings of common feeling with him. They both had been denied the feel of her arms. Before he could stop himself, he laughed.

The vizier paid no notice. He waited, his face bland.

"And who would you have me marry, Vizier?" Sarmin asked after rubbing his lips. "Wherever there is objection, there is alternative." From the *Book of Statehood*. Page two hundred.

For the first time Tuvaini managed a smile. "I would have you choose your own bride, Highness. From the Petal Throne."

Sarmin took his hands from the table as if it burned them. More treachery, and beneath the canopy of the gods, no less.

"Highness, hear me." Tuvaini leaned in, intimate across the smallness of the table. "Beyon has the marks. Within the month the patterning will kill him—or, if it does not, all who see him will know him as a Carrier."

In the drawer beneath the tabletop Sarmin's fingers found the dacarba. The steel felt cool to his touch. He recalled the despair that gave him the strength to take it. He ran his thumb along the top blade. "I don't believe you."

Tuvaini's eyes wandered to the window. "The emperor sent his royal body-slaves to the Low Executioner. He said they were marked. And yet their skin was clean when they stripped for the pyre, and each slave swore that it was the emperor himself who bore the pattern: from each man, the same story, until the Low Executioner brought me to bear witness."

"Then I would speak to the Low Executioner."

Tuvaini shook his head. "That man speaks no more."

"And the slaves?"

A whisper. "Burned."

Murdered. All murdered. Sarmin felt the blood drip from his hand. "Beyon is my brother."

"You had other brothers, Highness."

Sarmin remembered them all, their chubby, laughing faces: Kashim and Amile, one too young to walk, one not yet talking. Asham, Fadil, and Pelar especially. Pelar and his red ball. He bounced it in the courtyard, in the tutor's room, and in the kitchen. He bounced it against his brothers' backs and his sisters' legs. Sarmin closed his hand around the dacarba, felt the flesh of his palm giving way. "Tell me of the man who killed them."

Tuvaini startled. "It was Eyul's duty. He carries the emperor's Knife."

Consecrated by my brothers' blood.

Sarmin didn't know how long he clutched the blade, thinking of the assassin Eyul, of the look he gave that dark night. *One more for the Knife?* He only heard Tuvaini saying, "My lord… my lord… ?"

Sarmin shook himself back to the present. "Carrier or not, Beyon is still the emperor."

"No," Tuvaini pressed on, eager to explain himself, "the Carriers are not what you remember, Highness, wandering the Maze and staying to the low places. They become bold, attacking even on palace grounds. They serve some purpose, some other enemy we cannot see. A Carrier cannot sit on the Petal Throne, Highness."

The main door rattled; the handle turned, and Tuvaini almost knocked over the table as he stood. "I must go."

It took a moment for Sarmin to understand his urgency; the guards changed at the same hour every night, and at every changeover they turned the handle to confirm that the door was locked. It was a pointless tradition in Sarmin's view; not once had the door ever opened to their test.

"Better run, Vizier." Sarmin laughed again, though more quietly this time. Tuvaini hurried for the secret door.

The last Sarmin saw of him were his jewelled fingers pulling at the stone. "Next time, Tuvaini. Next time." Sarmin spoke the words to the narrowing crack, softly, but loud enough to be heard.

He leaned back in his chair in the darkness. Shadow hid the gods above him, but he knew they were there. The others were watching, too. He closed his hand around the cut he'd made, savouring the clarity of the pain.

Conversation, being rare, always left him buzzing. In the empty hours he would replay every word ever spoken to him, relive every moment, consider each nuance. But now—now the future held the excitement, not the past, and the possibilities left him intoxicated.

By two threads he was joined to the world, by his mother, and by Tuvaini, and each thread divided and divided again, spreading and reaching. The world came to him and he gathered his threads. He drew a circle with his palm, leaving a trail of blood on the wood. *A spider in my web.*

He stood and crossed to stand at the secret door. He pressed his cheek to the smoothness of the wall, holding the dacarba in his crimson hand. "Eyul? Assassin? Can you hear me?" He brought the dacarba to his lips and kissed it. "We will have our reckoning soon."

CHAPTER SIX

Mesema folded her wedding dress, careful not to snag any of the quartz beads dangling from its heavy skirt. The alterations from Dirini's size were hardly visible; the tiny darts and shortened hems had taken only a week to complete. She'd spent those days by the fire, the murmurs from the sewing circle flowing around her like a stream. The waters whispered war, but Mesema was unmoved. The summer had already wound its way towards harvest time. Her father had clearly chosen the path of peace, and she was one of his two emissaries. The Windreaders would be expected to defend the empire, just as the Red Hooves had before finding their strange god. But the empire was not at war.

She hadn't tried to run again. Every afternoon, Banreh left her father's side to teach her the language of the Cerani Empire. She hoped that perhaps she would find a new way of thinking inside those rough words, some new way of considering herself a princess; but her understanding was too limited.

Not like Banreh's.

Mesema turned and placed the dress inside her wooden trunk. She covered it with a layer of felt before reaching for her quilt, a wedding gift from her mother. It was made from the finest wool, and boasted shining threads of copper, more tiny beads, and even some pearls, bartered from the traders-who-walked. The quilt caught the sunlight as she lifted it and ran her hands along the edge. Tiny bells rang, soft as ladysong. She put it on top of her dress and folded the felt over it.

The box held all she would bring from her home, besides Tumble. She didn't want to close it; not yet. When she opened it in Nooria, perhaps her husband would run his hands along those bells, pull the wedding dress from its wrapping. She imagined him: dark hair and flat cheekbones, black eyes full of want. Would he dig through, heedlessly breaking beads and threads with rough hands?

A shift in the tent flap, the sound of wool brushing wool. Her mother approached down the centre of the longhouse to where Mesema's bed lay along the wall. Mesema didn't turn, or speak. She wasn't ready yet.

"I have something for you." A creak of ropes as her mother sat down on the bed.

"I have until midday," Mesema said, but more to herself than to her mother.

"Ah, but we won't have another chance to speak privately." Mesema felt her mother pull on her skirts. "Sit down, daughter." Mesema sat and folded her hands in her lap. She pressed her lips together to control the trembling. She would say goodbye like a woman.

Her mother held a small pine box in her hands. She put it down on her knees and opened it, revealing an oiled bundle tied at both ends. "They will want a son from you almost before you get there," she said, undoing the ties and pulling away the fabric. Inside was a stinking grey-brown resin.

"Your husband will come to you every night and day until it takes—your father was the same way. But it is your duty to choose the right stars for your child. You must make them wait."

"Why—? How?" It was bad enough that Mesema had no plains-children. Now she must pretend to be barren?

"Mesema, daughter, listen. The Cerani are strange and unholy creatures. Everything must be auspicious—*for us*." She put emphasis on the final words as she pinched off a bit of resin the size of a thumb. "Work this between your fingers until it's soft, then put it inside. It tricks his babies so they won't take root in you. In the morning, pull it out and burn it. When the Bright One is over the moon, burn it all and make your child. Do you understand me, daughter?"

"This doesn't offend the Hidden God? He chooses the stars for every child."

"The Hidden God doesn't live in Nooria. Outside His dominion, you do what you can." Mesema's mother rolled the resin back up in its fabric and retied the ends. "I will hide this at the bottom of your trunk." She paused. "Keep it out of the sunlight. Listen to me: if you have a son, I will send you more. Listen. You must have only one son."

"Mamma! I should have many sons—"

"Not in Nooria you shouldn't."

A Rider stuck his head through the door flap. "Chief wants Mesema," he shouted.

"I've done nothing wrong!" Mesema put one hand over the pine box.

Her mother drew in her breath. "Perhaps you will learn to hold your tongue among the Cerani," she said. "But never mind that. Go on."

Mesema kept her back straight as she walked out of the rear of the long-house. Fabric rustled as her mother hid the resin inside the wedding trunk behind her.

Outside, the breeze carried the scents of late summer: apples, manure, and the fresh blooms of sheepseye, heaven-breath, and mountain beauty. The sun shone over the crest of the hill and warmed her skin. She took a deep breath. Her new home would not smell this way—even the flowers and the breeze would be different there.

The Riders ran through their manoeuvres in the field, riding hard, slashing their swords through the tall grass, throwing their spears into the soil. New Cerani breastplates sparkled in the sun. Once it was harvest time, they wouldn't have any more days left for their manly games. And after the harvest, the peace of winter would be upon them.

Her father waited by the horse-pen, his shadow long and thin. His hair travelled two brown roads down his white tunic.

"Mesema," he said in the affectionate tone, opening his arms.

But she held back and looked to Banreh, who stood by his side as always, golden and small.

"Mesema," her father continued more formally, "I have a gift for you: a teacher. He will guide you in the language of your new people. After your wedding, he will return to us."

Banreh's eyes softened as she stared at him; did he pity her? A teacher to hound and scold her all the way to Nooria! Probably one of the captives from the Red Hoof Wars, someone not yet sold to the Cerani or to the traders-who-walked. The Red Hooves lived further south; they knew the harsh language of the empire. But such a man would despise her as the daughter of the clan chief who had enslaved him.

"Who, Father?" she asked, her eyes wandering to the horse-pen, where Tumble cropped the grass.

"Right here," he said, motioning towards Banreh.

His voice-and-hands. The tears came to her eyes before she could stop them.

"Daughter," said the chief, returning to the affectionate tone, "the son you will bear is going to seal our destiny at last. You honour us."

"Thank you, Father." Mesema stood a little straighter. A compliment from the chief was rare. But just as she smiled towards the sun, a shadow fell across it.

"I give you the greatest gift I can muster, but it must be for a short time only. I cannot spare him that long. Before the snows arrive..." Her father looked over his shoulder at the Riders.

So the women had spoken true over their needles. The Riders did not practise their skills for play. The wind felt cold against her wet cheeks. "Arigu will come back before the snows close the paths," she said. So he was planning a new attack on the Red Hoof tribe that lay between them both. Banreh would come home, to speak the words of war for everyone.

In the chief's voice he replied, "Our clan's future is too vast for one person to see. Do not concern yourself; you have your own duties. Become a mother, and soon. And learn what Banreh has to teach you."

"Yes, Father." She wiped her eyes and looked at his boots. So hard, such strong leather.

He took her hand, and dropped it. It seemed almost an accident. Then he turned and made his way through the mud to his Riders.

Banreh's eyes met hers with their usual composure, and he raised both hands to his chest, a sign of service. Clever hands. But those and his tongue were the two edges of a sword, concealed behind a patient expression. As terrible as a weapon could be, she knew it was nothing more than a tool for a strong man. She turned away from him and took three steps towards her longhouse.

"Mesema," he called out, his voice a croak, "are you unhappy?" She stalked back to him, her hands on her hips.

"Do you not remember the Red Hoof Wars, Lame Banreh?"

His cheeks grew red at the name. "I remember them."

"Do you remember my brother died that year? Stuck through the heart with a spear?" When he nodded, she went on, "Do you remember when some Redders got into our village and took Hola's daughter against her will? She was too little to have that baby, and she died trying to give it life. Do you remember that?"

Banreh nodded again. She could see from his eyes that he understood now, but she didn't stop.

"When you convinced me not to run, when you convinced me to turn back that day—you knew the war depended on it, and yet you said nothing to me."

"It is not for you to concern yourself—"

"Not for *me*? Don't make me laugh. You are barely more than a woman yourself, and my father uses you the same way." As soon as the words left Mesema's mouth, horror crept over her.

Banreh sucked in his breath, but his next words were mild.

"At midday, then."

"Banreh—" Mesema said, but he turned away.

"Tame your mouth before you meet your Cerani royal." He limped past the horse-pen, pulling his bad leg through the mud.

The first chill wind of autumn swept over her. Mesema looked down at her feet, still in their summer slippers with no linings. She wouldn't need to put the linings in this year. She would be warm. She would give birth to a prince in the summery sands. Or an emperor: a Windreader emperor, who might bring the two people, Felt and Cerani, together. Would that not bring a longer peace, over time?

Perhaps Banreh had been right.

"Greetings, Your Majesty," she said in Cerantic. "Yes, Your Majesty." The words felt sharp and unmanageable. But she would learn them.

She turned towards the fields, breathing in the scents of home. A sharp wind came, bending the grass, and Mesema's hair blew across her face in a dun storm. The grass thrashed, furious before the squall, and in the waving tumult she saw something, or thought she did. She shook her hair out so it streamed behind her and climbed the fence of the horse-pen for a better vantage point. A Red Hoof thrall, shovelling manure, gave her a look, half-smirk, half-sneer. She turned her gaze away from him.

In the rippling grass, ephemeral amid the seething green, gone and there again, a pattern lay, writ wide from West Ridge to East. Mesema gasped and blinked away the wind-tears. This was different from what she had seen before. Moons, half-circles and pointed shapes spread from one hill to the next, a pattern repeating and expanding in intricate themes, reaching out in all directions. The lines and underscores around the alien signs reminded her of Banreh's scratchings.

The wind cracked and Mesema fought for balance on the round logs of the horse-pen. A hare ran across the shadowed lines as if they held his path, binding him to a labyrinth. He turned wildly, this way and that, as if beneath the very talons of the eagle, drawing always closer. His brownish fur faded into the darker green. She could hear the rustling of his feet, but could no longer tell where in the pattern he ran.

Though she didn't understand it, she murmured a prayer to the Hidden God to thank Him for the message. The wind shook her once more, and fell still. Each blade of grass raised its head towards the sun, as if there had never been any message at all.

CHAPTER SEVEN

"The supplicant may now approach."

Tuvaini walked forwards and ran a sour eye across the young Tower mage. Though she kept her face blank, Tuvaini suspected some hidden enjoyment in naming the high vizier "supplicant."

"I would speak with Govnan." No titles or honorific from the supplicant.

"High Mage Govnan has been informed of your presence." The young mage met Tuvaini's gaze, her eyes the winter-blue of the wind-sworn.

So I wait on his pleasure, do I? Tuvaini held his peace. He craned his head to look up at the Tower. The stonework cut a dark line across the sky; he could make out no detail.

"We so seldom look up." Tuvaini addressed her in a friendly tone. "We go about our duties in this city that reaches for the heavens, and we so rarely raise our eyes above the first six feet of it all."

If you don't draw your enemy out, what have you to work with?

"The wind-sworn are ever watchful of the skies." Though she had Cerani coloring, something in the curve of her cheekbones, and in the way she clipped her words, suggested her homelands lay on the easternmost borders of empire. It seemed to Tuvaini that hardly a mage among the two-score of the Tower hailed from Nooria. Perhaps the local water left one unsuited to the pursuit of magic, or maybe it wasn't a calling fit for true Cerani. Either way, the presence of so many near-foreigners in the heart of the city always irked him. *Supplicant!* The word burned.

"And what have you seen in the skies?" He kept the scorn from his voice. No wind-sworn had flown the heavens in his lifetime, not since the great Alakal. He had always felt his father's stories of Alakal were tales for children rather than for men.

"Patterns." The half-smile she offered held a strangeness that silenced him.

In the Tower's courtyard minutes crawled by as if time itself flagged in the heat. The vast enclosure covered some twenty-five acres, and yet the Tower's shadow still reached the walls, overtopping them and delving into the palace sprawl. Tuvaini didn't need reminding of the Tower's reach. He glanced at the young mage again. He didn't trust her. He didn't trust any of them. He never knew whether he was speaking to the person, or to the elemental trapped inside.

"High Mage Govnan will see you now." She turned to face the door, the sudden movement setting her robes swirling around her. The brass door swung open at the touch of her fingertips.

Tuvaini followed her in. He remembered the heavy metal door from his last visit to the Tower. "The emperor does not have such a door at the entrance to his throne room," he said.

I don't have such a door!

"We are the emperor's door, his gatekeepers. There are foes to whom a door of brass is as nothing, and yet we keep them from the emperor." She led him through the entrance hall, past the statued relics of the rock-sworn.

"Invisible defences against invisible enemies. It puts me in mind of the old fable wherein the emperor buys a set of invisible clothes," Tuvaini said. He paused at the last of the statues. "Well, well. Old High Mage Kobar. His prisoner finally escaped."

The mage turned back. If she took offence, none of it reached her face. "All bound spirits seek release."

Tuvaini shuddered: *to have something like that inside, growing and gaining power, until at last it no longer serves, but masters...* The idea filled him with peculiar horror.

"Lead on," he said.

They reached the stairs. Tuvaini remembered them well; he saved his breath for the climb.

The high mage kept his rooms not at the top of the Tower, but in the middle. Tuvaini had no notion what the upper half of the Tower housed. His escort led him to Govnan's door, and took her leave with the briefest of bows.

"It's not locked."

The voice from behind the door took Tuvaini by surprise. He cast a glance left, then right, to see if anyone had seen him startle, but the corridor lay empty. He straightened the sash of his robe and stepped through.

Govnan watched him enter from his seat, an iron chair set against the far wall. The back rose over him and curled forwards in a vaguely claw-like manner, enclosing Govnan within its grip. He was a wizened ember of a man, but his eyes were bright in a shadowed face. Every Tower mage Tuvaini had met was either a youth or an elder, as though the burden of power stole away their middle years.

"High Mage." Tuvaini inclined his head by the smallest fraction.

"Vizier." Govnan waved away formality with an agitated hand. Tuvaini took two steps into the room. It smelled of char. The place lay bare, with no stick of furniture save the high mage's chair, nor any hint of ornament.

"I come on a matter of the utmost importance." Tuvaini returned his gaze to Govnan.

"What else would drag you to the Tower?" The high mage's voice held a crackle of irritation. The flame-sworn were always tetchy. "You have not seen fit to seek our counsel in eighteen years. I am fascinated to learn what has finally brought you to our doors."

"I am concerned for the health of the emperor," Tuvaini said. Govnan held silent. He could have been rock-sworn, for all the motion in him.

The silence stretched.

"And for the health of his brother." There was no way Govnan could know what was happening in the palace, but his gaze unsettled Tuvaini nonetheless.

A tight smile flickered across Govnan's face. "You never forgave the Tower for his brother, did you, Vizier?"

"You broke with tradition." Tuvaini let his anger speak. "You broke Tahal's law, and now we have a madman who might do anything—a raving prince who cannot rule." Tuvaini smacked fist to palm and strode forwards. "Beyon has no other heir—"

Govnan stood, sudden and unexpected. There was a fire behind his eyes. "If Sarmin is mad, that is no one's fault but your own, Vizier. The Tower spoke to save the child. It was you who incarcerated him."

"He had to be held secret. Any fool—"

Tuvaini staggered before a blast of heat. His words dried on his tongue.

Fire blossomed in Govnan's hands, and they burned as though soaked in oil. His lips peeled back in a snarl from blackened teeth in a mouth stretched so wide that it hurt to watch.

"Cage what you fear, and when it escapes it will consume you utterly!" A tongue of flame crackled from the mage's mouth as he spoke in an inferno roar.

Tuvaini could smell his hair smouldering. His skin felt tight, scorched before the heat, and yet some force held him so he couldn't turn away.

Fire spilled from Govnan's hands and ran wild over the stone floor; bright rivers encircled Tuvaini.

"Govnan!" Tuvaini fought down hysteria and put command into his voice.

For a moment the heat built, and then it broke. The flames died, and Govnan slumped in his chair, smoke wafting from his lips. "My apologies." The high mage spoke in little more than a whisper. "Ashanagur has grown strong. Sometimes he takes offence and slips my bonds to voice his will."

"It—It has a name?" Tuvaini said.

"He has a name." Govnan inclined his head. "And he will have a life beyond me. But you didn't come here to discuss the mysteries of the Tower. What would you have us do about Prince Sarmin?"

"Why did you insist Sarmin be spared the Knife?" Tuvaini asked.

"It was High Mage Kobar who—"

"Kobar is a rock. I passed him in the hall below. You tell me," Tuvaini said.

"He has about him that quality we seek for the Tower." Govnan gripped the arms of his chair and pulled himself straight.

"The Tower cannot recruit among the emperor's family." Tuvaini recoiled from the very idea.

"Once upon a time we did—it was a royal prince who founded this Tower, and Alakal himself was the grandson of an emperor. The royal family now consider it beneath them to serve, but if Sarmin were trained, he might make such a mage as has not been seen in three generations. Such a resource cannot be thrown away lightly. A time may come when the emperor has need of such talents. A similar provision was made in the time of the emperor's grandfather, though that child was lost in the chaos of the Yrkman War."

"Why did Kobar not say this when he demanded Sarmin's survival?"

Govnan shrugged. "I cannot know Kobar's mind, but it is clear that the more potential a weapon is felt to have, the more hands will turn to lift it."

"Well, this particular weapon of yours is mad," Tuvaini said. "He cannot be trusted to act in anybody's interest, not even his own. He sees treachery in every corner, and twists honest words into conspiracy."

Govnan fixed him with knowing eyes—too knowing. "If he twists your words, then speak none to him. You've wished him dead, buried him alive, so leave him be. If all is well with the empire he will die in that room of his, unknown and unmourned."

"All is not well, and yet there he remains." *Sarmin is of no more use to the Tower than he is to me.*

"No." Govnan stood with care. "All is not well."

"Your servant—" Tuvaini realised the young mage had never supplied her name. "She said the Tower protects the emperor from harm that doors cannot keep out. I know differently."

"Mura speaks with the certainty of youth." Govnan stepped towards Tuvaini, walking with an old man's shuffle.

Tuvaini backed away, his skin still hot with the memory of elemental rage. "We do not speak of a common plague. There is an enemy behind this—I sense his hand. The Carriers are his tools." Tuvaini heard the tremble in his own words; he feared the truth he had come to seek.

"An enemy? Yes, and we of the Tower fight him every day. We work to stay his hand; we work to keep him from claiming pieces for his game. A wall has been built around Beyon since the day of his father's death, a wall of enchantment like no other we have ever fashioned, but these are strange magics we fight. They are subtle and insidious, and in such a game the might of elementals may be circumvented. We stand at an edge now, a precipice, perhaps. Our wall is crumbling."

It will bury them all, Beyon, Govnan and Arigu. "I must return to the palace," said Tuvaini. "Meanwhile I expect you to focus on your work. I hope the empire will not crumble through your incompetence."

Govnan smiled. "No. It will not."

Tuvaini swept from the room. His hands were trembling, but he made sure Govnan couldn't see as he rushed down the Tower steps. He passed the statue of Kobar without a glance.

Sarmin would be of no assistance. It was time for Tuvaini to find out what his Red Hall bargain would yield. If he could not find an heir, one who was not mad or dying, all was lost. Satreth the Reclaimer had not driven the Mogyrk faith from this land only to have his own gods turn their backs four generations later. Blood had been shed for the papers he sought, the papers that held the key to the empire. He thought of Eyul holding his Knife, the blood on the floor by the fountain. It would be worth it. It *must* be worth it.

He passed the young mage, Mura, without a glance and hurried into the sunlight. Soon he would know.

CHAPTER EIGHT

Eyul scanned the horizon. What had looked to be a mere line in the distance now rose high enough to measure against his thumb. The Cliffs of Sight, with their sheer walls and flat tops, looked like clay bricks from the great dune where Eyul sat on his camel. They would reach the hermit in a day, maybe two.

Amalya stopped her camel beside his and waited. She spoke only when necessary, except during their dawn and evening meals, when they would share mundane details about the Tower and the palace, or swap some childhood anecdote. Eyul had grown accustomed to her companionship over the last weeks. At this time of night, with morning drawing near, he became impatient to make camp.

It wasn't unfamiliar, enjoying a woman's company, but Amalya was an unfamiliar sort of woman. In Eyul's world, females belonged either to the palace or the Maze. The women of the palace sashayed around in their silk and pearls, building schemes for revenge or entertainment. In the Maze, hunger drove women to please. But no matter whether noble or street-born, women were dependent on men for all their needs; they kept to their own sphere. Amalya, on the other hand, moved without censure from city to desert, spoke with boldness and honesty, and walked under the aegis of the royal family. Of all the women Eyul had known, only Beyon's mother had similar confidence—but even Nessaket could not leave the palace.

"Why are you smiling?" asked Amalya.

Feeling a fool, he scratched the whiskers on his chin. "Almost there," he said.

She looked beyond him to the cliffs. "Distance is hard to measure on the sands." They were so high up that dunes tall as towers looked like ripples on the ocean.

"I've been there before. Two days at the outside."

"Bad luck. Don't predict."

Having no rejoinder, Eyul pointed to the north-east. "If I remember rightly, there is a well not far from where we stand. We can camp there." He led the way and they reached the top of the dune, their eyes still fixed on the narrow line of the cliffs. His camel shifted, and sand slithered down into the shadows.

Amalya shook her head.

"No? Too far out of the way?" He surprised himself, being so solicitous of her opinion.

"No." She shook her head again, fiercely, as if shaking something off. Her hand clutched at her throat and she hissed, "Flesh comes— There are… people—"

—five of them, hidden beyond the dune's crest—

Eyul jumped off his camel, bow in hand, as the first man surged up the remaining yards between them. Blank of eye, his face patterned like a fine rug, he reached the crest of the dune on all fours. Eyul let his arrow fly and it travelled an arm's length before finding a home in the Carrier's chest. The man grunted and fell back over the side. Dead or wounded, it didn't matter; he wouldn't be climbing up again. *That's one.*

Eyul dropped his bow and reached for his Knife. The next Carrier found his footing and stood upright, a rusty sword levelled at Eyul's chest. Eyul ducked as the man rushed him. *Get in close.* He drew his blade across the Carrier's gut. *Two.* The old sword buried itself in the sand by his foot. Warm blood fell across his back.

A flash of blue to his right; scattering sand to his left. Two more Carriers came on the heels of their dead companions, trying to trap him between them. *So fast.* They clutched their small knives with confidence.

Another Carrier dragged Amalya from her camel and she screamed into the rising sun. Eyul couldn't help her, couldn't think about her now. He took the dervish position, arms out, ready to spin, and—

Now. He spun to the right, the sand sliding under his feet, and the Carrier in blue thrust towards his heart and caught him under the arm instead. By that time Eyul's elbow was in the man's throat. He registered the crunch of cartilage as he spun away, keeping his momentum, ignoring the sting of his own wound.

The Carrier behind him thrust, his dagger barely missing Eyul's neck, his sleeve brushing Eyul's shoulder. Eyul acted in the time between breaths, lowering his knife-hand, spinning against the sand, calculating the position of the other man's heart. *Now.* Mid-turn, Eyul's left hand blocked the Carrier's second thrust and half a heartbeat later his right hand pushed the emperor's blade between the man's ribs. *Four.*

Amalya. Eyul pulled his Knife free. As he ran to her, he scanned the dunes for more Carriers, but he saw just the one, kneeling next to Amalya's prone form, his hands around her neck. Eyul drew his hand through the sand to keep his palm from slipping over the bloody hilt of his Knife. He kept running.

Amalya lived. Blue fire wound about her arms, covering her skin from elbow to fingertip, and sizzled against the Carrier's chest. The Carrier opened his mouth; steam rose and evaporated in the desert air. His eyes bulged and turned milky. A ghastly smell of cooking rose around him.

By the gods—she was *boiling* him…

The Carrier's hands fell away from Amalya's neck and jerked in the sand before going limp. Eyul stepped forwards in time to catch the body before it collapsed on her. The flames wound away into Amalya's skin.

She lay there, staring wide-eyed at the sky for a time, but then she sat up, rubbing her arms and shivering.

"Have you ever done that before?" Eyul asked her, though he felt sure of the answer.

"Killed?" Her voice held incredulity. "Not people."

Eyul wiped his Knife on the Carrier's tunic, fumbling for words.

She stood and stepped away, staring at the body, relief and guilt mixed together on her face. It wouldn't do for him to compliment her deadliness, although that felt like the natural thing to say. It was hard, that first kill, he knew it. He remembered the first man Halim sent him after, a pickpocket, how the blood had spurted across the alley and stained the grey stone, and how he had stood trembling over the body until Halim slapped his face.

The Carrier with the crushed throat writhed in the sand, his hands around his own neck as he tried to breathe. Eyul would grant him mercy. He knelt and found the heart with his twisted Knife. He saw no change in the man's eyes as his struggles ceased; they were already dead.

Eyul cleaned his blade on the man's dirty clothes, then looked up at Amalya. She stood, arms stiff at her sides, lips drawn in a straight line, as her gaze passed over the four bodies around Eyul. Her eyes held an expression he'd seen too many times before: the look Beyon had when he found his dead brothers in the courtyard. The look said *How?* but didn't want an answer.

Eyul might have said something then, about how he'd saved her. He could say he had protected the empire from the plague-touched, or mention the safety of other travellers. But none of those would answer her question. He was a killer. That was obvious from his work.

Amalya turned away from him and went to her camel. She pulled her waterskin from a bag and took a long draught.

Eyul cleared his throat. "Do you think you can make it to the well? It should take us about two hours." When she nodded wordlessly, he said, "Good," and feeling the need to keep talking, "Well, no point in lingering here."

Amalya mounted her camel. Her shoulders remained tense. Eyul picked up his bow and did the same. "This way," he said. "With any luck…" He let his voice trail off. Nothing he could say would make him more like Amalya, a person unfamiliar with blood or its necessity. He started off down the crescent slope of the dune, turning leftwards. Waves of silent sand lay ahead.

Who had sent the Carriers? Nobody knew they were here except for Tuvaini and whoever had sent Amalya—and who had sent Amalya? Tuvaini would have chosen someone more ruthless, he felt, and Nessaket probably wouldn't have chosen a woman, believing all of them to be as duplicitous as herself. Only Beyon remained, but Beyon was not one for secrets or clever manoeuvres. If Beyon wished for an answer from the hermit he'd ride out himself, with a hundred warriors.

The question occupied him until the red stones of the well appeared, dark against the morning sands. They set up camp without speaking. Eyul set out the usual pile of dung, and Amalya unpacked her food, but when it came time to light the cooking fire, she sat back on her heels.

Eyul went to his saddle-pack for the flint and tinder, lit a flame and nursed it until the camel dung was smouldering. Amalya reached down and readied her pot, and Eyul walked a short distance away, standing guard.

Mesema leaned out of the carriage window, hoping for some wind, but the outside air only scorched her face and lungs. She retreated into the dark box she shared with Banreh. She was learning that the sun brooked no opposition here. All was bright and clear, and deadly hot. Only at night, when Arigu's Cerani soldiers sheltered in their tents, did she dare venture out onto the rocky terrain.

Banreh told her that they weren't really in the desert yet; when they got to the desert, he said, there would be naught but sand. They would sleep during the day and travel at night.

But she knew this had to be the desert. There couldn't be anywhere hotter than this.

"When you get to the capital," Banreh said, sitting still as if the heat and his leg did not pain him, "they will give you silks to keep you cool, and there will be tiled baths where you can soothe your feet."

"I don't want to get my feet wet," Mesema said, annoyed he'd used the formal tone.

Banreh smiled.

And she heard it, off in the distance, the bright jingle of little bells. She leaned forwards, listening, as Banreh's smile froze on his face and his eyes grew sharp and wary. He reminded Mesema of the god-statues up on the Great Plateau: still, but sharp. Hooves sounded on faraway rock, faded, sounded again. They were coming closer. She tried to count the bells. Six, a dozen, riders.

"Red Hooves," she whispered, putting a hand on the door.

Banreh grabbed her wrist. "They won't attack the Cerani. That's why you're in here."

Mesema paused. She could feel her pulse against Banreh's fingers. Those fingers belonged to her father.

"Wait," he said.

She nodded. The horses drew close now, so close she could hear their neighing and the murmurs of their riders. The coarse accents left no doubt: they were surrounded by Red Hooves, the least worthy of the Felting tribes, hardly of the People at all. She didn't dare look out of the window; instead she flattened herself against the wood, hoping no one would look in. Banreh's hand slipped from her wrist and wrapped itself around her shaking fingers.

"Listen," he said, "you are a Windreader. Windreader spears are coated with the blood of Red Hooves. You have nothing to fear."

His soft words gave her confidence. How strange that Banreh, who sometimes seemed so alien with his languages and his writing, knew exactly what to say in this moment.

"My brother was avenged a dozen times ten. His sacrifice made us ever victorious."

"Ever so." Banreh was not afraid. He looked her straight in the eye.

Mesema listened. She heard no clash of metal on metal, nor the shouts of injured men. The Cerani spoke to the Red Hooves. Their discussion sounded relaxed, almost casual. She could make out only a few words, but the ones she did hear made her shiver again.

"They're talking about a girl. Someone is going to give up a girl. Banreh, it's me!"

Banreh shook his head and slipped into the intimate tone.

"No, I don't think so."

She clutched his hand. She couldn't stop thinking about the Red Hoof thralls in her father's camp, their resentment, their unspoken fury. She'd felt it every time one of them was near. It was they who frightened her. She could easily imagine herself in the same position, abused and hateful, in disgrace.

The talking came to an end and bells tinkled as the Red horses drew away. Somebody shouted, "Don't bring her back unless she's proven!" and someone, another man, laughed. A horse neighed, excited, ready to run. And then the Red Hooves departed in a clatter.

Mesema fell to her knees and threw her arms around Banreh's middle. He was solid, not soft as she'd expected, and he smelled of ink and sweat.

He patted her hair. "When you are married, you will be safe. No one will dare harm you."

She didn't say what she was thinking: *I am safe now.*

At that moment the Cerani named Arigu stuck his head through the carriage window. He sneered at their embrace before turning to Banreh and speaking to him in his guttural language. Mesema recognised two Cerantic words, but she politely waited for Banreh to translate.

As she settled back on the bench, straightening her hair, he told her, "A Red Hoof woman has joined our caravan."

At sunset, Mesema walked along the stony ground to where two Felting horses stood side by side. One wore brightly coloured wool braided into its mane; the other showed hooves dyed deep red. The Red Hooves said their horses' feet were stained with the blood of their enemies, but Mesema knew it was only the dye from shelac berries—the Windreaders used the same dye to color their winter felt. She examined the Red horse. It was docile, so not a warhorse like Arigu's.

She ran a hand over her Tumble's flank. How he must hate this heat! Perhaps it was a cruelty to bring him to Nooria. She checked to make sure he had plenty of water. There was nothing else to do; the soldiers fed and brushed him, and Arigu wouldn't let her ride. Banreh said noble Cerani ladies rarely appeared in public, especially on the back of a horse, but he promised her the prince would let her ride within the castle grounds. It was written, he said.

She worried that Banreh put so much stock in his lamb-skins and symbols. Ink had no honour; ink had no history.

Mesema pulled her shawl around her. Ahead lay grey rock, dead land, except for the occasional scrubby bush. Their path stretched ahead, one plateau after another, lower and lower, until the mountains ended. It looked like water there, except for the colour, a band of white stretching out under the moon.

"The desert," came a woman's voice beside her. "The place where no thing grows."

Mesema didn't need to look; she knew from the accent that this was the Red Hoof woman. "My mother keeps a Red Hoof spear by our fire," she said. "She pulled it out of my dead brother herself."

"I pulled a Windreader spear from my sister's neck. After she died, I threw it out over the plains."

"That's not true," said Mesema. "No Windreader would kill a woman."

The Red Hoof did not speak for a while. Then she said, "These men are Cerani, but we are both Felt, the children of the grass. Shall we not be friends?"

"What's your name?" Mesema looked at her now. She was lovely, with creamy skin, light curly hair and roomy hips.

"My name is Eldra." Eldra wrapped both arms around her waist and shivered. She didn't have a warm jacket or shawl, but Mesema didn't care. A Windreader shouldn't care if a Red Hoof plunged right off the edge of a cliff. And who was Mesema, if not a Windreader?

"Why should I be your friend, Eldra?"

Eldra smiled. "I can tell you about my god."

The god of the Red Hooves had come over the eastern mountains to oppose the Windreaders even in death. And their god was dead, if the thralls in her father's care could be believed. He had passed from this world long ago, so he could speak to his believers only through old stories and songs. He was a useless god, blind, deaf, and dumb.

In the lands of the People many gods were acknowledged. Gods of the herd and harvest, water and winter, all were given their due at the appropriate times; but only the Hidden God kept the fate of the People in His heart. Only the Hidden God watched over them.

"We will not be friends, Eldra." Mesema turned and walked to her tent. At the flap, she looked back and saw Arigu dropping a cloak around the woman's shoulders. He talked to her a moment, gesturing with hands big as her head, before leading her towards his tent. With a shudder, Mesema crawled under her blankets. She still had time before she had to give herself to a Cerani man. Time to think, time to learn, and time to stay with Banreh.

Before she fell asleep, she made a prayer to the Hidden God, a living god among many. Her god did not fight for dominance, or to prove Himself to mortals. The Hidden God showed Himself only to those who looked for Him. She looked for Him now, in her heart and mind, because that was the only way she could carry Him into Nooria. As she closed her eyes, she felt the hint of a gentle wind on her face. It was enough.

CHAPTER NINE

Sarmin crouched by the head of his bed. Here under the shadow of the canopy none of the gods could see him, and the Sayakarva window was far to his left and out of sight. He was more alone than ever when he huddled here. Any guard entering through the door would not find him.

Ten years ago, one such guard had raised the alarm. Sarmin had held himself still, giggling silently, listening to the men shouting to each other as they searched. Not one of them thought to step around the bed. Sarmin had enjoyed the ruse and had hoped the excitement would bring his mother to his room. He didn't show himself until his window grew dark.

By that time, all the men assigned to his door had been killed.

Now Sarmin settled his back against the mattress and brought his knees up to his chin. He wished to think about his bride in absolute privacy. He remembered his father's wives, all five of them, with their dark scented hair and their soft breasts. He used to sit on the lap of the one called Lana and listen to his sisters learn their songs.

He remembered his sisters. Their gentle, wary eyes and their sweet voices. He remembered how they loved Pelar, his wild-haired, jolly brother. The girls had petted him like a kitten.

He remembered Pelar's red ball bouncing, Pelar running, Pelar laughing—very different to the ghost who appeared before him now, the ball in one hand, his face solemn.

"No," Sarmin said to his brother, "not now. Go away."

A Felting woman. He tried to imagine what she might look like. His mother had been true to her word and sent him another book, this one full of women in contorted, uncomfortable positions. He couldn't see any of their faces, no matter how many pages he turned. Sarmin fell to one side, staring blankly at the wall.

Pelar bounced his ball.

The door handle turned. It felt early for that, but Sarmin didn't care. Lost in thought, he rubbed his cheek against the carpet.

Light. A new sharpness of sound. The door had been opened. Sarmin rolled to his knees and peered over the bed. A man stood at the edge of the room, looking to his left and right in consternation until his eyes met Sarmin's over the sea of pillows and sheets.

Pelar's ball hit Sarmin in the chest.

Broad cheekbones, a bronzing of the eyes, a stubborn curl to the hair over the left temple. His brother's shoulders were broader than Sarmin remembered, and he was thicker of stomach than before. And he was no longer a boy. His eyes had grown wary; his hands restless.

Beyon. He looked well. Sarmin couldn't breathe.

No, not Beyon. The emperor. Lord of Blood. Lord of Dead Boys.

"My Emperor." Sarmin crawled around the bed to make his obeisance, placing his hand on the soft leather of one imperial boot. Toes moved beneath the leather, and the boot slid from under Sarmin's grasp. Fabric whispered. The door hissed over the carpet. The latch clicked.

A silence followed. Pelar's ball hit the back of Sarmin's neck, quick jolts that drew his shoulders together.

"Come here." The emperor's voice didn't belong in this room where everything was soft, where everything gave, even the vizier.

Bounce.

Steel for steel. I won't give.

Bounce.

He heard a crunch of stiff fabric. "Look at me."

Sarmin didn't move; he would face his brother, but not the emperor.

"Look at me," Beyon repeated. The voice sounded different now, lower. Softer.

Pelar's ghost took his ball and slipped away. The living crouched alone before the gods and demons.

Sarmin raised his head by hairs until he met his brother's eyes. They had once been merry, not like Pelar's, but easy and joyful. Now Beyon's eyes were older than his face.

Even old eyes can be shocked. Beyon covered it well, but Sarmin saw him flinch. "It's true—you've changed. But you are my brother," he said, "you of all people shouldn't grovel before me. Come, sit here." He indicated Sarmin's own bed. He wore three golden rings on his right hand.

Sarmin climbed up and watched Beyon through watery eyes. Heat rose in the back of his throat. "My Emperor," he said again, "why do you come—?" He stopped to wipe at his nose with the back of a hand.

"Sarmin—please understand, I'd have come sooner, but it wasn't safe for you. There are people who, if they knew you were here—" Beyon's eyes wandered towards the scrollwork, in the area of the hidden door. "Well. You wouldn't be here any more."

"But you come now." Sarmin wondered why his life was no longer important. Perhaps Beyon had conceived a child at last?

His brother changed the subject. "Do you know why he did it, Sarmin? Our father?" Beyon moved to stand at the edge of the carpet, by the opaque window. "Our grandfather had mercy and spared his brothers. Our father had to kill them himself, but not in the courtyard, on the battlefield. Father wanted to spare me that.

"But you—" Beyon turned back towards Sarmin. "You were the kindest, the gentlest child—the wisest of us. You were the one who would never lead an army against his brother. I went to our father's deathbed and asked him to let you live." His voice grew soft. "It was my very first decision as a ruler."

Sarmin's shoulders shook with denial. "No. It was Mother who begged our father to save me."

"No," said Beyon, "I asked Father to spare you."

A cold tear slid down Sarmin's cheek.

Beyon continued, "I believed it then, and I believe it now—even all these years later. You're the only person I can trust—Why do you shake your head? Is it not true?"

"It's true. It's true." Sarmin slid to his knees on the floor. He cradled his head in wet hands. "I would never betray you, Beyon."

Beyon knelt beside him, smelling of memories. The fatherly aroma of tobacco. A musky, female scent Sarmin almost recalled from the women's pillows. And then another, long forgotten until now: Beyon owned a dog. Sarmin longed to press himself up against his brother, soak in those memories and the fragrances of life, but Beyon grabbed his elbow and lifted it.

"Swear it," he breathed. "Swear it on my head, and I will take you from here. I will make you my first adviser."

Sarmin felt a moment of hope. He might sit at court. He might live among people, help Beyon run his empire, even breathe the outside air. But his imagination of these fine days quickly led him to thoughts of Tuvaini, followed by their mother and her general. He frowned as he placed his hand upon Beyon's clean hair. "Is that wise, my brother?"

"You question the Son of Heaven?" The emperor drew back, his eyes narrowing.

"Brother, if you anger those who have brought themselves up into power..." Sarmin thought of his knife, tucked away under his pillow.

"What do you care about that?" the emperor snapped. "Swear it!"

Sarmin said nothing. Beyon looked at the carpet. He lifted a hand, let it fall.

"I swear it," said Sarmin, at last, "as a brother. I will never betray you, Beyon."

"Yes." Beyon nodded and placed his hands on Sarmin's shoulders. "You have sworn." He exhaled a long breath.

Sarmin let Beyon hold him in that position for as long as he wished. He could feel Beyon's strength, and he could see the healthy tone of his skin. Beyon's breath wafted across Sarmin's face, pleasant and cool.

Tuvaini had lied. Beyon was not sick.

Beyon released him and leaned back. He looked at Sarmin as if he had just asked a question.

Sarmin opened his mouth, then said the second thing that came to mind. "I'd like to meet your dog, Beyon."

His brother laughed, and Sarmin watched him, the way his chin went up, the way his eyes cast to the side. This, he remembered.

Beyon was like a precious new book that he couldn't keep. If he told

Beyon about Tuvaini and their mother, Beyon would be angry and leave him here alone. But Sarmin couldn't keep the secret for ever.

"Sarmin," said Beyon, with a wide-lipped smile, "you have just told the emperor that he stinks of dog."

"My apologies, my Emperor—"

"No, no—don't apologise."

Sarmin looked at the small scar on Beyon's cheek, the stiff taffeta of his robes, the unadorned gold around his neck.

Beyon's hands moved to his sash. "I have something to show you. Don't be afraid." As his fingers moved, Sarmin tried to look away, tried to obey the cold hand that seemed to pull his chin to the side, but he could not. Blue-marked skin revealed itself, finger-span by finger-span.

Beyon slipped the red silk from his shoulders and sat bare-chested before his brother.

So Tuvaini had spoken true, after all. The emperor's chest and shoulders were as muscled and hairy as their father's once had been, but a curious patterning ringed his midsection with coils, concentric squares and half-moon shapes. Pairs of triangles, one facing up, the other down, appeared at regular intervals. A band of blue underscored each string and behind that, in fainter blue, a complex geometry marched beyond sight into finer and fainter detail.

Sarmin shivered. "But you look well." He couldn't take his eyes from the designs written upon his brother's flesh.

"I'm marked," said Beyon. "It began soon after I took the throne. At first I could hide the shapes —they were small enough—but of late, I go to my wives only in total darkness. My body-slaves…" His eyes focused elsewhere for a moment. "I was forced to have them killed. Now I let no one into my rooms."

"Are you dying?" Something lurked in the pattern: a threat, the language unknown but the tone clear enough.

"I don't think so—maybe." Beyon rubbed his chin. "You are my heir, should I be."

"So you're—" Sarmin's lips trembled around the word. He forced his eyes to the emperor's face.

"A Carrier? Not that I can tell. Everything I do is of my own will." Beyon buttoned his tunic.

Sarmin half-opened his mouth to protest as the pattern vanished behind silk. He forced himself to silence.

Beyon flicked his hair out of the way. "The dreams scare me. In them I do things not of my choosing." He looked at the stone window. "In my dreams, my body is not my own—but I can run away from the dream if I wish. I ran away when my dream made me threaten the vizier."

"The vizier?" Sarmin remembered the vizier's words: *The Carriers become bold, even attacking on palace grounds.*

"It's getting late. They'll be looking for me."

"Who? Who will be looking for you?" Sarmin's throat seized with fear.

"Slaves, administrators, wives, dogs." Beyon smiled. "The denizens of the palace."

Like Tuvaini. Sarmin again considered telling Beyon everything; to confess about his wife, the vizier, and his secret treasure under the pillow. *No. I have sworn to my brother, but I won't let the emperor take what is mine. Not yet.*

The emperor's commanding voice broke through his thoughts. "You have sworn. You will be summoned when it is time for you to serve." His brother was gone; the latch clicked.

Sarmin curled against the carpet until full dark, letting Ink and Paper step around him as they came to light his lanterns. Someone placed a tray of food beside his head. He smelled something new: the sour aroma of wine. Beyon's favor, or Tuvaini's, or perhaps his mother's. Whoever sent it did not expect him to wonder. He laughed to himself against the purple threads.

"Prince Sarmin of the Petal Court," he whispered to himself. "Vizier Sarmin." He thought another moment. "Emperor Sarmin."

Nobody answered.

He didn't know when Beyon would be back. How long would it take? Longer than a ride from the Felt? Longer than Tuvaini's trips through the secret passageways? Longer than the reach of their mother's arms?

Sarmin stood and pulled his knife from beneath his pillow. *I will not betray you, brother.*

He turned his desk upside down and hunched over it, intent. With fevered concentration he began to work. The point of the dacarba scored the wood time and again as he recreated the pattern: crescent moon, underscore, diamond within diamond, crescent moon, overscore. He missed no detail. Breath escaped him in slow rasps. *There's a secret here, for those with eyes to see.*

CHAPTER TEN

Eyul woke with a start. The last of the sun's heat sank through the cloth of his tent.

Something is wrong. He knew it, blood to bone. Sometimes it was like that. He knew better than to startle into action. He lay at rest, straining his senses, reaching for the wrongness. The sand between his fingers felt warm and gritty. Wrong. He sat up and moved to the tent flap. Veins ran across the dune, faint but visible in the low light of the setting sun: lines in the sand, raised little more than the thickness of a coin, no wider than his hand. Hundreds of them were stretching out in geometric profusion, crossing, intersecting, repeating.

He hurried out under a pink and orange sky. Amalya crouched by the remains of the fire, watching the lines at her feet.

"Amalya."

"It's a pattern," she said, staring at the shapes around her, diamond, half-moon, triangle, circle, square. "He has found us."

"Who has?" Eyul's fingers tightened on his Knife hilt. He didn't remember drawing it; his hands had made the decision.

"The enemy."

"I thought you said we were safe." Eyul stood scuffing at the lines of the pattern. They reformed as the sand fell.

"I thought we were," Amalya said. "My master told me he would hide us." She sounded defeated.

The pattern centred on the next dune, almost two hundred yards away. The heart was formed by interlocking diamonds arrayed around a six-pointed star. From each point, a design more complex than any palace carpet swept out across the slopes.

Eyul gasped as an electric tingle ran through him. Amalya gave a low moan and struggled to her feet at his side.

"The pattern is complete," she said.

The sands started to move. The entire facing dune began to flow, from the centre of the pattern, shifting with impossible speed, like water racing across a marble floor. He saw the tops of pillars first, then stone roofs, then archways from which the sand flooded, emptying long-buried halls. Within moments a lost city lay revealed before them, temple, tower and tomb.

Sarmin scored a line across the wood. One more stroke and the pattern would be complete. In his mind's eye he saw again the symbol-geometry emblazoned across his brother's chest, blood-red and blood-blue. He laid his dacarba on the floor and stretched his hands, noticing the ache in his thumb, the blister on his forefinger, and the sting of the old cut across his palm.

Sarmin's carved pattern contained what he had seen on Beyon's skin, but it reached out across the underside of the overturned desk to cover as much space again. He'd filled in the remainder as he would complete a circle two-thirds drawn, or fill in a mouth missing from the sketch of a face.

He sat back against his bed and rested his eyes on the more familiar intricacies of the walls. He'd long ago discovered all the watchers dwelling in the scroll and swirl of the decoration. Some of the faces he'd not found for the longest time, even after years of gazing, whole days spent staring, lost in the depths from daybreak to sunset, floating on strange and distant seas. He'd found them all before he'd grown his beard, though, the angels and the devils both. The wisest and most fearsome dwelt deepest in the patterning, hidden in plain sight, written in the most subtle twists. They had watched him grow, advised him, kept him sane.

Sarmin sought out the grim-faced angel whose gimlet eyes stared from the calligraphic convolutions above the Sayakarva window. "What will happen, Aherim?" He took up his knife again. "Should I complete it?"

Aherim held his peace. Sarmin frowned. The gods might watch in silence, but he expected answers from their minions at least. Aherim seldom missed a chance to offer advice if asked.

Sarmin set knifepoint to wood.

"It will be a stone dropped into a deep pool. No pattern can be made whole without a ripple."

He stared at Aherim. "Someone will notice? Who? Tell me who."

Silence. Sarmin felt unnerved. "I will ask Him." It was not a threat to be made idly, but surely one that would coax Aherim to speak further.

Sarmin waited. He pursed his lips. He had found Him last of all: Zanasta, eldest of the devils, speaker for the dark gods. He showed only as the light failed and grazed the east wall at its shallowest angle. Even then Sarmin had to unfocus his eyes to reveal Him.

"Tell me of the Felting girl. The bride Mother has chosen." There was time to kill before sunset.

"She comes." Aherim spoke again at last, his voice the dry whisper of fingers on silk.

"Is she pretty? Is she kind? Does she smell good?" Sarmin sat up and leaned forwards.

"She is sad, she is strong, she smells of horses." Aherim fell silent. He only ever answered three questions, and generally not the ones Sarmin asked.

"She is riding to me. That's why she smells of horse." Sarmin picked up his dacarba and sighted down the blades at one of Aherim's faces. "But why is she sad? Perhaps they have told her bad things about me. Maybe I'm ugly. Or is she worried that she will have to stay in this room with me? Maybe she will miss her horse."

Sarmin remembered camels, though not with fondness. His father had horses, but the princes were never allowed among them. "They kick worse than camels," he remembered a groom telling him. Still, he liked the way they looked. Perhaps a horse would be a good pet.

"I will make her happy, Aherim." Sarmin tilted the knife so that light danced along the blade's edges. "I will…" He tried to think how he might entertain her. When they came at all, people came to him with a purpose.

He couldn't recall a time when someone had come to his room simply to speak, simply to be with him. "Perhaps I will not make her happy, Aherim. Maybe I will share her sorrow. I will listen and hear of her life in the sandless wastes."

Eyul took one uncertain step, then another. Under his feet a thin layer of sand covered something solid: old stone, undisturbed by the passage of time or the magic that brought it to the surface. Amalya kept by his side, moving so close her sleeve rubbed against his. Eyul touched her elbow with his fingers and they each took another step forwards.

"Nothing could be alive in here," she whispered.

Neither of them wanted to test that idea too quickly. They took two more small steps. Sandstone houses lined the road. Square gaps in the walls showed where carved window-screens once had been mounted. Eyul could see nothing but darkness through them. Like Carriers' eyes, they watched their guests with quiet malevolence.

The sun was sinking towards the west, but still it blazed with heat. They wandered, separate from their shade and water. Eyul's leg ached with every step. This was a fool's game. He shook his head. "Let's get our camels and leave this dung in our wake." They turned in unison, for the first time moving with speed.

A stone wall had risen behind them, ten feet high and scoured by sand. It stretched to either side, curving out of sight in an unbroken arc.

Amalya let out a breath.

"Is there nothing you can do?" he asked her.

She blinked at the wall as if it had slapped her. "I can't touch my elemental here," she said. "It's as if he's gone." She said it the same way Eyul would tell her that every well in the desert had gone dry.

I have my Knife.

"Come on," he said, gripping her elbow and pulling her away from the wall. "They want us here, we'll be here. But it won't be that easy for them." With his right hand he pulled his weapon free. They turned again and walked up the street, the sun now in their eyes.

At a corner where the road split three ways, Amalya stopped.

"I feel something," she said. She leaned over and Eyul watched, spitting some fine grains from his mouth, as she ran the sand through her fingers. After a few seconds she said, "This way," and set off to the left. He glanced behind, then followed her.

They walked a hundred feet more. The road grew narrower.

"Does this look familiar to you?" Amalya asked.

Eyul shook his head before taking another look around. "Maybe." He wiped the sweat from his face, leaving a layer of sand. They walked some more. The sun slipped further down the sky. At least it would soon be cool.

"I want to get up high and see. If this was a city, there will be a gate."

"Not a good idea. These buildings don't look sound."

Amalya turned away, into the nearest building.

"Amalya, no!" Eyul ducked under the doorway after her.

"It's cooler in here," she pointed out. It was true. The stone remained chilled from wherever it had been hiding beneath the sands, and the sun hadn't yet found its way through the lower windows. Amalya pressed her forehead to a pillar and Eyul leaned against an interior wall.

"I have to find a stairway," she said, but neither of them moved.

The beating sounded first, a thumping sound like a distant heart. A spilling noise like the fall of a dry river came with it, outside the window to Eyul's right. Two beats later he heard a hissing through the window in the next room. Something or someone approached at a walking pace. He moved arrow-quick, grabbing Amalya by the waist. "Up, up," he whispered, searching for the stairs as he pushed her in front of him.

They found the stairs in the centre of the building. He was glad for her quiet movements, her lack of questions or fright. At the first landing he turned to survey the gloom below. "Stay to the side," he warned Amalya, not believing the calm darkness before his eyes. He spread his feet and relaxed, watchful, the emperor's Knife sure and ready in his hand. He was aware of everything at once: Amalya's stillness at his left, the sun's orange invasion through a hole in the ceiling, and the slow but steady approach of whispering sand.

The heartbeat stopped. The silence ached for the missing pulse, and then it came again, smaller, closer, quieter, somehow familiar. *Thump. Thump.* And again, on the stairs, like the bouncing of a ball.

A figure moved through the shadows. Eyul watched it climb the first steps. The red ball emerged into the sunlight first, then the boy's hand that held it. The light caught black curls and a smile, a smooth boy's face. "No," Eyul whispered. The boy climbed closer, pushing his feet into each stair with force, though the only sound he made was that of sand blowing in the wind.

Eyul forced himself to look into Prince Pelar's eyes. Black and cold, they stared both at him and through him. This was no longer the chubby, laughing boy he'd killed. This was a tormented creature from the depths of Herzu's hell itself. Dread soaked through Eyul's robes like cold rain. At his side Amalya drew in her breath.

"Kill it," she whispered.

"I can't," he said. *This is my creation.* Sorrow and horror weighted the Knife in his hand.

The creature smiled then, a skull-grin, and raised its arm towards the west. As it pointed with one finger, the red ball fell and bounced down the steps.

"Kill it!" Amalya had found her fright.

Eyul threw. A sound like grinding pebbles filled the stair. Sand swirled and stung for an instant, and fell before him, leaving only a scattering of stone and black grit.

"What— Was that real?" he asked Amalya, who crouched and ran her fingers through the dark grains.

"I don't think I saw what you saw," she said.

"What did you see?"

"Brannik of the Tower. Rock-sworn—or would have been; he died during the ceremony." She wiped her hands on her robes. "It wasn't him. He couldn't—"

He pulled her back from her memories. "Amalya, back at the camp you said the enemy put us here. Who is the enemy?"

She looked at him and placed one hand on the pendant that hung from her neck. "The creature pointed west. Should we go to the roof and see what's there?"

Sarmin sat, and the light ran from his blade. The dying rays slid across the east wall. He waited, enduring Aherim's silence until Zanasta came. It took more effort today, as if the devil had been hiding himself even deeper in the detail.

"Zanasta, show yourself." Sarmin furrowed his brow, squinting at the chaotic swirls where some long-dead artist had styled a rose from a froth of curling strokes.

"Show yourself."

And the devil smiled. Zanasta always smiled.

"This pattern is a key. Will something open when I set the final stroke?" Sarmin asked.

"I speak for the dark gods." Zanasta hated to answer questions.

"I know. What will happen?"

"I speak for Herzu, who holds death in one hand and fear in the other."

The light grew crimson as the sun plunged towards the dunes. Soon Zanasta would be hidden and silent.

"Tell me." Sarmin set his blade to score the last line.

"I speak for Ghesh, clothed in darkness, eater of stars. I speak for Meksha, mother of mountain fire."

"And they watch us now. Speak, Old One, or have the gods found a new Mouth?" The wood splintered under Sarmin's knifepoint. He began the line, his eyes on Zanasta.

"No!" The devil's smile vanished.

"Tell me." Sarmin cut half the distance. His hand trembled. *Zanasta always smiles.*

"A door opens. A door to everything. More than you can know or want. Hell and heaven."

The light fled, and Zanasta with it.

Sarmin held still, a hair's breadth from finishing. Mother had opened one door, Tuvaini another, and Beyon yet one more. He knew the things he wanted could not be reached through such doors. He wanted lost moments, fragile-feeling half-remembered old joys, Pelar bouncing his ball. He wanted to know what to say when people came to speak with no reasons. He wanted to know how to make a horsegirl smile.

He finished the cut.

For a moment there was nothing, only the thickening of the silence into something too heavy to bear. Sarmin stood. His knees ached. He could sense an approach. He felt it rising from unknown and unknowable depths, fast, then faster still, rushing at him. The hair prickled on his neck, the chill touch of anticipation reached down to the small of his back.

"No!" He spun, whirling, his knife held ready.

It hit.

The room rocked, then held still. Sarmin fell to the bed, clutching his blade. A pattern spread across the walls, the pattern he'd copied, but larger and more complex, deeper, carved in slashes from which a light bled, like that of dying suns, painting him with glowing symbols laid one atop the next. It lifted him. He stood transfixed, pinned, skinned in bloodlit patterning. His knife fell from a hand that seethed with alien geometries.

CHAPTER ELEVEN

E yul picked up his Knife, sheathed it and followed Amalya, his heart still beating a coward's rhythm. She reached the top before him and turned a circle before the red sky. He wondered at her calm and grace. He cleared the top step and automatically checked for safety; the shadows grew long, but he saw no threats in them.

"Look," Amalya said, pointing, "a wizards' Tower. This city is laid out like ours."

"There's the palace," he agreed. Were there silhouettes moving through the dusk of the courtyard? His hand closed around his Knife's hilt.

"This would be Stonecutters' Row." She turned to her left.

"This city has no river, though. And look—" She pointed westwards. "The large building, there—is that the tomb our emperor is building? It's in the right place."

"No, that's something else." Eyul had seen such a construction before, though Amalya was probably too young to remember; Emperor Beyon's great-grandfather had torn down all the temples to the Mogyrk faith and destroyed the heresy of the One God in Cerana. He couldn't remember if there had been a temple exactly like this one. It was square in shape and as large as three courtyards. Its tower rose into a point towards the heavens, as did each of its windows. He strained to see more, but the sun lingered on the horizon, cloaking the building in shadow.

"What is it?"

"Nothing good," he said.

They stood and watched, and the sun sank beyond the dunes. Myriad shapes lit up around the temple: triangle, line, half-moon. Eyul couldn't count them all; they were without number or end, with more appearing, forming a bright net around the dark building. Beside him, Amalya drew in her breath. The shapes lingered for a moment, prolonging the crimson light of day's end, before sinking into the sand and stone, disappearing like rain.

A tingling spread between Eyul's fingers and the twisted hilt of the emperor's Knife. "That's where we need to go."

Amalya turned towards the stairs without a word. They made their way down, stepping over the sandy remains of the demon that had worn Pelar's face. The street outside had fallen into a purplish gloom, but Eyul still felt uncomfortably hot. He passed Amalya his waterskin. "Be ready to duck into one of these buildings," he warned her. "Who knows how many of those creatures are loose?"

She said nothing as she took a drink from the skin and passed it back.

"This way," he said, leading her around one turn and then another. He kept his ears open for the telltale sound of shifting sands, but no more demon princes appeared and after a few minutes they were close enough to see the dark tip of the temple's tower. The next street would be under its shadow.

Amalya slowed to a stop. "I feel something," she said.

"Power?" He paused, still on the balls of his feet and ready to move on, but when she didn't stir he settled his heels in the sand.

"Yes, power. But it's all wrong. I can't go in there."

"But I have to go in there." As he said the words, Eyul knew it to be the truth. "I don't think we should separate."

"I can't go in there. I just can't. Try to understand—would you go into a place of—" Amalya's voice rose and broke off.

Eyul frowned. "A place of what?"

Amalya didn't respond, but cringed away, folding her arms over her chest.

"I don't get to choose." He drew his Knife and looked up at the Mogyrk steeple.

Amalya took a step backwards, raising one arm protectively over her face, and it hit him like a sword in his gut: she didn't trust him—and not only that, she thought he was capable of slitting her throat, right here, under the rising moon, for no other reason than her refusal to go into the temple.

And he could; in another situation, he would. The thought sank through him.

"Oh, by Herzu," he swore, turning his back on her. His feet felt heavy, but he walked on with determination. *What is this power, that allows me to leave a woman alone in a nest of demons?* He felt childish and cruel, but he discarded the idea of turning back. He was certain the answer to their escape was here, in the dark Mogyrk temple. He would come back for her—by then she would be scared enough to welcome his return.

He stopped just before turning the corner that would take him out of sight as a more familiar feeling washed through him: self-disgust. If he made her wait, made her wonder if he was coming back, she would despise him even more, and rightly so. He reached out and tapped the building to his left. "Get up on this roof so I can see you," he called out. "If something happens, scream for me. I will come."

He walked on, the sweat on his skin feeling clammy in the cooling air. When he looked back, he could see Amalya's white robes shining in the starlight.

She had no power against a sand-demon. He would have to hurry.

The temple's face rose before him, three storeys of carved stone. The One God of the Mogyrk faith looked down from his place above the mammoth door. The god who had been destroyed by his enemies, as Eyul understood it. A frail god of flesh, whose followers preached weakness, yet behaved savagely.

In the Cerantic pantheon there was a place for charity and love, and also a place for justice and righteousness. The empire could not have survived without the favour of its many gods. Therefore, with the Mogyrk madness defeated, Tahal's grandfather had wiped the empire clean of its monotheism. He brought down the Mogyrk temples and killed the worshippers. The religion persisted elsewhere, to the north and east, especially among the Yrkmen; but no more of their priests came to the empire.

The courtyard's chill pressed into Eyul's skin as he approached the entrance, Knife in hand. His foot slipped, banging against the stone on the sand-covered steps. The temple's door was of heavy wood, but the latch looked simple enough. He pressed his back against the cold stone for leverage and pushed, and the door opened enough for him to pass through. He could see nothing inside but darkness. Judging by the blast of air that hit his face, it was even colder inside.

He passed under the arch of the entryway and stepped into the wintry space. The arches had some sort of significance for the Mogyrk, he recalled. There were three in all: one at the entrance, one in the centre of the aisle and one over the altar. His Knife glowed with blue fire, giving him enough light to see. As Eyul passed under the central arch, his feet went numb with cold; the floor felt like ice rather than ancient stone. On either side benches stretched away into blackness. A thousand souls could worship in this vast space.

The cold grew harder, deeper. A man could not live in such a place; Eyul knew it would kill him. And then a sound, the first sound, like the scratching of a blade across wood, just a short scratch, but somehow more: somehow it was also a door opening. In his hand the emperor's Knife glowed more brightly, and twitched as if it were the scratching blade, as if it had made the final cut.

Eyul felt rather than heard the anger run through the church, through floor and wall. For a heartbeat, pattern-symbols flared. Something had changed. Somewhere a door had opened against the will of the pattern.

Twenty paces from the narrow altar, Eyul heard footsteps mirroring his own: as he approached so did another, from the opposite direction. When he paused, the other paused. Ten paces from the altar, he made out the shape of a man, heavy, broad-shouldered, though this man moved forwards as an invalid. Eyul recognised that painful, arthritic step and he fell to his knees. They seemed to freeze, instantly.

"Emperor Tahal." Without hesitation he pressed his hands and forehead to the glacial stone.

More steps. "Rise, child." The deep voice that sounded as if it were wrapped in rough cloth—this, too, he remembered.

Eyul rose, more slowly now, as the cold settled in his limbs and numbed his wound. He met the eyes of the Old Emperor, Beyon's father.

Emperor Tahal smiled. "Do you know how evil is destroyed?" he asked.

"With righteousness, Your Majesty."

Emperor Tahal's smile widened. "Think, boy: how is evil destroyed?"

"Thoroughly. Leaving no trace."

"There is always a trace." Emperor Tahal moved his hand in an arc, encompassing the huge temple in which they stood.

"The Mogyrk God? Is that who made the cursed?" Eyul frowned. "How did your ghost come to be here, Your Majesty?"

"A door opened for me, and I came." The emperor leaned forwards. "*Think,* boy. Think of the Carriers. *How* is evil destroyed?"

Cold fingers traced Eyul's spine. His lips were so numb that it was difficult to speak. "With the emperor's Knife."

The Old Emperor laughed. He tilted his head back and roared.

"The Knife," he repeated. "The *Knife,* Eyul."

Eyul's arm, half-frozen, was as slow to respond as his tongue, but at last he promised, "I will send you back to paradise, Your Majesty." His blade hit true as always, but it didn't freeze, as he had expected; instead, his hand burned with its heat, and its blue fire turned crimson. It took all his effort not to drop the Knife, and more to sheathe it again. He turned and started a slow run for the exit, feeling the building shake under his feet.

In the distance, Amalya screamed.

Eyul slid out through the doorway and stumbled down the steps. As he hit the ground he felt the last remnants of the day's heat burning through the soles of his shoes. "Amalya!" he shouted, searching the night until he found her on a roof, a glimmer of white surrounded by shadows. The building beneath her was shaking.

The city gave another judder and Amalya stumbled forwards. Eyul found his feet and broke into a jog, then a run, pushing through the leaden cold that pervaded his limbs still. "Don't move!" he shouted.

One more step and she would fall. The city shuddered again, and her robe blurred forwards. He forced himself into a sprint. The shadows around her resolved themselves into children's shapes. Amalya lifted her arm, fingers clenched, as if to raise her elemental, but she had no power here. Eyul plunged into a narrow street, taking a short cut, and momentarily lost sight of her.

The earth heaved, almost throwing him to the ground, and the windows that had been waist-high fell low by his ankles. The city was sinking. He rounded a corner and saw her again. *No time, no time to run up the steps—*

Amalya teetered at the edge of the roof. Black sand swirled about her. She made a motion as if to kneel, and then began to fall…

"No!" he shouted.

She twisted in the air and for a moment Eyul was reminded of a feather in the wind, but then she landed hard on her right side.

Two seconds later he lifted her in his arms. *If I had been faster…* His burned hand exploded with agony and as he fell to his knees the city sank another few feet. He saw blood in the sand. His leg wound had reopened. He couldn't carry her.

"Can you walk?" He set Amalya's feet on the ground. She clutched her right arm, raw and bloody, and gave a weak nod.

The demons' black sand had stripped the skin from it before she fell.

"Come on, then." He stood, wincing himself, and they picked their way through the dark streets, trying to retrace their steps. Where short walls had been, the sand ran down in channels; if he took a wrong step, they would sink, too. The half-buried buildings all looked alike. He chose a route, guessed, guessed again.

"This way," said Amalya, turning. Tears of pain ran down her face. Probably some ribs had been broken.

He followed—she was right, they were only fifty feet from the high wall—but then Amalya fell, screaming as the sand scoured her wound.

"We're close." He tried to help her up, but she pushed him off and stood by herself.

Two steps, and she'd fallen again. "Mirra!" she cried.

Eyul lifted her, ignoring the blood soaking through his trousers, and stumbled to the wall, which was only four feet high now. He pushed Amalya over onto the other side and she fell without grace, hitting the sand with a cry.

He'd have to lift himself over. He pressed down on the top of the wall with both hands, but his muscles failed at last. His body had given him up. He couldn't climb—he would wait for the wall to sink. He crumpled to the sand.

"Move, Eyul. Get up," Amalya whispered to him.

"In a moment," he promised.

"Get up," she whispered again, more insistent this time. She sounded so very young all of a sudden. "Get up, Eyul. Now!" And then, louder, deeper,

"Now, or you'll sink with the city."

He stood, and the sand moved beneath his feet. The wall stood just three feet high, but all he could see of Amalya was a bit of robe and her sandalled feet. He climbed over the stone easily enough now—why had it seemed so difficult?

Amalya lay crumpled against the wall on the other side. Her eyes were closed. Eyul gathered her up. She was quiet now, and her head lolled against his shoulder. Twenty yards away, to his left, he could see their tents, shining in the moonlight.

CHAPTER TWELVE

"Why are we going the long way?" Mesema fanned herself with her sleeve.

"The road follows the mountain range," said Banreh. While Mesema was restless, he was utterly still. He sat with his eyes closed, sweat soaking the collar of his shirt. "It seems long, but in the end it will be faster than going over the sand."

The Cerani had begun to hurry. At first they'd travelled the road only at night, but lately they set out while the sun still simmered low in the sky. Two hours had passed since they had climbed into the carriage, and Mesema was counting the burning seconds until nightfall.

Eldra made a little noise as the carriage rocked. "Why isn't there any wind?"

There was no answer to that. Without opening his eyes, Banreh said, "Let's begin another lesson. This time about the weather."

"I wish I could swim in a mountain stream," Eldra said in Cerantic.

"That was very good." Banreh smiled. "That's not easy to say."

Mesema shot him a look, but he still had his eyes closed. Not to be outdone by a Red Hoof, she bent her tongue around the rough Cerantic words. "Windreaders can tolerate any weather without pain." She used simpler grammar than Eldra, but she knew her accent was better.

Banreh cracked open one eye to give her a look of disapproval.

"I want to learn how to say something to Arigu," said Eldra. She smiled and shifted on the hard seat. "How do I say, 'I enjoy your manhood very much'?"

Mesema looked out of the window while Banreh told her. He was as calm as ever. She felt like kicking him.

"What about, "Cerani are very good riders'?"

"Stop," said Mesema.

Eldra giggled. "You're just jealous. These men don't want you."

"There are no men here," Mesema said, "only Cerani."

"Banreh's a man." Eldra put a hand on Banreh's good leg and squeezed. "Have you forgotten him already, Princess?"

Mesema turned away to the window, to the rock wall of the mountains. She would dash herself against them if she could.

"You're an idiot," she said to Eldra.

"*You* are," Eldra said. "This is a strong man, a fine man, but because of his leg you think he is a woman."

"I—I didn't—" Mesema hung her head out of the window and let the desert air dry the tears from her eyes.

Banreh kept silent.

Mesema looked up at the purplish rock of the mountains and the clouds that shrouded their peaks. There were Felting people up there in the cool, green valleys: Rockfighters and River People. She would never see them now. Her life would be sand, heat, and silk. In the spring, when her mother packed the wool into the stretcher, she would be idle, dipping her feet in the palace fountain. How strange, never to make felt again.

A flicker, and she saw it, or *him*; a man stepped back into the shadow of a dune. She watched him as the carriage passed. He kept his face turned her way, but it held no interest, nor fear. She felt a tingle along her arms when she remembered where she'd seen eyes like that before. When they had pulled her dead brother from his horse and lain him out on the ground, his face had held the same look.

The man grew small with distance before she could gather herself. "Banreh," she whispered at last, "there's a man watching us."

"Probably just a bandit. They wouldn't dare attack this caravan, not with so many imperial guards."

"A bandit?" She didn't know how to explain his eyes, so she said, "I don't know."

"Let me see." Banreh moved to the window and she pointed. The dune was too far away now, its shadows hard to discern.

"I can't see him. But we passed him all right, didn't we?"

"I suppose so." The man's gaze had her shaking still. She hugged herself and leaned away from the window.

The time passed; the sun lowered in the sky. Eldra sang little songs to herself about the strange god of her people. The tunes were not of the Felting folk; the rises and falls held the sounds of some distant place. When Eldra finished singing, she pulled a shawl from under her seat and wrapped it around her shoulders.

"Arigu will fetch me soon," she said, and it was true; the carriage stopped, and the general rode up on his horse. Behind it came Eldra's own horse, bedecked with bells and ribbons in the Felting way.

"Come now, girl," Arigu said to Eldra. He made Cerantic sound even uglier than it did already. His eyes were sharp as he glanced around the carriage.

Mesema wanted to tell Arigu about the strange man she had seen, but she was frightened.

Eldra giggled and jumped out of the box. Mesema could hear the horse's little bells ringing, moving ahead of them. Soon the carriage lurched forwards once more.

"Why does he... ?" Mesema let her voice trail off.

"He is a man," said Banreh.

"And so are you," said Mesema. Changing to the softer, affectionate tone, she said, "Banreh, before, I didn't mean—"

"I know." Banreh moved on the wooden bench, shifting his leg with one hand.

"Will you forgive me?"

He smiled. "As long as you promise to be nicer to Eldra." She liked his voice when he spoke as family. It sounded soft, like the rustling of the lambskins he wrote on.

The desert had already begun to cool. Mesema took Eldra's place next to Banreh and put her head on his shoulder. "I will. I want you to be proud of me."

He turned his head towards hers, so close she could feel his breath blowing against the hairs on her temple. "I am proud of you." He placed a gentle, ink-stained hand on her shoulder and pushed her away. "We won't speak of it again," he said in the formal tone.

We carry on.

Mesema slid across the bench to the other window. The west, beyond the desert, was a place of mystery: cruel fighting men who rode boats like horses, buildings bigger than her whole village, and an ocean so large that all of the Cerani and Felting lands could hide inside it. This was all true, if the traders-who-walked could be believed.

Wind rippled the sand, and Mesema tried to count the grains on her arm. How many questions would she like to ask Banreh? They couldn't be numbered, and she knew it. There was no way he could answer them all before he returned to her father and his war.

It hit her, as hard as the desert sun: Banreh would be gone, and she would be alone. There would be no intermediary, no protector, no adviser. An image of the dead-eyed bandit arose in her mind.

"Banreh," she said, still looking out towards the west, steadying one trembling hand on the window frame, "let's continue our lessons. I want to speak excellent Cerantic."

Sarmin moved through a darkened hallway. He passed a door to the right, two more to the left. He longed to turn and open one, but his body would not obey him. His feet moved forwards unbidden. Some force held his eyes fixed ahead to where, beneath shadowed tapestries, a man stood in a dim entryway. Above the man's head, tiles depicted a battle in shades of brown—perhaps the famous Battle of the Well, where the Cerani had defeated the Parigols once and for all. Sarmin tried to judge for certain, but he was too close now to study the tiles. He couldn't lift his head. Something forced him to look upon the man instead.

Tuvaini. Sarmin would have smiled, but his face paid him no heed. *A dream.* He left his room so often in dreams, and yet it always took a second miracle to make him realise he was travelling through nothing more substantial than imagination.

The vizier's lips curled back, revealing small white teeth.

He looked up rather than down at Sarmin, his eyes full of disgust, and held back, as if he thought Sarmin would make him dirty.

Even Sarmin's fever dreams had never seemed so strange. He'd never dreamed his body to be a traitor to his will—or taller, come to that.

Tuvaini's manner fascinated Sarmin. If everyone were to treat him with such disdain, he could move through the palace practically unseen. He tried to ask Tuvaini what had caused the sudden change, but his lips held still.

"I did my part; you can hardly blame me that you failed." Tuvaini held out a clean palm.

To Sarmin's surprise, he felt himself hand Tuvaini a rolled parchment.

"You've put me in an awkward position, to say the least,'
said Tuvaini, tucking the scroll into his robe.

"You have what you wanted," Sarmin said. His voice felt odd, gravelly.

"So I do. And next I will cleanse your stench from the palace."

Sarmin involuntarily glanced behind, to where he had started his walk. All lay dark. He turned back to Tuvaini. "I will leave, if it is in the design."

"In the design." Tuvaini's voice mocked Sarmin's.

For an instant a pattern flashed across Sarmin's eyes, overlaid on the scene, familiar, compelling and fearsome all at once.

Sarmin tried to reprove the vizier for his tone, but he could not. Instead he turned away, into the darkness, where he felt something shift.

The corridors melted away into night.

"Dada?" A young girl looked up at him with wide eyes, her hair wild with sleep.

Sarmin could see the pattern woven around his arm, spiralling to the hand that held the cleaver. A meat cleaver? Was Sarmin now a butcher in the Maze, chopping goat and mutton to sell in pieces?

"Dada?" the girl asked again. "Are you still sick, Dada?" Sarmin thought the girl very pretty. She was dark, like his sister Shala. He felt the blood from the cleaver running warm and powerful across his fingers. Shouldn't the man be practising his trade in his shop? But instead he stood in a dim mud-walled bedchamber, crammed with sleeping pallets pushed together. He had been sick. Patterned. Hidden away. Sarmin understood.

The man—Sarmin—both of them—they caught the little girl by the hair and raised the cleaver.

No!

With every fibre of his being Sarmin commanded his hand to drop the blade. The hand, bloody and dripping, hesitated, trembled. A hundred faint voices rose at the back of his mind, a thousand, more:

"The pattern finds no hold on her."

"The child resists. The wife resisted. The sons."

"She stands against the pattern."

"No, she is my child."

"She resists."

"Erase her."

And the cleaver swung, biting home with the wet sound of butchers' work, a clean cut between the vertebrae.

Sarmin howled, or tried to, but he didn't own his mouth. He tried to look away, but his eyes watched the meat open and the blood spurt. He tried to leave—with all his being he tried to leave.

Sarmin fell to his hands and knees, feeling sand beneath his fingers. No blood, no child. An unusual smell filled his nostrils and prickled his skin, but he couldn't identify it, not until he felt sand beneath his fingers. *Fresh air.* He lifted his head and peered over the crest of a dune. Fifty feet away he saw an older man and a dark-skinned woman, both injured. The man held the woman, who sat with her shoulders hunched inwards.

"Where am I?" he asked, but no sound came forth. The sun rose, fast and faster, and he stood beneath a different dune, watching a caravan go by. A young woman with wheat-colored curls stuck her head out of the carriage and looked at him. The world spun again and Sarmin was in his room, staring at the ceiling gods.

"What have you wrought of me?" he asked them in his own voice.

The gods did not have to tell him that his dreams were of his own making.

Mesema's lessons lasted until full moonlight, and her tongue and throat felt sore by then. Banreh asked for extra water from the soldiers, and when they brought it, she took a long drink and looked out of the carriage for the Bright One. He'd come halfway towards the moon since she first started watching. His inevitable journey, marking her own path from daughter-hood to motherhood, was too short, but she knew there was nothing she could do to slow the stars.

"Banreh," she said, but stopped; she heard the slow breath of sleep. She bunched a cushion behind her head and tried to close her own eyes. She thought of her prince, and made him like Arigu, only younger, and with curly hair like Banreh's.

She must have dreamed of him, for the next thing she knew was the faint light of dawn and the shouts of the soldiers as they set up camp. Banreh had already gone. She threw down her pillow and took another drink. The water still felt cool against her tongue.

She jumped out of the carriage and surveyed the wide landscape. Eldra was standing by her horse, facing the dark west, as she did every morning; she enjoyed watching the dawn spread across the desert. The Bright One hovered on Eldra's left. Mesema scowled at it, willing the day to come and make it disappear. Then she took a breath and prepared herself. It was time to be friendly. She wasn't doing it just for Banreh; when she got to Nooria, she would need a friend. She dragged herself to where Eldra stood, trying to think of a nice thing to say, but she needn't have worried, for Eldra spoke first.

"The sun comes from the east, as do my people. Soon it will light the entire world."

Mesema tried to think of a way to respond. Finally she offered, "I thought your people were to the north, like mine."

"God's people live in the east." Eldra closed her eyes, a faint smile on her lips.

The east. Mesema imagined it as a place of snow and high keeps, tall men of Fryth and Mythyck and Yrkmir beyond, shaggy mountain beasts, and strange, halting songs. From them the traders-who-walked carried many things, useful and pretty, but their dead god had never appealed to any People on this side of the mountains except for the Red Hooves. Mesema thought a moment, searching for common ground.

"I believe in the gods too."

"But there is only one god."

One god, dead, but with all the power of the many. It made no sense, but Mesema had to learn to guard her tongue. She switched to the intimate tone, a soft teasing between friends.

"What does Arigu think of your god?"

Eldra laughed. "Like any man, he doesn't care what I think." She spoke as a sister, crushing her consonants together like soft felt. "Anyway, God is not my god; he's everyone's god."

"Well, I understand that," Mesema allowed. "Anyone can worship a god, even if he belongs to other people."

"Mesema, listen. My god is everyone's god."

Mesema felt the heat of the sun on her back; she looked to the Bright One and was relieved to find him gone. "Why did your family send you to Arigu, Eldra? Are you to marry him?" Eldra glanced over her shoulder at the camp. "No... I never proved myself, and anyway, Arigu doesn't really care for me. I can tell." She turned back and squared her shoulders.

"Then what?"

"Never mind."

Mesema thought about Eldra's arrival. Banreh didn't appear to know why she was with them. Arigu had some design they couldn't see. Instead of one girl from the Felt, Arigu was bringing two. An honest assessment forced Mesema to allow that Eldra was prettier and more womanly than she was, but Eldra had two points against her. She wasn't a virgin, and she couldn't bear children, so she couldn't be meant for the prince. It bothered Eldra, the not-knowing; Mesema could see that now. All her jokes and flirtations served to disguise her worry.

"Well," Mesema said, taking Eldra's hand, "you're my companion, perhaps."

Eldra giggled. "I'd rather be Banreh's companion."

"You'd have to talk to him about that," said Mesema, hiding her stab of annoyance.

Eldra looked over her shoulder. "The general." She rolled her eyes and squeezed Mesema's hand. "I'll see you in the afternoon."

Mesema felt sorry for the girl. It was supposed to be fun, trying for a plainschild—or perhaps it was a sandchild in this case—but Eldra and Arigu didn't have a real romance, and as long as Arigu dominated their caravan, Eldra could never be with the man she really cared for. Mesema's cheeks grew hot when she realised she was glad of that. She wished the Hidden God had chosen a more blessed birthday for her, but instead she had been born selfish, under the Scorpion's tail. He'd also chosen her fate, in being sent away; she had yet to understand if that was a punishment or a reward.

She turned and looked for her tent. Banreh always tied a Windreader scarf to the pointed top so that she could find it. She crawled in and lay down on her mat, not bothering with her nightdress. She would ask for water to wash herself when she woke. The soldiers washed in the sand; they would consider it a waste, but they might allow it.

And then, without quite knowing why, Mesema cried herself to sleep.

CHAPTER THIRTEEN

"Let me see it," Eyul said. Amalya hunched in his arms, her back to him, as if even his gaze would sear her arm. He could see her pain, written into the lines of her neck and shoulders. He gritted his teeth as he drew himself up. Somehow he'd injured his own back.

Amalya turned slowly, holding her elbow with care, like a brimming cup. The sand had given her a new skin where the flesh had been scraped raw; only here and there could Eyul see the glistening of stripped muscle in patches the desert had not yet found. "Have you magic for wounds?" Eyul asked. The flies would come, and with them the taint that would sour the arm.

Her eyes held the glazed amazement of a man stabbed in the stomach.

He knew that look. "Have you a cure-spell?" He reached for her shoulder with his unburned hand.

She blinked, and some intelligence returned. "Herb law," she whispered, "I know a little herb law. My true magic lies in fire and in smoke." She managed a grimace and looked around.

"Herbs seem to be in short supply."

Eyul was relieved: she had her wits, at least. A Tower mage could be relied on for a well-trained mind.

"Wait here," he said, "I'll bring the camels."

Amalya crouched down, slow and stiff, sheltering her arm as though it were the most precious infant.

The stars lit Eyul's path across the dunes and he found Amalya's camel in the depths, between the starlit crests, where the darkness was almost tangible. He walked stiffly, dragging his wounded leg, as he scanned the ridges for the dappling of tracks left by his own camel. "An assassin wears the dark like a cloak," he quoted from the *Book of the Knife*. Darkness had ever been his friend.

No night terrors for Eyul.

And yet his breath came unevenly and his heart's rhythm guided his steps. For a moment he saw Pelar's ball, bouncing with every beat. Behind him Amalya's camel passed wind with unusual vigour, leaving the night's silence in tatters.

Eyul grinned and yanked the beast forwards by its tether. "You have the right of it, my friend." The horror sank with the city. The echoes that remained would haunt him only if he let them.

Eyul found his own camel a mile further on, waiting peaceably in the lee of a hundred-foot dune. He rode back, leading Amalya's beast and navigating by the light of the moon. For the last half-mile of his return, Eyul could see her robes at each crest, white against the moonlit sand, and motionless.

"You have magic for the pain?" he asked as he closed the last yards.

She looked up, dark gleams for eyes. "Fire and smoke, nothing else."

He helped her onto her camel. She held herself upright stiffly, moving with slow determination. Eyul still found her beautiful, despite the taut lines of her agony and the grim slit of her mouth. He felt guilty for it, even as he breathed her in. "There. Hold to the pommel."

She gripped with her good arm. "Tell him to walk steady. I'd rather not fall off." She managed a tight smile.

Eyul studied her for a moment. In the ruins she'd feared him as much as the ghosts, afraid he'd slit her throat. In a day or two her arm would swell, and she'd beg for that mercy. The knowledge sat like a cold stone in his stomach. The keen edge of the emperor's Knife would hardly notice her skin, but he noticed it. He didn't want her death on his hands.

"You never wanted any man's death." Eyul heard the words as if Halim were standing at his shoulder even now, risen from the grave and scarcely the more wizened for thirty years in the dry ground. "That is what makes you the ideal assassin: patience. Your lack of appetite lets you wait. Duty will guide your hand to make the cut."

Amalya returned his gaze. "What are you thinking?" A lover's question, asked through gritted teeth.

"That we should put space between us and this place," he said, mounting his own beast.

Tuvaini waited for her in the temple of death. Herzu watched him from eyes oflapis lazuli in a face of carved jet. He returned the god's stare as he approached along the central aisle. The sculptor presented Herzu as a thick-chested man with the head of a jackal, six yards tall. When Herzu visited Tuvaini's dreams, he came as a human youth, loose-limbed, robed, walking the dunes in the dusk, seen only in glimpses between the crests.

"My Lord High Vizier."

Tuvaini turned. Nessaket stood behind him, close enough to touch.

"My lady." He brought his fingers to his forehead. "You have a silent step."

She waited, impassive save for the slightest furrow between her brows.

Tuvaini moved aside, and as she passed he drew in the scent of her. Desert-rose, and a hint of honey. He watched Nessaket's smooth back, the motion of her shoulders, the gleam of olive skin as she made her devotions. Her personal guards would be waiting by the door, but in the temple of death they were alone.

At last she stood and turned. Tuvaini pulled his gaze from the sway of her breasts to the hardness of her eyes.

"You are a pious man, Vizier?"

"Only the foolish do not honour those with power over them," Tuvaini said.

"Herzu holds power in both hands." She spoke from the scriptures. "In his left he brings hunger."

"And in his right hand, pestilence." Tuvaini finished the line. A pause.

"And the emperor fares well this morning, I trust?" Tuvaini smiled.

Nessaket did not smile. "My son is well, I thank you." She walked to-wards the entrance and her waiting guards. She always left him this way, wanting. Set aside.

"But which son?"

Nessaket stopped, her shoulders stiff. For the longest moment she neither walked nor turned. Tuvaini wanted to see her face, wanted to see what his words had written there.

Another step towards the doorway.

"Herzu has his right hand upon Beyon's shoulder, Nessaket." Her name felt good in his mouth.

She stopped again. Sweat ran beneath his robes, liquid trickles across his ribs.

"Can Arigu find a child among the horse clans so young she is yet a virgin?" Tuvaini asked.

At that Nessaket turned.

Tuvaini felt his heart pound. "And if he can, will she reach Nooria? It's a long road from the grasslands, and we live in interesting times." He reached into his robes.

Nessaket startled, arms rising, mouth ready to call her men—

He pulled the scroll out quickly. "No weapons—we are not barbarians, Nessaket." He managed a smile. Their sins bound both of them to silence. Nessaket would not run to the throne room; she would stay and listen until he let her go. He held the scroll before him, level with his head. "There is an old man in the desert who remembers our history better than the most learned palace scribe. He holds treasures from the library of Axus, taken on the night it burned—papers, documents, books of record, sealed oaths, blood confessions spilled on cured skin." *And one has been stolen for me.*

Nessaket approached, a sway to her hips, silks flowing, a memory from dreams on nights too hot for sleep.

"And what does your paper say, Tuvaini?"

"I—" She had never spoken his name before. "I—" He looked to the scroll and its wax seals. His hand shook from wanting her. "It shows the lines of succession, back past the Yrkman incursion. Where we have speculation, it has names; where we have hearsay, it has dates. Fact in place of argument."

"And what is that to me? Or the emperor?"

"Herzu watches us. May we speak of death, Nessaket?"

She was close, her scents surrounding him. "I married the death of children, Tuvaini. I am no stranger to such talk."

Tuvaini lowered the scroll, unrolling it. "This page shows the path Herzu has set before me. It tells a tale of failed lines, premature ends, assassination. It shows how, with enough time, the seed that falls furthest from the tree can flourish."

She took a step closer, her head tilted in question.

"Beyon will die soon, or become something worse than a corpse. And fifteen years' solitude has broken Sarmin; he could never rule. Let that line end, and the next step is written here." He pointed at the bottom of the scroll.

Nessaket drew in her breath. "Treason."

"I do not speak of betrayal. I would never raise my hand against the empire. I love the empire." He traced a finger down the longest line upon the parchment, reaching his grandfather's name. "And it falls to me to safe-guard the empire."

She was silent a long time, and he listened to her breathing, watched the light on her hair. She raised her head from the parchment and looked at him, truly studied him, as she never had before. What did she see, he wondered.

"I very much enjoy being the emperor's mother," she said at last.

He resisted the urge to wet his lips. "And how did you enjoy being the emperor's wife?"

"One of many wives." She turned towards the statue. "It was tolerable."

"Tahal was a great man, deserving of many honours," said Tuvaini. "But I am a humble servant of the empire, who has never once asked permission to marry."

"I see what you mean." She fingered the pendant that hung between her breasts.

Another silence.

"Beyon has been to see Sarmin," he told her. "He wishes to circumvent you and make Sarmin his own servant."

"He will fail." She dropped the pendant and faced him.

"They were close as boys. Apart, they are easily controlled, but together, they might be difficult."

"While you are not." Nessaket showed him a slow, secret smile, and for an instant she was the girl he had loved in the happy days of Tahal: the graceful young girl who danced for the emperor in his private rooms, the boy at his feet forgotten. Tuvaini had always been overlooked. But no more.

"While I am not," he agreed. "A sick son and a mad son, Nessaket. There is no future there."

She stepped closer, so close he had to clutch the scroll to keep himself from touching her. "I will consider your words," she said. "And your offer."

Tuvaini swallowed. "Nothing could please me more."

A brief incline of her head and she was gone, brushing past him and to her guards without another word.

Tuvaini lowered himself to the stone and stared up at Herzu's face. His breathing slowed; his fierce need abated. He gathered himself for his next confrontation. It was as he had told Nessaket: together, the brothers created a difficulty. It was time for Herzu's fury to tear them apart.

Eyul and Amalya rode through another night. Eyul slouched in the saddle, his mind clenched around the visions the ruins had shown him. Every so often he looked up, checking that Amalya still kept her seat. She swayed as though in her cups, jolting with every footfall.

A chill wind picked up two hours before dawn, snatching sand from the ridges to give each gust a stinging edge. Eyul wrapped his desert scarf in the manner of the nomads to hide his face, reducing his view to a slit. In the palace treasury Eyul had seen the iron helms taken from the Yrkman invaders; those men had chosen to confine their vision to a slot, showing as little of the world as Eyul saw now. Perhaps such helms sat well on men whose narrow view of the world led them across treacherous seas to impose their will and die at such a distance from their homes.

For a while Eyul rode beside Amalya. "We were meant to die in that city," he said. "That pattern was set to crush us."

"Yes."

"But something went wrong with it—something changed. Somehow a door was left open, or forced open, and an old ghost found his way in."

"Old ghost?" Amalya spoke through teeth gritted against the pain.

"The Emperor Tahal. He showed me how to break the pattern. I thought it would be difficult, or complicated, but it was simple."

How is evil destroyed? With the emperor's Knife.

Amalya managed a tight smile. "The solution is generally simple when you know what it is. Strike at the centre. But sometimes that's most of the problem—finding the centre."

They rode without speaking from one dune crest to the next, until he asked, "What did you fear in the Mogyrk temple?"

She turned. Her eyes rolled white in her head for a moment before she found focus. "Everything."

"What's to fear in a new god? The invaders, men of Yrkmir and Scythic and other places you can't say without spitting, they carried Mogyrk with them. What's to fear in that? There's no magic in their lands, just coldness and mountains without end. All peoples bring some or other god with them and Cerani swallows them whole." Eyul realized he was quoting Tuvaini, and stopped.

"The Mogyrks see no shades," Amalya whispered. Her camel jolted and the pain sharpened her voice. "They see only one path, one design, and they have just one evil. Think of that, assassin: one temptation, one Lord of Hell, with dominion over all things dark. The devil the Mogyrks carry on their back can turn the hearts of many men." She straightened in the saddle and watched him with a quiet intensity. For a while only the creak of leather and the soft noises of padded feet in sand filled the space between them.

The wound on Eyul's leg burned as if new. "You think such a devil would find easy meat in the Knife-Sworn?"

"You've taken scores of lives." The moonlight caught her cheekbones, sculpting her beauty. "Women and children, perhaps?"

We live in a world of sorrow, of pain and hard choices, Eyul wanted to say. Somehow the words that had always brought him comfort felt too hollow to speak here in the desert. "I—" *I bring peace. I send souls to paradise. I give an end both swift and kind. Few in this world have one at their side strong enough for mercy in their final moments.*

He said nothing.

"You think loyalty will hold you safe against corruption?" Her words stumbled and she swayed. Already the wound was poisoning her blood.

"I am loyal to the empire," Eyul said, "if nothing else."

Amalya coughed a laugh and then muttered, "Loyalty is the easiest of all virtues to subvert." Her words rang like steel on steel.

Caution bent Eyul's lips. "Who gave you the Star of Cerana?"

She struggled to lift her head. "Are you loyal to the Star? Or the honesty of its delivery?"

"Who gave it to you?" Eyul fought the impulse to shake her. Amalya bent over the pommel of her saddle, the breath harsh in her throat.

"Who!"

"Ask me again, at the end." And she would say no more. The moon dropped in the sky and still they rode on, an hour of ups and downs, punctuated by grunts and winces. "We could rest." Amalya's voice came dry and cracked.

Eyul pulled up his camel and dismounted. A lost hour held no water. It made no difference whether Amalya found her end on this dune or on the sands another day to the west. He told himself it made no difference.

Amalya dismounted like an old woman. Something had broken in her, to make that plea for rest. Eyul felt it break when she spoke. She caught his eyes in the grey light and manufactured a smile. "I could make us a fire," she said.

"Are you cold?"

"Burning up." She tried a grin, but sudden pain erased it. Eyul imagined he could feel the heat coming off her. At sundown, when he had lifted her onto her camel, he had smelled the wound and felt the fever on her skin. *Why?* he almost asked aloud, but the answer closed his mouth. She didn't want to die useless.

"A fire would be good. It will be a while before the sun finds us," he said.

Amalya's brow glistened where her sweat ran in trickles. He started on the straps to his saddle-pack. "I'll find us something to burn." He remembered Amalya's fastidiousness when it came to cooking over camel dung.

"No." The word held a crackle that made him drop the ropes and turn to her.

Her dark eyes caught the crimson hint of dawn and threw it back at him. A wisp of flame played over the skin of her wounded arm and was gone. Amalya held her good hand before her, brown fingers clawed; she spoke one hot syllable, and fire woke on the dune. A white flame leaped up between them, higher than a man. Eyul stumbled back, the heat beating at him like a fist, and his already burned hand roared a protest.

"Amalya!" he shouted over the camels' terror, reaching out for one as it broke past him, and missing.

The flame made no sound save for a faint but angry roar, higher pitched than the wind. It neither wavered nor flickered but stood like a white lance against the sky from which all trace of dawn had been driven. Eyul could smell his headscarf smouldering and he stumbled backwards.

"Amalya!"

She stood before the flame, one hand extended as if she were pouring out her fever into its hungry brilliance. The desert sun at its zenith in a steel-blue sky would shed a kinder light than that which now lit the dune. Under its illumination all color fled. Amalya stood robed in utter white, her flesh cut from pieces of night.

For a moment the flame flared brighter still. Eyul raised one hand to his eyes, but his vision had already left him. An echo of Amalya against a white-lit sky lay in every direction.

She gave a short cry, and the fire fell cold and silent. Amalya's after-image died with the flames, leaving Eyul in a world of black.

"Amalya!"

She didn't answer.

Eyul groped a blind man's path to where he'd last seen her. For the longest time he thought himself lost beyond redemption—his hands could find neither Amalya, nor any sign of their camp. Questing fingers caught only sand, sand, and more sand. He called out, softly at first, and then more stridently, but only the wind answered, filling his mouth with grit. He crawled in an ever-widening circle, though his leg and hand smarted and his back protested. He ignored them. *He would find her.*

At last there was a soft whisper to his left. "Here…'

When at last he caught a handful of cloth he sighed with relief and reached out again, this time finding firm flesh within the robes. He'd had no plan beyond finding Amalya, and so he gathered the woman to him and sat with her cradled in his lap. He could feel that the fever had left her, expelled with the heat of the flame. She was limp, unstrung, but breathing smoothly.

"You lost control of your fire," he told her, "but I suppose it's better this way. You can't feel it now."

Eyul sensed the dawn, felt the fingers of its warmth pushing back the chill of night. He turned his face to the sun and stroked her hair as a mother would her child's. A tear rolled down his cheek. He checked the Knife at his hip. The hilt felt warm beneath his sore fingertips, reassuring. There might be little call for a blind assassin, but the emperor's Knife would make his end a quick one. And hers.

I send souls to paradise.

The heat built quickly, and with it came flies. Eyul covered Amalya's arm as best he could with his cloak. She stirred once in his lap, muttering something incomprehensible, and he ran his fingers across her lips. "Shhh."

An hour passed, or maybe four. The sun parched Eyul, and his tongue felt like old leather when he spoke. "Perhaps it is time." *Before she wakes. She won't feel it.* He reached for his Knife, faltered. He didn't want it to be time.

"Nice knife." A stranger's voice sounded at his shoulder. Eyul pulled the blade clear.

"They say a blind man's other senses get sharp." The stranger spoke with mild amusement. Somewhere on the dune, others whispered.

Eyul knew the accent; only one people spoke the true-tongue with such reckless disregard for vowels.

"But it can't be true. I watched you cuddle that pretty slave girl for so long that Jarquil had time to find your camels."

Eyul set the emperor's Knife to Amalya's throat.

"Hey now!" The nomad's surprise set a grim smile on Eyul's lips.

"Wh— What?" The touch of metal to skin brought Amalya from whatever dark seas she floated on.

Eyul flinched, finding his own surprise.

"Who?" Amalya asked the question in a croak.

"Nomads," Eyul said. "You should let me cut your throat. I'd be doing you a favor."

CHAPTER FOURTEEN

"Hey now," the nomad said again, softer this time, "the sun rises. Time for you to come with us, blind man."

Amalya's fingers curled around Eyul's wrist. With a sigh he drew the Knife away from her throat. He bent his head over hers, seeking the hollow of her ear. "Can you see them?"

She stirred and spoke into his chest. "No weapons in their hands."

"What do you want?" Eyul asked the nomad, raising his head as if he could see. He heard the soft bray of a horse.

"Me? Nothing. The old man is expecting you. Come, now."

"It's all right," Amalya said.

Eyul sheathed his Knife. He kept still as someone, a nomad, from the smell, wound fabric about his eyes.

"Jarquil brings water." Done with Eyul's bandage, the nomad tapped his shoulder, then tapped it again until Eyul raised his knife-hand to accept a clammy water-bag, cool against his burned palm. He held it to Amalya's mouth first.

Afterwards, the nomad took the skin from his hand. "Come, now. The pretty girl, too."

Eyul drew his right arm in front of her. "She stays with me."

This drew a hoot of amusement. "If you think you can hold onto her, blind man."

He did. She was not as helpless getting onto the camel as he expected, but he wrapped one arm around her anyway, holding her firmly in place. With his good hand he grabbed the pommel.

The nomads led them on, and they travelled in silence under the hot sun. Amalya rested her arms on Eyul's, and nestled her head under his chin. He supposed she was drifting. Her hair was hot from the sun, wafting a fragrance he remembered from the palace courtyard: the yellow flowers that sparkled on their bushes like the stars at night. He had never learned the names of the different flowers, not even for the making of poisons, for he did not work in secret, or with cowardly tools. If a man died by the emperor's Knife, he and everyone else would know it. And so he didn't know the name of the yellow flower. He regretted that, among many other things, today.

Eyul had never questioned any of the decisions and beliefs that had brought him to this moment. Every step felt pre-ordained, difficult but necessary for his service to the gods. At the same time he knew that any different choice might have brought him a different life—one where he would be quietly fishing along the river, perhaps, or collecting ink roots in the desert. Maybe he'd have sons instead of dead princes to dream about.

He felt Amalya's fingers close around his elbow and surprise drove away the last of his wistful thoughts: she was alert.

That small touch of fellowship encouraged him. Without sight, the hours left to him promised to be small in number and low in comfort. Sweat and sand chafed his skin; pain held his back in a scorpion grip. The nomads' high-pitched calls roiled in his ears. Even so, the gods might have chosen a worse ending, for he was not alone.

"How are you feeling?" A stupid question. Soon she would ask him to free her, to give her up, and he would do it.

She turned until he could feel her breath against his throat.

"I think we're going to be all right."

She lies for me. "Yes," he said, "maybe so."

Tuvaini passed through the Low Room where the fountain made soft lapping sounds and patterned sunlight fell through the latticed stone above.

Two of the Old Wives sat upon the fountain's rim, washing their arms in the cool water. One met his eye and whispered in the other's ear, and they both giggled. Despite their grey hair and sagging breasts, he was no doubt too old for their taste.

This room held no more solace for him. When he looked at the tiles, he remembered Eyul's blood, and he wondered whether the assassin had survived his mission in the desert. If it were any other man, Tuvaini would assume him dead, but Eyul's years of killing hung around him like chain-mail. He might survive. The idea was pleasing.

He passed the guards, who bowed, and the slaves, who prostrated themselves; he paid no attention to either.

The doors to the throne room stood open. Tuvaini had liked the great doors very much, in Emperor Tahal's time. It felt right for the gods to smile upon Tahal, who had earned the throne with both strength and spirit. But when Tuvaini realised the doors favoured all emperors indiscriminately, he became disenchanted. Under the aegis of those carved gods, the Boy Emperor had thrown tantrums in his chair, refused to listen to his adviser, and even struck his mother when she tried to whisper in his ear. That was when the nobles had first drifted away from the city, pursuing power in their own provinces, unhindered, while the boy pursued maturity in his.

It would be a long time coming. Even now, as Tuvaini approached, Beyon played a loud game with the slave children and his mangy dog. "Catch the ball like that," he said, as a little brown-haired boy laughed. "Then— quick!—throw it and turn—"

The boy threw the ball towards a little red-haired girl; her hands darted out to catch it, but she missed. Squealing with laughter, she raced the shaggy dog for the prize.

"Get it, get it!" the boy called after her. But the dog got the ball, and Beyon and the slave boy collapsed with laughter.

"Your Magnificence." Tuvaini made a quick obeisance. Beyon looked at him like a man coming awake, his eyes clearing, his smile fading. "Tuvaini," he muttered. In a louder voice he said, "All right, children, have some honey-nuts—here; here—and now back to your master and the chores he has for you. I'll see you again tomorrow."

The children plodded away from the dais, their heads low, their shoulders bowed.

"Do you know, Your Majesty," said Tuvaini, "that their master might well beat them for their presumption, interacting with you?"

Beyon raised his eyebrows as Tuvaini put on a look of concern.

"Then I would have their master killed," said Beyon. "It is not for him to judge."

"As you say, Majesty." Beyon rarely had any other solution. It bored Tuvaini, but also he depended on it. "But remember, these slaves will grow up one day, and they will expect special favors from you." *Or me.*

"Unlikely." Beyon patted his dog and stood up, his gaze taking in the empty room. "By the time they're grown, they'll understand how things are. They'll be all hollowed out."

Are you all hollowed out, then, my emperor? Tuvaini cleared his throat. "Then why bother, Your Majesty?"

Beyon didn't answer. He squeezed the red ball between his fingers. "The little red-haired one—her parents sold her. They came from the Wastes. She told me they were clanless, and had too many children and no food. They got a good price for her pretty face."

Tuvaini thought of Lapella and looked out across the tiles.

Beyon continued, "How do you think they choose which ones to keep and which to sell? Do they choose the oldest? The youngest? Or do they decide which of the children is more useless to them?"

"What is useless to one family," said Tuvaini, "may be of great use to someone else."

"That comes later," said Beyon, waving a dismissive hand. "I am interested in the choosing: how can you see potential in a child, or the lack of it? How can they be sure they made the right choice?"

"I suppose there is no point in dwelling on it once it's done. That road leads to madness." Tuvaini smiled to himself.

"It's madness from any direction you come at it, to discard your own children." Beyon looked down at his hands, turning them over to examine his palms. Tuvaini had noticed this habit in him of late. Perhaps there were some small marks appearing there.

Soon, now. Soon.

Tuvaini looked back at the doors, making sure there were no waiting supplicants. "Your Magnificence," he said, "I came to speak of serious matters."

"Oh?" Beyon sat down on the throne. He always looked too big for it, too broad in the shoulders and hips. His dog settled at his feet and pricked up its ears.

"You remember I spoke to you of Lord Zell, Magnificence, and his concerns about pirates beyond the western shore. He complains the White Hats of his province do nothing, and would raise his own army as in days of old. I have written strong words—"

Beyon waved a hand. "Lord Zell and his blusterings bore me. Send your letter."

Tuvaini made his next move, the words coming from his mouth as if he had practised them a hundred times. "My words would carry more weight if delivered by a hundred Blue Shields, Magnificence."

"I won't send my own guard. I need them." Beyon shifted upon the throne and sighed. "Who is the general there? Send Arigu to replace him."

And there it was. In less time than it took to eat a date, Tuvaini had reminded Beyon both of his vulnerability and his dependence on Arigu. The emperor was in position. All he needed to do was set the tiles to falling. "That is the other subject we need to discuss, Magnificence." He paused for effect. "I have heard whispers: General Arigu plots with your brother. Prince Sarmin means to sire an heir, to rule in your stead. Movements have already been made in this direction."

Beyon went still and said nothing.

"Arigu asked permission for a brief return to Vehinni Province, but my family confirms he never arrived there. Instead he fetches Prince Sarmin a horsewoman from the north. The prince means to marry her without your permission." Tuvaini stopped talking and cast his eyes down. *Let him chew on that.*

After a silence, the emperor said, "Arigu has wanted to see the Grasslands for some time now. But something is missing from your story."

"I'm sure I don't know the whole story, Your Magnificence."

"You've always been too kind to my mother, Tuvaini, but Arigu takes no action without her standing behind him. I suppose she is tired of this son and wants to try the other."

Tuvaini said nothing. He hadn't meant to implicate Nessaket. He'd expected Beyon to lose his temper, to be rash, to behave as Beyon had always behaved.

Instead the emperor leaned back in the throne, breaking into a smile.

"My mother is clever, but she is not clever enough. You are my faithful servant, Tuvaini. She didn't plan on you, did she?"

Tuvaini steadied himself on a pillar.

"I shall frustrate her in the getting of this heir, and amuse myself in the process. When is this woman expected?"

Tuvaini forced the words from his mouth. "I believe very soon, Magnificence."

"Then I shall go to the desert and fetch her. I will present her to Sarmin myself, as a gift from the emperor." Beyon laughed. "And when the child is born, my bitch of a mother won't even see it. She'll have no leverage with either of my heirs."

Tuvaini felt a pressure at the top of his head, heavy and sharp, like the tip of a sword. A pain shot from his scalp to his heels; a strike from Herzu himself, who held agony in one hand and loss in the other. Tuvaini welcomed the pain. He relaxed, breathing deep, and let it fill his veins with steel, strengthen his mind with a warrior's keenness.

He opened his eyes and saw Beyon, the Boy Emperor, staring back at him. He looked foolish and scared. "And the general?" Tuvaini asked.

Beyon shrugged. "He will make an oath, or die."

This boy was no emperor; he was worth *nothing*. Beyon murdered powerless guards but allowed treacherous generals to live—and why? Because they were powerful; because he needed them. Because he was weak. So weak, he had the marks; so weak, he would die, soon, alone and outcast.

Tuvaini made his obeisance. He was already deciding on his next move. Herzu had touched him, and so blood must be shed. If he felt a slight hesitation, a moment of pity, imagining a girl's blood in the desert sands, he put it aside. The gods and the empire forced his hand. It must be done.

CHAPTER FIFTEEN

Eyul woke to the whispers of men and the sound of dripping water. A cool rag rested on his forehead. The air felt still and warm against his skin; he guessed he lay inside a tent.

"He wakes," a nomad said.

The last thing Eyul remembered was dozing in the saddle. *Amalya*. He tried to sit up, but hands, more than two, pressed him down onto his blanket.

"You put something in my water."

Someone else spoke. "You wouldn't have let us take care of the woman if they hadn't. We had a hard enough time of it as it was." The voice was cool and rich. A river in the sands.

"You sons of whores! If you—" His hand went to his hip. The emperor's Knife was gone. He reached for his eye bandages and tore the first layer away, but once again, hands stopped him.

"Such impatience." The voice felt familiar. "Not the temperament for desert travel." Water dribbled into Eyul's mouth and the man continued, "Your friend is alive."

Eyul ceased his struggles. "Where is she?"

"Elsewhere."

"I need to get to the hermit." Laughter rang out around him.

"You don't know my voice, assassin? You have arrived. And once you are well enough, you will have a choice to make."

Eyul lay on his back and allowed the hermit to tend to him. First the old man rubbed a harsh-smelling salve on his burned hand. Then he washed the wounds on his face and leg with cold water. Eyul considered the hermit's words. An assassin didn't make choices.

"Does your role still fit you like a tight slipper, Eyul? Do those boys still haunt your dreams?" The tone was conversational. Eyul didn't reply. He remembered the last time he'd come to see the hermit. The hermit couldn't stop the nightmares, but he'd offered his water pipe, and that had eased Eyul's mind for a time.

Fabric rustled as the hermit finished his ministrations. A waft of air told Eyul that one of the nomads had either come in or gone out of the tent.

"I regret what happened in the desert. I was powerless to change those events." The hermit's voice was still close.

Eyul considered this a moment. "You saw?"

"I saw," the hermit said.

Eyul tried to gauge how many people were listening. The nomads could hold their silence for hours if they needed to, a skill gained from years of hunting sandcats or ambushing hapless merchants. They could sit motionless in their dun-colored robes until their prey was tricked into foolishness. His mother, from the sands herself, used to sit by his bedside with the same rocklike silence.

"A taste of what you've come for," said the hermit. "The Carriers share a common vision: what one sees, they all see. Each Carrier is a piece of the whole, a part of a larger pattern, and the pattern itself is like a river, or a song, flowing into itself, writing itself, making itself heard."

"The pattern is of nature?"

"No, the pattern is man-made; that is for certain. But that is not to say it doesn't have a life of its own."

Eyul listened again, but heard nothing but the hermit's slow breathing. He would not ask Tuvaini's question; the hermit could not live past answering it, knowing the pattern had found Beyon, and Eyul doubted now that he could kill him.

"Who is the enemy?" Eyul made a new question.

"Ah, now you are riding ahead of me." A whisper of sand, and then the hermit's voice came from above him. "You will learn more after you've made your choice. I give no information for free, Eyul, especially to those who've come to kill me."

"I am not here to kill you." Eyul spoke the truth.

"Disobedient in your old age?" The hermit didn't wait for an answer. "I require the wizard's protection. Leave her with me and I will tell you what you need to know."

Eyul rolled his head from side to side. "That's not my decision to make."

"It is now," said the hermit. Cloth rustled, and Eyul caught another gust of fresh air. He was alone.

"Amalya," he said out loud. Nobody answered.

Mesema kicked the sand beneath her slippers. It still held the night's chill, though the sun threatened in the east. She could see why Arigu called this land the White Sea: its waves, some cresting higher than ten horses, rippled away into the western darkness. The Bright One blinked above them, making his last few steps towards the moon before the sun chased him away.

Eldra brushed Mesema's elbow with her fingers and offered a fig. They stood together, taking small bites, facing the west. Once, Mesema had seen Eldra as a woman and herself as a girl, but now when she looked at their shadows she saw the same curved hips, the same narrowing at the waist. They were of a height, and sand-coloured curls fell around both of their faces. A stranger might take them for twins. A Red Hoof and a Windreader; it was no longer so strange.

"Tell me about your prince," said Eldra.

Banreh had asked Arigu about the prince, but he hadn't received an answer. Perhaps Arigu didn't know him, or maybe he kept silent for another reason. She told herself it didn't matter—only the child mattered. "You know as much as I do," she said.

"Maybe he has the nose of a rat, or the wool of a sheep," Eldra said with a giggle.

Mesema had to laugh too. "I shall close my eyes."

"There's only one part of him that needs to work right." Eldra nudged her with an elbow.

Mesema drew in her breath, feigning shock. "Eldra! You are truly wicked!"

"Does that mean you won't speak well of me to Banreh?"

Mesema tried to smile at that, but her cheeks felt stiff as old leather. She turned away, buying time. As she struggled for something to say, something sparkled at the corner of her eye. She turned to catch it in her sight, and heard the desert groan, low and resonant, bringing a tremble to her legs. "Eldra...'

The dunes shifted and whispered. The sand fell off them in sheets, spilling into the valleys between, revealing shapes of glimmering silver in the fresh sunlight. A pattern lay across the sand, a geometric weaving from dune to dune, beginning at a point she could not see and ending just where her slippers cast their shadows. Triangle, underscore, circle, dash, square: this was the same pattern she'd seen in the grass at home, when the hare had made his mad run to safety.

Something urged her feet forwards along the hare's path. Curiosity, dread, rebellion: it was all of a piece as she walked away from Eldra and into the mystery laid across the sand. *Follow this arc, this line, turn here where the circles intersect... Yes.*

She heard someone shouting her name—Eldra!

Wait.

The hare had dashed under these two parallel lines. *Turn here where the circle is not quite complete; pass through the diamond.* Here Mesema stopped, confused. Where had he gone next? Through one of these smaller shapes, into the paths that hid, small as lace-point? She knelt and stared into the depths. Perhaps he had.

"Mesema!"

Banreh ran up behind her; she knew it was him from the sound of the sand under his boot where he dragged his right foot. He grabbed her around the waist and pulled her back, away from the hare's hidden ways. She was surprised by the strength of Banreh's arms. He had pulled her well away from the edge of the pattern, almost to the camp, before she even had a chance to protest.

"What are you doing?" he said, tightening his grip and pressing her back against his chest. "Are you mad?"

"You're the one who said to look for patterns." She relaxed against him, tilting her head back against his neck, and he let her go.

"But look—"

She followed the motion of his hand, and in the distance, at what must be the centre of the pattern, a building shone in the sunlight, the tallest Mesema had ever seen. Its white stone rose in a series of jagged points that cut away at the sky, and at the centre was a tower, rising even higher into the blue, straining towards heaven. As she looked, the shapes and lines that had surrounded it flashed and disappeared.

Mesema kept close to Banreh, feeling his warmth, smelling the ink on his hands. "What is it?"

Banreh didn't answer.

Eldra came to them, her feet light on the sand. Her eyes showed no fear; instead she smiled at them. "The traders-who-walk speak of these pointed houses. They are holy places for my people."

"Did the pattern bring it here? It—It wasn't here before. Was it?" Mesema shivered, though the heat grew all around her. Perhaps it had been behind a dune.

"It's a gift," said Eldra, glowing now with excitement. Mesema gathered her lips around another question, but Arigu suddenly pushed between them, tall, and wide as the front of a horse, blocking the light of the dawning sun. He grabbed Eldra by the arm, his big hand crushing the fabric of her sleeve.

Eldra stumbled backwards, kept from the sand only by his iron grip. Then he hit her, and she fell.

The whole camp gathered about them now, taking in the scene, muttering among themselves. Banreh knelt by Eldra and touched her cheek. They exchanged soft words. They looked so intimate, with their foreheads almost touching, Banreh's hand now on Eldra's shoulder, that Mesema drew her mind away. She tried to focus on another conversation, but all the other voices distorted in her ears.

Mesema turned to the general, putting her hands on her hips. "Apologise!"

Arigu looked down at Banreh. "Scribe: tell your charge I will do no such thing. We cannot stop here in this place of sickness." He turned away and shouted for his men to break camp.

"Only a coward hits a woman!" she called after him. Out of the corner of her eye, she saw Banreh watching her from his place on the sand.

Arigu stopped and pointed to where the pattern had shimmered on the dunes. "Did you see that pattern?"

"Of course—I've seen it before. I'm not frightened!"

His mouth twisted as he took a step towards her. "You're lucky I don't hit you, too, Princess. Do you know how many soldiers I have lost to that pattern? How many good men have died with those marks on their skin?"

"Died?" Surprise won over Mesema's anger.

"You've seen the pattern, but not the death?" He stepped closer, his nose twitching as if he smelled bad meat. "What are you, then?"

Mesema waved her hands in denial. "I saw a pattern on the grass. That's all." *Maybe the pattern was not the Hidden God's, just the hare, showing a safe path through.*

Arigu calmed. His sharp eyes studied her. He looked thoughtful, and for a moment he reminded her of Banreh, only less kind. "And what were you looking for, out there on the sands?"

She swallowed. "A path."

Eldra was sitting up now, steadied by Banreh's arm, and Mesema looked away. Watching them touch made her stomach twist around.

Arigu wasn't finished with her. "A path to that building?"

She shook her head, no.

"Good. That kind of building has caused more trouble in Cerana than even the pattern." Arigu motioned her forwards. "Come, girl. Let me look at your arms."

"Why?" she asked, confused, even as she moved towards him.

"I need to see if you have the marks."

She held out her arms and Arigu folded back the sleeves of her tunic. She noticed that his hands were trembling, but his fingers were light on her as he examined her skin. He was gentle, for a big, gruff man. "Well," he said after a few minutes, "you don't have the marks."

"And if I did?"

Arigu ignored her question. "You said you saw the pattern in the grass. Did somebody put it there?"

"Just the wind."

"And you never saw it before that?"

"No." Mesema brushed her sleeves back into place.

"Would you remember what it looked like? If someone asked you to make a picture of it?"

"The bigger shapes, maybe." *The path is important, not the pattern.*

Without another word to her, Arigu turned to Banreh. "Come with me," he said. He pointed at Eldra. "Don't touch her," he called out to his men. "Let me deal with her." He tapped Banreh's shoulder and the two walked together, away from Mesema. "I have to ask you—" he began, but they passed out of her hearing.

Mesema knelt by Eldra. "Did it hurt?"

Eldra nodded, still cradling her cheek. "I want to go to the church."

"You can't. We're moving on."

"Mesema, who can outride a Felt? I'll be there before they can even—"

"Listen. The pattern *kills* people. Arigu just said so. If the church is part of that…" She remembered Banreh dragging her away, remembered seeing the church for the first time. How had she not seen it before?

"The Cerani lies." Eldra rose and brushed the sand from her skirt. "And the pattern is not the church; our faith is older than patterns." She walked to the carriage, her posture straight and sure. Mesema was relieved that she went to the carriage and not the horses. Eldra's words were just words; she wouldn't ride off to the strange church alone.

In the distance, Banreh nodded to Arigu and limped back towards them, step by step. His face remained patient and still, even as sweat dripped from his hairline and soaked the collar of his tunic. She stood up to face him as he drew close, lifting her chin and putting her hands on her hips.

They looked at one another for a long moment.

"It is as I told you; you must learn to curb your tongue," said Banreh.

"Because I see things?"

"Partly. They have never heard of windreading before. But mostly, Cerani women don't speak as you do." He gathered himself. "Arigu says the pattern is a soul-stealer. Those marked by it become its servants. Those it can't use, it kills."

"How can a pattern make such decisions, Banreh? There must be—"

"There must be what? Do you know something more?"

Did she? Mesema lost her grip on the tiny thread she'd been following in her mind. "No."

"Well, then. Keep your thoughts close."

Mesema twisted her hands together. "I understand. Banreh, where did that church come from?"

He looked puzzled for a moment. "I suppose it was behind a dune and then the wind moved the sand…" He stopped, then said, "I have to tell you something."

She waited, watching Banreh massage his hip with one hand. He paused overlong, his eyes still cast down. *Something bad, then.*

"Tell me," she said at last.

He looked at her. "The emperor doesn't know you're coming. Until he dies, you must keep your betrothal a secret."

"But I'm to go to the palace!"

"No, we will wait in the city."

"For him to die?"

Banreh sighed, and said, "Yes."

Mesema took a breath. She'd known it would be hard, coming to the desert and living among the Cerani, but she hadn't expected treachery. She stepped forwards, putting a trembling hand on Banreh's shoulder. "Banreh—Arigu doesn't mean to kill the emperor, does he?"

"No, the emperor is already dying."

She breathed a sigh of relief. "But why keep it a secret? Imagine, if you married someone and my father didn't know…" Mesema caught her breath. "My father was deceived."

"Not exactly."

"My father was deceived, and Arigu's only warning us now because it's too late for us to turn back." She spoke, though her throat felt hollowed by sand.

Banreh kept silent, staring at the church in the distance.

"Arigu has been disloyal, Banreh, and caught us up in his game. I don't like it. I don't like it at all."

"As you say, it is too late for us to turn back."

She couldn't read his voice. "Is that why Eldra is here? In case we make a run for it and get lost in the desert? So she can be the Felting bride if I run? We look alike." Mesema gathered her hair in both hands and pulled.

Banreh hung his head. "When the emperor dies, you will be a queen, as Arigu promised, and your father will be satisfied."

"And the war can go on, because nothing is more important. Not even this pattern that kills."

Banreh looked over his shoulder at the packed horses and the waiting soldiers. "Come. It is time for us to move to a new camp."

Mesema wiped at a tear and turned her back on Banreh. The dunes stretched out before her, their valleys offering shadow and secrecy. Without thought she started running, between one dune and the next, the sand shifting under her slippers, until her legs were shaking with effort. At last she fell against a soft, shadowed slope, gasping for breath. The sand cushioned her back and coiled around her feet like a rug. She was well hidden from the soldiers, and the pattern.

Mesema closed her eyes and listened for Banreh's uneven gait. When he came around her side of the dune she said, "You will never let me run away from it, will you, Lame Banreh?"

"When Arigu chose you, your great-uncle looked into the grass."

Mesema made a snort of disbelief. She didn't open her eyes. She didn't want to see his face.

"The wind showed us the future. You are to create a new leader, and with him, more glory than we have ever seen."

"Glory that comes from fighting?" Mesema sighed. "You have used your honeyed tongue on me once already, Lame Banreh. I listen more cautiously now."

"Then hear this." But he said nothing for a time.

Mesema kept her eyes closed, listening to the falling of the sand.

"Mesema," he said at last, "I would not let you go unless I believed it."

"Go to Nooria?"

"I meant, go away from me."

A sob escaped her, but she caught the second one and held it. "If you don't hold me right now," she said, "I will never forgive you, Banreh."

Movement, and she felt his arms around her, the damp of his sweat and the roughness of his tunic. She laid her head against his chest. "This is the last time," she said. "I will be braver in the future."

He said nothing, only smoothing her hair.

"Damn my great-uncle and damn the grass," she said after a time.

His voice fell soft against her ear. "It's time to go."

"Yes." She stirred against him.

He kissed her where her hair met her forehead. His lips were soft, but the touch of them burned her.

"Don't." She opened her eyes and stood up, arranging her hair with her hands. The feel of him radiated through her, even now that the sun bled its full heat into the air. It would have to last. She took a breath and felt the hot air fill her lungs.

The high, pointed tower of the church peeked over the ridge of a dune. She shivered, remembering what Arigu had said about his dead soldiers. She couldn't fathom how the deadly shapes related to Eldra's religion. Perhaps the church worked like a sword: a power, to be used by good and evil alike. Mesema understood swords, and she could only grow to understand them better as time passed. But if the god was a sword, the pattern was something else again. Where a sword cut and laid bare, the pattern bound and kept hidden. Much like Arigu.

She didn't trust Arigu. Worse, something kept her from saying so. Instead she turned to Banreh, motioning towards where she knew the Cerani general waited, putting aside the thudding in her stomach. "Let us leave this place," she said.

"I think there is someone behind the Carriers," Tuvaini said. "A man."

Lapella made no indication that she had heard him. She lay across the bed, turned away on her side, her smooth curves bare for his inspection.

He ran a finger along her hip. He knew she listened. Lapella would always listen to him. "And those who fall ill hear his voice and become his creatures."

She moved, a slow, oiled motion, turning her face to the pillow, her hip to the bed.

Tuvaini watched her, watched the lantern gleam on her skin. He knew she held tight to his words. She thought he was giving something to her, sharing secrets, making a bond.

"He has touched the emperor, this man."

Lapella stiffened at that, her fingers knotting in the sheets, then she drew a deep breath and relaxed.

"He plans for the day he will speak and Beyon will follow his will." Tuvaini pictured Beyon's face. He wondered when the light in the emperor's eyes would die. The Carriers were already preparing the ground for their advance, buying favors within the palace walls, even from Tuvaini himself.

Lapella moved to receive him, though still she did not speak, even as she lifted herself.

Tuvaini thought of the enemy's purchases. Entry through the Red Hall to kill the emperor's Knife. Access to Prince Sarmin, through the secret ways. Tuvaini had sold them both when the price offered exceeded their value. Though the first time, with Eyul, he hadn't known the target.

Lapella sighed beneath him and he twisted his fingers within her hair, pulling her head back.

The man behind the Carriers—the enemy—he might walk the palace even now. He had failed once already, and he would fail again.

There had been a moment when Eyul had been locked in combat with one of the Carriers, a moment when it had seemed their intention had changed. The Carrier pretending to attack Tuvaini hadn't moved to finish Eyul, though Eyul was injured; instead, it ran. Eyul lived. Beyon and Sarmin lived also, occupied with the prince's wild bride.

Tuvaini need only wait for his moment.

The enemy had failed, and he would fail again. A wild bride, with wild ways.

He would fail again.

Tuvaini, spent, pushed Lapella from him. Sweat ran across his ribs. "He buys favors, but he doesn't know what he has paid."

Lapella lay silent, gleaming, soft motion in her hips.

He could hear her breathing now. "He will take Beyon, but I hold the keys to Beyon. And when I choose, Beyon will be undone."

"What then?"

At last she speaks.

"The empire will be great once more." A strong empire would defeat the curse at last. Once the Pattern Master showed his hand Tuvaini would strike, and the Cerani would no longer live in fear of his design. They would reach for magnificence, as they had in the Reclaimer's time. There would be art and song, and trade to be had. The light of heaven would fall once again upon the throne.

Lapella rolled to face him. Already he wanted her again: her ripe curves, her dark curls, the faint scars of the wounds that made her his, the way she bit her lip when their eyes met. She ran a finger down his cheek and a lump came to his throat, surprising him. "I'm afraid for you," she said.

He rolled over and entered her once more, pinning her hands against the pillows. This time would be even better. He liked to see himself in her eyes. "Worry for the Carriers and their Master."

CHAPTER SIXTEEN

Eyul dreamed of the young princes. He dreamed of blood running across shining tiles, reflected in a child's dead eyes. In his dreams, the young Beyon spoke to him in the courtyard, though in life he had not.

"Why are we always here?" the child Beyon asked him once.

"We are not here. It is a dream." Eyul closed his eyes to shut away the blood. "I am ill, and so I am always dreaming."

"I'm tired of this dream," said little Beyon. "I'm tired of dreaming altogether."

"I'm sorry, my friend; I will try to wake."

It took days. When at last he opened his eyes, Eyul could make out the blurry faces and hands of those who tended him. As day passed dry thirsty day, he dreamed less and moved about more. Soon he was able to see to his own needs in the morning, so that by the time the female nomad arrived with his tea he had shaved and bathed in the sand. A man could not remain an invalid too long in this harsh land. He wondered if they'd have killed one of their own as helpless as he had been.

Eyul decided he was ready, though he was not sure of the days; at least six had passed since the woman first brought him tea. He dressed in a fresh linen tunic and waited for her, sitting cross-legged on the ground. After a time she pushed aside the tent flap and entered, tray in hand. The light of the desert shot through his eyes, leaving a spiderweb after-image. He covered his face, but the sun had already driven its nails deep. Through the pounding in his head he could hear the woman pouring tea, respectfully ignoring his weaknesses. From prior experience Eyul knew she didn't speak Cerantic, but she understood one word, and he gritted it out through his teeth: "Hermit."

"Arapikah." Coming. He uncovered his eyes and tried to meet her gaze, but her face remained blurred.

He tried a second word—"Amalya?"—but the woman shook her head and moved towards the flap.

This time Eyul turned his face away.

He took a swig of the strong, dark tea and let the dimness of the tent soothe his pain. He would have to depend on his tongue today. His words would come out blunt and transparent, but there was nothing to be done about that. Tuvaini was the master of words, knowing when to thrust, when to parry, and when to leave himself open, while Eyul was the Knife, always pointing.

He protected his eyes and looked away as the flap shifted once more.

"Eyul," the hermit said, as if praising a dog. He was not what Eyul had been expecting. Ten years ago, the hermit had been thin and wasted, with a beard grown past his knees. Then, as now, he'd worn nothing but a loin-cloth. But this man was more muscular and cast a heavier shadow. He was older than Eyul by at least a quarter of a century, but the way he sank into a squat, with no stiffness or hesitation, spoke of a man far younger. Eyul squinted past the hermit to where shadows played against the fabric of the tent. Two nomads, standing guard.

The hermit smiled. "I suppose you are anxious to get back to your master. Time is running out. Will you make that deal?"

Time is running out for you, perhaps. "Amalya carries a Star of Cerana. She's not mine to barter."

"I see." The hermit ran a finger across his mouth. "Is she Beyon's, then, or the vizier's, or do you mean she is her own person?"

"I mean she is not mine."

"And that's the essence of it." The hermit's eyes were all that Eyul could make out of his face, and they were so coppery bright that it hurt to look at them.

Eyul thrust his fist into the sand. "I want to see her. If she's agreeable, then I'll make the deal."

"I have anticipated you." The hermit's eyes turned to the flap. "Arapiki!"

Eyul turned his head to the side again as the desert sun filled the opening, making a show of reaching for his empty knife belt. Island-pepper tickled his nose, and beneath that, blood. Amalya. She settled on her knees between them. Again he wondered how long he'd lain drugged and blind in the tent. Amalya's generous curves had gone to angles. One arm lay inside a sling. He searched, but her eyes remained in shadow.

He would not leave her here.

The hermit watched both of them. "It doesn't matter who asked the question you carry. I have the answer, and I need this wizard. Will you trade, Eyul of Nooria, son of Klemet, Fifty-third Knife-Sworn?"

Eyul turned to Amalya. He couldn't make out her expression. "What say you, Amalya of the Tower, of the Islands?"

Movement, as if she wet her tongue in preparation to speak, but in the end Amalya only nodded. Eyul watched her for a long moment, but heard nothing beyond the wind against the sides of the tent.

"I have to hear you say it, Amalya." He didn't speak to her the way he wanted to, because the hermit was there, listening. His words felt rough, sand against skin.

"I want to help the emperor," she said at last. She kept her head bowed.

Eyul turned to the old man. "No."

The hermit's white teeth showed in a smile. "Then you have come here for nothing. What will your master say?"

"I need only my Knife." Eyul smiled, relaxed now with the rightness of his decision and the presence of Amalya beside him.

"Then I will propose another deal." The hermit turned and said something through the cloth of the tent. In that brief moment of privacy, Eyul turned to Amalya, hoping for a sign, a word, or a look. But she remained motionless, her head bent low. The hermit turned back to face him. "Your Knife is on its way. It's… an interesting blade."

Eyul held his silence until two nomads entered, carrying his Knife between them like a temple offering. They laid it on the mat by the empty teacup and withdrew without a word, just as Beyon's slaves would have done. Eyul picked it up, remembering how it had burned his hand in the ruined city. A warmth rushed up his arm. Out on the sands, someone sighed with happiness, a long, low breath.

Here in the tent, though, work remained. Eyul pointed the tip at the old man, sighting down the blade, and grinned when the hermit drew back slightly.

"My payment for Amalya will be a sacrifice," Eyul said, "but you must tell me whom to kill."

The hermit threw his head back and laughed. "Oh, my child," he said, still chuckling. "How I wish you had been born to noble blood. You are wasted as an assassin. Of course it is all nonsense, the idea of royal blood, *noble* blood. Power is a different thing. But it matters to a foolish mind and keeps you from where you should be. And on the matter of where people should be—" He turned to Amalya. "My dear, this is now between me and your friend. Please wait in your chamber."

Amalya rolled to her feet, showing more strength than Eyul expected, and walked to the tent flap. Just before she passed through, she looked at Eyul and moved her chin back and forth by less than finger's width. *No*, she was telling him, but she didn't want the hermit to see. He jerked his head away, avoiding the sun, knowing how she might interpret it, knowing that, too, would be something true.

When the tent flap fell shut the hermit said, "Amalya is comfortably installed in the caves. You remember how many there are—the Cliffs of Sight have been occupied since before the time of memory. We live among the ancients' paintings, their offerings to the gods, even their old sandals, and yet the ancients themselves have been swallowed by time."

"Whom shall I kill?" Eyul asked again, full of doubt now that Amalya had said no. Nomads outside the tent spoke in whispers, too low for him to hear.

The hermit continued instead of answering, "It makes a person wonder. Who were these lords, and did they accept the offerings of the cave-dwellers? It makes a person think about our own gods and goddesses, does it not? Are our offerings, even those of our emperor, in vain? I tell you, I have searched for the truth all these years, and I believe I have found it." The hermit drew his fingers through the sand, scoring it with parallel lines. "I know how to please heaven and make our empire the strongest in the world."

"Then you should go to the emperor," said Eyul.

"Did you go to the emperor and tell him of your journey, Eyul?"

Eyul put his Knife into its sheath, where it belonged. The tent seemed quieter all of a sudden.

The hermit smiled. "I didn't think so. You were wise. You and I both know Beyon cannot be trusted."

"Who, then? Tuvaini?"

"Danger surrounds the palace, and Tuvaini plays a game."

Eyul relaxed, now on familiar ground. "Then let us speak of the danger."

"Govnan is a danger," said the hermit. "Govnan of the Tower stands between heaven and the throne."

"Are you saying that Govnan has put the marks on Beyon? That he—? That Beyon can be saved?" The hermit knew already—the hermit *always* knew.

The hermit laughed. "You choose interesting words, Eyul. There is more than one way to be saved. But with Govnan gone, there is hope."

Govnan ruled the Tower, and the Tower shielded the emperor. Each mage was chosen as a child and raised to understand his or her role as a guardian of the throne. How could an enemy arise from the Tower?

Eyul hid his confusion from the hermit. "Then Govnan will be killed."

The hermit hesitated only a moment then gave the answer that Eyul had travelled so far to hear. "What it means for the pattern to take an emperor is that a new emperor must be found. Kill or cure—but cure quickly; once the pattern has him he will be dead or gone, beyond your help either way. With Govnan removed there is hope for Beyon. His blood is fierce blood, difficult to write upon." The hermit stood and walked towards the door flap. "Your camels will be ready in a sand's turning. Feel free to go and find your friend."

Eyul sat a while in his tent, rotating the teacup in its saucer. Could it be true that Govnan was involved with the pattern-curse? Would Amalya ever believe such a thing?

There were things going on here that he did not understand, but he knew from working with Tuvaini that it wasn't good to show too much thinking. He wouldn't put Amalya's freedom in jeopardy by lingering here. He placed the cup upside down on the saucer and fastened his belt around his waist. He found the bandage that had covered his eyes and wrapped it around his head just twice, blocking the worst of the light but leaving him able to see his path.

Outside, the vague forms of pilgrims rose from the bright sand and the sound of soft voices and different accents filled the air. On his previous visit there had been blond-haired folk from the north, Cerani, Islanders like Amalya, and even men from the west, their hair neither black nor blond, though he couldn't see such detail today. He didn't linger, but hurried up the stone path and entered the first narrow opening he found.

Darkness swallowed him. He unwrapped his bandages and listened to the cave. Far ahead, low voices murmured in reverent tones. He took a tentative step and kicked something hard and light. It rolled a short distance before hitting the wall, and he stopped again. The objects in the cave, dark against black, gained shape. He turned in a slow circle, trying to get his bearings.

He had kicked an old jug, the kind made for oil or honey, but its round belly had long since broken open, losing its contents. Long ago someone had placed it beneath a painting on the rock wall, together with other now-mouldering objects. He leaned in towards the painting and made out a woman, outlined in red and brown, with both hands held up to the sky. She looked rather like Mirra, and he remembered the hermit's words: what had become of these ancient worshippers? He picked up the old jug and replaced it beneath the goddess. *Do not take from the gods what is theirs.*

He heard a shuffling on his left and twisted towards the sound, one hand at the ready by his sheath.

Eyul smelled fire, and Island herbs. Amalya, clothed in white, from her robes to the bandages around her arm, cut out from the darkness like a star. He willed his feet to stillness. "How… how is your arm?" he asked, rooting his shoes into the rock.

"Better." Amalya turned to the painting. "The hermit makes a great deal of these."

"I respect the gods," said Eyul, "but it doesn't do to think overmuch about them." Tuvaini's words. "Why does he frighten you so?"

She swallowed. "Do you think he believes in them?" She looked sideways at him, more at his shoes than his face.

"If anything, this shows that Mirra has ruled these lands for more than an age."

She touched the painting, drew her fingers across the figure's bare breasts.

"I thought this was Pomegra, mother of the wise."

"As I said, it is not prudent to think too much about them."

"It makes you uneasy." She turned towards him, and he remembered holding her up on the camel, and the feel of her hair against his chin. "It makes me uneasy, too."

"The gods should make anyone uneasy." The cave came alive with orange light as the sunset spilled its color over the cliff face.

Amalya drew closer. "I didn't mean the gods. I meant choosing. You're a man who follows orders, but now that you've had a choice—" She grabbed his left hand, and for a moment he couldn't move for the feel of her soft palm squeezing his knuckles.

"You're wrong." He stepped back, and she wrapped her hand around her bandaged arm instead. "Choosing was easy."

"You bargain with death too readily," she said. "We need to be careful."

He could have told her then about Govnan, but instead he moved deeper into the cave, avoiding the sun's light. Amalya stood where he'd left her. She was brave. She wouldn't be frightened for long.

She took a breath and asked, "When do we leave?"

"They are readying our camels now."

"And who—?"

"Later."

Her fingers worried at her bandages. "Eyul… Thank you." That was what he needed to hear. He turned his eyes towards the darkness.

Sarmin lay on his bed. Moon-glow from the Sayakarva window picked out a corner here, an edge there, enough to hint at the room. Sarmin filled in what he couldn't see from memory. Hints and memory, mortared with faith, the raw materials from which a man might construct a palace, or a prison, or both.

When the pattern-magic had washed over Sarmin, dreams had swept him away: strange dreams, where he saw with eyes that were not his own. In their wake he felt burned-out, empty, and sleep would not come.

Sarmin closed his eyes and again the pattern hung before him, an after-image in red and green. The longer he kept them shut, the tighter the focus became—and more: he felt the Many. He felt them crowd about him like old ghosts, and their silence pressed on him. They drew closer still, standing beside him, whispering in his ears, flickering at the edge of vision.

The Many murmured in the darkest recesses of his mind, a multitude of distant voices, one laid over the next, and overlaid again. He felt the Many as a burden on his shoulders, scores of them, hundreds, maybe even thousands. He carried them all.

Without warning the pattern flared, and once more a dream took him in its jaws. Sarmin moved through the hollow of a mountain. Light showed at the end of his path, the bright colours of sunset. He lowered himself from the cave-mouth, balancing his feet on a narrow, rocky ledge. Below him a big man and a dark-skinned woman stood by a pair of camels, their heads bent close together as they talked. The man wore cloth around his eyes. Sarmin watched them mount and move away from him. Their camels were sluggish and loud.

Sarmin realised that, like the Many, he too was an observer, watching from behind eyes he didn't own. *Carried.*

Sarmin didn't recognise the sleeve that covered his arm, but he recognised what emerged as the cuff slid back along his wrist: triangle, half-moon, diamond within square, square within diamond—

"The pattern!" Again the voice that was not his spoke his words, softly, and with the accent of the low-born. In answer, whispers rose around him, like sand lifting before the storm.

All see what one sees. All know what one knows. All want what one wants. All live what one lives. This the pattern. This the price.

And then through it all came a clear voice, cool as a river in a desert: "Is there a stranger here? One who is not the Many?" It was a man's voice, redolent with age and wisdom and power. The Pattern Master had found him. "I have felt you, stranger. You opened a door that should have remained closed."

Sarmin held silent.

"Show yourself!" The command brooked no refusal.

Sarmin shrank into himself, imagining himself a dot, a mere speck amid the bulk of a dune.

"Beyon? Is it you? Have you joined us at last?" the Pattern Master asked.

Sarmin heard amusement bubbling beneath the words. He fought back the outrage that rose in him, as hot as it was unexpected.

"Hide, then." The slightest ripple of anger swirled in the current of the voice. "You serve me, no matter what you think you choose. The pattern will be complete: one pattern, one future. There will be one to whom all will bow."

Sarmin kept his peace, silent and hidden among the multitude. More than anything, the lack of imagination in the Pattern Master's ambitions irked him. *If I were Master I'd want...* Sarmin wondered what he would want. He needed more than bended knees, less than that, too... *Many patterns. That's what I'd want, many patterns.*

A sound came behind him: pilgrims on their way to worship. He crept down the ledge and dropped to the sand, running into the shadow of a rock.

Amalya lifted the ladle from the stew and motioned towards Eyul, who sprang to service. She'd done everything with one arm except pour the water from the well, and he had been waiting for a chance to help. He put a bowl on a rock beside her and held it steady while she poured, then did the same with the second bowl.

When both were filled he handed her one and squatted down to eat. "Smells delicious."

She gathered her next bite. He could see that she smiled.

"It's nice to have a full night between us and the cliffs." Amalya nodded as she chewed, bent over her next spoonful.

She moved her bandaged arm freely, and there was no sign of the fever that had plagued her.

But she remained gaunt; Eyul could make out the sharpness in her cheekbones and the hollow of her throat. She looked up, and Eyul busied himself with his stew. He felt a fool, to be staring. Part of him wished this trip to be over; it was far easier to follow Tuvaini through dark corridors, listening to his thoughts on everything from warcraft to the supremacy of coastal olive oil...

Easier, but less interesting, perhaps.

She was still watching him, not moving, her hand on her knee. "I trust you, Knife-Sworn."

Eyul put down his spoon and spent a few seconds balancing his bowl between two curved rocks next to the fire. It gave him some time, but he still couldn't think of a response other than, "Pardon?"

"At one time you frightened me. But not any more."

"Now the hermit frightens you." He focused on the flames, her flames. Her magic.

"I feel great power in the hermit, though he can't do the simplest tasks of a Tower mage," she said. "I don't understand it, and it frightens me. Metrishet hides from him."

"Metrishet?"

"My fire."

Eyul had heard hints about the elementals, that they had personalities and thoughts of their own. "Does he— Does it think?"

"Yes, he thinks, and he communicates." A dark look crossed her face. "He does not like our world."

Amalya carried something alive inside her, while Eyul carried only ghosts. Did Metrishet resent Amalya? Did the elemental beg for his freedom the way his ghosts begged for justice? He cleared his throat, looking for a way to frame his next words. "The hermit says he can help Beyon against the Carriers."

She took another bite, then said, "That would take a great deal of power, to stop the disease from spreading." Clearly she knew nothing of Beyon's markings; the words held no special meaning for her.

"Would it? Perhaps it just takes some learning. He has old texts, documents, things that aren't available to everyone."

"Could be." Amalya leaned over her bowl, her brows drawing together in thought.

Eyul picked up his food and said nothing for a time. He didn't know how to broach the subject of Govnan. Amalya herself had told him to find the centre and use his Knife. The hermit had shown him the centre. And yet, when he opened his mouth to speak of Govnan, no words came forth.

Guilt filled him. Amalya had told him she trusted him, and yet he kept silent. Eyul put aside his bowl again. So many of his victims he knew nothing about. What use was it, when drawing a blade across a man's throat, to know his likes and dislikes? To know who had loved him, and who had trusted him? And yet he couldn't resist. "What about Govnan?" he asked.

It was Amalya's turn to be confused. "Pardon?"

"You trust me—what about Govnan?"

"Of course I trust him." She put her empty bowl next to his half-full one. "We both serve Beyon."

"The mages serve the empire," he said, thinking of Tuvaini.

"People sometimes differ on what that entails." She drew in her breath. "Beyon is the empire."

"All right," he said, taking the bowls and standing up.

"What do *you* think the empire is?" she asked. "The buildings? The army? The scribes?"

"No, you're right." He took a handful of sand and poured it into her empty bowl. "We both belong to Beyon."

"The Tower belongs to Beyon," she said, "and Govnan is the Tower."

"All right," he said again, not sure why he was unable to say more. He scrubbed the bowls, watching her outline against the sky, and she watched him, not speaking, until at last she crawled into her tent.

Eyul could feel the morning's heat on his shoulders, weighing him down, the burden of another day. He missed working for Tahal, who had been sure and fair. He had never struggled with doubts under Tahal. He'd been a strong emperor, never weak, until the very end, and even then Tahal had taken steps to ensure the empire would remain whole. The deaths of his boys ensured a unified palace and a unified army...

And yet, what was good for the empire had been poison for Eyul. Tahal had loved him, and Tahal had destroyed him. He'd given Eyul the Knife, knowing what was to come. He had doomed him—

No; before Tahal there had been Herran, and before him Halim, and before that, Eyul himself. He had been chosen for his nature.

He threw the bowls to the sand and looked at his tent. The nightmares waited for him there. He did not wish for sleep, nor did he wish to wait here for the full light of the sun.

A sandcat appeared over the crest of the dune, its lithe body slinking towards him. Dawn gleamed along its yellow hide. A good hunter, it could overwhelm its prey in seconds—as could he. The animal watched him, its head low, its green eyes shining in the rising sun.

Eyul met its gaze, his shoulders falling in relief. "I am tired of hunting, my friend. If you want me, I am here."

"No."

Eyul was startled—had the whisper come from Amalya? The cat took one step towards him, then turned away, drawn perhaps by an easier kill beyond the dune. A flick of its paws, and it disappeared from sight. It was only then that Eyul felt his fingers on the hilt of his Knife, ready to draw. *Not so ready to die then after all.*

He unbuckled his belt. The leather, worn as it was, felt rough in his hands. He laid it out, checking it from buckle to pointed end. The Knife looked small, powerless in its sheath, the metal of the hilt twisting dark against the lighter color of the dune. A gusting wind kicked sand against Eyul's back, tiny needles pricking his neck, and he stretched, feeling light without his weapon.

Wrapping the bandage around his eyes, he counted fifteen steps to Amalya's tent. He dropped to his knees and scratched lightly at the flap.

A rustle, and then her voice came, velvety with sleep. "Eyul?"

"When we met, you asked me how I became an assassin." She was silent, but he felt her listening on the other side of the cloth.

"There was a man—a cruel man. Jarek. I spent many days with him, weeks, maybe months."

"He taught you to kill?"

The simplicity of her question caught him off-guard. "No—no, at the time I was just a boy lifting purses." He remembered hiding in a doorway, slipping after his mark, the soft feel of leather against his fingers, and the shouts, the chase.

"The guards said I'd lose my hand, but first they put me in Jarek's cell." For a moment he felt Jarek's breath on his neck, heard the shouts of the guards taking bets. *When will the boy scream?* Eyul cleared his throat. "He didn't know how to kill, at least, not on purpose."

"I see."

He drew his fingers through the sand, as he'd seen the hermit do, and closed his eyes against the morning light. "One day—I remember it was a cold day—they passed a sword through the bars to me. They said if I killed Jarek, they'd let me go. A visitor came and watched me try. He was young, well-dressed." No bets were taken that day, in deference to the visitor with green robes and serious eyes.

Halim had always been serious. Each turn of the blade, every thrust and step, could save or end your life, he'd said. In training there had been no cause for levity. In the end, Halim had been a better teacher than an assassin. He'd died when Eyul's beard was still new and soft on his cheeks. Halim never knew grey hairs or creaking joints, but he had known regret. The one thing he never taught Eyul was how to live with it.

"Eyul?" Amalya's voice brought him to the present.

He shook off the memories. "I couldn't, even after all the things he'd done to me... When he was on the floor, pleading for his life, I couldn't do it. I had to tell the jailers to take my hand after all."

"But they didn't."

"No." His right hand went to his hip, searching for the familiar Knife, and found nothing there. "It was a test. The assassins look for mercy in their young recruits. Then they show us how death itself is a mercy."

She reached out to him then, soft fingers on his wrist. "It can't have been easy for you."

Eyul thought of Beyon and his dead brothers; Prince Sarmin in his room, longing for death; a young Island girl, leaving her family for ever... "It's not easy for any of us."

"No, so it isn't," she said with a sigh. "It isn't."

Eyul drew a breath. "Amalya," he said, "the hermit wants—"

"No." Her hand tightened, fingers digging into his skin. "You don't have to tell me," she whispered, her voice so soft he had to press his forehead to the tent flap to hear her. "I don't want to know. But I beg you, as we are Beyon's instruments, to tell the emperor first."

So it was Beyon who gave her the Star.

"Beyon doesn't like to speak to me," he said.

"Do you promise?"

"I promise." He wrapped his fingers around hers and squeezed. He felt relieved to have the decision taken out of his hands, but something nagged at him.

The white fabric shifted. He could feel the heat of her breath against his nose. "Eyul," she murmured, "it means a great deal to me that you made a promise to the hermit. But I'm afraid it's too much."

"Let me worry about that."

A silence. "If you say so."

"Thank you, Amalya." He drew his hand away and stood up.

"Eyul?" She raised her voice now. He imagined her, inside, turning her face towards him. He imagined the sun lighting her features.

"Yes?"

"Do you have trouble sleeping?"

"Yes."

"Me too."

Metrishet. The desert grew hot around him. He stood, the light driving long nails through his eyes. He watched her tent so long that he wondered if she still listened. "I'll see you at nightfall."

She answered. "At nightfall, then."

He climbed into his tent at last, leaving his Knife in the sand. Today he would not sleep as an assassin.

CHAPTER SEVENTEEN

Mesema and Eldra prepared for sleep. They laid their mats side by side and ran bone-picks through one another's hair. It felt strange, after so long away from home, to braid Eldra's curls when they were so close to the colour and feel of Dirini's, and it was stranger yet to sit idle, doing girlish things, when the pattern waited. It felt so odd to fiddle with hair-beads while deceiving an emperor.

"What about Arigu?" whispered Mesema.

"He didn't come for me, and if he had, I'd have told him I still had the Woman visiting."

They giggled as the sun burned its way through the tent.

"What is he like?" asked Mesema. No amount of worry could keep her from being curious.

"He's mostly nice, when it's just the two of us," said Eldra, tilting her head to Mesema's fingers. "Gentle."

Mesema remembered Arigu's hands on her arms, how he hadn't squeezed or poked when he'd looked for the pattern-marks. She thought about the chief coming to her mother in the longhouse, how his eyes went soft at the sight of her. "Sometimes strong men are soft in private."

"And sometimes soft men are rough."

Mesema thought of Banreh. "I suppose." She secured a bead at the end of Eldra's last braid.

"There," said Eldra, turning to face her. "Now we are both beautiful."

"You're the pretty one, Eldra." Mesema picked up her quilted bag and placed the pick inside. It also held bracelets and hairclips, the kinds of things she would wear on her wedding day. Would her husband like them? She didn't expect to know, nor would she ask. She wouldn't be able to talk with him as she could talk with Banreh. She couldn't tell him about reading the wind, or about the resin, carefully hidden in the bottom of her trunk.

She was learning that her life in Nooria would be about hiding: hiding the truth and, in turn, hiding from the emperor, and the pattern. Thoughts of the pattern had dogged her all day, just as the heat surrounded and suffocated her, but no matter what she tried to think about instead, a shape or path kept entering her mind. She was learning how to hold her tongue, but she didn't know how to keep her thoughts from turning.

"Have you ever seen a pattern like the one that came through the sands?" she asked Eldra.

"No, but I've heard of them." Eldra leaned forwards, almost bumping noses with Mesema. "I wanted to go to that church."

"Well, you couldn't," said Mesema.

"When you're a princess, you'll command them to take me back."

"If I can spare you." They giggled together under the bright canvas.

Mesema yawned. Sleep dragged at her, but her mind wouldn't stop. Just as notes made no song without the touch of a musician, shapes and lines made no spell without the touch of a mage. A thought came to her, and the sweat on her back went cold. "I don't think that church is a good place to go," she said, dropping onto her mat. "We should forget it."

"What shall I make of myself, then?" asked Eldra, her voice sharp for the first time.

Mesema rolled to look at her. "Listen. If you had gone to the church, what would you have made of that, with no food and no water?"

Eldra sighed and turned her back.

"Let's go to sleep." But in truth Mesema couldn't close her eyes. She tried to decide whether a pattern could enforce a man's will. How had it been created? Each shape seemed simple in itself, but together they created something beyond her ken.

Mesema rolled onto her stomach. She wanted to forget the pattern. She was meant to have a child. Her duty lay in that simple and difficult task. It didn't matter what the prince looked like, or how he treated her: when the Bright One came over the moon, she would lie with him. There were more frightening things than making a child. For the first time, she was not frightened of her prince.

She did fear his brother, the emperor. She wondered how long it would be before he died of his illness. But as much as he frightened her, she couldn't make herself wish for his death.

At last she drifted off to sleep, sung along by the sounds of sand and the familiar neighing of the horses. She dreamed of home, of the songs by the fireside and the women with their needles. She dreamed that the women embroidered her receiving cloth, a circle of white as big as the longhouse, in blue and yellow and purple; they employed the costliest dyes for the baby emperor. And when Mesema tied off her thread and looked at their work, she recognised the shapes and twisting paths of the sand pattern.

She screamed—no; she woke to a scream: Eldra was sitting beside her, tears running down her face, fingernails scraping at her own skin.

Pattern-marks ran across her chest, a spiderweb of color marked with moons and half-stars.

Outside, men were shouting. Weapons hissed out of their sheaths. Sand spilled under fast-moving boots.

Mesema thought quickly. "Gather yourself together, Eldra!" She reached out and slapped Eldra's cheek. Eldra fell silent, her eyes dazed and blood-shot. "Good," Mesema said, buttoning her friend's nightdress with shaking hands.

"What's happening in there?" Arigu's voice.

"A nightmare," Mesema called out, hoping he wouldn't hear the squeak in her voice. If it were Banreh, he would know instantly that she lied.

Eldra grabbed Mesema's wrists. "What are you doing?" she whispered.

"I don't know what they'll do to you if they find out," said Mesema, too low for the general to hear.

"I'm dying anyway." Tears gathered in Eldra's eyes. "I heard what he told you. The pattern kills."

Arigu's shadow rose and flickered over the canvas. Mesema thought he had turned away and was surveying the camp. She covered her eyes with one hand. The Hidden God truly did not live in the desert. What terrible fate had befallen Eldra, without the guiding hands of rain and shade? And she herself—? Mesema gasped and ripped open her own nightdress, but she saw only the blue marks of her veins beneath pale skin. "Why—?"

"My bad luck." Eldra tried to smile.

Mesema hugged Eldra, her throat burning with sorrow. Eldra patted her back. "I'm going to heaven." But no matter where she was going, her hand trembled.

Mesema held on, her eyes squeezed shut. She wanted to go back to the morning, when they had picked the prettiest beads for their hair, back to when they had eaten figs in the light of dawn, before the pattern came, but there was no going back, no going home, and there was no saving Eldra. She looked back at Arigu's shadow, but he'd moved on. "I'll take you to your church," she whispered.

"No. You will go to your prince—"

"No!" Nooria was a place of evil. She knew it now for certain.

"You must promise me—listen!—you will go to your prince and help him stop this pattern." Tears continued unabated down Eldra's cheeks, but her voice came steady and sure. "Promise me."

A promise to the dying held the sanctity of a promise made to the gods. Mesema sniffed and wiped her cheeks. She had been unkind when Eldra was scared and alone. Even after that, try as she might, she hadn't liked her as much as she could have. And then there was Banreh. Mesema owed Eldra a kindness. She tried to swallow, but her throat was too dry.

"I promise."

"Good," said Eldra. She turned and slipped a tunic over her nightclothes. Eldra was leaving. Eldra was dying. Mesema could do nothing but watch.

Before going through the flap, Eldra kissed her on the cheek. "You will be a wise and brave princess," she whispered. Then she was gone.

Mesema fell onto her side and lay staring at the walls of the tent. She heard nothing extraordinary, no threats directed at Eldra by the soldiers. She wondered where Eldra was now; mounting her horse, maybe, or disappearing behind the first dune. She buried her face in the desert sand. She heard a familiar sound, a saddle, creaking under a man's weight, and then laughter.

A short cry rang out: a woman's cry, frightened and sudden. *Eldra.*

Mesema shot up. Outside her tent, shadows moved, and men shouted. She listened, frozen with fear, too frightened to look.

She thought of Banreh. *We are Windreaders. Our spears are coated with the blood of our enemies... Ever victorious...*

The tent flap moved, and she screamed.

A young Cerani soldier peeked in, his brown eyes narrowed.

"The general says to stay in here. Hide. Don't come out for anything."

She wanted to ask about Eldra, but her tongue had turned to stone.

He left, and Mesema took a deep breath and counted her fingers. Her mother had taught her counting when she learned to sew. She missed the feel of the hard bone in her hand, the tension of the thread as she pulled it through the wool. She thought of the designs she used to make: three stitches and then a cross for a bundle of wheat. Five circles for a flower, caught at the tips.

The shadows stilled. Voices lowered to a murmur. She could not bring herself to go outside. *Four and five, catch. Four and five, catch.* She'd just counted her fingers for the seventh time when Banreh poked his head inside. Something in his eyes made her afraid to ask.

"You should get dressed and come out now." He used the intimate tone.

Mesema pulled on her clothes, kneeling on Eldra's empty mat. Something terrible had happened; she knew it in her stomach and behind her eyes. She crawled out and stood up in the bloody light of the setting sun.

"Mesema." Banreh came and stood at her side. He always knew just where to be. He took her elbow and steered her to the left, where the horses stood over their barrels, and further on, where the scattered crates and tents of the camp gave way to the dry sea. There, in the trough of a wave of sand, Arigu stood by Eldra's horse.

Mesema walked closer, though her feet were as lead.

"Where—?" And she saw her: Eldra lay in the sand, an arrow rising from her chest. It looked just like the spear that had risen from Jakar's.

"No!" Mesema cried. Banreh took her hand.

"Why did you kill her? She was going away!" Mesema started towards Arigu, but Banreh held her firm.

Arigu looked down at Eldra with a tired, sad expression.

"Why would I kill her? I liked her well enough."

Banreh squeezed her hand. "Horsemen came—I saw them, Mesema."

"He more than saw them; he took Jouhri's bow and knocked one clean off his horse. Not an easy shot." Arigu nodded at Banreh and then jerked his head towards the north. "Man's over there."

She studied both their faces. They didn't know about the patterning. Someone else had killed Eldra. It was a cruel joke of the desert gods, to kill her twice.

"Why?" Mesema knelt by the still body. Someone had closed Eldra's eyes. Her hands, though, were still splayed across the sand. Mesema crossed them over her abdomen in the way of the Windreaders. The familiar smell of wrongful blood rose around her. She'd forgotten that smell until now. Mesema arranged Eldra's braids and touched the beads she'd placed at their ends. The arrow, of white wood topped with bright blue feathers, was strangely beautiful. She worked one of the feathers free and kept it in her hand.

Banreh answered the question she'd forgotten she asked. "I think they mistook her for you."

"For me?" Assassins? Was that why she was kept inside the carriage, while Eldra rode with Arigu every night? She remembered thinking how she and Eldra looked like sisters. How nobody ever told her—or Eldra—why she was there...

Realisation brought anger. "You wanted her with us in case the emperor found out about me. You knew she might get hurt." Banreh seized her shoulders, but Mesema didn't stop talking. "I suppose, since you didn't like her religion, that it was all right to let her die."

"Guard your tongue," said Banreh.

"She knew you didn't care for her." Mesema looked into Arigu's black eyes. She saw anger there, but also pity, and that made her look away.

Arigu spoke. "This is an empire, little girl. Affection is costly." With a look at Banreh, he added, "You can't let it change things, no matter what you feel."

Mesema clutched the feather against her palm, felt the hollow spine snap beneath her fingers. "You play with lives."

"I am not playing," Arigu said. "In twenty or thirty years, when your son cuts his brothers' throats, talk to me again about the value of life. Talk to me again about affection." He pivoted on his heel and walked away.

Mesema said, "I *hate* him. People are nothing more than instruments to him, like needles for sewing."

"Did your father not use you?" said Banreh. "And does he not care for you?"

"That was for the sake of our people. You know it well, Banreh."

"And Arigu does what he does for the sake of the Cerani people." He sounded right. He always did.

Banreh stepped out before Eldra's horse. "What is its name?"

She hesitated, knowing his mind. But it was the Felting way. "Crimson."

"Crimson," he repeated, drawing his blade across the horse's throat, "lead your rider Eldra to the lands of summer."

When the horse went still, Banreh and Mesema gathered what straw and rags they could, covered them with lamp-oil, and sent Eldra to the next life.

As they walked back to camp, hand in hand, she said, "You killed the man who did this?"

"One of them." There was a measure of pride in his voice. He was Windreader, after all.

"Good."

They said no more.

The camp was struck and the caravan was ready to go before the sun had managed to set. As Mesema and Banreh prepared to climb into the carriage, Arigu rode up to them. He was not a bad rider. His big shoulders stuck out on either side of his mount; she'd never noticed before, but he resembled the ancient statues of centaurs. He looked from Banreh to Mesema, opening his mouth to speak, but saying nothing.

She grew impatient. A man did not hesitate when something must be spoken.

At last Arigu said, "I am going ahead to the city." He addressed Banreh. "My men will protect you as far as the river. There my man Aziz will meet you and lead you into Nooria."

"Sneaking around like horse thieves," Mesema sniffed. Arigu ignored her, addressing Banreh again. "If it is too dangerous for you to proceed to the city, Aziz will take you to my estate by the sea."

There was fear in the general's eyes. The assassins had frightened him, and with good reason. The emperor would have his revenge. Mesema's skin prickled. She realised she might not live to meet her prince, but what of the prophecy about her son? *The Hidden God does not live in the desert,* her mother had said. Perhaps He hadn't seen everything.

Arigu pulled away, kicking his horse like a savage and galloping over the sand. Mesema watched until he was a dark speck against the horizon. She didn't like him, but she dreaded to see him go. It meant the end was near—the end of her journey, very likely the end of her life. She followed Banreh into the carriage, feeling the heat but no longer caring.

"Arigu's men rode to the body. A bandit, they said." Banreh didn't wait for her to sit. "They looked like soldiers to me, or guards, Cerani." He frowned. "But if the emperor knew of us, wanted us dead, he would send five hundred men, or a thousand, not three."

Miles passed in silence and in heat. As the wide wheels turned in the sand, Banreh mentioned something about her language lessons. She ignored him, staring out of the window instead.

"Mesema."

She watched the sand anxiously for a sign of the pattern, or further assassins.

"Mesema." Banreh touched her arm.

His strength poured into her through that connection. She took his wrist in her other hand. "Banreh."

"Are you well?"

She shook her head no.

He watched her, his green eyes thoughtful.

She wanted his thoughts. She wanted his calm. She wanted everything about him. "Will you kiss me again, Banreh, as you did before?"

He pulled his wrist from her grasp and pressed himself against the other side of the carriage. "I cannot."

"Yes, you can. And nobody will know or care. Arigu's gone. Eldra's gone."

"I will know. I will care."

She knelt on the carriage floor, her arms over his legs, hands clasped as if in prayer. "This could be the last day we ever spend together. If that were so, wouldn't you want to hold me?"

He ran a hand through her hair, a different look on his face now: the look of a Rider just come in from the hunt. "Of course I would. But this is not our last day."

She ran her hands up his chest and kissed the front of his shirt. Hard muscle lay beneath her fingers. Strength, but trembling, even so. "Please,

Banreh," she said, rising up on her knees, touching the back of his neck with her hand. He exhaled, a shaky, breathy noise, and she knew she had him then. He pulled her in with his strong arms and pressed his lips against hers.

She held to him, skin against skin. His chest firm, his neck soft, his cheeks rough. His lips fell over her arms and face; his fingers pulled at the lacings of her shirt. This was as it should have been. They should have made a plainschild.

"Lie with me, Banreh," she whispered in his ear.

He slowed his kisses. His hands let go of her laces and went still. "No," he said. He pushed her back and leaned against the side of the carriage, away from her.

"No?" She threw her arms around him and kissed his face. "Why not, Banreh?" His soft hair tickled her cheek.

"Mesema, you know why not. Stop. Stop!" He pushed her away and before she could say anything else, he hit the roof of the box with his fist, requesting a halt. He opened the door while the carriage was still moving.

"Banreh, what are you doing? Don't leave me!"

He jumped down into the sand. It hurt his leg, she knew, even though he didn't show it. He pushed the door shut and limped away from her. He would ride, then, with the other men. She would be alone. The carriage moved forwards, uncaring.

Mesema wiped at a tear. Banreh couldn't go against her father's wishes, not even for love, not even if this were the last day of his life. She hated him. He was no more than a thrall, and Eldra had been braver. She reached in her pocket for the blue feather, her reminder of Eldra's wish. She rubbed the feather against her cheek, wondering if she'd live to fulfil her promise. The not-knowing felt like torture. She wished she could jump out of the carriage like Banreh, run to the palace and the emperor, find out for certain.

At last Mesema pulled herself together. She sat up and settled on the bench. It was no use feeling sorry for herself; she would wait with dignity, like a woman. She sat with her own thoughts through the dark night, until the sun rose and the caravan came to a halt. When she climbed out of the carriage that morning, she held her back straight and her head high. Marry or die, she would do it like a princess.

CHAPTER EIGHTEEN

"A caravan." Eyul studied the parallel tracks in the sand.

"We're close to the buried city," Amalya said.

"Horses, twenty or thirty of them, and a carriage." Military, without a question. Whether they were White Hats or Blue Shields, Beyon's Imperial Guard, he could not tell.

"Too close."

He looked at her now. She was shivering, her hand clutching the pommel. "Then we will go wide around them."

Eyul mounted his camel and steered it westwards, away from the road. The Scorpion looked down upon his back, while the Maid pointed to the palace with one starry finger. They steered their camels in and out of shadow, the dunes guarding their path.

"Do you think it is safe to sleep without your Knife?" Amalya asked after a time.

They passed between the dunes in silence. Eyul closed his eyes and felt the weight of the weapon at his side. "I will sleep with my Knife, then."

"You are the emperor's Knife, the Knife of Heaven," she said. "Your weapon is the holy connection between you and Beyon."

"Beyon would not care for there to be a connection between us," he said.

"Why do you say that?"

Did the Tower really know so little of the palace? "Because I cut the throats of his five brothers. The eldest had reached ten years of age. The youngest was in his silk wrappings. I killed them all." There; he'd said it. She wanted him to keep his Knife; this is what it meant, for Beyon as well as Govnan.

Amalya did not speak for a long while. They moved, side by side, the sand blowing like fog around their camels' knees. When dawn broke over the mountains, Eyul pulled up to bind his eyes.

Amalya looked towards Nooria and said, "*Tahal* killed his sons. You were nothing more than his instrument, no more worthy of blame than the Knife that made the cuts."

Eyul drew out his bandages and listened.

"I've been thinking of when you joined the assassins. You said they looked for mercy, but I think they were looking for something else, too." Her voice sounded regretful. "They gave you a choice: kill or lose a hand. Some would have tried to get out of both, but not you. You accepted those as the only options."

"But they were."

"No, there are always more options, Eyul. They needed to be sure you were—"

"What?"

She moved as if to speak, then shrugged.

They needed to be sure I was obedient. He pulled his bandages tight. He wasn't one of Beyon's dogs, to run hither and yon fetching rubber balls. He looked her way, but the fabric made it impossible to see her face. "I am loyal, but no lackey." He dismounted.

"No? You're still following orders. As long as you think it's for the empire, you obey." She climbed to the sand, disappearing behind the blur of brown that was her camel.

He played for time. "You said the emperor and empire are one and the same."

"But you said otherwise."

He pulled the tents from their bindings.

"You must decide for yourself, Knife-Sworn, whom to heed."

"Maybe I'll find my own way." He threw down some water-skins and the dried camel dung for cooking.

"Not if you can't see beyond the choices you're given." She stood facing him, not moving. He imagined the look in her eyes, patient but firm.

He moved away and began to assemble his tent. He was still learning how to do it by touch alone. So she didn't think he was capable of making the right choice? Next she would try convincing him to stick close to Beyon, to be truly his Knife, as he had been Tahal's. She didn't know the emperor was marked, didn't realise what a farce that would be.

Why had he not told her? Eyul could see her shape moving around the fire, hear the water pouring from her skin, smell the pepper rising into the air. She stopped her work, turned her face his way.

He asked a question. "What did Beyon want with the hermit?"

"The emperor did not want the hermit," she said. She bent over the fire and lifted the pot to hang over it. "He wanted you. He wanted to know if he could trust you."

The tie snapped and the poles fell in opposite directions.

"You came to spy on *me*? For *him*?"

"I came to *assess* you."

You are as brave and obedient as I have been told. Her words. He felt naked under the sun, as naked as the boy in that prison so many years ago. "Then tell me, Amalya of the Tower, did you find me wanting?" He wished he could see her expression.

"I told you," she said after a moment, "you are loyal to the empire, but not to Beyon."

He picked up the poles and began his task a second time. He would make her the fool this time. "You do know Beyon is marked?"

She caught her breath. "What do you mean?"

"I mean, the pattern has marked him. Half the palace knows."

"I don't believe you."

"Now I'm a liar?" He grunted with false amusement. "He had his bodyslaves killed to keep them silent. And their executioner. Where do you think the links in that chain will lead? Now Carriers walk unchecked through the centre of the palace, attacking the vizier himself. Beyon can't be trusted."

Amalya's voice wavered. "It's impossible. The Tower has many enchantments, protections over the emperor. Govnan—"

Eyul tensed at Govnan's name, dropping another tent pole. She continued her protest: "Govnan has done everything he can to protect the emperor, even placing patterns of his own around the palace walls."

Placing patterns of his own? Eyul cleared his throat. "The vizier already searches for an heir. The—"

He heard a sizzle; untended water boiling over and falling into the flames.

Amalya didn't move. "Have we failed, then?" Her voice sounded thin, scraped by sand.

He didn't think she wanted an answer. He stretched the tent cloth over the poles. His mouth tasted sour. He felt as if he'd stuck himself with an arrow. Amalya had believed in Beyon, believed in the Tower's ability to protect him. He finished erecting his tent and walked around her to pick up the second set of ties. He could see through the bandages that she sat before the fire, shoulders slumped.

When both tents were up, gleaming in the morning sun, Amalya began to finish her work. Steam from her pot wafted past Eyul's nose, speaking of the barks, peppers, and flowers of her homeland. Her scents. He wondered if he would ever smell that lively, fertile aroma again once he left the desert. He settled down in the sand and watched her silhouette, cut out against the sun, though it sent a bright pain behind his eyes.

She looked over her shoulder. Somehow she always knew when he was watching her, even when her back was turned. Eyul stared down at his fingers, blurs against the lighter-coloured dune.

"I'm glad you told me." She stood and turned to face him; her shadow fell across his lap. "Have you seen his marks? Is that how you became a Knife with no emperor?"

He shook his head.

"Then how are you sure?"

"I was there when the Low Executioner swore to the word of Beyon's body-slaves. The vizier was with me."

"And then he was attacked?" Amalya knelt facing him. Though he struggled to, he couldn't see her expression.

"Soon after. I protected him…" He remembered the Carrier who'd circled Tuvaini at the fountain and then run away.

"When did you last see Beyon?"

"Just before I left."

"So did I." She paused. "He didn't seem any different." This was true.

"What are you thinking, Amalya?"

She waved her arm. "I'm not sure. Give me some time."

"The line of the Reclaimer has come to an end." He took her hand. He remembered what she'd said: that loyalty was the easiest of virtues to subvert. She had been right. "I know every well and oasis between here and the western mountains."

"What are you saying?" she asked, studying him. "That we should run away?"

"Are you saying the two of us can save the empire?"

She came to him then, close enough to embrace. "What would we do in the west, you and I?" Her breath fell across his lips. He put a hand on her neck and traced her cheekbone with his thumb.

"I don't know. Go fishing."

She laughed. "Fishing?"

He smiled at himself, but he was more interested in the feel of her skin under his fingers. "It was the first thing that came to my mind."

"Well," she said, resting her head on his chest, "it's a long way to go for a fish or two."

"You're the only woman I've ever invited to come fishing with me." The only woman he ever would.

"I'm flattered. But there is nothing for us in the west."

"There may be nothing for us in Nooria," he said.

She raised her head to him. He longed to see her eyes. "There is hope. Beyon remains well. Hope failing, there is death."

"Shall we go to Nooria, then, and die?" He traced the line of her waist with his hand, from her ribs to the flare of her hips. Was this what he had wanted all along? Had he ever tried to do what he could for Beyon?

She leaned into him. "We will go to Nooria and learn our fates. Together, as we are."

"If that's what you want." Their lips met and held, smoke, pepper and sand. He turned his head to look out over the dunes, but she said, "We're alone." She released his weapon belt and let it fall.

"I could be your father."

"You don't look like my father." She kissed the edge of his chin, where his beard grew in sharp and rough. "And your body is strong and lean."

"Try living in it."

"Be quiet," she said, pushing up his tunic. Her mouth traced a jagged scar on his chest.

He let out a hard breath and pulled her closer. She ended on his lap, hand running through his hair, lips dancing over his neck. He pushed the fabric of her robes aside, his hand finding the curves of her skin. Her fingers moved over him, too, running across his old scars and healing wounds. He whispered her name, as he had so many times in the hermit's tent.

Amalya pushed him onto his back and placed her knees to either side. She touched her hand against his mouth. "You are just like a man."

"I hope so."

"Come into the tent." Amalya scooted away from him and through the flap. Her sandals fell off her feet and lay, small and dainty, in the sand, one on either side of his belt. Eyul fingered the beaded leather. So delicate. He wondered why they hadn't already broken.

She called out for him. "Eyul?"

"Here I am," he answered, dragging his belt with him through the flap. She knelt in the sand, her eyes bronze in the diffuse light. He tossed the old leather aside, Knife and all.

"Make it good, Knife-Sworn," she said. He did his best.

Afterwards, as they lay entwined, her head against his neck, she said, "There is another heir." Her voice sounded breathy, sleepy.

"Beyon's brother." He ran his fingers over her thigh.

"Govnan says he's a powerful mage."

Eyul frowned. Tuvaini had said nothing of this.

"We could go to the prince, tell him everything." She lifted her leg to rest on his hip bone. "Perhaps he can help us, help his brother."

"He's mad," Eyul said. "The vizier has already tried to rouse the prince to his duty, to no avail."

"But he was alive when you left." Not a question.

"The Empire Mother sought a wife for him in the Wastes. Once he makes an heir…" He knew the vizier intended for him to kill Sarmin. He fell still as he let the idea rush over him, let its bitterness sink in. "It is bad luck to kill the mad."

"Everyone wishes to command the emperor's Knife, but that right belongs to just one man."

"Which man is that?"

She didn't answer, instead running her finger over his lips.

"Emperor Beyon doesn't know about this woman from the Wastes?"

"Not unless the vizier told him." Which was unlikely, Eyul decided. He thought of Tuvaini, and how he would react to the things Eyul had learned. "The hermit thinks Beyon can be cured."

"So that's what you meant, before." She shook her head. "I don't trust him."

Neither did Eyul, but the hermit had restored some of his sight and saved Amalya's arm. Eyul believed the hermit could help Beyon. All he had to do was kill Govnan, and the hermit's way was clear.

Amalya's injured arm lay between them. He touched the bandages, yellow with sand. "Is your wound still clean?"

She twisted away from him, looking up at the roof of the tent. "We'll change the bandages later."

"Later," he agreed, kissing her again, and there was no more talking.

Tuvaini took the folded letter from his pocket once more. The handwriting looped across the page, curved and voluptuous. *I would like to speak with you concerning the temple of Herzu. Come to my rooms this afternoon.* No signature. Perfume on the paper. She'd been confident he would know who had sent it.

Too much doubt had forced Nessaket's hand. There had been no word from Arigu, of this Tuvaini made sure, and now, with Beyon running off to the sands, Arigu's fate was even more uncertain. All that remained to Nessaket now was her mad prince, and Tuvaini. She had no choice. He kissed the letter and laughed.

He walked from one end of his room to the other and back again. He wished he could go to Lapella, but this was one thing he could not tell her. In any case, she would not be there; she rarely waited for him at this time of day, occupying herself instead with mysterious female tasks.

So he was left to pace, and had no one with whom to share this moment.

The sun lowered in the sky. He'd planned to make Nessaket wait, but not too long. He lit his lantern, stepped out into the corridor and made his way to the mosaic at the end of the hall. He pressed the golden stone that was the eye of Keleb, and the panel swung open. Once inside he pulled the latch closed, listening hard and holding his lantern high. Ever since he'd divulged the secret ways to the Carriers he felt nervous travelling through them, though he'd left out many paths. This one, for example, which ran closest to his own room, he'd kept secret; but that didn't mean a Carrier wouldn't stumble across it.

The family history he'd gained outweighed the risk. It wouldn't be long now.

Satisfied he walked alone, he hurried across a stone bridge and up the stairs to the next storey. After stopping to listen again, he walked down a corridor, slower now, not wanting to be out of breath when he met her. At last he came to the door that would open across from Nessaket's room. He fumbled with the keys for a time; he didn't know the feel of the right one. At last the lock turned and he opened the door, just a crack.

He didn't hear any women's voices, or soft footsteps, or shutting of doors. Most of the wives, old and new, would be at the fountain at this time. He and Nessaket would have their privacy. Nevertheless he took care in stepping out; being caught here was a good way to get his throat cut, even with Beyon in the desert.

He moved towards Nessaket's door, listening to the silence. He remembered how once this corridor had run with happy children. Even then, Beyon had dominated, lording over his brothers and sisters in both height and will. They had loved him and obeyed him without complaint. It was foolish of Tahal to rid Beyon of his most devoted servants; the only foolish thing he'd ever done.

The mechanics of his journey had kept him distracted, but now, knocking at her door, Tuvaini's body tensed with excitement. To be at her door, to be invited to her private rooms, was to stand on the threshold of success. Soon he would preside over a secure, bountiful empire, with a beautiful queen at his side. He would invite the greatest poets and philosophers to court. He would establish a laboratory, where the seers could view the stars. He would build monuments to Cerani greatness all around the world.

The first statue would be of Tahal.

Nessaket let him in and quickly pulled the latch closed. She stepped away, her chest rising and falling with rapid breaths, her hands clenching and unclenching at her sides. He'd never seen her this way, but he liked it.

"My son is ill," she said, "and my other son mad."

Tuvaini said nothing. It was better she saw it for herself, though his tongue, body and mind were itching.

"In that family, only Tahal kept his sanity. Even Satreth the Reclaimer drank Yrkman blood and slept with a sword in his bed, though nobody speaks of it today." Her words came out in a rush. "The line was ever volatile. It is said there has never been madness among the leaders of the horse tribes. I hoped…'

Silence. Sweat gleamed between her breasts. "I could wait for Sarmin to get a son."

Tuvaini willed his hands to stillness.

"Or I could have another son myself. I still could; I was only twelve when Tahal first took me." She turned away and wiped her brow with a silk cloth. Her dress tightened around her hips when she raised her arm. Two steps away, her bed curtains hung open, inviting.

Tuvaini licked his lips. "And what do you want?"

She turned back to him, her eyes wild. "For years I struggled to be Tahal's favourite wife, to make my boys his favourites. I taught my sons the craft of the palace, how to survive with no friends and no trust. Four of them, I had. One died as a baby, I lost one in the succession, and one to the Tower. And then it was all for nothing; Beyon pushed me away."

He picked his words carefully. "You have allied yourself with the army. Some would call it treasonous."

She shrugged. "It was something to stand on. If I am tall enough, the emperor will see me."

"And Arigu?"

She turned away again and wove her hands together.

"Do you renounce him?" he asked, hearing the quaver in his own voice.

Her shoulders tensed. "Yes."

He moved closer. "An army wants things the palace doesn't see, cannot see. One cannot trust a sword for long. You are right to renounce him."

"Yes." Her voice came out a gasp.

Another step closer. "What now? Another emperor, another child?"

She relaxed, preparing for his touch. "It is the easiest way." He paused behind her, breathing her scent. "Starting over from the beginning."

"Tuvaini." The way she said his name, hoarse and breathless, sent a thrill through his body. "There will be no wife but me, no son but the first."

"Why would I want anyone else?" He drew a finger down her back now, closing his eyes as he reached the end of her spine.

"Then we are agreed." She turned to him and put a hand on his chest, but she did not push him away. It felt strange to stand so close to her, to have her within his power, that for a long while he simply stood, looking down at her.

"I remember you," she said, "always running errands for us wives. When the slaves brought the sweets on a tray, you would pick the best fig and bring it for me. When I had to kneel at Tahal's feet, you brought me two cushions instead of one."

He couldn't speak for a moment. "You remember?" For so long his thoughts had centred on owning her, wanting her—now she reminded him why.

"I remember. Mostly because I thought you'd ask me for a favour. Nobody in this palace does such things out of kindness. But the years went by, and you never said a word." A tear ran unheeded down her cheek.

Tuvaini brought his hands up to rest on her shoulders. "You were his favourite. And mine." He looked at her as he once had, back when they were young and the world a simple place. He saw the pretty girl instead of the cruel beauty who walked his dreams.

The years have stolen away that boy and that girl. We have both become twisted things. But maybe now we can make each other better.

"I never forgot you, Nessaket."

"That is why I put my faith in you now, Tuvaini. I will make you a son, and you will make me a queen—a real queen, not someone who hides in the shadows."

He pulled her towards him and lowered his face to hers. The feel of her eyelashes brushing his skin, the touch of her breath on his lips, almost made him forget his words. "You will never have to hide. There will be no enemies, no Carriers, and no other wives. No mages or generals under our feet. It will be you, me and our empire."

Nessaket took a quick breath. She tilted her head, her lips parted, her eyes half-closed. Another tear fell into the hair at her temple; Tuvaini didn't know which of them had shed it. He kissed the wet spot on her skin. She was sorry to let Arigu go; she loved him. But compared to himself, the heir to the throne, Arigu was no more than an upstart foot soldier. She would be glad that she chose him soon enough. He would make her glad.

Eyul woke in the heat of the tent with a growling stomach. Amalya slept by his side, her breathing smooth and easy. Her bandages had loosened during sleep and were beginning to unwind. He smelled no sickness in her wound, and his own cuts had healed well under the hermit's care. Still, he thought it best to keep her arm clean. The fresh bandages were outside, in his pack. He should also get their food from the fire. He hoped it hadn't burned to a cinder.

He crawled out of the tent and stood up, yawning, feeling the afternoon sun on his naked body. *I'll be scorched if I don't hurry.* He opened his eyes before he remembered not to, and light cut through his mind, turning the desert to black and white. He knelt, groping in the sand for his Knife. He slipped it free from its belt and hefted it, the weight of the hilt reassuring in his hand.

"Listen." The whisper came to his ear just before the sound of horses. Eyul held his left hand over his face, squinting in the direction of the noise. Two silhouettes rose over the dune: riders, pulling a third horse between them. Two recurved bows rose up over their shoulders.

The riders slowed to a halt, heads turned his way. They moved as if they were wearing something stiff. Leather, maybe. They turned to one another, some silent message passing between them. In unison they brought their bows forwards and set arrows to their strings.

Eyul laughed. He laughed so hard that his stomach cramped. Blinded and naked they'd found him. This could be the end of the Knife-Sworn, just as the emperor's life also came to an end in Nooria.

The riders looked at one another again and Eyul knew what they were thinking: it was bad luck to kill a madman.

It gave him the moment he needed. He threw himself sideways, the hot sand searing his shoulder and thigh, and two arrows struck the ground beside him. Eyul rolled closer and found his target. He could see the archer on his left, a sore outline against the sky: too distant a target for any real hope. They managed to miss him with arrows. He could hardly expect to hit back with a thrown blade. Eyul flung his Knife anyway, on a high arc, and rushed forwards. The closer man let out a soft, surprised grunt. He had a right to be surprised. He slid from the saddle without further complaint and Eyul raced on, putting the man's horse between him and the second rider. His mark landed on the sand, a blur.

"Herzu!" The other man's voice sounded familiar.

Eyul pounded up to the vacant horse, a well-trained beast that kept its place and let him use it as cover. He had only moments, and little hope, despite his lucky throw. He felt around the fallen man for his Knife. It had to be lodged somewhere vital since the archer had only twitches left in him.

"To your left."

Who spoke? He found the hilt jutting from the dead man's throat. The horse he'd ducked behind whinnied in pain and ran; the surviving rider had kicked it. Eyul tumbled away, too late, and a spear-thrust grazed his side. The other horse bore down on him now, a dark shadow, and Eyul rolled under it, lifting the bloody Knife over his head and slicing a clean line from foreleg to flank. He dashed clear as the horse fell screaming.

The rider jumped free as well; Eyul heard his boots hit the sand.

"Try me, old man." The voice came from over by the fire, near Amalya's tent. Eyul recognised that smooth tone now: Poru, from the palace guard. He remembered the man as an easy-going fellow from the sea province, given to gambling and racing boats along the river. Now he cut circles in the hot air with his sword, leaving dark traces in Eyul's vision.

"What are you doing here, Poru?"

"What does it look like?"

"Eyul?" Amalya stepped from her tent.

Poru's stance relaxed. "Is that a girl? Not bad, old one." He backed towards the tent, still on guard for Eyul's Knife. "I'll just take her, shall I?" He moved, leaving a series of dark after-images.

Eyul took his aim, tried again. "No." He lowered his knife-hand.

Poru stopped. "You're blind, aren't you, old man? A lucky throw on Bazman, that was. You won't be any trouble."

"If you're so confident, come closer."

Instead, Poru took a step back, towards Amalya. She had wisely retreated inside the tent, but nevertheless, Eyul felt a shiver in his knife-hand.

"Why don't I just take your girl, your food and your water, and let you find your own way home?"

"And when I find you in the palace, what then?"

"You won't."

"And why is that?"

Poru laughed. "Throw that Knife or let me go, old man."

"Twenty feet, a line from your left shoulder." Another whisper; not a woman, he realised; not Amalya. It never had been. Instead it was a child. Eyul froze, confused. "Now." It came again, more insistent. He threw, snapping his arm out, allowing no warning.

Poru fell against Amalya's tent and slid, jerking, into the sand. He made high animal noises as he died.

Eyul stepped back, looking around. He made out no other figures against the white of the sky. "Who spoke to me?" He felt something solid beneath his boot; Bazman's bow. Crouching, he ran his fingers along the wood. Yokom of the royal armoury was the only bowyer capable of creating these recurved masterpieces, fitted with bone and gut-string. They were among the most powerful weapons the city had to offer.

"Who sent you, Poru?" he muttered, plucking the string with his finger. He walked slowly to his victim. Faces passed through his mind: Beyon, Nessaket, Tuvaini.

It took effort to free his Knife. The blade had pierced Poru's forehead and sunk hilt-deep. Eyul yanked it clear at last and wiped it through the sand.

Amalya's voice brought him back to the desert. "Blue arrows."

She was safe. Little else mattered at that moment. He dropped the Knife and went to her. "I'm sorry," he said, "I didn't want to leave you in danger."

"You killed both of them, blind. I'd hate to see what you'd have done if you could see." She pulled at Poru's quiver. "Can you see these? Bright blue. What kind of bird—?"

"Those fletchings are reserved for the royal family."

A pause. "Beyon?"

"I don't know."

She drew in her breath. "So these were assassins?"

Eyul knew all the assassins of Nooria. There were few enough of them. "No, palace guard, but dangerous men. I should have died."

"Then why—?"

"I don't know." He considered it as he pulled on his clothes and knife belt. His head ached from the light; he felt as if his teeth were vibrating from the pain. He picked up the Knife from the sand and slid it into its sheath. "It's afternoon. We might as well start moving."

After breaking camp they mounted their camels. He noticed Amalya no longer had any trouble commanding her beast; she did not need him for that. The horses Eyul let loose. They would follow their noses to water. Eyul and Amalya set out towards Nooria, leaving Bazram and Poru in the sand.

CHAPTER NINETEEN

Three days. Three days, and yet she lived. Mesema folded her hands in her lap. Riding in the carriage without Banreh or Eldra there dulled her mind and spirit, so, to keep herself sharp she concentrated on remembering the pattern, savouring her own fear; other times, she thought about embroidery. She would hold herself in one position for hours on end—anything to keep herself disciplined, for she would need discipline, to go to her death with dignity. If news of her death travelled to her father, she would not want him to be ashamed. And if she lived…

If she lived, she would need discipline, just to keep on living.

She shifted on the bench. The muscles of her back complained with every jolt and bounce of the carriage, and her rear ached. The felt padding she had complained of so much back in the grasslands would be a blessing now. Her neck felt stiff, too—these were minor complaints compared to what had happened to Eldra, or even what Banreh suffered every day, though she told herself she didn't care about that. She maintained her position, counting stitches in her mind.

The caravan slowed and stopped. She could hear the men talking, low and scared. They had found something, but what?

Perhaps it was time. She smoothed her hair and straightened the beads around her neck. She would look well for this.

She waited. She did not fan herself, or squirm, but kept still, listening to the voices of the men and the nickering of the horses.

Banreh appeared at the carriage window. She looked away from him, at the opposite seat. She didn't want to see his eyes.

"What is it, Banreh?" She used her father's tone, formal and clipped.

"We have come upon the emperor's camp," he said. "We have been commanded to stop here."

She imagined the emperor, frail and sick, being carried on a litter to oversee the destruction of those who plotted against him. "Very well."

Banreh said nothing else but waited near the window as if expecting her to speak. Finally he urged his horse forwards, beyond the carriage.

Stupid thrall. He values words far too much. Mesema closed her eyes and took a breath. She would be brave. Every woman must be brave eventually. She realised she'd made fists in her lap and relaxed them, placing her hands loosely on her knees.

She waited.

The air grew heavy. She couldn't breathe, but she remained still. She heard women's voices, giggles, and it made her sad for Eldra. She cocked her head, listening.

The door swung open, revealing a wizened, dark woman with chestnut eyes. Her gaze ran down Mesema's body, taking in her clothes and jewellery. Mesema sat straight in her seat, resisting the urge to bite her lip.

Four men ran towards the carriage, carrying large sticks wound with fabric like great scrolls. Mesema jumped back, startled, but the men paid her no attention. They stood on either side of the old woman and unwound the scrolls, creating red screens made of silk which they held aloft, forming a corridor. The corridor led to another, and another, each held up by four men, leading to a place she couldn't see.

The woman watched her, smiling. "Come, come," she said in Cerantic, motioning with one hand.

Mesema slid off the bench and down the steps. The woman took her arm and led her between the swathes of fabric, turning here and there until finally she walked through a tent flap—or at least it had looked like a tall tent flap from the outside. Inside, it resembled a small house. The red walls slanted towards a high, round ceiling of white. On the sand, rugs and cushions offered comfort for her sore body. A sleeping mat and a large tub full of water occupied one end. Oil lamps provided light and scented the air with lavender.

This tent was not for her; this was someone else's tent, where she would wait for the emperor's judgement.

The old woman touched her arm and pointed to the tub.

"Wash first," she said.

"I speak Cerantic," said Mesema. "You needn't speak to me that way."

The woman nodded, grinning. "I am called Sahree. Now you take off your clothes." She pointed at the tub again. "You have sand ground into your skin, like a nomad."

Mesema almost asked why the emperor should care, but she held her tongue. Her fingers worked the lacings of her blouse as she looked around the tent once more. Two other women, both young, had come in behind her. When she looked at them, they giggled and huddled together. One had blue eyes, but she didn't look Felting. The other looked Cerani.

Mesema's heart gave a twinge when she thought they might have been her friends, had things been different. If Arigu hadn't been such a liar and Banreh such a fool.

When she took off her blouse, the women exclaimed in laughter again. Mesema burned with humiliation and began to undo her skirt.

Sahree must have seen the expression on her face, for she tapped Mesema's shoulder and smiled. "This is good," she said, pointing to her chest. She motioned to the blue-eyed woman, who stepped forwards and put her hand right over one of Mesema's breasts. "Good skin. Tight," she said. An odd compliment, Mesema thought; Cerani might not be the girl's native language, but the message came across in any case. She nodded encouragingly at Mesema.

Mesema tried to smile back, but her body had begun to shake. Would the emperor be looking at her chest? She wondered where Banreh was, and if he were still alive.

"Don't be frightened," said Sahree. "It's just some soap and a brush." Her eyes betrayed a hint of impatience. "Willa, help her." With that, the blue-eyed girl took Mesema's arm and eased her towards the tub.

Mesema climbed in while the young women exclaimed over her thighs and buttocks. The water felt cool against her skin as Sahree cleaned her with gentle hands and rubbed soap into her hair. She hadn't been washed like that, by another person, since she was a baby. It made her think of her mother. When she climbed out, the younger women dressed her hair. As their soft fingers unwound her tangles, tears ran down Mesema's cheeks. She missed Dirini and Eldra.

"No, no," said the Cerani girl, the one Sahree had called Tarub, "don't ruin your eyes."

Willa fetched a wet cloth and pressed it over Mesema's face.

"Better," said the other.

"Now for the difficult part," said Tarub.

Mesema panicked: what did they mean, the difficult part? She calmed her breathing. She was a princess. She would not scream, or be frightened, but she did push the cloth away. She wanted to see.

They laid her back onto a cushion and held her legs apart as Sahree gave her a gentle smile. "We need to be sure you are a maiden. Please forgive."

"It will just take a moment," said Tarub, grasping her hand. A few seconds later, when Sahree's fingers found their way inside her, Mesema squeezed Tarub's hand so tightly that she feared she'd injured her.

Sahree laughed and let her go. "Maiden, for certain."

"This is good," said Tarub, extricating her fingers from Mesema's grasp.

"Now we dress you," said Sahree cheerfully, splashing her fingers in a bowl of water.

Mesema pressed her legs together, but she still hurt. A Windreader could not be humiliated this way. "Who are you?" she asked at last. "Why are you here?"

The women looked at her as if she were mad. "We are the body-slaves to the Old Wives, the emperor's mothers and grandmothers," said Sahree.

"Are the Old Wives here, then?"

Sahree shook her head, amused. "Of course not."

This didn't answer anything at all, but Mesema chose not to pursue it as the women started holding up filmy pieces of cloth, more like scarves than dresses. "See this one?" Tarub shook out some fabric and held it against Mesema's face. "It looks well on you."

Mesema wrung her hands together. The bath, the maiden check, the clothes—none of it made any sense. Why wasn't she dead already? Was it a game? If so, all she could do was go along with it. "I choose that one, if I am allowed to choose."

The women exchanged glances. "Of course you may choose," said Sahree. They gathered the fabric over her shoulder and pinned it with a jewelled brooch. It felt softer than the softest wool, softer than skin, as it fell cool against her body. Another piece went around her waist and they tied it all together with a patterned sash. They placed jewelled sandals on her feet and stood back to admire their work.

Mesema lifted her arms. It felt strange to have no fabric between her arms and her ribs. She felt naked. "How do you name this color?" she asked. It looked like the grass and the sky mixed together.

"That color is named ocean," said Tarub. "It is good for you."

"It is very good," said Willa.

"What now?" Mesema held her hands awkwardly at her sides.

"I will see if it is time," said Sahree.

Once again she had received no answer, but Mesema couldn't ask another question, for Sahree had already disappeared through the tent flap. She kicked at the rug. Tarub and Willa smiled at her in encouragement, but still she felt awkward.

After a minute Sahree returned and clapped her hands together. "Soon," she said. "The emperor, heaven keep him, is almost ready. But you must learn the proper behaviour. First, when you come within your height of him, you must give obeisance. Do you know obeisance?" Sahree put her knees on the rug, then bent over, her hands stretched before her on the ground. "Now you try."

Mesema did the same.

"Good," said Sahree. "Then you wait until someone tells you to get up. Don't mutter or fidget, now."

Mesema didn't need to practise keeping still, but she did it anyway, for Sahree's sake.

"Good," said Sahree at last. "Rise. You must do the same if he leaves the room before you. Now, when you speak to the emperor, you must address him properly as "Your Magnificence" or "Your Majesty"."

"All right," said Mesema, folding her hands to keep them from shaking.

"There is more," said Sahree, "and we used to be very strict in his father's day, may he live in heaven for ever, but we haven't the time."

"Because the emperor is ill?"

Sahree gave her a sharp look. "Ill? He is not ill."

Banreh, you fool. Mesema stared at her feet. If she allowed the tears that stung her eyes to come forth, they would throw cold rags on her face again. She bit her lip and dug her fingernails into her palms. The pain cleared her mind.

It was clear the emperor didn't intend to kill her quite yet, but it was also clear that Arigu had lied again. The emperor was not dying. She wished she could hit Banreh for believing Arigu's nonsense. She sighed. No; she couldn't hit Banreh. She would be too glad to see him.

An invisible signal stirred Sahree to action. "Come!" she chirped, taking Mesema's arm. Outside, a new series of red corridors appeared for her.

"Why do they make silk paths for us?" she asked.

"So that the common men cannot see you," said Sahree. Mesema could tell from the morning sun that while her tent had been to the west, the emperor's stood to the south. Their journey ended at a tent flap where two men stood guard. They wore round blue hats topped with feathers, different from the pointed white hats worn by Arigu's men. They gaped at Mesema, and she looked at her feet, small in their jewelled sandals.

After a few minutes the tent flaps parted, pushed from within, and a man wearing blue robes bowed slightly to her.

"Enter," he said, his voice crisp and cool. She couldn't tell his age; he might have been twenty-five or forty.

She took a breath to steady her nerves and moved forwards, taking tiny steps over a silk runner. Without looking up she could tell the tent was large, three or four times the size of the bathing tent, but she heard no voices or movement. It felt as if she were alone.

After ten steps she looked up; she didn't want to get too close for her proper obeisance. The emperor sat twice her height away, reclining on a pile of cushions. She saw his face first, the face of a Rider in his prime. He looked confident and strong. A smile played around his lips, and yet he seemed angry. She took a few more steps and faltered, now seeing Banreh, crumpled in obeisance, on her left.

"Approach the emperor," said the man who'd let her in. Mesema swallowed, ashamed of herself, and continued to walk forwards. She realised that she was staring at the emperor; she couldn't remember if Sahree had told her not to look at him. He smiled at her, with the look of a man about to tell the end of a joke, but as she got closer, his expression changed to one of surprise.

She knelt and put her face to the silk. She congratulated herself: she had made it this far. Banreh knelt just beside her and she wondered how long he'd been waiting. She worried about his leg. Her skin tingled. She refused to scratch herself.

The emperor let them wait. After a minute she began to count stitches again. Perhaps this was their punishment: he would sit on his cushions and wait them out, until they starved to death. But soon after the thought passed through her mind, the man in the blue robes said, "The emperor will receive the lady now."

She sat up and faced him. He looked down at her with almond eyes.

"I've seen you before," he said.

Mesema couldn't meet his gaze any longer. She looked at his hair, straight and black.

"Do you speak?" he asked.

"Yes, Your Magnificence."

He leaned forwards, to a tray covered with silver goblets and pitchers. "Do you drink?"

"Sometimes, Your Magnificence."

He snorted and poured two goblets full of red liquid. He handed one to his servant, who handed it to Mesema. "In the desert, one must provide food and drink to one's guests," he said.

"Thank you… Your Majesty."

"Messeeema." He downed his in one gulp and stared at her.

"I saw you in a dream."

She sipped her drink and found it sour. Nevertheless she took another sip. She didn't know what to make of his words, and in any case she was having difficulty speaking.

The emperor twirled his goblet, lost in a daydream. Then he bounced back on the cushions, propping his head with one hand. "Do you ride?" He'd changed his mood as quickly as the wind in a storm, and he still hadn't so much as glanced towards Banreh.

"Your— Of course." She lowered her goblet. "My horse's name is Tumble. He's very fine."

"Will you ride with me tomorrow? I should like to see a woman ride."

"Y-yes, Your Magnificence." Fear blossomed in her chest.

The emperor motioned towards Banreh. "What about him?"

Mesema sighed with relief. "He has a horse too. He—"

He cut her off. "I didn't mean for him to join us. I am asking who he is."

"His name is Banreh, Your Majesty. My father's voice-and-hands. His am-bass-a-dor." Banreh had taught her that word.

"So he is the one responsible for bringing you here?"

And there it was.

She steeled herself, concentrating through the buzzing in her ears. "Your Majesty, General Arigu is responsible. He lied to my father. Then he left us when the assassins came."

"Yes, I have heard about this."

Mesema took another drink, letting the sour liquid scour her throat. She hated the Cerani; they were liars, all of them. A familiar feeling rose in her chest, the kind that couldn't be stopped by fear or etiquette or anything besides Banreh.

"They killed my friend. Her name was Eldra. She was pretty and brave." A real man had to take responsibility for his actions. He would know what he had done. "I took some fletching from the arrow in her chest. A blue feather." Banreh didn't move—couldn't move—to stop her. "I'll be holding it in my hand when I die. So let me know, and I will fetch it."

The blue-robed servant rushed forwards, his hands reaching for Mesema, and she flinched. She wasn't sure whether he meant to strike her down or throw her from the tent.

The emperor held up one hand and stilled him. "You are brave, Mesema. But I don't kill women, and I didn't send any assassins."

She looked down into her drink, overcome with confusion. Not even Banreh could stop her tongue so well.

Silence fell between them. His servant stood on Mesema's right, poised to intervene.

"Well. Your father must be made aware of my displeasure." The emperor motioned towards Banreh. "I will send him this one's head, but then all will be forgiven. You will marry as planned, and your father will receive the goods and weapons Arigu promised."

She knew that she must save Banreh, only not how. "Your Majesty," she said, her mind racing, her hands shaking, "if you send my father the head of his voice-and-hands, the man he considers to be a part of himself, he will never send you the wool you expect every year in tribute. Worse, he will refuse to send his Riders against your enemies. He has influence among the other tribes—the Black Horse Clan, the Blue River Clan, the Flat Earth Clan, even the River People and Rockfighters. He will bring them all to his side."

He gave her an appraising look. "And what threats are these, that we need the aid of the Windreaders to address?"

Better not to mention treacherous generals; that might anger him. Her mind reached out and grabbed what it could. "The pattern-maker who kills your people, Magnificence."

His hand jerked, spilling his drink on the purple cushions, and he rubbed at it as he said, "And what do you know about the pattern, or its maker?"

"I've seen the pattern twice now. I know nothing of its maker."

"Has the pattern reached the horse tribes, then?"

"No, Your Majesty. I saw it only in the wind."

"In the wind." The emperor threw aside his cushion and stood. He was as big as Arigu, and as muscular, but he moved with far more grace. He walked a slow circle around Banreh.

"We will speak of this wind later. Now you will give me a better way to chastise your father, or I will kill this one."

She did not doubt him. She turned, her heart beating fast.

"My father has sent many gifts for your family as my dowry, Your Majesty. His best wools and dyes, amber and rare healing plants. Send them all back."

"I would be doing him a favor," said the emperor, pausing near Banreh's shoulder, a smile playing about his lips. "You are sneaking your tiles off the board."

Mesema shook her head emphatically. "No. For the Felt the return of a gift is a great humiliation. It will mean that the gift was poor and inappropriate. My father will be shamed before everyone. And the power will be on your side, Majesty, to forgive or not to forgive."

The emperor considered this and laughed. "You are clever, Mesema Windreader."

She looked down at her silver goblet, out of words at last.

"You may go. The ambassador will be returned to your father, along with his gifts. I will summon you when it's time for our ride."

Mesema stood and curtsied. She felt dizzy; her ears hurt. The emperor turned his back, facing the red walls of the tent, looking at nothing. The man in blue robes tapped Banreh's spine. Mesema turned; she didn't want to see Banreh struggling to get up and walk. She hurried back along the runner and at the flap, Sahree's wrinkled hand seized her arm and dragged her through. Full morning blasted across the sky—it had seemed night in the emperor's tent. Time was galloping ahead. She would never see Banreh again.

Sahree led her through more corridors, her fingers digging into Mesema's arm, until at last they pushed their way back into the tent where she'd bathed. The three women changed Mesema's clothes and combed her hair once more, and rubbed creams into her feet and hands. Then, as the sun rose high in the sky, they laid her on her mat and stood over her, waving huge fans.

CHAPTER TWENTY

E yul studied the charred corpse. "A horse. They hadn't the fuel to do much more than scorch it."

Amalya crouched over the twisted remains. The heat had tightened tendons and left the beast contorted. "There's a body underneath, a woman."

"Tribesmen, then, Felting riders off the grass," Eyul said. "A long journey that, to die in the desert."

Amalya lifted her hand. "Wait." She kept still, her lips pressed tight in concentration. The smell of sulphur rose in the air, making Eyul cough, and blue flame flickered in Amalya's eyes before orange bloomed there, wild and hot. When she opened her mouth again, smoke issued. Her words were rough, as if ash filled her throat. "Young, female. Stone around her throat and feathers on her chest. A horse with metal on its tail. A waste. The fire was not allowed to kill them."

"How did the female die?" Eyul had never addressed Metrishet before. The elemental unsettled him. He knew one day it would consume Amalya.

Amalya closed her eyes and stood up, coughing. "An arrow."

"This is the Felting girl." Eyul studied the hollow between the dunes. An empty barrel and a ripped canvas lay discarded in the sand. Someone had camped here and left in a hurry.

"So it is. Beyon's doing?"

Eyul looked towards Nooria. "For all his killings, I've never known the emperor to cause the death of a woman or a child."

"But the pattern… Perhaps it has him now?"

"Or he didn't do it." He looked at the bodies again.

"Let us move on," said Amalya. "There is nothing more for us to learn here."

"All this to bed a queen?"

Bed her? I have done that. Next I will own her. "Why set my sights so low?" Tuvaini asked. "Can I not hunger after power like every other man?"

"With you it always has to be personal." Arigu looked up from his goblet, a certain humour in his dark eyes. "There has to be someone to defeat, to humble… or covet."

"Perhaps you know less of me than you think, old friend." Tuvaini wrinkled his nose at the sour whiff of Arigu's ale. He'd picked up the taste on distant campaigns.

"Perhaps." Arigu acknowledged the possibility. "But I'm right, aren't I? It's Nessaket." Drops of amber glistened in the tight curls of his beard as he lowered his goblet again.

As Arigu grinned Tuvaini felt a pang of old hatred. So often he'd wanted to sink a fist into that broad, amiable face, though he'd probably break his hand on those raw-boned features. Rumour had it that the blood of Mogyrks flowed in the general's veins; a grandmother raped when the Yrkmen rode the desert with sword and holy fire. The slander spread well; Arigu's build and colouring fed the whispers. Tuvaini had never regretted starting that rumour.

I had Nessaket. Soon I will have the empire. "You mistake me, Arigu. I'm as loyal to the emperor as you are." *Let him play with that.* He returned his gaze to the Settu tiles between them. The game had run to plan. The game always ran to plan: Arigu had never beaten him in all their years of play, and yet here he was again, accepting one more challenge, showing no surprise that Tuvaini had discovered his return to the palace, no fear that he might be arrested at any moment. He sat calm, patient, ready to stand the tiles once more.

Arigu had nothing, just the tenuous loyalty of soldiers camped in the desert. Even so, Tuvaini felt uneasy. His Fort tile and his Rock tile stood central to the board, dominant, flanked by Tulwars with a string of River tiles to the rear. Yet he felt disquiet.

"What game are you playing, Tuvaini?" Arigu pushed a Spy stone out to the furthest corner of the board.

Tuvaini placed the Tower, setting the tile squarely before the Rock. "Why, Settu, of course, Glorious General." *He doesn't play to win, he plays to learn. To learn* me.

Tuvaini had his men waiting outside. He need only light the lamp in the window and they would rush in and seize the general. Yet he remained in his seat. Arigu led ten thousand loyal soldiers. What would they do, seeing their leader in chains? And he'd met no commander strong enough to take Arigu's place. It troubled him, a loose thread against his finger. It did not escape his notice that he had cursed Beyon for the same hesitation.

"So you have run back to the city alone." Tuvaini waited for Arigu to admit the girl had died, that his plan had failed, but Arigu only fingered his tiles. Tuvaini continued, searching for the words that would provoke a reaction. "It would be a mistake to bring this Felting girl to the city with Beyon searching for her. And for you."

Arigu smiled his broad and friendly smile. "You have not arrested me, old friend."

"To ally yourself with the horse tribes is perilous. You risk the empire, and your throat, for your ambition," he said.

Arigu's smile widened. "Whereas you risk only the emperor?"

I risk nothing that has not already been lost. Tuvaini set the fifth and last of his Army tiles, white, for the White Hat Army. Taller than any tile on the board, it stood now at the head of an unstoppable advance into Arigu's heartland. Tuvaini steadied the tile and drew his hand away quickly, spreading his fingers. It had been a long time since accident had felled any of his tiles before the Push. Settu was a game for steady hands. All games were.

"Tuvaini, old friend, no man can risk the empire." Arigu set another Spy stone.

His tiles stood in scattered confusion. Tuvaini had the game.

"The empire cannot be taken. It cannot be lost. It's too strong," Arigu said. He reached for his Dominants, the tiles he should have played at the start. They were useless now, but his to play if he chose. "The empire rests on three pillars, and each in turn could bear the load alone." Arigu set out his own White Hat Army, the first pillar. "All the grass tribes, stretching out even to the trade lands of Kesh and the Vaulcan Marches, with the nomads from the dunes to sharpen their spears, would be held by the army at the Cerani gates. Not through numbers—there could be five Riders to each man of Cerani—but because war rests on the science of supply and method, not bravado and the application of warpaint."

"I'm not a schoolboy," Tuvaini said, but Arigu went on.

He set his Fort tile behind the Army tile. "The walls of Nooria are the second pillar: a stone currency with which time itself can be purchased. And with time, aid will come from the four corners of the empire." Arigu tapped each of his Army tiles in turn, spread out at random across the board.

Behind the Fort, Arigu laid the Tower. "And the third: the mages cannot be turned from their service to the throne."

"My tutor always taught me that the empire was indestructible." Tuvaini pursed his lips. *What about the girl?* "But I am not reassured." He reached towards his Assassin tile to claim the victory.

Arigu waved Tuvaini's hand away. "The empire is in no danger." He laid a finger on his Emperor tile. "But there can be change."

Arigu made the Push. His Emperor tile fell. The Emperor caught the Assassin, and the Assassin the Vizier. The cascade continued, splitting, dividing around the Spy stones, spreading out across the board with the soft, rapid click of tile felling tile. Patterns Tuvaini had neither seen nor imagined emerged, grew and died, and still the toppling continued.

Tuvaini stared at the ruin before him. Fallen tiles covered every inch of the Settu board. Six tiles only remained standing, the same on each side: the White Hat Army, the Fort and the Tower.

"A draw." Arigu drained his goblet and stood to leave.

"Your plan is finished, Arigu." Tuvaini couldn't keep the anger from his voice.

"Not yet." Arigu straightened his tunic and reached for his swordbelt. "The girl comes."

She lives? His men had failed, and Arigu stood there smiling. Knowing. Tuvaini rose to his full height, fury guiding his words.

"To seed claimants to the Petal Throne among the grass tribes? You would grow a pet emperor with relatives who live on horseback." He made a sharp gesture towards the board. "Men who can't even play Settu."

"We can all learn new games, Tuvaini. If enough emperors die, the king-makers will eventually come to your door. You even have Beyon's look, though scraped a little thinner, it's true." Arigu tightened his belt, jiggled his sword in its scabbard and flashed a dark smile. "We can't all stake our hopes on ties to the royal bloodline, however tenuous. Some of us have less regal ancestry… or so the gossips say."

"She will die." Tuvaini spoke the words to Arigu's back. It would happen. He had the means and the will to make it happen.

Arigu paused at the door, looking every inch the general.

"I need an emperor who needs me, Tuvaini. I need an emperor who can see that we stand poised to take the world. I've seen it, Tuvaini. I've seen all the nations between the seas. There is nothing like Cerana."

The general's unexpected eloquence struck Tuvaini. He'd spoken the truth: the empire set its sights too low. More could be found over mountain and water. Gems to the north, spice to the south, wood to the east; they spread out before him, dates for plucking.

Tuvaini said, "Wait."

Arigu turned, the door half-open, his face drawn in question. Tuvaini swept the tiles away, clearing the board. "We can talk about that."

CHAPTER TWENTY-ONE

Mesema had heard nothing of Banreh. Perhaps he had already set off over the desert. Perhaps he sat in some other tent, scratching on his lambskin. Perhaps the emperor had killed him after all.

Sahree had not allowed her to get her own riding clothes from the trunk on top of the carriage. Instead she had, after much fussing, dressed her in thin silk pants and a long tunic. A wide blue scarf protected her head from the desert sun. "No padding?" Mesema asked Sahree, tapping her behind, but Sahree just shook her head and sighed.

She moved through the silk corridor once again, but this time it ended not with a tent flap but with open sand and a group of horses. Mesema's heart lifted when she saw Tumble at last, waiting next to a tall steed; she hadn't quite believed she would be allowed to ride. She clambered into the saddle with a yelp of joy and patted his mane. "You're a good boy, you are, getting through all that heat and sand for me," she said. From her elevated position she could see the entire camp: waggons were being loaded, tents struck, fires doused. Men in different colored uniforms—Arigu's in white hats and the emperor's in blue—hastened to their tasks. She didn't see Banreh.

Everyone fell quiet, and she knew the emperor had arrived.

He mounted the powerful horse on her right. He wore a rough tunic and breeches, nothing more than what a thrall might be given at her father's holding; only the gold on his fingers showed him to be something more. Behind him, two soldiers in blue mounted their own horses. A fourth man waited well to the emperor's right, his white robes fluttering, though no wind stirred. He looked at Mesema with eyes the color of the winter sky and she quickly turned away.

The emperor gestured towards the mountains ahead. "We'll ride to the east."

She didn't ask where he was taking her—she didn't feel that it mattered. He was the emperor, and if he wanted to take her to the top of a mountain or drop her down a well, it couldn't be prevented.

He smiled then, a natural smile from a Rider in his seat.

"Let's see you ride." He set off, and she could see he treated his horse more as a thrall than an equal. Still, he rode well, and she had to struggle to keep up with him. She wasn't used to the soft feel of the sand under Tumble's hooves. The emperor rode ahead for the most part, but she managed to pull alongside for a few moments at a time. They exchanged no words. The blue-hatted soldiers followed at a distance, and behind them rode the strange man in white. When she turned, she could see them, sitting straight and awkward on their mounts.

The mountains towered before them, lit by the evening sun. In time the rock grew distinct, shadows marking lower peaks, crags and ridges. They passed from the dunes to where the sand rose in tiny ripples. She could see a great rise of mist from the rocks to her right, and a swathe of green that trailed away, heading south-west. This could be no other than the River of a Hundred Names, which fed the Felting in the valleys and flowed down into Nooria and beyond.

Mesema rode on, trailing the emperor, until the orange-lit rock face filled her vision. Here the mountain threw out two great stony arms, boulder-strewn and riven with deep clefts, in a protective embrace around an area of sand. The emperor steered his horse into the gap. Mesema looked up at the huge rocks that looked poised to fall and crush him.

"Come," he called back to her. Cerantic did not have the authoritative inflection her own language provided, but she recognised the command in his tone. She followed, clinging to Tumble's mane.

Once through, she drew in her breath. A riot of colours, yellow, purple and blue, danced from rock to rock. It could be the plains for all the flowers, except for the pale, shifting earth that lay beneath them. She slipped off Tumble and knelt by a sky-tinted blossom. She ran her fingers over the thick and fleshy petals.

"It looks like you," he said. He'd come to stand beside her.

"The zabrina."

Mesema stood and backed away.

"I meant the color is the same as your eyes." He leaned over and snapped it from its stem.

Mesema frowned at the flower as he twirled it between his thumb and forefinger. "Why did you bring me here, Your Majesty?" Behind him, the soldiers had dismounted and were standing guard. She didn't see the man in white and was glad for it.

"Do you see nothing here worth the bringing?" He threw the flower aside.

"It is pretty." Mesema looked around at the colours, intensifying now in the last light of the sun. "Where is my father's voice-and-hands, Your Majesty?"

Shadows reached across the valley.

"He has gone to join the rest of his body."

She hoped he spoke truly. Mesema fingered the blue feather in her pocket. More questions bubbled up inside her. "Why didn't you bring your brother the prince to greet me? Are you angry with him because of the general?"

"No." He studied her with copper eyes.

She hugged her arms around herself. "Did he not wish to come?"

"He—" The emperor glanced back at his guards, but they were not within earshot. "He's not like us."

"Us? I am not like you, Your Majesty." The words came out before she could stop them. She braced herself, but he only laughed.

"Correct: nobody is like me. I am the Son of Heaven." He laughed again. "The gods' favour is obvious, is it not?"

Mesema watched him laugh, feeling uncertain. Cerani humour eluded her. She took a few steps away, admiring the flowers that rose impossibly from the sand. The desert: this was the heart of the Cerani Empire. Her father had told her that a person who can live in the desert can live anywhere—fight anywhere. These flowers looked delicate, but they must be strong, to survive here. Indomitable.

The soldiers pierced the ground with long torches and touched them with flame. Flowers did not look so pretty in firelight, but Mesema could still smell their perfume, and if she closed her eyes she could imagine springtime on the plains.

Mesema felt something hard underfoot and when she drew back her shoe she could see metal, glimmering low in the sand. She glanced at the emperor, but he had turned away and was looking at something in his hand. Mesema lifted the item and turned it over in her palm. She'd seen such round discs before, in the sacks of the traders-who-walked. It was a coin, for people to use when they had nothing to barter. The face stamped on the coin looked like the emperor, but older. She dropped it and studied the desert floor. Other objects glittered in the flames, and she picked up each in its turn: a colored gemstone, a ring, a charm. She lifted the charm and held it up to the light of torches and sunset. A golden ship, held aloft by great clouds, twirled from her fingers. She turned it this way and that, trying to imagine if such a ship existed, one that could fly through the air.

Sand shifted behind her and she tensed as the emperor spoke. "These are offerings to Mirra, goddess of beauty, children, and healing."

One does not take what belongs to the gods. Mesema gave a solemn nod and replaced the cloud-ship, but not before its golden mast pricked her index finger. She hissed and pressed her thumb against it to stop the bleeding. "Your goddess has blessed this place, Your Majesty."

He said nothing, but she could still sense him at her back. He expected her to make an offering.

Perhaps the goddess could be a friend. She might ensure Mesema's child would be a glorious ruler as her great-uncle had foreseen. Mesema fingered the beads around her neck. Glass and ceramic brought across the mountains by the traders-who-walked, strung with some of her mother's gold on a woollen string. She had nothing better other than the silk clothing Sahree had given her.

No sooner had she begun to lift the necklace over her head than she felt the string snap between her fingers. The beads cascaded over her palm and onto the sand, a fall of sparkling colour. She watched them roll and bounce between other, half-buried offerings, until they came to rest in a serpentine line.

A wind blew from the west, sweeping the sand from around her feet and casting it against the mountain face. A long note sounded from the stone, higher and fuller than anything blown from a singing-stick. It seemed the final note of a longer piece, the last broken-hearted syllable of a mourning-chant; it spoke of all the unheard notes that had come before it, chords that told of beauty, sorrow and violence. She felt it vibrate in her chest, and she knew that the entire song would have been too much for her to bear.

The guards fell into a whispered chant, while the emperor laughed once more. In a voice meant for only her, he said, "The ignorant say that Mirra sings for those She favors."

The wind shifted then, bending the flower-heads towards the south, where she knew the city lay. The sand scattered around her feet, hinting at shapes and lines, moving towards something she almost recognised. The Hidden God offered at first only two vague figures and a few spidery lines, but then the wind blew harder and for one moment the image lay clear before her: a woman, knife in hand, with a fallen man at her feet. The sand offered no detail but she knew them even so: herself and the emperor.

Mesema felt each hair on her head standing on end. Her palms hurt where her fingernails dug deep. Her lungs began to burn before she remembered to inhale, and even then her breath came in gasps and gulps. She was more frightened now than when the Red Hooves had flown through her village on their cursed horses. Why would she kill an emperor? What would happen to her after she did?

She had to run away.

If she could get to Tumble, and start riding, the River of a Hundred Names would take her to the folk in the mountains, and they could take her home.

She swung about. The emperor stood directly behind her. *No.* She put out her hand and tried to push him away. The cut on her finger burned, and she screamed.

Darkness. Flowers, tobacco and leather. Someone held her.

"Mirra's song was too much for her. Bring me the water, now, quick!"

The emperor. She opened her eyes and looked at his face. He glared over her at the soldiers in blue, his eyes wild and furious, and she saw the cruelty there, the other side of his strength. Had he killed Eldra, after all? How long before she too became a problem best solved with a cut throat or an arrow?

He looked down at her and put a hand to her cheek. "Are you well?"

She closed her eyes, fighting nausea. A message from the Hidden God. Its meaning was clear, and unavoidable, the most definite and most terrible message He had ever sent. It filled her mouth like a bitter root. "It is sometimes hard to serve the gods, Your Majesty."

The emperor snorted. "Then don't, unless you want to find your efforts wasted."

He held her in silence for a time and she gathered herself. The emperor felt different from Banreh. Softer. His hair reminded her of her father's. *But my father doesn't kill girls.* Or did he? She remembered what Eldra had told her about pulling a spear from her sister's neck. She didn't know what to believe. *I may be a killer, too.*

"I'm better now," she said. Her finger hurt.

As they rode towards the caravan, Mesema held tight to her reins, feeling so dizzy she feared a grain of sand might knock her from the saddle. The Hidden God had shown her a future, but she hoped it wasn't true. *Gods do not lie. They can be unclear, but they do not lie.*

The emperor rode beside her, as lost in thought as she. The movement of sand filled the silence between them as the moon rose in the sky, a wide crescent. The Bright One moved closer, his long journey three-quarters finished.

"Tonight you will dine with me," he said, and spurred his horse forwards.

Eyul left his camel in the valley and crawled up the dune on his elbows. Amalya waited below in the darkness. He looked out over the campsite and slid back down to her.

"The emperor's caravan, a large one, with his and Arigu's soldiers both."

"Do we join him?"

Eyul considered it. *No. Get to the city first. Deal with Govnan.*

"They're bound to move slowly. We'll go around. If the scouts stop us, they stop us."

"Eyul." She looked at the crest of the dune, where the sounds of men and horses carried. "Since he's here, do you think he was the one—?"

"I don't know." He gathered his camel's tether and pulled. "There are more important things than a girl."

Amalya moved her lips, but said nothing. She took her camel's rope and followed him.

Sarmin closed his eyes and let his mind seek the Many. He moved among them, their whispers brushing against him as he passed. Their words shimmered on the edges of the pattern-shapes and pulsed into the threads, strengthening the pattern-bonds he passed between. Sarmin kept to the dark spaces, unseen, unnoticed.

A flash, and the Many turned as one, called by an unfamiliar touch, a vibration at the heart of the pattern. Sarmin felt it too, a prickling against his skin, a hollow in the design. One of the Many drew away. Sarmin followed, curious, ever cautious of the pattern's Master.

"Rise." Mesema rose from her obeisance and the emperor motioned her towards a low table. "Please, eat."

Torchlight danced over the red cloth covering the table, revealing apples and gleaming oranges, flat pillows of bread, and bowls of steaming lamb decorated with zabrina blossoms of deepest blue. The scents of garlic and thyme reminded her of home.

She stood over the feast and stared at her reflection rippling in a golden plate. The body-slaves had crushed berries against her lips, giving them a bloody look, and swept her hair into a cascade of curls. She did not look Felting. She would never look Felting again.

Is this what a killer looks like?

She knew the emperor would not eat. Emperors were descended from the gods, Sahree had told her, and they did not break bread with mere mortals. He did, however, pick up a goblet and gulp down the sour red brew he'd shared with her before.

Mesema settled down and picked up a piece of bread. The emperor kept his eyes on her, as if she were giving a performance. She didn't think she could eat, no matter how delicious it smelled. She crumbled a bit of bread between her fingertips.

"We should arrive at the palace soon." The emperor's voice fell deep and heavy, as if just thinking about the palace made him tired.

"You'd rather stay in the desert," she murmured. Not a question.

"Always."

He reminded her of a Rider in winter, restless, waiting for the day the raids would begin, but for the emperor there would be no raids. The empire was at peace, if living with the pattern could be called peace.

"What is the palace like, Your Majesty?"

He smiled. "Like a garden full of snakes."

Like me. Mesema tried to bite the bread, but ended up just brushing it against her lips. The crust felt sharp and tough. She tried to push the evening's vision from her mind.

"Something worries you, Zabrina."

"Yes." She took a gulp from her goblet—*wine*, they called it. She shaped the Cerantic word as the wine ran over her tongue, deciding how much to say. "The wind showed me something in the sand, Your Magnificence."

He raised his eyebrows.

"I saw the pattern." She left out the rest, for now, and it made an empty space in the room.

He stared at her, his hand clutched around his goblet. "You play a game with me?" He lifted it in a rough movement and the wine sloshed over the side and ran across his fingers, but he didn't take a drink. "There are enough women in the palace who play games. Perhaps I should have sent you home to your father."

"I…" Banreh had warned her to keep silent. Mesema looked down at her hands. A smudge of blue showed on her fingertip, a threatening touch of colour. Everything seemed to slow as she wiped the mark against her skirt. She felt the soft threads against her finger, the fabric moving against her thigh, the sweat on the back of her hand. *It's just a mark from the colour they put on my eyes. It's from the soap. It's from the dye in my clothing.* But when she looked at her finger again, the spot remained, taking the shape of a crescent moon. It sent a message she couldn't read, though she knew it to be fearsome.

"What is it?" the emperor asked, putting his drink aside. She had nearly forgotten him. He would kill her now.

"Nothing." *Run. Go now—find Tumble and go.* But she hadn't run the first time, when she saw the vision in Mirra's garden, and she wouldn't run now. The emperor stared across the table at her, and she kept still as a tent pole. His face remained that of a stranger, his expressions alien and unreadable, except when transformed by anger.

"Show me." He knocked the pile of food aside with his elbow and grabbed her hand. Fruit fell and rolled against her slippers as he examined her fingers. He must have felt her hand shaking. He must have felt her fear.

To end here, in the desert… She had seen death fly through her village on the back of red-hoofed horses. Jakar's clouded eyes made a hollow in her that she felt to this day. Iron was terrible, but the pattern was worse. The pattern wrote your end upon you. It made you wait, knowing your death, wondering to what sinister goal you were to give your life's breath.

At long last the emperor looked up and told her what she already knew. "A tiny moon."

"No!"

"A pattern-mark." His lips grew tight.

"It's not!" Her mouth lied without asking permission.

He let go and patted her hand. "Don't let anybody see it." She watched him. He should kill her, or at least call his guards and have her removed, but instead he drank again from his goblet. If she were to guess at his expression now, she would call it worried. *No, he will not kill me. It is I who will kill* him. Would the pattern make her do it? At last she said, "I'll… I'll be careful."

"When we get to the palace, I'll have the mages protect you as they do me."

They fell silent for a time. She thought about Eldra, first with the marks across her skin, and then lying on the desert sand with an arrow sprouting from her chest. She thought of herself, standing over the emperor with a knife.

"Your Majesty, why are you helping me?"

He smiled. "You have spirit. I wish I had known you before."

"Before the pattern touched me?"

He shook his head. "In Mirra's garden—when you touched me—my robes fell open. Isn't that when you saw the pattern?" She stared at him, a dark idea taking form in her mind. Banreh had spoken of the emperor as if he were sick, as if he were going to die.

"You really do see things in the wind? And all this time I thought you played Settu with me. The way you always hinted at the pattern—"

"The pattern… was inside your robe?"

"But you are exactly as you seem. How do you do that?" He stood and un-tied his sash. Mesema thought she should turn her head, or tell him to stop, but a terrible fascination won her over. A truth hid behind his silks, ready to be revealed, and she wanted to see. The knot came loose and the purple silk fell to the floor of the tent.

"See." He lifted her chin with one hand. She saw.

His flesh showed line upon line of red and blue, the larger shapes followed by smaller and yet smaller again, so that looking at his skin, she felt as though she gazed into the distance. His arms, too, were banded by pattern-shapes. In the centre of his chest, where a crescent moon floated above a series of smaller circles and polygons, she could see a smear of her own blood.

"I touched you, there," she said. "I cut my finger on a little air-ship." Would her skin look like this also?

"I have been patterned for years," he said, "and I am still alive." The crescent moon drew her eyes, the twin to the one on her finger. Blue outlined with red, her blood a brown smear across it, it seemed to stretch with each breath the emperor took. Stretch, and reach towards her.

She touched her finger to it, moon to moon.

Sarmin felt it again, a brightness between the pattern-threads. He moved towards it, feeling the silence around him. The others hung back, silent, wait-ing, though for what, he didn't know. Closer to the brightness he felt many barriers, lines that stopped and twisted the pattern-threads and made them wrong. He studied the ugliness until he found a way to slip through.

The emperor drew in his breath, long and hard. "I remember,' he said, "so many things."

Mesema saw them too, the boys running in the throne room and hiding in the women's wing. She heard the Old Wives singing and nibbled the honey-cakes the cooks slipped into Beyon's pocket. She could feel the taste of them on her tongue. She saw Emperor Tahal, laughing and reaching for her to sit on his lap. She saw her brothers, dead. She never stopped seeing them. She screamed and beat her fists upon the throne. She pushed her mother down the dais steps, seeing the hurt and confusion in her eyes. A gutted nobleman lay prone before her, his blood soaking into a silk runner. Then another, and another. Tuvaini spoke in her ear, soft and urgent, making her stomach twist. Then he left her, and the dark throne room echoed with her finger-taps. Light came and with it children, running across the courtyard, chasing a dog, laughing—but not her children. Never hers.

And the dreams carried her away from the palace. She spied on a caravan, watching a girl with wheaten curls. She thrust her knife at the vizier. She laughed at an assassin, knowing he was trapped.

I was an emperor.

She gasped and pulled her finger away. "Memories."

"It can't take mine. There are protections woven all around me." His hand shook as he replaced his robe.

"But there were things you had forgotten until I touched you." That, too, she had seen.

"I hadn't forgotten them, not really." He sat down, grasping at his purple sash. "It's more that I stopped feeling them."

"Your Majesty," she said, meeting his copper gaze, "listen. We are both trapped in the pattern-web."

"In that case you should call me Beyon."

Was he joking with her? She tried his name in her mouth. "*Beyon.* What shall we do? We have to stop it." She thought of her promise to Eldra, not forgotten even when the feather lay beneath heavy wools in her trunk.

He laughed. "What shall we do? You are ever brave, Zabrina, Windreader."

She didn't feel brave, but she tilted her chin at him anyway.

"I am Felt. We carry on."

"Well, Zabrina, Felt, Windreader," he said, moving to the door flap, "why don't you have something to eat before you get some rest? We'll reach the city soon enough, and then we can... do something."

He didn't sound convincing, but Mesema nodded before falling into her obeisance. He remained the emperor, and she would obey.

Sarmin had found a way through, only to discover new barriers before him, barriers made of moving ghosts: Pelar. Lana singing a melody in the women's wing. His father, grunting with pain as he lifted himself from the throne. Every time Sarmin tried to move forwards, a new image from the past blocked his way. On the other side he heard voices. Beyon's, and a woman's. The woman's accent was soft and sibilant. He wanted to stay and listen.

A voice purred in Sarmin's ear, unexpected, smooth as the silk on his bed. "You move in my place, Stranger."

Sarmin kept his mind still.

"The emperor is troublesome, isn't he?" The Master took a conversational tone. "So many protections to move through. Nevertheless, he is mine. Not yours." The last reverberated with anger.

Fury beat its wings in Sarmin's chest. The Pattern Master didn't sense it, or didn't care.

"Beyon will serve me, alive or dead, broken or no. It is too late for him. And you…'

Sarmin felt himself falling.

"You do not belong."

Sarmin fell past the whispers and calls of the Many, through the dawn-tinted desert sky and the dark places suspended in the pattern, between the gods painted on the ceiling and through the purple light of his room, and onto the pillows and comforters of his royal bed.

CHAPTER TWENTY-TWO

Eyul stared at the dim canvas roof of the tent. Near midnight, close to the city, they'd stopped and tried to sleep, in an attempt to reacquaint themselves with city-time. Soon they would walk the stone streets in the burning sunlight, conduct their business when it should be time for making love, and sleep when the cool breezes rushed across the sand. Sleep when the stars formed their patterns in the sky, pointing to other destinations, and to the time when they would not be together.

Amalya slept beside him, her breathing even and easy. The Tower comforted her; she harboured no suspicions against Govnan. She had faith that everything would work as it should, and that Beyon would be saved; otherwise, he hoped, she'd have run away with him as he'd asked. He thought once more about the west, and what was said to exist there: an ocean full of fish, islands peppered with fruit trees, and space. Specks of land lost in seas wider than deserts, places where a person might stop and think, even for the rest of his life.

Everything would change after today, with Govnan, with Beyon, and with Amalya. Whatever decisions he made regarding Govnan, things would be different.

Unless Beyon had turned—then everything was already too late.

He rolled to face her. "Are you still awake?" A question for children whispering under the covers.

Amalya pulled her blankets up around her shoulders. "Mmm."

"Do you think Beyon sent those guardsmen?"

"You said not."

"But if the pattern has him—"

She sighed and fell quiet until he thought she was sleeping. Then she spoke again. "We won't know until we see him. But you should give him the benefit of the doubt."

"Why?"

"Because you never have before."

"That has no effect on whether or not—"

"It has an effect on you. It matters to you."

He pressed his lips against her arm. "And you?"

If he could hear a smile, he thought he heard one then.

"Very much. Now sleep."

Instead he rolled to his other side and looked at his Knife. Something had happened to it in the buried city when he freed Tahal. It whispered. When the sandcat had come upon him, the Knife had kept him from dying. It had helped him kill the guardsmen when he couldn't see. And yet it spoke with the voice of a child.

He was not even sure it spoke with just one voice.

Perhaps he had gone mad, after all. But he thought not. He'd never noticed madness help a man as much as the Knife had helped him. This was something else; some other magic that was neither elemental nor patterned had infused the Knife.

He reached out to touch the warm blade and he heard it: a child's voice. "Eyul. Assassin." It blew over his skin, soft and calm as afternoon wind, and fell still.

"Who are you?" he whispered, but the Knife had nothing more to say.

Sarmin stood by a fountain, its gentle music the only sound in the circular hall with red walls. Oil lamps burned low and smokeless in well-spaced niches. He turned, making a slow survey of the chamber. He couldn't see a door, but what he could see looked familiar.

"Find the Red Door," he said. They were his words, but he didn't own the voice that spoke them.

The fountain room. We have bled here. This is the red heart of the palace of the Cerani emperors. This the pattern. This the price.

Sarmin crossed the hall, seeing the marble fountain in the room beyond, and set his hand to the wall.

Sarmin watched the Carrier's fingers search until they found hidden studs. A door swung inwards, noiseless, invisible until it began to open. The whispers came again.

The Carrier took an oil lamp and trimmed the wick so low it could barely sustain a flame, then passed through the doorway into a narrow corridor hewn from undressed rock. This building, the whole city, had been constructed about a rocky outcrop where nomads had once found shelter. Hidden pathways ran through the palace, accommodated within walls, making stone-filled voids. Sarmin could feel the rough floor through the Carrier's slippers, the coolness of the stone as he brushed his fingers along the wall. The Carrier moved with purpose and caution, making turns without pause where the ways split. *Left. Turn here. The lower way, Tuvaini said. The fool said. Take the lower way.*

An unease grew in Sarmin, an unease he couldn't name. The Carrier seemed to feel it too. *Close. We grow close.*

Ahead, flickers described a rock wall, torchlight from around the next corner. The Carrier slowed, pressed tight to the stone now as he moved forwards. From among the Many, several rose to guide the Carrier.

I was a thief; step like this. I was a spy; breathe shallow. I murdered; move in slow.

The stone scraped beneath Sarmin's chest, or rather, beneath the chest of the one who carried him. Hugging tight to the wall, edging forwards by fractions of an inch, the Carrier peered around the corner. Three royal guardsmen waited around a stone span crossing a chasm. Sarmin recognised them all. Over the years he had gathered their names and even sketches of their lives, all sewn from fragments dropped by lips sworn to silence. These men came from his personal guard: Rotram, Ellar and Connin.

None who stood guard by his door was permitted to speak with him, to answer his questions, or even to acknowledge he had ever spoken. Few men, though, can keep their mouths from framing a single word day after day, month through month. Sarmin knew them from hours spent with his ear pressed to the door. Rotram the gambler, Ellar with his visits to the women of the Maze, Connin with his twin girls and, last year, a little boy, born blind and coughing, and dead within the month.

The Carrier set down the lamp and drew a dacarba from a scabbard beneath his tunic. From the host of the Many a single voice spoke out with confidence. A single will took the knife. *I was an assassin.*

Two of the guardsmen leaned against the rock wall, facing the chasm, looking away from the Carrier's approach. The third, Connin, straddled the length of stone crossing the void, careless of the blind depths beneath him.

The Carrier waited.

"I hate the tunnels," Rotram said. The torch in his hand coaxed sparkles from the light mail over his chest and struck gleams from his conical helm.

"They cut throats in the east wing last month," Ellar said.

"The Carriers who attacked the vizier came through the tunnels. We all know that."

"So we guard the tunnels," said Connin. He spat into the depths.

The Carrier pulled back from the corner towards his lamp, the flame a mere glow around the wick. He changed his grip on the knife, making it an extension of his arm. *I was an assassin.*

"El, isn't your brother on the rota for the west wing?" Connin asked.

But Ellar had no chance to reply. The Carrier stepped around the corner and in three quick paces reached the bridge where Connin sat with a leg dangling on either side. Sarmin tried to cry out a warning, but no sound came. Connin struggled to rise, but the Carrier caught him across the temple with a rising kick. His helmet flew free and he flailed for a moment. Then, like an inexperienced rider rolling from his saddle, he pitched into space.

The Carrier scarcely broke stride. By the time harsh reunion with the earth had silenced Connin's screams the Carrier had reached the far side of the chasm and turned, his knife ready.

"Damn!" Rotram pulled his scimitar clear of its scabbard, surprise making him clumsy.

"You filth!" Ellar reached the bridge-stone first. Sarmin had never seen such hatred on a man's face. It scared him more than the glimmering reach of the guards' scimitars.

Ellar advanced, his steps wary despite his rage. Each of these men was a veteran, and the training of a royal guard ran deep. The Carrier's wrist flickered and in an instant his blade was jutting from Ellar's throat. The Carrier moved swiftly and surely across the bridge-stone, batted away Ellar's weakened thrust and pulled his dacarba from the guard's neck before he fell.

Sarmin marvelled that palace guards could be killed with such ease; as a boy he'd been taught they were invincible.

The whispers rose around him. *Good kill. Slay the last. Bleed him.*

Rotram charged. Rotram the gambler. The Carrier dived at Rotram's feet and a pain like scalding water ran along the Carrier's back. Sarmin felt it and cried out, and the Many cried out too. The Carrier's knife struck out to the left and he rolled to his side and lay prone, his legs extended out over the drop. Rotram carried on for three steps, rolling like a drunkard, the tendon behind his left knee cut.

"Carrier Witch!" Rotram screamed as he fell. His cries trailed off. Sarmin heard a sick, wet crunch, then nothing.

Witch? The pain in the Carrier's back made Sarmin's stomach churn with nausea. The Carrier stood, and Sarmin felt hot blood running down his legs.

The Carrier moved on, unsteady, and reached a patterned hand to the wall for support. He moved on, steps up, steep, curving.

"Three palace guards. You did well." The Pattern Master spoke.

I was an assassin. The will that had held the Carrier retreated back into the Many, its voice growing fainter.

"A pity you could not slay Tuvaini's servant. Three of the Many to guide against one old man and still you failed," the Pattern Master said.

He is the emperor's Knife. Even to cut him was more than could have been hoped for.

"No matter. He works for me now."

Sarmin stopped listening. The Carrier had climbed a narrow, spiralling stairway to a door of stone. Bloody fingers guided the dacarba's point into a slot in the lintel. Inch by inch the knife slid home, hilt-deep. Without sound, and by degrees, the door opened. Sarmin saw his room. He saw his bed, and on it a young man sprawled in sleep, sweat plastering black hair to a pale olive brow.

Me!

He opened his eyes and saw her there, framed in Tuvaini's secret door: a woman of the Maze, her white robes dark with blood around the hips and legs, the pattern-symbols reaching out along her arms, running up along the veins of her throat. She stood at the foot of his bed, dacarba in hand, raised high. And the eyes that watched him were windows to the Many.

Eyul whispered over his shoulder, "What kind of magic would a ghost command?"

Amalya didn't answer; she was asleep. He rolled towards her and gathered her close. He could feel the beating of her heart, the joy of her firm, soft, curved shape. If they could lie like this for ever... But Nooria's walls lay close, and things would move quickly inside; it was as if his thinking about the city sped the coming of day. Now, in the dim glow of early dawn, the light did not bother his eyes. Later, he would suffer.

Amalya's bandages hung loose from her hand. Eyul smiled to himself; she was too fastidious to show dishevelment when awake. He sat up and reached for her pack, where she kept the fresh bandages, and cradled the clean fabric in his lap as he pulled the dirty linen away. Tossing it aside, he lifted her arm and prepared to wrap it up once more.

He leaned closer, his eyes straining in the low light. A bit of dirt, or a smudge, darkened her skin near the old wound. He wet a piece of the fabric and rubbed at it, but it remained, clearer now, three definite lines forming a shape under his thumb.

Eyul let out his breath. He didn't know how the pattern worked, whether it tattooed itself from the inside or stained a body from the outside, like ink on a page. It didn't matter. A blue triangle took its place on Amalya's wrist, its head pointing towards her hand.

Sarmin rose to meet his assassin. She stood at the secret entrance. The Carrier flesh held the Many, each will bent to his destruction. Unbidden, his hand found the hilt of Tuvaini's dacarba beneath his pillow. It had become dear to him, the embodiment of all his secrets, new and old, a treasure kept close to which his fingers returned time and again.

"See, I have a knife, too," Sarmin laughed as the patterned woman closed on him. None of it felt real—or if it felt real, it didn't feel important.

The woman circled him, looking for an opening. Sarmin knew her caution to be misplaced; the *Book of War* had taught him nothing of knives beyond their names.

"Tell me, Pattern Master, what am I to you?" Sarmin asked. He thrust his blade at the woman, hoping to buy a little time, and she skipped back, scattering black drops of her blood on the carpet. She moved as if to music, her knife part of her dance. Sarmin saw his death in the moon-gleams it sliced from the air, but the need for answers cut deeper than his fear.

"You've sunk your hooks into my brother, so what harm am I to you, here in my hidden room?"

The woman kept her lips pressed in a thin line. She looked young, perhaps five years his junior, hair cropped close, limbs thick with the hard labour of her class. She was the first woman beside his mother Sarmin had seen in fifteen years, and she came to kill him. The patterns drew his eyes though, more than her feminine charms. Patterns like Beyon's, but different, and more complete.

"Tell me!"

She moved too fast for Sarmin's eyes to follow. His knife-hand stayed motionless, paralysed by the moment, as the woman twisted beneath it, coming up to catch him in an embrace that bore him to the bed. The weight of her drove the air from his lungs in a crimson spray.

I'm stabbed.

Sarmin felt only astonishment that her knife could enter him without pain. The warmth and closeness of the woman woke memories of lost days. Sarmin lifted a hand heavier than lead to the arm that bound her to him. His precious knife lay lost in the sheets, but it didn't seem important any more, now that he was dying.

Sarmin felt the woman's blade twist inside him, metal on bone, a grating sensation between two ribs. Pain brought a sharp cry and another spray of blood from his lips, but he no longer had the strength for agony. He lay with his cheek beside her head. Her short hair was softer than he had imagined.

Even now the pattern drew him. One finger traced the half-moon on her shoulder.

A glow kindled within the assassin's flesh. Under the idle scroll of Sarmin's fingertip, blood-light illuminated the symbol and ran like fire beneath the symbols on either side, waking the pattern. It seemed to Sarmin that he was lifted from the silken bed and with another's eyes he saw the two of them bound together, as tight as a lovers' embrace, the penetrator and the penetrated, both bleeding.

Sarmin saw his fingers walk a path among the pattern-marks, waking a flood of light as if the markings were cut into a skin beneath which fire burned. His attacker strained, but managed no motion beyond the ripple of muscles. With each symbol brought to life, a memory or image flooded Sarmin, one upon the next, faster and faster, until he could pick just a glimpse here and there from the deluge:

Beyon, walking across the sand.

An assassin, older but vital, holding his knife over a young woman.

Felting folk on red-hoofed horses, spying on a caravan, the pattern-marks on the leader, hidden, but calling to Sarmin with the voice of the Many.

Tuvaini, a Settu board before him, a frown on his face.

The Tower, stark against a steel sky, a great nail driven through the city of Nooria to fix it in the world.

The images rushed through Sarmin so fast they left him breathless. More, and more again, and he rose above them, borne on a spike of pain. And in one instant the pattern lay revealed beneath him, awesome in its complexity, beautiful in its simplicity. A pattern of many dimensions, reaching for the past and the future, enclosing, incorporating…

"It is wonderful, isn't it?" The speaker stood at his shoulder.

"Almost perfect," Sarmin said.

"Almost?" A tone of reproach.

"There." Sarmin tried to point, but found he didn't have arms. He didn't need them. The Pattern Master saw it too: a dark line cut through the pattern, a wound it sought to seal. Sarmin reached to touch the damage and the glories of the pattern resolved into a single moment.

"You opened a door." The Pattern Master reproached him.

"Now the Knife stands before your plans." Sarmin reached along the pattern, back through the weeks, and he saw the ruined city rise from the sands. "You tried to kill Eyul." *I would kill him too, given the chance.*

"I failed," the Pattern Master said without emotion. "It is no matter."

Sarmin withdrew from the vision, taking in the entirety of the pattern once again. "You no longer wish him dead?"

"The Knife is better broken."

Sarmin saw it, an epiphany of fearful symmetry. "There are two sides only: yours and the Knife's. The Knife can never serve you, but broken—"

"That would be perfection."

No.

Sarmin ran from the Pattern Master. He hid in the details, driving his will along the twists and coils of the great pattern, seeking the symbols that marked his quarry, until, amid the vastness of the grand pattern, among the near infinite variations on the theme of the Many, Sarmin found the individual he wanted.

He made changes, subtle alterations that might escape unseen. The power came to him as naturally as breathing.

Sarmin could sense the Pattern Master seeking him, and remembered old games, hiding from his brothers, squeezed into closets deep among the silks, and the scent of sandalwood, the sound of footsteps passing close by, the rattle of a hand on the slatted door. *Close now.*

A pain beyond any he'd known blossomed between his ribs. He screamed, and screamed again, and opened his eyes to see the gods gazing down upon him from the painted ceiling of his room.

The Knife whispered to Eyul, one voice after another, "Do it fast."

"Yes, before she turns."

They were right. Eyul ran the hilt across his lips, a rough metallic kiss, not soft. Not like hers.

"Why do you wait, Eyul, Assassin?"

Amalya murmured in her sleep, a sweet sound that made him grit his teeth.

"Do you want a mage among the patterned?"

"Quiet, now," he whispered.

Choices. As decisions went, this one should be easy. He didn't know if Govnan was truly the enemy, or whether to trust Beyon, but a Carrier must die. It was the law.

And yet...

She'd told him to see beyond what was shown. There had to be something more here, something else to find.

"Do it now."

He remembered holding the Knife to her throat before the nomads came; he should have done it then. He'd been too soft, too hesitant. Eyul touched the shining point to her skin.

Skin was far too easy to breach; a fault in design, like so many others.

Amalya opened her eyes and smiled. Eyul pressed the blade home.

CHAPTER TWENTY-THREE

The Carrier lay across Sarmin, the pattern on her skin faded. She lifted her head, slowly, as if rising from a deep sleep. Their eyes met. She looked puzzled. Together they turned their faces to the knife in his side. She snatched her hand away from the hilt as if it burned.

"You're stabbed," she said.

"I know."

"I'll get help!" She struggled up, glanced left, right. "Where in hell are we?"

Sarmin smiled at her language. He tasted blood.

She ran for the door and pounded on it. "Help! There's a man stabbed!"

Sarmin could see the wound in her back now, where the blade had sliced her tunic open. He saw the pattern, dull reds, dull blues, and the play of her muscles under dusky skin. Beneath the clotting trickles of blood from her cut Sarmin could see the two slight changes he'd made: circle to ellipse, blue triangle to red. It was almost lost in the sweep of her patterning, but enough to free her from the Many.

"Help!" she shouted.

"They're dead." Sarmin coughed up blood, bright crimson on his fingers, "dead, or ordered away."

She ran for the window.

"Don't—" It would be a sacrilege.

But she put her fist through it anyway; three blows cleared all but the jagged fragments of alabaster from the frame. The sound took him to back that distant night and a new pain narrowed his eyes.

The Carrier stood motionless, stunned by a view Sarmin had never seen. Only once had Sarmin looked from that window, long ago. He had broken it himself, the night they brought him to the room. Darkness had not hidden the assassin and his bloody work. Years had not softened the memory.

"Come back to me?" he asked.

She did, her steps slow, noticing the richness of the carpet for the first time.

"What did you see?"

"A palace. A whole city—as if we're flying above it."

"We're in a tower, the tallest in the palace," Sarmin said. He coughed. His side felt cold now. Before it had been so hot, with the blood flooding down across his ribs.

"It isn't the tallest."

Sarmin found his hand reaching for the *Book of Etiquette*, but he stopped it. The book told him that a prince does not speak to those of the Maze. The book spoke of punishments for any of her caste who even looked upon royalty. And yet she spoke to him. She contradicted.

He coughed again, then said, "You look touchable to me." He'd not meant to say the words aloud.

"What?"

"That Tower isn't in the palace. You're looking at the mages' Tower. It's the only spire that overtops the palace," Sarmin said.

"Mages?" Her eyes returned to the knife in his side. "We should go there. They could help you."

"I don't think I can walk," Sarmin said.

The Carrier cast an eye around the room, checking out the door, the window, the ceiling, the narrow entrance to the passages that had brought her to his room.

"Wh— Where am I?" she asked at last. "What are we doing here?"

"Do you have a name?"

"What?"

"A name, do you remember your name?"

She frowned, and after a moment said, "Grada."

"Your name is the start, Grada, the corner of a pattern. Think on it, and you'll see the rest." He met her gaze, but his sight had started to dim. He was glad not to be alone. "You've been sick, Grada. Look at your arms. You're a Carrier."

"No." She didn't look, but her voice lacked conviction.

"The mages could help me, perhaps. I need to speak to them."

"Yes!" Grada's face lit up, as if the prospect of some concrete task were stone amid the sand. "I can carry you. I'm strong. Like the ox, Jenna says." She reached for him, took his wrist in her hand.

"No—" Sarmin winced at the idea of being thrown across her shoulders, "I would bleed too quickly."

She frowned. "But you said—"

"You remember the Many, Grada?" Sarmin asked. She shook her head.

"You remember them," he said, "you carried the Many, and that is how you can carry me. We will be two. I'll guide you to the mages' Tower."

"No." She released his wrist but didn't move away.

Sarmin shrugged. It didn't hurt—nothing hurt any more. He smiled and laid his head back. The gods watched him.

"It's my knife, isn't it?" Grada asked, her voice soft.

"Yes."

Sarmin watched the gods. He thought of Beyon, and of Grada. He was glad not to be alone.

"I will carry you." Grada leaned over him. "Show me how." Sarmin released a sigh he'd not known was inside him and set a trembling hand to her neck. Warm flesh pulsed beneath his fingertips. A star became a moon. And they were joined: Grada and Sarmin.

"Grada?" He spoke from inside of her. He could see himself through her eyes, pale against cushions dark with his blood.

"Grada?"

He could hear his breath rattle into shallow lungs.

"Herzu's member! You're a prince!"

"I'm going to be a dead prince unless you start moving, Grada."

"I'm in a palace and I stabbed a prince!" She was yelling, but her lips did not move.

"Grada!"

She started towards Tuvaini's secret door. Sarmin shared the pain lancing out from her sliced back.

"Who is Tuvaini?"

"Cerani's high vizier, a cousin of mine, I think, if you go through enough genealogy."

"Genie what?"

"Pay attention, those stairs are steep."

"The high vizier? Camelspit! The *high* vizier comes to see you?" She reached the bottom of the stairs and paused. She looked out over the bridge.

"Rotram?" she asked. Another memory had escaped Sarmin's keeping into Grada's mind.

"A royal guard. He died here."

"Died?" Grada asked out loud.

"Was killed."

"I remember a dream—" Images fluttered through her mind: the hatred on Ellar's face, Rotram falling into the blackness.

Sarmin moved within her and turned her head from the chasm. "Don't."

"They killed him—*somebody* killed him," she said, "with my hands." She looked at them, still rusty with his blood. "But it wasn't me?"

"No."

"It wasn't me." Prayer rather than conviction.

Together they made their way across the bridge and through Tuvaini's passages—the secret ways pre-dated Tuvaini by three hundred years, but Sarmin thought of them as the vizier's. Tuvaini, keeper of secrets—what other hidden paths had the man trodden?

Grada retraced her footsteps, bringing them through the forgotten bowels of the ancient palace. A concealed door gave before experimental fingers and she crawled through, emerging behind a patterned urn, man-high, in a dusty corner of a corridor lit by lanterns.

"This is the under-palace?" Recognition thrilled across Sarmin's shoulders, though he had never walked the halls where servants went about their business.

"I thought the emperor must live here when I saw it," Grada said, "I didn't know there were such places." Her words carried images of the Maze in their wake: dark rooms, small and dirt-floored, sewer stink, and rot in the gutters.

She found her feet and looked both ways along the corridor. To her left was a low door, and above it brown tiles picking out a scene from the Battle of the Well, showing Cerani and Parigols locked in combat.

She moved to go past, but Sarmin stopped her and they almost fell. "I've seen this before—this decoration."

Grada said nothing.

"I saw it," Sarmin continued, "I was with the Many, and I saw Tuvaini here. And something was given to him—something precious. It was his price for betrayal. His price for opening the secret ways to you."

Grada frowned. "I remember… almost."

"He plays Settu, my cousin," Sarmin said. "We're tiles on his board. He tried to use me and found that I was not a tool he could turn to his purpose, so he sold me to the Many, and charged a high price for his treachery. He plays the Pattern Master at his own game. Or he thinks he does."

Grada shook her head and for a moment Sarmin felt himself fade, losing substance, as if he were a memory or an idea ready to be overwritten by new thoughts. The image came to him of cushions black with blood.

"Quickly," he murmured, "we have to reach the Tower." They had taken four steps before Grada remembered her robes and retrieved them from the throat of the urn. The sun robes were ill-suited to fighting, but essential to the outdoor life of the Maze. She gasped as she struggled into them, but the rough cloth would hide her wound.

Sarmin retreated to the back of Grada's mind and watched as they passed a hall where women, old and young, sat at long tables, cutting and stitching with swift fingers and quicker voices. The corridor split and from the left men came, hefting amphorae heavy with sweet-wine for the palace kitchens. They passed without a glance for Grada, who hurried down the passage to the right.

They passed by a well, low-walled and secret in a window-less hall. The air felt strange to Sarmin; it was clammy on Grada's skin. She took a wooden bucket from a row by the wall. Sarmin found himself listening to her breathing, wondering at the soft strength and strangeness of her body beneath the robes. As she reached for a cover for the bucket Sarmin turned her hand, studying her palm for a moment before she took command again.

The corridors became more crowded, with servants, scribes, craftsmen, all bound for unknown destinations. Grada stepped aside and passed unmarked, beneath notice, a ghost within the machine of government.

A low door gave onto the grand courtyard. As a child Sarmin had left the palace carried within a palanquin, taken through the Elephant Gate, a vaulted portal with doors of spice-teak, tall enough to admit gods. The door before them now was not for gods, or princes, or even merchants. Even so, a palace guard waited, a scarred hand resting upon the hilt of his hachirah. His eyes flitted to the bucket in Grada's hands and he wrinkled his nose and said nothing. Grada passed through, silent, into the sun. Sarmin could hear the words unspoken: night-soil. Hachirahs meant nothing to the Maze-born.

The noonday sun bludgeoned the flagstones of the grand courtyard with such violence that none lingered there. Only Grada and a distant patrol of the Blue Shield Guard moved in the heat. Sarmin felt the hot stone through Grada's sandals and through the slits of her eyes he saw the great expanse of the sky. After fifteen years beneath a painted ceiling the sight robbed him of thought. His scream escaped Grada's lips and he ran, throwing himself back into her skull, into her mind, into the darkest recesses, diving under the blackness, burrowing—

"Grada?" A man's voice in the night of memory.

"Grada? Why are you hiding?" Closer now. "Father always finds you."

And there, buried from the sun, in a stranger's nightmares, Sarmin learned of other ways to lose a childhood.

CHAPTER TWENTY-FOUR

Eyul stood by the burning tent. He watched her funeral pyre through his white sun-mask, Knife in hand. It had taken only seconds for Metrishet to free himself, to blister Amalya's smooth skin and envelop her blankets in a crackling blaze.

Someone would die for this. He twisted the hilt of the emperor's Knife in his hand, ignoring the whispers pouring forth in his mind.

There was no point in collecting Amalya's pots, her spice-sack or anything else that spoke of her. Let the desert claim them, as the pattern had claimed Amalya. Let them be forgotten.

But first, someone would die. Perhaps many.

He mounted his camel and turned towards the city.

The sun in the west hit the white walls of Nooria and filled Mesema's vision with orange light. She covered her eyes against the brightness, wishing she knew what lay beyond that orange veil. Her stomach twisted with the not-knowing. She wished she could stop the carriage, but it creaked and bounced along, moving inexorably forwards. She longed to turn back, back home, back to the desert, back anywhere but here.

The pattern had not appeared anywhere else on her skin, but remained on her finger, a small dusty-blue moon. Twice she'd slept and twice she'd awakened, frightened and pleading to the Hidden God. One day would be the bad day, the day she'd find those lines and shapes running across her ribs. She hadn't yet decided what to do on that day.

Sahree sat opposite, her eyes averted; it had been so ever since Mesema's visit to the emperor's tent. Everyone thought she was his now, the property of the divine. The other girls no longer spoke to her; they only murmured to each other in awed tones. They did everything for her, without ever meeting her eyes. If she sighed, they fanned her. If she yawned, they offered her plump cushions. If she stumbled, they rubbed her feet and cursed the ground.

For the first time she realised how lonely the emperor must feel. And yet it kept her safe; they looked away from her, away from the blue mark on her finger.

She embroidered a pattern in her head. Somewhere, something burned; the smoke caught in her throat. Mesema tried not to swallow. If she swallowed, Sahree would think she was thirsty, leap from the carriage and cause the whole caravan to stop until the second-freshest water and second-best goblet could be found. *Almost there. Loop, stitch, stitch.* She kept her blue-tinged finger pressed against the cloth at her knee. She missed the feather from Eldra's arrow. She used to work it in her hand, but Cerani women had no pockets; she kept it in her trunk now, next to the resin Mamma had given her.

After a time, the stench of burning faded and Mesema smelled food, meat with heavy spices, flowers, the stale smell of wheat-brew. She heard chains swinging in the wind, and a baby crying. Why were there no voices? A glance through the window answered her question: mothers, traders, and soldiers all prostrated themselves as the emperor's caravan passed by.

Sahree held out a piece of sheer fabric. Mesema was to cover herself so that nobody could see her. She had come to know this in the last day. She shook it out and pulled it over her hair and it settled on her cheeks gently, like a butterfly. When she breathed, it pulled against her nose. Everything she looked at turned hazy-white.

A twinge shot through her finger. Beyon approached. She imagined him wending his way between the soldiers and pack-animals, careless on his mount, his eyes hard and tired. No sooner had the image crossed her mind than he leaned in, looking first at Sahree and then taking in her silken veil.

She was relieved that he couldn't see her face.

"We will enter the city soon," he said.

As if I don't know! Mesema looked at Sahree, at her veined, thin hands, and wondered how many years Sahree had worked for the palace, how many emperors she had seen live and die.

He didn't wait for a response but drew away. She could hear him galloping towards the wall; she imagined the common folk dashing out of his way as he charged ahead, arrogant, heedless, as she cradled her finger in her left hand. It hurt now, when he moved far away. Sahree might see the tears streaming down her cheeks and think it was all for love of Beyon; better she not know the truth.

"What— Who am I?" Sarmin didn't think to ask, "Where am I?" Where would he be? Where had he always been? In his room. Through the blurred slits of his eyes he could see the only sky he had ever really known, the patterned gods of his ceiling.

"You are Sarmin, prince of Cerana. Grada remains in the mages' Tower. You are separate, again, and whole, or as whole as I can make you." The deep voice had the crackle of age in it.

Sarmin rolled his head towards the speaker and realised he was lying flat, on his own bed. His fingers sought out the tear in his tunic, and the wound below, but they found nothing, just tenderness, and the crusting of dried blood on silk.

The man stood beside the bed. Sarmin's eyes refused to focus, giving him only a smeared impression of a figure wreathed in light, alive with the ghosts of flame. Sarmin kneaded his eyeballs and looked again, seeing an old man now, shadowed, with wisps of white hair haloing a bald head.

"I have no skills for healing," the man spread his hands, and for a second the wraith-fire played across them again, "but I spent thirteen years in the desert, in the Empty Quarter. There is a rock there, a rock that bleeds. I used a little of that blood to knit your flesh and call you back to it."

"I don't know you." Sarmin felt weak. He felt empty. He wanted Grada.

"My name is Govnan. I am High Mage of the Tower."

"You are two pieces. A puzzle of two pieces." Sarmin still felt lightheaded; he spoke the words without thinking. "Fire and flesh."

Govnan raised a brow at that and stepped closer to the bed. Sarmin struggled to sit.

"As the slave carried you within her, I too carry another. It is not the same magic, but similar—simpler. Ashanagur is bound within me, and his strength is mine. At one time he danced across the molten sea before the City of Brass where efreet dwell, but now he dwells in me, until the day comes when he consumes me and I will live inside the fire."

"I remember the Tower. The high mage was Kobar, before… when I was a child. He made us laugh. He knew tricks, made talking faces in stone walls… He touched Pelar's red ball and it grew so heavy we couldn't lift it." Sarmin smiled at the memory.

"High Mage Kobar was rock-sworn. The time came for the earth-spirit bound to his flesh to find its freedom. For ten years I have held the Tower for Emperor Beyon."

"Beyon." Sarmin remembered his brother, the patterns on his skin, the dead guards outside the door. "There are assassins—you must save him!"

"Grada came for you, Sarmin. There are no others. Beyon's enemy seeks to break him. If he fails to break him, he may try murder, but he is not failing. Even with all the protections we have woven around him, the pattern closes in."

Sarmin stood. His legs felt strange beneath him. He walked on stilts once as a child, and this was not so different. He found himself taller than Govnan, an odd feeling, as he had been sure the mage would loom over him.

"You're wrong. Broken or whole, Beyon serves his purpose for the enemy. I have seen that enemy." Sarmin's blood had turned black and clotted on his silks. For a moment he felt it again, running hot down his side. "I saw him behind the Many, the Carriers: a Pattern Master."

Govnan bowed his head. He focused his gaze upon his hands, his knuckles large, and whiter than skin should be. "You have the talents of your line, Prince Sarmin. The throne was purchased with such skills in the earliest of days, and the potential runs through your dynasty. Beyon's potential has helped to keep the pattern at bay. Your potential kept the emperor's Knife from your throat."

"*You?* You put me here? In this room?"

"No—the Tower spared your life, no more. Envy put you in this room: ambition."

"How many?" Sarmin asked. "How many boys have lived out their lives like this, under this curse?"

"It is a gift, Prince. Life is always a gift." Govnan met his stare, and Sarmin could feel the heat of the man. "And there have been no others in my lifetime. There was a child in the time of the Yrkman incursions, but his quarters were sacked when Nooria was overrun."

"I want *Grada*." And as he spoke the words Sarmin knew that he did want her, more than his lost years, more than close-held memories of stolen things, more than his mother or brother.

"Grada is at the Tower, and it is best that she remain there. She has been a tool of the enemy. I will return her knife and—"

"I want Grada." Sarmin had seen with her eyes, spoken with her breath. He had held her whilst he was dying.

"Even if no taint remains, she is low-born, gutter-kin; she has her place, and you have yours."

"You are a two-piece puzzle, High Mage." A cold anger held Sarmin, iced fingers on his neck. "And even if I have no book on the subject, I am nothing if not a man of patterns."

"Prince, you must calm yourself. I do not understand—"

"No!" They had held him too long; they had schemed in their corridors and towers, painted him into their plans, and at every turn they had thwarted him. Twenty paces, left turn, fifteen paces, left turn—

"No," Sarmin said, "I am done with turning."

He drew two symbols, one with the index finger of his right hand, one with the left, one symbol for fire, one for man, and they hung in the air between them.

"Sarmin, don't."

"Your magic is wrong."

Sarmin moved his hands apart, and the symbols with them. And in that motion, Govnan lit up like lamp oil before the taper. New flame flowed across old skin, pooling, pouring, building, and as Sarmin's hands parted, so Govnan parted from Ashanagur until the two stood side by side. Govnan was a dark twin to the being of light beside him, standing straighter now, more sound, as if something had been added rather than taken. Ashanagur wore his fire like a cloak, the lithe, long limbs beneath it the color of molten iron. Around his feet the carpet charred, but the fire and the heat did not spread.

"Ashanagur," Sarmin said, "you are free."

White eyes sought Sarmin's and something passed between them, warmth rather than heat. An understanding. There was a sound of cracking, perhaps the stone beneath the carpet, perhaps the foundation stone of the world. A jagged line of incandescence opened between them, and in a heartbeat Ashanagur was gone, leaving only a faint coil of smoke.

The angels and the devils watched from the walls and were silent.

CHAPTER TWENTY-FIVE

Eyul turned another corner of the Maze. Smoke from the Carrier-pyres overlaid the more familiar scents of blood and excrement, the flavours of his old home. The familiarity of the twisting alleys reassured him as much as the Knife at his hip. He felt more surety here than in Tuvaini's dark passages. The Maze was honest, in all of the ways most people didn't wish to see.

He moved towards his destination with confidence, memory guiding his feet for his vision was hazy behind white linen. The alley where he'd made his first kill ran alongside the ruins of an old Mogyrk church. These days he doubted anybody could have identified the fire-darkened, crumbling mortar for what it had been, but Eyul remembered from Halim, who knew it from his father. Only memories kept Satreth's victory alive, though here in the Maze, it hardly felt like a victory. The Mogyrks, Halim had told him in a hushed whisper, had given out food and clothes to the denizens of these twisting streets. The only charity they saw now happened on feast-days, when the palace discarded its old clothing and spoiled food, and expected the Maze-folk to be grateful.

Eyul paused at the final turn, listening to an altercation in the narrow street ahead: two men and a woman, and the woman was screaming. He felt a grim smile on his lips. *Don't let them run from me.* He touched his hand to the hilt of his Knife and moved forwards.

"Not this. Go to the palace." The Knife-whisper, authoritative, for a child. "Quiet."

The low-born men turned. He could see the lines of their bodies, their heads turned attentively in his direction: they thought he'd been speaking to them. They had the woman bent over the lip of an old well, one holding her arms while the other was making ready to take his pleasure.

Eyul pulled his Knife free.

"Can you not spare the tin to pay for that?" Eyul's feet tingled with the pleasure of the upcoming dance.

"I'm no whore!" The woman's shadow quivered as she struggled.

"Liar." One of the men punctuated his word with a slap. "This is no concern of yours, blind man."

Eyul smiled. "True." This would be too easy. Disappointment crept in. Maybe this wasn't what he wanted after all. "But I'd still like you to go." He hefted the Knife in his hand. "I came to visit this place, and you're disturbing me."

The men exchanged glances. The woman lay still and said nothing. He could guess at their thinking: either he could take them, against all logic, or he was mad. Either way, it was bad luck to fight him.

"Herzu take her anyway." The man to Eyul's left backed off.

"Don't think we won't remember you, Khima."

The second man followed him, and the woman, Khima, crumpled to the stony ground, a dark lump in the centre of Eyul's vision. He walked past her to the opposite wall and lifted his bandages. Decades of grime had obscured the arterial spray of his first victim. He ran his fingers along the brick.

The child whispered to him from the Knife, "Leave this place. You are needed at the palace."

"Hey," said Khima.

Eyul backed away from the wall to where he'd stood when he slit the man's throat. Yes; he remembered. The sun shot through his vision, a welcome pain.

"Hey," she said again, and now he could feel her warmth, her breath on his arm. He could kill her as easily as scratching his nose, add her blood to the wall. He felt free, powerful.

"I could lift my skirts," she offered. That would do.

She was not just skinny but wasted, not much in his hands, but his body didn't seem to mind. He finished, one hand against the brick where he'd drawn first blood, the other on her bony hip. Afterwards he offered her a drink from his waterskin.

"It's fresh, from a well in the desert."

"Tastes sweet." She smacked her lips together. They were still full and round, not cracked and bleeding as they would be in a few years' time. "What's it like outside the walls?"

"Same as inside the walls."

She laughed at that. He let her keep the waterskin. Already his mind itched for something else, something more. Govnan.

He left Khima sipping the sweet water in the alley. He judged she had a few hours before those men came back and took their revenge. No matter; he had a revenge of his own to finish. He covered his eyes again and slipped through the Maze, his gaze on the Tower, cutting a shadow from the sun. He dodged a galloping horse on Palace Road, twisting back to throw a curse at its silhouette of a rider.

The Knife-voices spoke together at once, loud but unintelligible.

"Be quiet, or I'll throw you in the smith's fire." It was no more than a whispered threat; Tahal had given him this Knife twice over. It was all he had left.

Eyul made the rest of the way to the Tower in silence. He knew from Tuvaini that Govnan would be somewhere on a higher floor; he'd have to get past the other mages first. He paused, looking up at the Tower's sheer walls. He couldn't climb. He would have to hurt people.

The door swung in easily. Perhaps there was no need to lock the gate to the Tower; only a madman would enter the home of the mages with violent intentions. A young woman with light-colored eyes gave him a shallow bow. "I am Mura. What does the supplicant—?"

She didn't finish her sentence; Eyul had spun behind her and wrapped his arm around her throat. Pointing the Knife at her heart, he said, "The supplicant wishes to see High Mage Govnan."

She coughed, but he didn't ease his pressure. Her elemental was trapped inside her; let it remain there. They moved through the courtyard like a clumsy four-legged beast. He saw no one else. Were there so few mages? He kicked open the brass door and looked through it, past the statues filling the entry hall. Still nobody.

The young mage began to stumble, losing air, and he let her fall. She writhed on the threshold, coughing, her hands to her throat.

"What's your name?"

"M-mura."

"Where are the other mages?"

"We are just… five," she said hoarsely, "me, Govnan, Hashi who travels with the emperor, Amalya and Suresh."

Only four mages left? "Where is Suresh?"

"Top floor… library." Tears ran down her face. She was young.

He tucked the Knife in his belt. "I will go and see Govnan. Would you stop me?"

"You can go up, but he isn't there." Mura turned her face to the floor. "A Carrier came here before you, and Govnan ran to the palace."

CHAPTER TWENTY-SIX

The caravan plodded through the city gate. Twilight dimmed the carriage-box, making a shadowy form of Sahree. Mesema closed her eyes and listened to the carriage-creak, the horses and the distant camels, and the buzz of the city, like a thousand bees, getting louder every minute. Voices, raised in laughter, argument, trade, and love—Mesema had never heard so many voices. The sound made her glad, but when she looked out of the window all she could see were walls, high and close, rising to either side. She felt like a lamb in its pen and shivered.

The voices grew distant as the carriage passed through yet another gate. This new place held a stillness, and the soldiers, when they spoke, used hushed tones. They had arrived. The carriage pulled to a stop and Mesema jerked her shoulders back, seized with a sudden panic; she felt she might be sick. Sahree scrambled from her seat and left Mesema alone in the darkness. Mesema wanted to shout out, to ask Sahree to return, but instead she clutched her hands together and took careful breaths. *Here I am. I have made it this far. I'm not dead, nor have I hurt anyone.* Another thought came to her, an exclamation in her mind: *Banreh!*

She waited. Outside the window, torches lit a wide courtyard. Soldiers unpacked their animals with quick, efficient movements, and others ran up to assist them, leading away the horses and the camels, carrying the boxes, offering water to the travel-weary. Mesema waited, but Sahree did not return, and as night fell in earnest, fewer soldiers could be seen. Those who remained were now leaning against the barrels, speaking casually to one another, or smoking some sort of weed in a pipe. She waited, and at length even those soldiers wandered away, leaving her alone.

Mesema opened her carriage door and paused to see if anyone would come to stop for her, or assist her. She heard no footsteps, nor the rustling of Sahree's skirts; only a distant chanting reached her ears, falling soft and rhythmic on the night air.

She stepped out. It was a long drop to the courtyard tiles. The soldiers had always set out steps for her before. Her sandals made a slapping noise against the stone, but still nobody noticed, or came for her. At the top of the walls that encircled the courtyard she could see soldiers on patrol, but if they saw her, they didn't show it.

The palace rose over Mesema, all sheer walls, domes, and rounded windows, bigger than the stone temple she'd seen in the desert, bigger than any structure she'd ever seen. It glowed brightly, even against the night sky. Across from where she stood, white brick outlined a small wooden door. It didn't look impressive enough to be the palace door. Another, larger, stood beside it.

She tried to fathom having many doors, each assigned to an appropriate station. The Felt had their leaders, to be sure, but there were not so many differences in status. Every Cerani had someone above and someone below, excepting the emperor and the most miserable slave.

And which door was meant for her? She felt it best to use the low door; though she guessed it was the wrong one it would surely be better than using a door meant for the emperor alone.

A modest hallway led her between the soldiers' lodgings. Boots struck stone floors. Cerani voices called to one another, giving and accepting orders. Somewhere, lamb was roasting in garlic and rose petals. Her stomach grumbled. She turned, and turned again, following the passage towards the centre of the building. Soon she entered a well-appointed corridor, with hanging tapestries and marble floors. She paused. The pattern-link told her Beyon lay above—she felt it in the pricking of her finger—but she couldn't see a staircase anywhere. She wiped away a tear, feeling foolish. *We are Felt.*

On her right, a dark room opened onto the corridor. She ducked inside and found a crowded space, with statues and benches cluttering the floor without perceptible order. Stone walls supported a high ceiling lost in shadow. Candlelight flickered from the far end of the room. Curiosity gripped her, along with a sense of recognition: Beyon knew this place. She discovered a path on the far side of a sneering marble gryphon. At the end rose a golden figure, a horned, twisted beast three times Mesema's height. Its feet were candlelit, and its eyes lay hidden in the shadows above. Fangs shimmered beneath sneering lips. It held a dead baby in one hand and an apple in the other, both withered and sunken. The place stank of rot.

Dirini had told her that Cerani made such tributes to their gods, statues fashioned of more gold than the tribes could gather from all their lands in a generation. She'd thought that a story for the sewing circle.

And what sort of god was this? Despite her horror, she ran her hand along one of the god's feet. He felt cold and smooth against her skin. *Who are you? The God of Sickness? Killing? I think I know you—I think I will come to know you even better.* His metallic eyes looked down at her, curious, but not hungry. He knew her to be his subject already.

She shivered, seeing the stiff hair of the baby in his left hand.

Footsteps sounded behind her. Mesema turned, feeling the soft fabric of her dress slip low on her shoulder. She adjusted it as her eyes met those of the woman who had entered, wide and dark, as cold as the god's, and more familiar. Mesema no longer had Beyon's memories, but she still had the feel of them. She took a step back.

"What sort of disrespect is this?" The woman tilted her head, speaking over her shoulder. Only then did Mesema notice a host of blue-topped soldiers at the end of the aisle. She took another step back and felt the god's toes poking into her skin.

The woman addressed Mesema next. "Do your duty!" As she moved her head, her long black hair shifted, revealing bare breasts. Mesema had never seen a woman walk about naked before.

Mesema started, "I—I'm sorry, I don't—"

"Do you even speak the civil tongue?" The woman stepped forwards and slapped Mesema's face. "How dare you stare at me and give no obeisance." Close up, Mesema could see tear-streaks on the woman's cheeks. "Do you not know who I am? I married the great Emperor Tahal and gave birth to the Son of Heaven." Two of the soldiers moved behind her, their swords drawn.

Beyon's mother. *Of course.*

"Show your respect to the Empire Mother," one of the soldiers said, moving his sword up and down.

Mesema fell to her knees and spread her arms out before her. She knew better than to ask forgiveness. She would be patient, as she had practised. In the corner of her eye she could see the other woman's slippers, green and gold.

"Find out whose serving-girl this is." The Empire Mother sounded tired now, sad. "Beyon's wives let them wander like goats."

The slippers moved to go past her, but Mesema spoke first, her eyes still on the tiled floor. "Your Highness, I am not a serving-girl. I come from the Felting tribes. I am the daughter of the Chief Windreader."

"Did I give you leave to speak?" Mesema kept silent this time.

"Get up, girl, and let me look at you."

Mesema stood, her eyes focused on her sandals. Her feet, she noticed, were dirty.

"The emperor, my son, joined your caravan, is that so?"

"Yes, Your Highness."

"Hmmph. Beyon always did like children." With a thin smile the Empire Mother lifted Mesema's chin in one hand. "And Arigu chose a pretty one, didn't he?"

"Thank you, Your Highness."

"And what of him?"

"Of whom, Empire Mother?"

"You're stupid, aren't you? I'm asking about General Arigu." The Empire Mother ran her hands along Mesema's arms now, as if she were judging the strength of a horse. Mesema pressed her index finger and thumb together to hide the crescent moon-mark.

"He left our caravan, Your Highness, to reach the city before us."

The Empire Mother frowned. "I suppose we can still use you." Mesema didn't understand her meaning, but she kept silent. "You will stay in the women's wing from now on."

"Yes, Your Highness."

The Empire Mother smiled, but not in a friendly way. "Were you not assigned a body-slave? Where is she?"

"Sahree, Your Highness. She left me in the courtyard."

"That old bat. We'll get you someone better. But no more wandering the palace."

"I apologise, Your Highness. Thank you, Your Highness."

"Keep quiet, too." She turned in a swirl of black hair and swept past the soldiers who filled the room. Mesema stumbled after the Empire Mother, her heart beating wildly against her ribs.

"High Mage Govnan is here to speak with you, Lord Vizier."

If the fact that the high mage waited at the door surprised Azeem, none of it reached his face. Tuvaini had kept him on all these years for good reason. In many ways the Island slave reminded him of Eyul. He would have made a good assassin.

"Well now." Tuvaini put his scroll down. "We live in interesting times. A high mage has never called on me before. Robes." He snapped his fingers at Tellah, waiting in the shadows.

"Azeem, you may show the supplicant in."

Tellah finished with the last robe-tie as Govnan followed Azeem into the chamber. The high mage looked older, hollowed, but the same intelligence glittered in his eyes. Tuvaini felt his hand tremble and could not still it.

"Govnan, good to see you." Tuvaini did not rise from his chair. "Might I offer you some tea?"

"Prince Sarmin is dead," Govnan said.

"Dead?" Tuvaini put only faint surprise into his voice.

"An assassin."

"The royal guards did nothing?" Tuvaini asked. His mind raced. He had waited so long, and now events were unfolding with frightening speed.

"They died."

"And the Tower?" More pointed.

"The assassin had supernatural aid. Our defences were too slow."

"The body?" Tuvaini wanted to see Sarmin. He wondered if those dead eyes still held the same madness.

"Burned. The Tower's defences were slow, not absent. A servant arose from the lake of fire. The assassin burned. The prince's remains are badly charred. His room and the staircase below are unsound—they will need to be demolished in due course."

"Well." Tuvaini let his gaze slide across the room, skipping from Tellah to Azeem to Govnan. "Well, this is terrible."

"Indeed."

"The emperor must be informed," Tuvaini said. "The council must be summoned. Such a threat must be addressed. The hand behind this act must be found and the emperor's safety assured."

Govnan nodded. "The wind-sworn have sent word to the council; the priests of Herzu and Mirra will meet us in the throne room. Generals Hazran and Lurish will represent the armies of the Blue Shield and White Hat. Master Herran will speak for the assassins."

"Well and good." Tuvaini got up from his chair and took the scroll from the desk before him. It weighed nothing in his hand, but so much hung upon it. "It is fortunate the emperor is returned from the desert. We will attend upon him immediately."

"I have one other errand. I will see you there."

And so it was alone that the high vizier walked the corridors to Beyon's throne room.

For secrecy he took the Forbidden Passage, past the wives' hall where silver waters ran beneath jewelled ceilings.

A pale beauty waited by the entrance, a prize from the heathen kingdoms. He couldn't help but look: her skin was as white as fish bellies, her hair nearly as light as mountain snow. Red silk stretched tight over her breasts: Beyon's second wife.

Tuvaini had left that thread loose. Beyon's seed had never found purchase in any woman, but it didn't hurt to be sure. He would have to deal with that quickly.

Only his own son would be born in the wives' hall. The next Son of Heaven.

Govnan had given him the world in two moments. With one breath he had taken Sarmin away, and with the next he had assembled the only authority that might judge an emperor. Before such men, before such a gathering, Beyon's sickness could be revealed. Before such men a right of succession might be claimed and proven. Mages and assassins, priests and generals— the old men whose caution had sealed the fate of Beyon's brothers, the old men who would take Beyon from the throne and set Tuvaini upon it. And then his work would begin.

CHAPTER TWENTY-SEVEN

Eyul slipped through the Low Gate and the Low Door. He kept one hand on his hilt; Govnan's fire might be fast, but the Knife would be faster. It had fallen silent, which pleased him. Nighttime brought a clarity of vision he lacked in the day and now he could see the faces of the soldiers he passed; each shuffled out of his way, mumbling apologies. They knew who he was and what he could do. He was home.

He passed by the temple of Herzu, which was always dark, no matter the time of day. Inside, blue-hatted guards gathered around Nessaket. Her voice cut daggered slices in the air. In days past he might have paused and tried to look across the crowded room; he might have wondered. He'd had Nessaket once, in the dark days after Tahal's death, when Beyon would not allow either of them in his sight. He'd pulled at that golden skin, bitten those smooth shoulders, tried to give her the sense of danger she sought. He'd lived in the service of Tahal's family, whether for killing or pleasure. Now when he remembered Nessaket's bed it was as if some other man had been there. Some other man had been in the courtyard, too, drawing metal across those little throats.

That man had cared.

He turned another corner and sniffed the air. Govnan had a distinctive scent of fire and soot, but Eyul smelled nothing like that here.

"Eyul."

Eyul turned at the familiar voice. "Master Herran." Only another assassin could take him unaware; Herran stood but two arms' lengths away.

The old man looked at him without moving. The wrinkles around his grey eyes tightened in a disconcerting way. Assassins were always watching—yet there should be nothing for Herran to see.

"I have been summoned to council," Herran said at last.

"There will be much to discuss." Eyul took a step forwards. "Govnan is—"

Master Herran held up his hand. "You would speak of such things in the corridor?"

The emperor's Knife stood half out of its sheath, warm in Eyul's palm. Master Herran had noticed; a flicker of an eyelid had given him away, but he made no movement towards his own weapon.

"Something has happened, Eyul. I want you by me."

"First I have a task."

Master Herran raised a white eyebrow. "Indeed. But do you know what it is?"

Soldiers' boots sounded in the other corridor: Nessaket's men, leading her back to the women's wing.

"You stink," said Master Herran. "You smell of the Maze, and of fire."

No remnant of Amalya's spice on him, then.

"It will annoy Tuvaini," Eyul said. Tuvaini washed in rose water and jasmine petals, but it didn't mean his hands were clean.

Master Herran chuckled. "We assassins delight in annoying the vizier. You will go with me, then?"

Govnan would likely be there, if it were a true council. Eyul nodded.

"Very well." Master Herran walked towards him. One leg was noticeably stiffer than the other. Eyul could have the Knife in his throat before he took another step.

Or in Nessaket's. She rounded the corner now with her usual grace; often she looked as if she were floating. Bodyguards made a clumsy circle around her, their balance skewed by an unfamiliar young woman who stumbled in their midst. Her pale face had been slapped to redness and yellow hair tumbled free of silver pins. Wide cheekbones: she had come from the horse tribes.

Impossible. I saw her dead.

Her eyes, blue as zabrinas, met his gaze and turned away. He frightened her. Good. From all over the world the palace claimed souls, and went on to destroy them. This one would at least be wary.

A smile crept across his lips.

Master Herran touched his shoulder. "Let us go." Eyul turned and walked with him.

Sarmin sat where he had so often and for so long, upon the bed in his room, legs crossed, hands folded in his lap. The gods watched him from the ceiling, the angels from the walls, and the devils—the devils watched from the walls and beyond. The Pattern Master looked for him with a thousand eyes.

Sarmin wondered how many people Govnan had told so far. He wondered how they might react, to hear that someone they had forgotten was now dead. There would be few tears shed.

His mother might dab one eye, smudging the lines of kohl beneath her lashes. Beyon would rage, but Sarmin wondered, would he mourn? Perhaps—not now, but later, maybe, in a week, when the anger had burned out.

"And my bride from the grasslands? Will she mourn me, Aherim?"

Sarmin looked for the eldest of the angels and found him without struggle. Since the pattern first washed through him Sarmin saw things more clearly. Once he had to strain to picture the grim angel among the swirl and scroll of the wall painting; now the faces never hid. Even Zanasta, whose wise and evil eyes could be found only in the last moments of the setting sun, now appeared whenever Sarmin spoke his name.

"She would mourn you, Prince." The angel whispered his answer.

"Why would she mourn me, Zanasta?" Sarmin found the devil's eyes. Other, lesser demons, the ones who haunted each corner, clamoured to answer, but Sarmin ignored them.

Zanasta smiled, a convolution deep within the complexity of the patterned walls.

"I speak for the dark gods."

"Answer the question."

"I speak for Herzu who holds death in one hand and fear in the other. I speak for Ghesh, clothed in darkness, eater of stars. I speak for Meksha, mother of pestilence and famine."

"Zanasta—"

"She would mourn the idea of you, Prince. She would mourn the lost chances, the step not taken, windows unopened. She would mourn for herself, which is all man can ever truly mourn, for the fact that she lives in a world where lives are lost, broken, trapped."

Sarmin thought of Grada, safe in the mages' Tower. He wondered if the horsegirl would be like Grada, or his mother, or both. He thought of the soft voice he'd heard with Beyon. Is that how she sounded? What did she look like? He scanned the swirled pattern of the walls. Was she in there? Did her face watch him?

"Aherim?"

"Yes?"

"Will I ever leave this room?"

"Yes."

"Alive?" Silence.

"Zanasta, will I leave this room?" His skin crawled with cold horror.

"I speak for the gods of darkness and want."

"Will I—?"

"You will die here, Prince."

The Empire Mother led Mesema up the stairs, a spiral of marble and gold that rose higher than any tent in her father's holding. It seemed so airy and light that she was terrified it would collapse under their weight. The high domed ceiling told the story of the empire in colorful mosaics. In the pictures worked from stone and glass she saw battles and proclamations, but few women.

At the landing the Empire Mother suddenly turned, her black hair swirling. "The throne room is that way." She pointed to her left. "The women's quarters are this way." She motioned towards the right.

"Thank you, Your Highness."

"I told you to keep your mouth shut."

Mesema clenched her teeth and followed to a double door inlaid with silver and gold. Her finger ached, and she sensed Beyon was closer than before. She wanted to ask him what had happened to Sahree. The disappearance of the old woman became more ominous with every moment she didn't arrive. Her fate now sat like a cold stone in Mesema's stomach.

The Empire Mother pushed open the great door. Sahree was not waiting in the room beyond, but the emperor stood with his back to Mesema, speaking to an older woman.

"What do you mean, she's not here? Lana, where else could she be?"

The woman called Lana answered him, her voice soft but audible, as the Empire Mother pulled Mesema into the room.

"I didn't know to send anyone down for her, Bey-Bey—how could I have? Don't worry; the guards will find her."

Beyon wore stiff robes edged with golden threads. Mesema had never seen him so richly clothed. Lana rose almost to his shoulders. Her short dark hair curled around her ears.

The Empire Mother spoke. "I have again succeeded where the emperor has failed."

Beyon turned, his eyes so dark Mesema might have thought them black. Lana shrank away, looking frightened, and suddenly very small to Mesema's eyes.

"Lana." The Empire Mother made it sound more of a statement than a greeting.

"Nessaket." Lana made a small curtsey.

"Nessaket." Beyon pronounced her name as if it were an insult. His mouth twisted into a false smile. "So. I missed the honour of seeing General Arigu in the desert. I am concerned for his wellbeing."

His mother did not look in the least bit concerned. She laughed. "Two steps behind. You always were slow, Beyon." She looked at Lana. "This is the horsegirl. Put her in the ocean room. I don't want to see her again."

Lana curtsied again and turned to Mesema. "Come." She led the way down the corridor. "I sent a maidservant to bring you here, but she said your carriage was empty. You must learn to wait—the palace is all about waiting."

Mesema left Nessaket and her son with relief, though not quickly, for Lana walked with mincing steps. This gave Mesema time to appreciate the beauty of the women's wing. A longhouse had no corridors: it consisted of one great room, sometimes divided by skins or curtains. Every room here was the size of a whole longhouse, with these corridors leading from one to the other, big enough for everyone to sleep inside.

The corridors were more than functional: they showed who should walk in them. Mesema remembered the plain corridors on the lower levels, where a few faded tapestries graced their walls; that was enough for the soldiers and servants. She could not even make out the color of the women's walls, for all were covered with tapestries, tiles or paintings. Niches hollowed away from her at intervals. Some bubbled with water, while others held cushions or flowered vases. Images of women appeared everywhere, even on the door handles. Mesema wanted to see who they were and what they were doing.

They passed a dark-haired woman who looked at Mesema as she passed. *One of Beyon's wives.* She remembered this, though it was not hers to remember.

Lana stopped almost at the end of the hall and opened a gilded door, motioning for Mesema to enter first.

Mesema walked in before her and gasped. Blue ocean moved along the walls, captured in swirls and strokes of paint. White birds circled lazily over grey fish jumping in the waters below. A wooden ship, big enough to hold five thousand of those grey fish, ploughed through the waves. Mesema touched its textured sails, rubbing the thick paint with her marked finger.

"Clouds," she said, "I thought these were pulled by clouds." But clouds were painted upon the ceiling. These ships travelled the waters, she realised, and the sails were made of cloth. The white curtains of her bed were designed to match these great sails.

"Well… goodbye," Lana said, ducking her head slightly before turning to the door.

She nearly collided with Beyon, who smiled. "Hello again, Little Mother. I'm sorry about all that."

Lana stood straighter as they clasped hands. Mesema found herself looking up at her now.

"It is good to have you back, Bey-Bey." Lana's voice even sounded deeper and louder in the emperor's presence.

Beyon turned his smile on Mesema. "Do you like it?"

"My room? Yes. I've never seen the great ocean." She remembered her wedding dress, Eldra's feather and her secret resin. "Will someone be bringing my trunk?"

Lana glanced at the emperor and then back to Mesema, shocked. "The emperor does not deal with such things!" she said. "I'm sure someone will bring your trunk."

"It's all right, Lana," Beyon said, kissing her on the forehead. "I'll talk to you in a bit."

Lana made a little curtsey and left the room. Mesema hadn't wanted to mention Sahree in front of Lana, but now that they were alone, she stepped forwards. "Your Majesty—"

He lunged and grabbed her around the waist, hands rough against her skin, one thumb moving beneath her silk wrappings. He pressed his mouth against hers so tightly that he flattened her lips against her teeth.

Mesema stood still, arms numb and limp at her sides. Through the open door she could hear women murmuring and the swish of silk.

Then, just as suddenly as he had grabbed her, Beyon let her go. He stood back, and their eyes locked.

Mesema saw the man she had met in that tent in the desert, with Banreh crumpled at his feet: fearsome and terrible, a spoiled boy elevated to godhood, beyond anyone's reproach. She gathered herself. "Beyon, where is Sahree? My maid-servant?"

"She might have seen your finger." Not an answer.

"She didn't. I was careful."

His eyes narrowed at her. "Even while you were sleeping?"

"Is she dead, Your Majesty? What of the others? Tarub and Willa?"

"That is not your concern." He stepped forwards again, and she cringed. He frowned, and she saw a trace of the other man she'd touched, the boy with the honey-cakes in his pocket. "Very well. I will take my leave."

Mesema knelt and pressed her forehead to the silken rug. She kept her position for the count of thirty stitches. She couldn't hear the emperor move. His slippers were soft, the carpet, soft, but her finger told her he watched her still. At last he left the room, but he lingered nearby. Soon the smell of jasmine told her somebody else had entered. She sat up to see the dark-haired woman from the hall smiling at her from the doorway.

"Hello."

"Hello." Mesema tried in vain to fix her silk.

"I'm Hadassi." She had the black hair and golden skin of the Empire Mother, but she didn't have the same piercing look. The Empire Mother saw so much that Mesema was already afraid of her dark eyes. Hadassi's eyes were dull and wide as she looked Mesema up and down, and her lips formed a pout. "Third wife."

"I'm Mesema."

Hadassi took a step forwards, looking around the room. "This was Tahal's mother's room. Nobody has lived in it since before Nessaket came."

"It's a beautiful room."

Hadassi took a seat on the floor. "Mine is better." Her dress shimmered in greens that made her skin seem to glow. Amber gleamed from her neck and wrists. In the palace everything beautiful was made even more so, until the eye became tired, jaded.

Hadassi took Mesema's left hand, the unmarked one. Her brown eyes crinkled as she smiled. "You are to be fifth wife?" Another wife, blonde, appeared in the doorway, wary and watchful.

Mesema shook her head. "No."

"But he likes you, no? You have been with him?" Hadassi waved at the second woman, who entered and took a seat next to Mesema. "This is Chiassa, second wife."

"You are concubine?" Chiassa didn't speak Cerantic as a native. Her hair suggested eastern origins. "You go on cushions with emperor, heaven bless?"

It struck Mesema that both women had asked the same question—were they genuinely curious, or worried, or had someone instructed them? *Snakes*, Beyon had warned her. Arigu had gone to great lengths to bring her across the mountains and the desert, to arrange for an heir that was not Beyon's. And now someone wanted to know whether she and Beyon had lain together. Mesema pretended not to understand. She curled her marked finger against her palm.

"Well," said Hadassi, patting her leg, "we'll know soon enough."

Mesema kept her silence. She must be careful. The women would be in and out of her room every day, asking questions until everything was revealed, even her pattern-mark. She would never be safe here. The room felt close and stifling. She stood up.

"Blessed be the day," said Hadassi, rising also.

"Blessed be the day," Mesema repeated. It felt like the thing to do.

Chiassa stood, brushing the wrinkles from her pink skirt.

"Blessing, where do you go?"

"Blessing," Mesema repeated. "I'm going to go—" Nessaket didn't want to see her. "For a walk." Perhaps the wing was big enough for that? She walked out of the door, and the other two women followed behind her like ducklings. *Well, this won't do.* She quickened her pace and rounded a corner, nearly colliding with an Old Wife, who stood against the wall chewing black leaves that smelled of rot. A dark froth bubbled between her lips and ran down to drip on sagging bare breasts. She did not speak, but glanced at Mesema's covered front and stuffed another stinking leaf into her mouth.

Mesema curtsied and kept on walking until she reached the great room inside the main doors. A red-headed woman sat upon the cushions and fiddled with her jewellery. She looked at Mesema with piercing dark-blue eyes. "Well, hello there."

"Hello." Mesema gave up on finding a place in the women's wing with no women. Resigned, she sat down, and Hadassi and Chiassa sat opposite. There was a moment of silence as everyone looked at one another, comparing, measuring, wondering. The red-haired one twisted a jade bracelet around her wrist.

Chiassa laid a soft hand on Mesema's arm. Her touch differed from Hadassi's. Hadassi had been curious and false, even greedy, while Chiassa felt sisterly. "Nessaket say to keep out of sight. You should do that."

"I'm to stay in my room all day? What of my horse, Tumble?"

Hadassi almost jumped off her pillow. "You have a horse? You don't ride it, do you?"

"Of course I ride him—or I did, at least."

"Well, they won't let you now." She thrust her lips out in another pout.

"But they said… It was written." *Dry plains take you, Banreh.*

The redhead let go of her bracelet and it dropped to the carpet. "You meant a real horse?"

"This is Marren," Chiassa said, motioning.

"Fourth wife," said Hadassi. Marren made a face at her.

"Yes, a real horse. His name is Tumble. He is somewhere here at the palace. Bey— The emperor let me ride him in the desert, but I don't know what will happen now."

All three of the young women leaned forwards.

"He let you— You rode with him?" Marren asked, and the others leaned back again, eyes cast down, thoughtful.

Careful, now. "Oh—I think it was just amusing to him."

"Even if Beyon allowed it in the desert," said Marren with a cold smile, "Nessaket and First Wife would say no in the palace." At the mention of those two women all the other wives went quiet. Mesema reached for Beyon's memories, but could find nothing of his First Wife except for a lingering sense of dislike.

"Where is the First Wife? What is her name?"

"Atia." Chiassa said. "She's sleeping, maybe."

"She is speaking with Beyon," said Marren. The wives exchanged looks at this and said no more.

Mesema studied the floor. Did Atia have a grievance about her? She shifted on her cushion and looked up to see Marren watching. Perhaps she'd given them enough to talk about and could now return to her rooms alone. "B-blessings," she said, rising. "I think I will retire."

They smiled at her. She judged that it would not be long before they were deep in gossip.

Mesema went out into the corridor and worked her way towards the ocean room. She paused to examine the mosaic in a wall niche: a woman, her eyes made of polished jade, held out a red fruit to a reclining man. Her placid face was almost a challenge; many people—her father, Arigu and now Nessaket—wished she herself were this calm and unquestioning. She couldn't be, especially not now that the pattern stood so close, its colours scratching at her skin, ready to be revealed.

Voices intruded upon her thoughts, distant, but raised in argument.

"Perhaps Nessaket sent for her, but you went to the desert to claim her and never said a word to me!"

"The tale was carried quickly enough."

"Lana, explain to him that I have the right to refuse new wives and concubines!"

"Why did you drag Little Mother in here with you? To make sure I keep my temper? Because I won't. I am the emperor, and you have affronted me.

If I say the horsewoman comes, she comes. If I decide to make you fifth wife and her the first, that's how it will be."

Me, First Wife? What about my prince?

"Bey-Bey—"

Mesema could not hear what else Lana said.

As she strained to listen, the jade-eyed woman swung away from the wall, ruby fruit flashing in the lamplight. A corridor revealed itself on the other side, dark and reeking of smoke. Mesema backed away as a cloaked figure moved forwards, but she found nowhere to hide among the tapestries and cushions. She felt naked and vulnerable: someone in the desert had tried to kill her, but killed Eldra instead. Now she stood here defenceless, with no generals or look-alikes to protect her.

She remembered her vision: *No, it's impossible; I can't die before Beyon does...*

How could I take comfort in that!

The stranger pushed back his hood, revealing white hair and a long nose. Bright eyes examined Mesema's face. The old man stepped into the corridor and closed the hidden door behind him. His shoulders were stooped and his skin sagged, but she sensed a strength in him that didn't come from swinging a sword or throwing a spear. His strength was more like Banreh's.

"My dear, I am sorry to frighten you," he said, taking both her hands in his. She feared momentarily that he would notice her mark, but his eyes were on her face. "And you are the girl." He cocked his head. "Ah, I could not have chosen better myself." His eyes held her still and she realised, too late, that his kindness covered something else. He expected something from her: some unnamed duty.

But Mesema would get something from him, too. She looked back at the tiled woman, swinging towards the wall now, her fruit still uneaten. "How did you come through that wall, my lord?" *And who are you?*

The old man tapped his head with a grin. "I am an old man, but I still have some secrets." He linked arms with her and turned back towards the entrance. "I heard the emperor was here."

"He is... talking, my lord."

"Then I shall wait. Would you be so kind—?" They entered the great room, and the women on the cushions all turned their heads, craning their necks for a better look at the old man.

Mesema caught sight of Beyon at the back, white-faced and motionless, and beyond him Lana, pointing with a shaking hand, her lips trembling.

Then Lana screamed.

CHAPTER TWENTY-EIGHT

Tuvaini waited before the throne-room doors. He had waited a lifetime. He could wait some more.

Govnan arrived to stand beside him, head down, as if lost in his thoughts. The high mage looked different; something had changed in him. He seemed both less than he had been, and more, though Tuvaini couldn't determine why he thought that.

Tuvaini watched for Master Herran. His voice would carry further than most at the council table. Men like Eyul were the sharp edge of Herran's organisation, but the assassins did more than kill: they were the Emperor's ears, his secret eyes, his police, the long arm that reached those who worked against him.

Dinar, Herzu's priest, joined them, surrounded by a dark flock of acolytes. His followers peeled away to the corners of the antechamber as he approached Govnan.

"High Mage. Vizier." Dinar inclined his head.

They acknowledged him, then continued to wait in silence. The doors towered above them, the wealth of a small nation in cedar wood, carved with the many gods of Cerana.

General Hazran arrived, worry in the hard lines of his face. His aides lined the grand corridor, lamplight gleaming on their polished leathers, the royal guard almost lost in their number.

General Lurish accompanied Mirra's priest, bringing more soldiers and more clerics.

"A bad business," Lurish muttered to Dinar, "I remember the boy…'

Tuvaini caught a snatch of the conversation.

Without warning the great doors parted, swinging silently inwards on well-oiled hinges.

"Where's Master Herran?" Tuvaini looked to Govnan. "Who will speak for the assassins?" The council was not yet complete. Beyond the doors a gong tolled, a slow beat, repeating and repeating.

Govnan only shook his head and walked in. Tuvaini followed.

Before the dais where Beyon was seated upon the Petal Throne, the council table had been set out: a long, gleaming slab cut from the same forest giants that had yielded the doors. Two figures were already seated at the eastern end, both cowled in assassin grey.

Govnan took his seat at the western end. Tuvaini sat at the mage's right hand. His breath came shallow now; his hands were numb, except for his fingers, which prickled. He hadn't felt such fear since his childhood, when he first came before Beyon's father to pledge his service. Funny how so trivial a thing could make him sweat. The stakes had grown. For some reason an image of Lapella swam before his eyes, but he shook her away.

At the far end of the table, Master Herran pulled back his cowl and looked at the high mage. Eyul, on Herran's right, also uncovered his head. The sun had burned him to a dark oak. He met Tuvaini's stare, but nothing passed between them.

Why had Eyul not come to him first? Tuvaini's hand tightened on the scroll beneath his robe.

"We are met." Govnan parted his hands. "Emperor Beyon, your council is before you."

Beyon rose from his throne and clasped his hands behind him. Tuvaini watched him: a powerfully built man in the prime of life, with a bearing the Cerani called "the look of eagles." Every inch the dynamic emperor.

"How stands my empire?"

"It stands strong, Emperor." Govnan gave the traditional answer. And Cerana did stand strong; Tuvaini knew of no other empire so great, no people on the face of the world more blessed with wealth. But like the emperor, the empire's outward strength could be deceptive.

"Strong?" Beyon's gaze swept the council. "The empire is attacked from within. An invisible worm gnaws at our very heart. My own brother has been slain within these self-same walls that protect us all."

Tuvaini suppressed a smile. *All your brothers were slain within these walls, Majesty. Sarmin merely balances an old account.*

"My brother is dead," Beyon strode to the table and circled it as he spoke, "and I will have the author of his murder face justice. I will have *justice,* and if the lands of Cerana must be sliced open from belly to throat before it is found… then so be it. An evil grows among us, and it must be cut out."

Beyon stopped at the eastern end of the council table and rested one hand upon the shoulder of the emperor's Knife. Eyul made no move, but his gaze fell on Govnan with a dark intensity.

Tuvaini wet his lips. His mouth felt dry, and tasted sour.

The words he had to speak built behind his teeth. He felt sick with them. He could swallow them down, hold his peace, and let the moment pass. He could live his life in the quiet luxury of his office, loyal, with honour. He could take his frustrations to Lapella, all that bitterness, and the hollow, aching certainty that there must be more for him—he could take it all to her, and she would bear it all.

"We have an enemy who works against us," Beyon said, "a secret foe who poisons all our efforts. Someone who seeks to wound us on every level. Govnan and his mages fight a war that ranges from the vaults of the sky to the deepest caverns. Our enemy moves behind the fire and amid cold ocean depths. Master Herran's assassins chase the foe's agents in shadow. My own Knife has killed them before the fountain—the place my father named as the palace's own heart."

Beyon walked the length of the table to stand by Tuvaini.

"We have endured these attacks too long. It is time we struck back." A hand upon Tuvaini's shoulder. It had been an age since last the emperor touched him. "What say you, Lord High Vizier? Where must we strike?"

Tuvaini stood. One did not stand at council, and the guards beside the throne moved hands to swords, but the words he needed to say could not be spoken seated.

"We must strike close to home, my Emperor. Closer than any here would ever have wished." The time to hold his peace had slipped away. In minutes and moments it had escaped him, beaten away by a pounding heart.

"The worm that has burrowed among us has been discovered." Tuvaini raised his voice and found its power, and the men along the table watched him, some with surprise, some with concern, none able to look away. "The sickness must be cut out."

Beyon took a step back.

"Emperor Beyon, blood of my blood, lord of all Cerana, before these servants of empire, before this council's witness, I declare you marked. I name you Carrier, slave to the plague that haunts us, and unfit for rule."

Beyon took a second step backwards, one hand splayed wide across his chest. He stumbled as his heel touched the lowest step of the dais.

"Tuvaini!" Govnan launched to his feet, his chair toppling behind him. "You have—"

The words died on his lips as Eyul jumped up also, his hand on the hilt of his Knife. Master Herran put out a hand to stay him.

"Ask him!" Tuvaini pointed at the emperor. "Let him but show his chest, naked and without paint. Let him show clean skin, and I will bow my head to the executioner's sword."

"I have heard the rumours." Dinar's rumble cut the silence before it stretched. He laid his staff, black with Herzu's death runes, across the table. "Uncertainty is a sickness in and of itself."

"My officers speak of it when they think I don't listen." General Lurish pulled at his upper lip, his gaze upon the table.

"Emperor?" Tuvaini asked, voice quiet now.

Beyon backed towards the throne, his eyes wild, finding nothing to fix upon. His two sacred guards, peerless slave-bred warriors, took their places, one at his left hand, the other to his right. The royal guard held their positions at the walls, uncertain.

"Beyon, you carry the marks. You cannot rule. The enemy has killed you already." Tuvaini could taste his triumph, a quiet storm rising within him.

For a moment the emperor found focus, as if seeing Tuvaini for the first time.

"Look at your hand, Beyon."

He lifted it, turning his palm to his face. A pale-blue diamond marked both front and back, so faint one might think it a bruise, and across his wrist Tuvaini saw a slim red crescent.

With a cry Beyon ran. He made for the door, and his sacred guard ran with him, trailing their blades. The men of the royal guard stood as if rooted, their heads bowed, their sapphire plumes lowered.

"Eyul." Tuvaini turned and held the assassin's gaze. "You know your duty."

Eyul rose. The emperor's Knife gleamed in his hand. With a last glance at Govnan he left the table and followed Beyon from the room.

The great doors closed behind Eyul and for long moments all eyes remained upon them.

Govnan's voice brought Tuvaini back to the council table.

"The emperor is a Carrier and his brother is dead: what remains to us? Who will guide the empire and keep it whole?" The old man looked unsettled.

"The emperor may yet be healed." The priest of Mirra drew his cream and gold robes about him.

"Has any Carrier yet been cured?" Tuvaini asked. "Any single one?"

Dinar studied his palms, stained black with the Tears of Herzu. "Beyon's own law requires the death of all Carriers, death by stone and fire."

"Eyul knows his duty. Beyon's remains will be cremated before sunset." Tuvaini felt his heart quicken. He reached for his scroll and resumed his seat at the table.

"We must look to the records," General Hazran said. "Texts remain sealed in the royal treasury. Beyon's father worked to prune the Reclaimer's line for two generations, but there will be an heir if we reach back far enough."

Lurish snorted. "Some minor noble from the outer provinces? Some half-savage who knows nothing of the empire?"

"Perhaps a solution lies closer at hand?" Master Herran spoke in a soft voice, but the table listened. He fixed Tuvaini with his pale eyes. "Have you a suggestion, Lord High Vizier?"

Tuvaini returned the gaze. *This man misses little.*

"I have a document here. The Reclaimer's tree, taken from the Axus Library before the fire. It shows the line from the time of Beyon's great-grandfather." He unrolled the tightly bound parchment and smoothed it out upon the table. The great and good of Cerana left their seats to crowd at his shoulders.

"Here." He laid a finger on Jemal, second of the Reclaimer's sons. "A prince set aside when his father died and his elder brother took the throne."

"The child had talent," Govnan said. "The Tower petitioned that he be spared, just as we sought to protect Prince Sarmin, but he was lost when the Yrkmen looted Nooria."

"He was lost," Tuvaini moved his finger down the scroll, "but not without issue. There was a girl, a servant, I suspect—she is unnamed—but there was a child born before the Yrkmen came."

"How could such a child have been spared?" General Lurish asked.

Tuvaini shrugged. "The emperor had his own sons by then. Perhaps a younger, illegitimate, cousin was not considered worth killing."

"And who was this child?" Dinar's deep voice commanded attention.

"My grandfather on my father's side." Tuvaini rose from his seat. "We have an heir, gentlemen." He climbed the first step of the dais. "And it is I."

He took the second stair and turned to face them. "You have your heir: a man who knows the empire and its ways, a man who knows *you* and *your* ways."

The throne-room doors swung inwards, so silently that none of the council noticed, or turned their heads.

Tuvaini stepped backwards, reaching the Petal Throne. "You have an heir: a man who will destroy our hidden foe and who will let this empire be greater than we have dared to dream."

"I would follow such an emperor."

The men of the council looked at the newcomer. From the doorway Arigu smiled and bowed.

Tuvaini returned the smile and sat upon the throne. He set his hands upon black stone armrests, amid silver flowers. It felt like coming home.

CHAPTER TWENTY-NINE

Fifteen paces, left turn, twenty paces, left turn. Sarmin trailed his fingers across the wall fabric, listening to the whispers beneath the hiss.

He thought of Tuvaini's door, of Grada coming from the tunnel, her knife in her hand. His walls were less solid than he had thought. The ceiling gods were paint and gold leaf, the work of deft fingers and a skilled wrist.

"There are no angels." He set his hands across Aherim. "I could scratch you away, like an itch. A man could make a blank page of this room with a bucket of plaster."

Silence.

"Answer me." Silence.

"I will not die here. I can leave at my will."

Sarmin crossed to the door. Govnan had said it would be left unlocked. He set his hand on the wood. His fingers trembled; his whole hand, his arm, his body shook.

"I can leave." Bile flooded his mouth, burning the back of his throat.

He steadied himself against the wall with his other hand, head down. His hair fell over his face and a trail of sour drool extended from his lips. "I have opened doors before." He gasped the words. "Doors where men don't go."

His fingernails bit into the edge of the door. Ten breaths, deep ones.

"I… can… open… *this one.*"

He hauled, and the door swung inwards, crashing against the wall, shockingly loud.

And there it was: the world beyond, an area of paved stone six feet by six feet, empty now, but polished to a shine by the feet of hundreds of bored guards, and the tower steps curving down, out from sight in a tight spiral.

Sarmin tried to step through, but his legs failed him. He crouched on the carpet, retching dryly.

What would she think of him now, his horsegirl? Grada, Mother, if they could see him weeping and broken before an open door?

He tried to crawl forwards, though his tears had left him blind and his arms had no strength.

For an age he lay there, a wet cheek to the rug, the silk fibre tickling his lips, staring at those steps. The threshold was a precipice. It held all the terror of the fall from his window, the long drop to his dead brothers, before they sealed it again with a thin alabaster pane.

Out there they thought him dead—out there he was dead.

"I can't."

He crawled back to his bed.

My bride. Sarmin turned once more to his walls and what might be seen there. Among a million twisting lines he found the curve of her cheek. He traced it with a finger and found her smile. She watched him. She was close, he knew it. Out there, beyond the threshold, she was close enough to hear the call of the Tower mages. *Come to me. Please.*

Mesema struggled with the pomegranate. Even the fruits here were strange and unhelpful. Still, her efforts had won her a small pile of segments, like pale rubies in her dish. They were beautiful, but disappointing in the mouth. She would have preferred an apple.

"Who was that man who scared you?" she asked Lana. The old man who had come out of the wall and spoken to Mesema as if he knew her.

Lana frowned and considered every word she spoke, as if picking her way through a field of secrets.

"His name is Govnan."

Mesema added another segment to her pile on the silver plate. Something tugged at her: a memory of Beyon's? Imagination?

"And who is Govnan?" He was clearly someone important, for he had sought no permission to enter the women's wing.

"He is High Mage Govnan," Lana said.

"A mage?" Mesema turned a seed in her mouth, thinking of the pattern. "What kind of mage?"

Lana kept her eyes on the floor, studying the mosaics. Juice beaded her nails as Mesema tore the remains of the pomegranate apart. The mage hadn't looked dangerous, he had looked tired and old—and yet he had called freely upon the emperor's time.

"What did he say to the emperor?" Mesema had seen them exchange words by the door. Govnan had spoken only once, and Beyon had nearly stumbled, putting a hand on the old man's shoulder, as if for support. They left together with no goodbyes.

"I don't know." Her voice trembled, and she kept her eyes down.

"Has someone died?" Mesema didn't know why she asked it, but as the words came she knew them to be true. She felt the pattern closing in, stronger now.

Lana kept her head down, but the tears fell in a steady rain. Mesema felt her eyes prickle. It couldn't be Sahree; the high mage would not concern himself with a mere servant, nor would Beyon react so to her death. Nevertheless a sudden grief welled in her, blurring the lamplight that gleamed on her plate. She pushed it away.

"I'm sorry." She put her hand on Lana's, her fingers pale against the dusk of the woman's skin.

Lana pulled her hand back. "I had a son, Pelar. They will be together now."

For a moment they watched the floor together. From nowhere, maybe from memory, Mesema felt the tug of a cold wind, and with it a longing for the wideness of sky and the endless grass of home. Nothing here gave the eye peace; the walls, the ceiling, the floors, they were all worked and scrolled, all intricacy and convolution, like the essence of a lie without the substance.

"What happened?" She wanted to insist, but the words sounded faint, as if spoken into a vast cavern.

Lana ignored her, and Mesema wanted to take her by the shoulders, to demand an answer, but it would be useless. She put the remains of the pomegranate on the silver dish and rose to her feet. She walked past scroll-work and gold leaf, carvings and tapestries, until she saw darkness through the curved lattice of a wooden screen and found, beyond it, a balcony overlooking the courtyard.

The soldiers below were joking and shouting among themselves, relaxing in the torchlight, reminding her of the Riders back home, but when they saw her they fell silent and scattered from view. From up here she could see the courtyard's stones formed a diamond pattern of black and brown. Its far end pointed towards the city, a confusion of roofs and awnings illuminated by orange bonfires. Each fire was tended by a lone silhouette. Mesema shivered.

She ran her fingertip along the stone railing. Perhaps the rough surface would rub the mark away, but even without looking, she knew it clung to her still, telling her of Beyon's distant movements.

A wind blew up around her, hot as fire-stones and smelling of char. A flag atop one of the towers cracked and strained against its fittings. She pushed her hair from her eyes and looked at the Bright One, stepping near the top of the moon. *Just a few more days—a week, perhaps.* She put it from her mind.

Then she saw it: the highest tower in the palace, the topmost window gaping. Though the night was dark, the room beyond the window appeared darker still.

Something held her gaze—*there!* Something or someone was hidden there. She could almost remember, and the lost memory pulled at her, the half-formed image—something of both softness and cruelty. Beyon knew who or what crouched there alone, removed from the rest of the palace. Perhaps he had put it there.

Mesema rubbed her fingertip, trying to bring forth those things she had touched in Beyon, but she had lost this piece of his past, as she had lost so many others. She knew only that it felt like grief. She didn't know what the pattern meant for her or Beyon. She didn't know whether Arigu's games would change the empire, or what role Banreh would have in that, if he lived. She didn't know what had happened to Sahree.

But she could find out what was in that tower.

She left the balcony and passed the scrollwork, the tapestries, and the tasselled cushions. The floor mosaic caught her eye: the pattern seemed to flow, a slow rotation, with only one line constant, unmoving, like a single certainty, a thread, drawing her. She passed Lana, who did not even raise her head, and as she followed the line Lana made no move to stop her; she gave no sign of having seen her. A silence pressed on the room, so profound that even breathing came hard.

The line left the mosaic swirl and crossed two plush rugs, dividing their patterns. Mesema followed it to the doorway, never raising her eyes. Almost in a dream she pushed open the doors and passed between two guardsmen dressed in splendid colors; neither man so much as twitched.

The line led on, along the centre of the corridor. Mesema pursued it, and silence followed in her wake.

The magnificence of the palace should have taken away her breath, but Mesema saw it only from the corner of her eye; the line filled her purpose, a simple constant amongst the lies and confusion, and where it led, none blocked her way. She moved as if she were invisible: as long as she watched the line, no one would watch her. A simple truth.

She passed courtiers, servants, guards, and then more guards, and silk and woven tapestries gave way to bare stone. A spiral stairway took her up, turn after turn promising the sky, and the line grew as broad as a river, as black as pitch, until, suddenly, it was nothing but a crack in the flagstone beneath her slippered feet.

Mesema found herself at the top of the stair, before her not the sky but a door, open just an inch, just enough for her fingers. She pushed it.

Sarmin pulled, and with slow certainty she came, not drawn against her will, but because of it. Sarmin watched the door. Pale fingers, nails painted like blood, glistening with moisture, and then she stood there.

"Hello." He smiled. He hoped it was the right thing to do.

"Hello."

She looks so young.

"I'm Sarmin," he said.

"Mesema." She glanced around the room then her eyes returned to his. "I don't remember why you're here." A strange thing to say, and a strange way to say it. She spoke the words with hard corners on the vowels. The oddness of it made him laugh.

"I'm Beyon's brother."

"His brother?"

Her lips made a circle. Everything about her made him glad.

"His brother." It didn't sound like an explanation, but it was. She walked into the room. Sarmin watched her, wondering if he looked foolish. She sat upon the bed, so close that if they both reached out, their fingers would touch. He could smell soap on her, and fruit.

He cleared his throat. "I had other brothers, but they died."

"I'm sorry." And she was, he could see it in her eyes, a sparkle of tears. No one had ever said they were sorry, not for his brothers. "They were… killed?" She knew they had been. She paused because the words were ugly in her mouth. He could see it. "My brother was also killed."

Sarmin nodded.

"It was wrong."

"It was." He blinked to keep his eyes clear. He didn't want to cry. But it was wrong. "I worry for Beyon. He's sick. I don't want him to die, too." The notion that he might keep secrets from her was silly.

Mesema looked away. She pressed her cheek to her shoulder and held her hand towards him, fingers extended. A pattern-mark challenged him from a fingertip. *No—not my princess.* In the darkness of his mind he recalled the Pattern Master's mocking voice.

Sarmin took her hand. Her skin felt cool, but fire passed between them. *Mine.* He turned her fingers in his and knew this to be another reason why men fought: the touch of her skin and the way her hair fell over her cheek as she looked at their joined hands. He would not let the Pattern Master have his bride. He spoke over the pounding of his heart. "I can take this mark away," he said.

She pulled her hand back and fixed him with strange blue eyes. "It copied itself from Beyon when I touched him. My finger was bleeding." She looked past him, at the carvings on his headboard. "When I touched him again, he remembered things—good things and bad things."

Sarmin thought of Grada, how she had rushed back into herself. What Mesema described was different and accidental, but somehow the same. "You held Beyon to Beyon. The Pattern Master tries to lift him away, to leave only meat, but you held him within himself."

"Leave the mark," she said, with no hesitation.

Something in that stung him. "You love him? Beyon?" An ache opened in Sarmin's chest, a hollowness. *She was to be mine: the horsegirl brought from the grass clans.* She had been his only gift in a million lonely years. Beyon's now.

But she shook her head, her eyes fixed on the broken window. "Not him."

Someone else, then. "The— The Master will come soon," he said. "The pattern is almost made." *And I will die in this room.*

"What will you do?" Again her eyes settled on his.

"What *can* I do?" Sarmin asked. "I don't think I can stop him—I'm sure I can't."

She looked at him, waiting.

"I do have a kind of magic," Sarmin admitted. "I can see the Pattern Master's plans. I can see how much power he has, how he holds everything in his hands. He scares me."

"You can see his plans, and you say that you can remove his marks." Mesema held up her index finger. "Doesn't that mean you can stop him?"

"I'm like an eagle that can fly over the city and see it whole. Then I can squawk about it to the mice who see only the walls around them."

"And the marks?"

"I can change only one person at a time. There are too many."

"Beyon—"

"I can't help him." He spat out the truth like a bitter pit. The Master had known it when he told Sarmin there was no hope. "I would have to remove Govnan's protections, and the Master is always watching, waiting for that to happen." He saw now that he had almost opened the way for the Master. Mesema had saved Beyon by raising his memories; it was her voice Sarmin had heard that night. *Can she use patterns, then, as I can, as the Master can?* He looked at her again. How did mages identify one another? The High Mage travelled the empire every few years, searching for children with talent. How young were they? Younger than Mesema, surely. Once identified, they spent the rest of their lives with the Tower.

Sarmin felt a sudden panic. He'd worried Beyon would take her, or the pattern, but he hadn't thought of Govnan. Govnan had already taken Grada away. He might take Mesema, too, and still call Sarmin fortunate. He made fists in the covers. *If I could leave here…*

"What would he do then?" Mesema asked her question as she studied the calligraphy on the wall.

Did she see the faces hidden there? "Govnan?" *If I could leave here, then I would give orders to these old men instead of taking them.*

"The Pattern Master."

Sarmin reached back in his mind to their previous conversation. "I think the Master would be happy to see Beyon dead. Once he hoped to control the emperor, but now he has waited too long, and I sense he is a vengeful man."

"A vengeful man makes mistakes," Mesema said. Her words sounded wise, but Sarmin couldn't imagine the Pattern Master making a mistake. The only fault he could think of was one of omission: if there was something the Master didn't see or couldn't see…

"Listen. I've seen the pattern," Mesema said, "in grass, and in sand. A hare ran through it in secret paths."

Sarmin said, "I've seen the pattern, too. I've run through it, lived in it. But it doesn't help. His pattern is perfect." *As are you.*

"You're sure?" She pinched her lips together.

Sarmin winced. Remembering the flaw made his stomach turn, like nails on chalkboard. The emperor's Knife. The pattern—the whole pattern—was not drawn on parchment, or written on Carrier skin; it was bigger than that. The whole pattern was written through every*thing* and every*one*.

Except the Knife. Only the Knife remained as a taunt to the Master, inside the pattern, yet not part of it.

"First he must break the emperor's Knife. Then it will be perfect."

"Beyon's knife? But surely—"

"Not Beyon's knife, not the one he carries, anyway—it's more than that, much more. The Knife is both holy and unholy." She turned to him, her eyes flashing with a new idea.

"Sarmin, listen. In the desert, the pattern led us to a church of the Mogyrk One God."

One god, one pattern, one way. He looked past her lovely face to the gods on the ceiling. Many gods for many choices: could this be what the Master was missing?

Mesema touched his hand, calling him back. "Do you think the Pattern

Master believes in the One God?"

He spoke, trying to make his consonants soft and his vowels hard, as she did, "I don't know. Surely it is how he sees himself—one Master, with all powers—but he needs others as much as I do. The Carriers."

"If he needs them, we will stop them." She thrust her chin out, just a little.

"Is this how all your people are?" Sarmin asked. "Ready to fight? No surrender, even when your horses are gone?"

Mesema grinned. "Yes, we're famed for it. That, and for speaking out of turn. We are the Felt."

"I imagined you, when Mother told me you were coming. I wondered how I could make you happy." Sarmin felt the blood rise in his cheeks.

"Fight him. Fight this Pattern Master and his plague. That would make me happy." She looked fierce now. Sarmin had never imagined her more lovely.

"Then I shall," he said.

"And me?" Mesema pointed her finger Sarmin's way, and his soft brown eyes turned to the moon-mark there.

Mesema loved Prince Sarmin's voice, the first Cerani voice too soft to scratch against her ears. Nothing about Sarmin had edges. The emperor had made her ears hurt; the wind ran around him like a storm. Sarmin's voice rose and fell with the rhythm of Tumble's tether-bells. She closed her eyes and imagined lying next to him under his blanket. His window had been broken, and the cold desert night gripped the room.

Now he took her hand as he had before, his gentle touch reassuring. "Your blood made that mark—or you marked yourself. I think that makes a difference." He looked at his own hands. "Blood must be the key to the pattern. It's how I freed Grada."

"Grada?"

"She was a Carrier."

"You love her?" She didn't know why she said it, but she knew there must be a truth to it. It made her sad.

"She's from the Maze." When she looked at him, not understanding, he went on, "She's low-born. She helped me, but I can't be with her, not like that."

Mesema knew the explanation didn't reveal everything, but then maybe he didn't know everything. He looked away, and she studied his face in profile. At first, shyness had kept her from doing so, then she grew so comfortable with him that she forgot to look. But now his face drew her eyes.

Olive tinged Sarmin's skin, and yet still he looked pale. Sweat plastered his dark curls to his temples, and she remembered the smell of vomit outside the room. Her hand crept out over the silk blanket that covered him. She meant to touch his face, to check for fever, but her fingers met something cold and sticky first. Of course: the other smell she hadn't identified when she entered. Blood. "What's that? Are you hurt?"

Sarmin didn't answer. Night darkened the room, and light came from only one lantern, far away in the corner. Mesema feared what she might see, but forced herself to walk to it anyway, her footsteps slow and dragging. She studied the red stain on her hand with a cold certainty. "You're bleeding."

"Not any more." Sarmin's big brown eyes creased at the edges when he frowned. He looked like his brother the emperor, but with finer features. He would have been as handsome as Banreh if he weren't so thin and wasted.

"Do you have a wound? I know how to sew—" She had done much sewing of flesh during the war. Sometimes it helped. Other times the wound only festered. You could never tell…

But he waved her off. "You should go. People might be looking for you."

Mesema frowned. Only Beyon would look for her. She realised with a start she hadn't told Sarmin about her vision; she'd put it from her mind, and therefore kept it from him. *No secrets from my prince.* She opened her mouth, but Sarmin's eyes had already closed. *Another time, then.*

"You need your rest. I'll be back," she promised, but he didn't respond. His chest rose with a slow breath. She crept towards the door.

"Wait."

She turned. Her prince reached under his pillow to draw out a long dagger. It had a three-sided blade, and the hilt sparkled with red gems. "Take this dacarba. I don't need it any more."

Mesema stepped forwards and lifted the weapon. It felt light and cool in her hand. She'd held her father's sword once, when he wasn't looking, and her brother's boning-knife; they'd both had been heavier than this. She wrapped her fingers around the hilt, feeling the sharpness of the gems against her palm. She shut her eyes and thought of Beyon. *I will not kill him. I won't!* "No. I can't take this," she said.

"I command you. Take it—keep safe." Sarmin closed his eyes again. His head drooped back upon the silk. He slept.

"I don't want it," she whispered, though he couldn't hear. She crept to the door, dagger in hand, and began her descent to the palace.

Eyul pushed in the eye of Keleb and stepped through the wall into the hidden corridors. He guessed that Beyon had chosen these dark passageways—he would have, in the emperor's place. He carried no lantern; better that he come upon the emperor unawares. When he had finished with the emperor, he would come back for Govnan.

A rustling sounded above him and to the right. He smiled to himself and crept towards the spiral staircase. Beyond that would be the bridge. It wouldn't do to send Beyon's body into the chasm; it had to be burned in the courtyard, before witnesses. He'd wait until Beyon had arrived safely at the other end.

At the top of the stairs he crouched, listening. Somewhere ahead, Beyon breathed. Clever for the emperor to stand on the bridge. He knew the law better than anyone.

"Eyul, is that you?"

Eyul listened. He heard only Beyon; the two bodyguards had either run or been sent elsewhere.

"Eyul, you are my sworn protector. You will not kill me."

"I am sworn to protect the rightful emperor."

"I am Tahal's chosen successor."

"You are a Carrier."

"No."

Silence. The darkness felt bitter, pressing in on Eyul's skin. A smell of rot wafted up from the deep. His palm grew sweaty around the Knife's hilt. He could hear whispers, soft as leaves in the wind, too low for him to understand.

"What do you say?" he murmured, twisting the hilt in his hand. The voices fell silent. Eyul stood and addressed Beyon, fixing his eyes where he knew the emperor stood. "I've seen the marks on you."

"I carry the marks, nothing else."

The stench of rot grew stronger. Eyul stood and peered into the dark.

Beyon lowered his voice. "My brother is alive."

Eyul listened now to the above and the below, for any footstep that would reveal another listener. Beyon was careless to speak out in the darkness.

"My brother is alive," Beyon repeated, "and I am no Carrier. The true Carrier who stabbed my brother knew the secret ways. Someone had revealed them to her. Someone from the palace."

Someone from the palace. Eyul knew who that must be, but his mouth was slow to follow his thoughts. "The attack…" He cleared his throat. "It's not the first time. I believe…" Dangerous to say the words, unfamiliar. "Tuvaini arranged for the Carriers at the fountain." Working with Govnan? The two of them, conspiring to bring down the empire. *Why?*

"You see," said Beyon. "Come with me, and—"

"No. You're still marked." Eyul readied the Knife in his hand. "Tuvaini may be a traitor, but your brother is the emperor now, and you must die."

He took a step forwards. He heard Amalya's voice then, strong enough in his memory to bring back her warmth and her scents of spice and smoke. *You should give him the benefit of the doubt. It matters to you.* He paused, his leg extended, his grip faltering. It did matter. He lowered his Knife.

"You must die," he said again, "but it won't be me who kills you."

A long silence fell between them. Fire crackled, and a lantern illuminated the bridge. Beyon stood at the midpoint of the crossing, the darkness on either side, his eyes darker still. He smiled, a tight stretch of the lips. Eyul couldn't remember if Beyon had ever smiled at him before.

He sheathed the Knife and joined his emperor.

CHAPTER THIRTY

"And the girl, Your Magnificence?" Azeem stood by the bottom step of the dais, his face polite, respectful, blank. Elevation to Lord High Vizier had wrought no discernible change in the man.

"Not important." No grandson of Tahal would threaten him now. Tuvaini eased back into the throne. It was not a comfortable seat. He drummed his palms against its stone arms as his mind rushed through the corridors of the palace, out into the winding streets of the city and along the wide roads that led to every corner of the empire. He had so many plans that he could not decide where to begin.

"I wish to invite some of the greater lords," he said at last.

"We must make it clear that we will work with them. Lord Zell of the western province is the loudest when it comes to complaint. Send five men with silks, gems and fine wood—it must be a good load. And remind me, is Lord Zell married?"

"His wife died in childbirth three months ago, Your Majesty."

Tuvaini thought a moment. *The girl.* The gods had arranged everything perfectly for him. "The Felt are good breeders. Keep the girl here." She wouldn't marry a prince, but surely her father would be almost as pleased to see her with the empire's richest lord. That would in turn please Arigu.

"And Lord Zell will be further indebted, Your Majesty." Tuvaini ignored Azeem's flattery and looked around the bare room—Beyon's room. "Bring the cushions back, and the tapestries. It feels like a tomb in here." Everything of Beyon's felt empty and cold, as if he had just been waiting to die. Well, tonight his time had come: his pyre would light the dark courtyard. Tuvaini thought he would enjoy looking down on it from Lapella's window. He stood. "Where is Govnan?"

"In the treasury, Your Majesty, examining the texts." Azeem met his eyes and the message was clear.

Examining my claim, seeing whether the supplicant, the last of a bastard line, has true right to warm the Petal Throne. No matter.

"Then I shall retire."

Azeem fell into his obeisance. For a moment Tuvaini almost looked over his shoulder for Beyon or Tahal, for the emperor, but instead he walked from the dais and towards the doors. Everyone hugged the floor at his approach except for the blue-hatted guards at the door. They stood to attention, ready to follow him wherever he meant to go. Their eyes betrayed worry and sorrow. While not many had cared for Beyon, it had been said his soldiers loved him. Tuvaini had never seen that until now. He passed them without comment.

He walked, lost in thought, following long habit to Lapella's quarters. Zell had been the obvious lord to invite first, but things would be more difficult from now on. He would consult Donato in the morning about trade in the provinces. Whom he invited, how, and in what order would affect his plans for the city markets.

He passed the fountain and remembered Eyul's fight with the Carriers. How simple the man was. Tuvaini rubbed his tired eyes. He must reward the assassin and see to the finishing of Beyon's tomb, empty though it would be. Work would be stopped by bureaucrats as a matter of course because of the succession. The wheels of empire, powered by the slaves of pen and scale, were designed to turn with little guidance, but Tuvaini would guide the wheels in this. The common folk must not know the Carriers had struck so deeply into the empire. It was important to renew work on the tomb, to make it great for the city's unknowing eyes.

The familiar sight of Lapella's door drew him back from his worries.

Tuvaini wondered if she slept, and how long she waited for him every night before surrendering to dreams. He turned the handle as the guards took up position in the hallway. They must wonder what business he had in the servants' quarters. *Let them wonder.* He smiled to himself, picturing her reaction when he told her that he sat on the Petal Throne at last.

Tuvaini stepped into the night of Lapella's room. A single wide candle burned on the windowsill, its flame nearly drowned by melting wax. He crossed the dark space and lifted it, his gaze drawn downwards to where Beyon's pyre should be. The courtyard swam in darkness. "Lapella." His whisper sank into the unseen edges of the room, unanswered. In her mirror's dim glass he saw the gleam of the light in his hand, and how it lit the curve of his palm and the line of his jaw. He stared into the black spaces of his reflection and shivered. It was a cold desert night.

"Lapella?"

A dark pool yawned before him: Lapella's bed. He took a step forwards and a twisted shadow flickered against the wall, a crouching demon. He drew back, crying, "Lapella!"

The room kept its silence. Tuvaini took a breath and listened to the distant sounds of the city. *Foolishness*, he thought and moved to the bed. She faced away from him, her dark hair spread out across her pillow. His relief escaped in a short laugh as he reached for her shoulder. "La—"

No. She lay arched backwards, her elbow twisting down into the mattress, one leg folded beneath her and the other sprawled off the side of the bed.

Tuvaini opened his mouth and made a croaking noise. He ran his fingers through her hair, thick and soft as always, and touched her cold cheek.

"I—" His breathing filled the quiet room. "Lapella, wake up. I have news for you."

He waited, but Lapella didn't move. Her right hand stood in the air, a frozen claw. Her left reached towards an over-turned dish. He leaned across the bed, his stomach pressing against hers. Five plump dates rolled towards him as the blankets shifted. He lifted one, and the dark flesh yielded under his fingernail to reveal a mixture of crushed nuts, honey and candied flower petals.

Lapella never bought such things for herself, and they hadn't come from him. He dropped the sweet and wiped his fingers carefully.

"I didn't know this would happen." He spoke into her small, perfectly proportioned ear. A golden hoop was strung through the soft lobe. Her eyes were turned from him, and he was glad of that. "I'm sorry."

He imagined the way she used to shrug at him, her way of saying that all the waiting and disappointment were nothing to her; that she didn't mind bearing it all, everything he had to bring her. He searched across the dark room for the outline of Mirra's statue. "Perhaps Mirra wanted you beside her and so she took you away." He'd heard such sentiments expressed in the past and he knew they were words she'd like to hear. Inside, he knew that Herzu had taken her, and not out of love.

He returned to the window. "How would you have me feel?" He stared into the darkness a while. The courtyard showed no movement, no fire. The room grew colder.

"I am the emperor now," he said to her. "Everything is going to change. Nothing would have changed for you, though. I'm sorry." He turned and looked at her twisted form on the blankets. Poison could pull a person's muscles in strange ways. He had seen it before. "I must go. Goodbye, La-pella."

The door felt heavy, his shoes, heavy. The corridor was too bright. The soldiers followed him, their boots noisy on the floor. It set his teeth on edge. Eyul had always been silent when they walked together. Perhaps as emperor he would set up a new guard using only Herran's men. His eyes prickled. He blinked, staring at the tiles to keep from seeing her twisted arm. *Silly.* He shook his head as if to rid it of foolishness.

He turned a corner. He had no idea where to go. He passed the women's wing and kept on walking.

Mesema crept down the tower stairs, the three-sided dagger in her hand. The weapon frightened her. Its sharp blade had already torn through the top of her skirt. She paused at a landing, listening for voices, but she knew the tower was not guarded—at least, not by people. Something else tickled at her skin. The tower stank of fire—not cooking fire, or the kind that kept the longhouse warm on winter nights; this smelled like dead fire, the stench the Red Hooves left behind them after killing Jakar and forcing Hola's daughter. It had filled the air during their funeral rites, this smell of blackened stone and dark tears.

Ash covered the last flight of stairs, a black powder so fine that it rose up around her sandals like a cloud. As she moved towards the door she heard faint voices.

"Another five—put your coins there—" Laughter.

"No. Again."

Mesema pushed the door open by finger-widths, and when nobody raised their voice in alarm she slipped out into the wide hallway. Bright lanterns lighting the wall at regular intervals made her feel exposed, though the corridor was unoccupied. The voices came from her left. Young men—soldiers, she guessed—played a betting game of some kind. They were using words Banreh hadn't taught her.

"Hey, Sazz, what are you doing here?" one of the men called out. "Did you hear the emperor—?"

Mesema didn't catch the rest. Her finger told her Beyon was in the palace, but always far away, no matter how much she moved. She peeked around a corner to find another empty hallway.

"You're in the wrong place, my lady," said a blue-hatted guardsman, quiet on his feet. "I'll take you to the wives' quarter, yes?"

She let him lead the way, past the barracks.

"—madness, to spend the whole winter in the north—"

"—say the girls there open their legs for nothing more than a smile. They'll keep us warm enough—"

The soldiers stood with their backs to the corridor, paying no attention to her or her guide.

"I heard they all have behinds wide as cows."

A second man laughed. "Then I hope we can tell the difference before it's too late."

Mesema's ears burned, but she kept her head down and followed close on the guardsman's heels. The corridor ended in a dark entryway, and she recognised the temple of the terrible god, Herzu. Her stomach clenched with hunger. She longed for the smell of rain and the sound of Banreh's voice. The god would not let her pass without reminding her of these things.

The guardsman led her down a new corridor. On the wall to her left, thousands of tiny stones formed a battle scene: warriors of jade and onyx, raising swords behind their king. The king wore red, and his eyes gleamed topaz. On the other side of a great green field waited the enemy, their white robes flowing, their faces flat and indistinct. She kept the dagger across her belly, shielding the blade behind her arm, the point nearly at her elbow. Fighting the pattern was not the same kind of war, but already Eldra had given her life and Sarmin his blood. Would she have the strength to use her weapon when the time came? She picked up her pace to match the guard's strides. She would have to be strong. She had promised Eldra, and now Sarmin had promised her.

They climbed stairs laid with the plush carpet of the women's quarter. At the top the guardsman opened his mouth to speak, but a glance along the corridor stopped him; he threw himself into obeisance, and when she stood, confused, waved her down beside him with some urgency. Mesema turned her head ever so slightly on the carpet, squinting for a glimpse. She had spent quite enough time with her face pressed to the ground—a lifetime's worth, in just a few days.

Five men approached the steps, a white-faced man in blue robes and four soldiers in blue. Each looked lost in his own thoughts, sad, confused. What had happened? They paid her no attention. The man in blue looked everywhere, but saw nothing. His eyes searched for something else. She saw his face for a moment. It was narrow, touched with some of Beyon's features: the strong nose, the wide mouth.

The man passed and went down the stairs, the soldiers behind him.

Her guardsman stood with caution. "Go on, quickly—and don't wander again. This is not a night for it."

He left her without another word and hastened after the men.

On the far side of the landing stood a wooden bench piled high with cushions. Mesema had just one more hallway to cross, but suddenly she felt too exhausted to move. The bench reminded her of her longhouse bed. She could have curled up among those cushions and slept for a week, if her stomach hadn't been twisting with hunger. Instead she grabbed a cushion, cut it open and shoved her dagger inside. The cushion was not stuffed with wool, as she had expected, but fine white feathers that rose in the air like snow. She hurried on, not pausing until she passed the grand staircase and saw the heavy carved doors. What would they think, to see the Felting woman in a torn dress smeared with Sarmin's blood, carrying a ripped pillow? The sound of soldiers on the stairs gave her no time to think. She pushed against the wood and ran through into the women's wing.

Lanterns cast low light, glimmering off the golden trim in the ceiling. Nobody sat on the cushions or wandered the dark corridor. All the women must be sleeping. Mesema rubbed her tired eyes. There were so many doors, she could barely remember which was hers.

Under the window, as high as her hips, stood a green vase with a golden lid. Perhaps she could hide her dagger inside until the morning? She leaned down to open it. A familiar scent tickled her nostrils and brought her back home to her mamma, sitting in the longhouse that last day. She reached in and touched the contents to be sure.

Her mother needn't have given her the resin for stopping babies. They had enough of it here, at the palace. That was why Beyon had no heirs: they'd been denied him.

When a Felting girl showed herself barren, she became the property of her father and brothers for ever, forced to play whatever role they decided she should play. But perhaps for Beyon the opposite was true: if he played a role, then they would give him a child.

But he hadn't, and so they had turned to his brother and fetched Mesema from the Wastes.

But who were *they*?

She sat next to the vase, the pillow dropping from her hands. She remembered Arigu's deceptions, and Eldra's death. She remembered how Nessaket had mocked her son the emperor, telling him he was slow—slow to understand that there was more to fear besides the pattern and its Master.

Beyon was not, as he claimed, the final authority in the palace. Others—the Pattern Master, his mother, Arigu—wrapped strings about him and pulled, and when they were finished with him, they would get rid of him, just as they had his brothers.

And then what would happen to Sarmin?

Mesema grabbed her pillow from the floor and hurried down the hallway, looking for her ocean-painted room.

Sarmin sat on his bed, running his mind across the pattern-threads like a musician would bow his strings. Meeting Mesema—his bride—made it difficult to concentrate.

He'd lived with his five books since he came to this room. They told him of the empire, statecraft, the gods, war, and how to behave at court, and now he had a new book, that made his skin feel hot. But none of his books spoke of love. He thought of the poets who had come to his father's court. With the women cleared from the room they would sometimes speak of their hearts, though Sarmin couldn't recall the words they had used.

He wanted Grada. He recalled the closeness of her, the intimate touch of her skin and her mind. Mesema's lips invited him, but he knew Grada, muscle to bone. Was that love? He hadn't been able to answer Mesema on that point. It disturbed him, a flaw in the design.

The diamond that was Grada's soul hid in the Tower, but he felt it gleaming at him from across the city. He concentrated, moving lightly along the pattern's threads, bypassing charms of ice and fire set to protect the Tower's residents from intrusions such as his.

"Grada."

"Prince!" Surprise and relief, followed by hesitation. "You need me?" A flash of a white room, simple clothes, more than she'd ever had, but nothing too rich, nothing that felt wrong to her.

He felt foolish. "No, nothing—"

"What of the pattern? Have you freed more of us?"

He sent a simple thought, a negative.

She fell quiet, occupied with something. Her hands moved and pulled—weaving, perhaps—but so late? He could move into her, watch from behind her eyes, if only it didn't feel like invasion, him sliding into her as she had slid her knife into him. "It is late. Forgive me." He began to turn away.

"Prince!" Her hands went still. "What have you learned?" With those words she lifted a weight of stones from his chest.

"I will tell you." He told her of Mesema, of her pattern-mark, and of the church that rose from the sands. Sometimes he told her in words, other times he grew tired and instead offered images, scraps of ideas, and the tinge of questions that ran along the edges of his mind.

When he finished she was quiet, though her thoughts were turning. Then she opened her own mind and showed him her room, the door ajar and the ladder leading down, the streets of the city, loud and dark, and at last, the Low Door, the one he had never seen before, that led out to the desert sands.

"I can be a knife hidden in your sleeve. I can help you," she told him.

CHAPTER THIRTY-ONE

Sarmin sensed his brother's arrival long before the secret door swung open. He felt the draw and the power of the pattern, the full force of the design wrapped around his brother's soul, and the way Govnan's protections struggled against it. He sat up in his bed and turned to where his brother would appear.

Beyon slipped through. His hair shone like black marble. His eyes, eagle-sharp, scanned the room and his hand lay strong on the hilt of his great sword. But he stooped, and his skin looked sallow and waxlike.

Then Beyon smiled, like the dawn sneaking through the broken window, slow and bright.

"Brother," said Sarmin.

"Brother."

Beyon had always looked the emperor, broad-shouldered and powerful. When they were just boys, the wives would say, "Look at Sarmin, such a pretty boy." But whenever they saw Beyon they would use just one word, always: "Strong." And he had been strong, fighting the pattern these many years. Now he grew tired. Could Mesema keep his head above the quicksand?

Beyon reached for the bed and sat down, but his eyes were elsewhere.

"When I came before, I spoke of bringing you to court."

"I remember." Sarmin smiled. How long ago that seemed.

"But they have seen the marks on me. Now my court is just two people," said Beyon. "You and the assassin. My throne is a crumbling bed in the old women's wing. Do you remember how we used to run and hide in those halls?"

"I do." He took his brother's hand.

"I spent much of the night in the secret ways."

"You are lucky to know the ways so well, how one leads to the next, like secrets, one after the other."

"Yes, just like secrets. I hope to use them all the way to the desert."

"They go that far?"

Beyon grinned. "I think so. I've heard tell that they do."

Sarmin thought about Mesema, somewhere in the women's wing. He could not leave his room—he could not protect her. He imagined her travelling across the desert, free. They could keep going, all the way to the west and the great ocean there.

"My bride—" *Mesema.* Her face came to him: a good face, with strong lines, like Beyon in her way. She had that look; she gazed at the world as if she knew she belonged to it.

Beyon answered quickly, "I can take her with me." Their eyes met, and Sarmin saw the doubt there, the hope. Beyon had lost everything, his health, his family, his throne. Mesema was all he had.

Sarmin used to think he had nothing to risk, nothing to lose. He laid a hand on his own dried blood, felt its stiffness rub against his palm. *I gave this blood for you, brother, and I will give yet more.* "Good," he replied, staring into Beyon's eyes. "I have other things I need to do."

Beyon hesitated, but he was the emperor: he wanted, he needed, and so he took. He put a hand on Sarmin's shoulder.

"Won't you come with us? To the desert?"

Sarmin remembered the dizzying space beyond the door.

"I'll stay. The mages will protect me." He felt a rush along his skin. Grada would soon leave the city. Sarmin wanted Beyon to leave him in peace so that he could join with her and see the desert through her eyes.

He still had Grada.

Beyon stood, his shoulders more square than before. *Good.* Mesema would continue to give him strength. Sarmin didn't need strength, only courage. Courage, and Grada.

"If I should die, brother…" Beyon's voice trailed away. "You must fight for the empire. It will be yours."

"And Tuvaini?"

"He is a traitor. Be strong, my brother."

"I will be strong." Grada had left the Tower and now she moved through the city streets, covered, unnoticed in the dark. He wanted to walk with her. "You must go, my brother. The Pattern Master watches you."

Beyon bowed in the manner of equals. "I will see you soon," he said.

"And I you," said Sarmin, inclining his own head the same way.

And yet Beyon paused by the secret door, his finger tapping the stone. "Eyul told me of a city that rose from the desert—a city just like ours, except that in the place of my tomb there was a Mogyrk temple. He saw strange things…'

It came in a flash, the pattern laid over Nooria, the desert city a map of things past and things to come. More than ever, Sarmin wanted Grada by his side. "You must go, brother."

Beyon slipped away and Sarmin leaned back against his pillows, reaching out for Grada in his mind. She moved along the riverfront now: in the low light of dawn, the fishermen hauled their nets and serving women filled their barrels. Where Grada walked, her feet sank into cool mud. She directed her gaze to the white flowers floating on the surface of the water. They were precious and delicate, the sort of thing you didn't expect to last. It made him feel braver.

"Do not be afraid, Grada," he said. "I know what you must do."

CHAPTER THIRTY-TWO

Eyul stalked the dark corridors, watching the guards, searching for the ones who looked indignant or grieved, the ones who turned away, their mouths tight, when the subject of burning the former emperor arose: the ones who showed hate in their eyes when they saw Eyul, believing him to be Beyon's killer. His task was to find these men and tell them when and where to honour their oaths.

It was not easy; most were reluctant to share their true thoughts with him. He had to avoid the ones who were shaking and frightened, though even they might turn to Beyon's side when the time came.

Beyon had not revealed his plan; he had only told Eyul to send half of the loyal men to Mirra's place in the desert and leave the other half here, in the palace, ready to turn on their fellows and Tuvaini. So to every other man Eyul told the path through the secret ways to where the river ran down the mountain at the edge of the desert. After three days he had sent a total of fifty-three men through the dark passages. Not enough to take back an empire.

Perhaps, as the days went by, Tuvaini's leadership would create more men who were loyal to Beyon. He wondered; Tuvaini could come across as a good man, concerned and pious, and he did care about the empire. It was just as Amalya had said. Caring for the empire meant different things to different people. Tuvaini felt that meant he must lead. Eyul felt that he must not.

How odd it was that Beyon had turned to him, of all the people in the palace: the man who had killed his brothers. And he had meant to do so even before Tuvaini's betrayal; weeks ago he sent Amalya to sound him out. Beyon had never been a friend, but he had known better than Eyul himself what it meant to be the Knife.

In the last hours Eyul had told Beyon about the city that rose from the desert, and how Pelar's demon had directed him to the temple. He told him about Tahal's otherworldly visit. He told him of the dead girl in the sand, and how two palace guards had tried to kill him. He told him Amalya was dead, and that only four mages remained in the Tower.

He held back that he had killed Amalya; he held back the voices in the emperor's Knife; he held back his meeting with the hermit, and the deal he had made to kill Govnan. He did not want the Carriers to learn these things should Beyon lose his battle against the pattern-marks.

He turned a corner and came upon another guard standing alone. The feather on his blue cap tilted forwards sadly as he contemplated his hands. Eyul settled back against a dark wall to watch him. Finding the loyal men took time, time they didn't have. He wanted to kill Govnan now, but he must attend to Beyon's tasks first; Amalya would have wanted it.

How he longed to draw the Knife across the old man's veins, taste the blood as it sprayed in the air. His throat almost hurt with excitement to think of it. This thirst for a kill was something new. It was ugly, but part of his soul now. He would have his revenge, and then the hermit could work his magic.

Soon now, soon.

The Blue Shield guard looked up and registered Eyul's presence. His lips curled in disdain.

Eyul moved forwards.

At dawn Tuvaini rose from his chair and called for his body-slaves. He looked through his window at the courtyard where a few White Hats leaned in the shadow of the wall, their heads bent in conversation. The tiles spread

out bare and white from their boots to the palace door. A quick movement caught his eye, but it was just a slave-boy, running after a ball—one
of Beyon's favorites, always playing when there was work to be done. He
would not want to throw his ball in the courtyard once the pyre was lit. If
it ever were lit.

Almost four days, Eyul. Where are you?

Tuvaini extended his arms so the slaves could remove his robes and wash
him with scented water. Their gentle, slow touch made him impatient. He
was neither their child nor their lover. He kept his gaze on the soldiers until
soft hands drew fresh clothes over his nakedness. He fingered his blue sash.
All his silks were simple, unassuming. He needed a tailor.

Dressed and perfumed, he opened the doors to the adjoining room where
Azeem waited, forehead to the carpet.

"Did Eyul report during the night?"

Azeem shook his head, eyes down. They had had the same exchange every
morning.

"Rise, Azeem." Beyon persisted like a stone in Tuvaini's slipper. He poured
some water and let its coolness soothe his throat. A night without sleep had
left him parched and dizzy.

"I will see Donato, then I would see the potion-master. What is his
name?" Tuvaini knew his name well enough; he had purchased from him
poisons aplenty, but Azeem did not know that.

"Kadeer, Your Majesty."

"Kadeer." Tuvaini lifted a date from the golden breakfast tray and brought
it to his nose. Biting into it, he said, "Yes, I'll see him, too."

"As you wish, Your Majesty."

Tuvaini smiled. He could afford that much for Azeem.

"The Empire Mother waits upon your attention, Magnificence." Tuvaini
chose another date and bit its dark flesh. "Does she," he murmured. Nessaket of the flowing robes and dancing hair waited on his whim. He let that
roll around in his mouth with the sweet fruit. "Let her wait. Come with
me, Azeem."

He had walked the emperor's path to the throne room countless times,
first with Tahal, and then with Beyon. Azeem walked beside him now, playing his own former role as faithful servant. Tuvaini hoped Azeem would be
more faithful than he had been. He warranted watching.

On the dais the throne sat, tall and gleaming. He ran his fingers along the cool armrests and looked out over the room. Slaves hung tapestries and leaned soft pillows against the wall. Closer, at the foot of the dais, Arigu knelt in obeisance, waiting for him. Tuvaini waved Azeem off to fetch Donato.

As the great carved doors closed behind Lord High Vizier Azeem, Tuvaini said, "Rise, General."

Arigu rose to his feet, but kept his gaze low to the floor. Tuvaini smiled. Everyone, from his slaves to his generals, was wondering how much he would remain the same, how much he would hold to his former habits and promises. "Why have you come, old friend? Is there a problem?" Arigu should be on his way into the desert by now if he wanted to get to the horse tribes before winter.

Arigu raised his eyes, concern painted on his face. He spoke loudly enough for everyone to hear. "I wanted to express my regrets at the terrible loss of your cousin, and pass along my best hope that Beyon will be captured."

"I pray the same to Keleb, good General."

"Our gods are strong, my Emperor, stronger than any other that might try to insinuate itself in our land."

A look passed between them.

"You speak of the Mogyrks."

Arigu had the feel for the common people—he always had. It was something Tuvaini lacked, but he could appreciate the value of a little rabble-rousing.

"I do. In the desert, Your Magnificence, I happened upon a Mogyrk church, and around it, I saw the pattern."

"The same pattern that marked our emperor." Tuvaini lifted his hands above his head, getting a feel for the drama. He met the eyes of everyone in the room, especially the guards, and raised his voice. "An assassin silenced Prince Sarmin's heart. An assassin, brought to the palace by Beyon himself."

"A Mogyrk assassin," Arigu met his eyes again, gaining confidence as he interjected, "from Yrkmir."

"A foe once distant in both leagues and time," Tuvaini said.

"But now so close as this very palace, Majesty." Arigu stepped forwards, ignoring the bodyguards who drew steel and blocked his way.

Tuvaini kept his face still. This was Arigu's moment. He would let him talk.

"We had forgotten the dangers of that faith," Arigu continued. "They worship the dead god. They brought the pattern-curse to the emperor and killed Prince Sarmin."

A cold shiver ran along Tuvaini's spine. Arigu's words made him feel something was missing, a gaping hole he hadn't noticed before, as if he might step off the dais into empty space.

"A Mogyrk assassin," he said. He looked out across the throne room at the tapestries depicting the Reclaimer's victory. Once they had felt celebratory to him; now they read like a warning. "We will have our revenge." *Where is Eyul?*

"The army loved Beyon well enough." Arigu placed his boot on the first step of the dais. "He had a warrior's soul. But the army best loves the man who puts it to its intended use."

Tuvaini brought his eyes back to the general. Arigu smiled inside his beard. Behind him the guards looked at one another, excited. The wisdom of Arigu's performance impressed Tuvaini.

"Nothing pleases the people like holy war, Majesty, old friend." Arigu pushed a bodyguard's blade out of his way and leaned closer. "That faith flows around our borders, a stinking tide, waiting to overwhelm us." He spoke softer still. "Yrkmir is at the heart of what is not ours."

Tuvaini rose and addressed his audience of slaves, guards and stray administrators. "The Yrkmen came to our doors with their evil faith in the time of my grandfather's father. The years have weakened them and made us strong, and in their jealousy they took our prince. Let us now pay them a visit in return. If we take Yrkmir, the gods will be pleased, and will open all roads to us." He nodded at Arigu. "You speak wisely, General. We shall attack in the spring. Go now to the horse tribes, before snow closes the passes. Win their allegiance."

Arigu bowed. "As you command, Your Majesty." He straightened, and spoke again, in a different tone, his voice lower. "There is something else."

Tuvaini put the assassin from his mind. "What is that?"

"The wives—Beyon's wives. There is a risk they bear the marks." He leaned closer. "Or an heir."

Arigu echoed Tuvaini's own thoughts. "You never know. Beyon was cursed indeed, but it is not impossible." Tuvaini had wondered about Beyon and his wives. He'd never shown any attachment to them, though they were beautiful, the prettiest flowers within reach of the empire's plucking. Beyon must have been proud of that.

"Your Majesty?"

"Use them—draw him out. You know Beyon." Tuvaini shrugged. "He may do something rash."

Arigu gave another bow, tighter this time. He backed away from the dais, almost bumping into Donato and Kadeer as he exited the room. Tuvaini was no longer interested in Donato and his analysis of the provincial markets. Arigu's performance had both excited him and left him unsettled and dissatisfied. With Beyon and Eyul unaccounted for, there was the question of his own protection. Arigu had spoken true: the soldiers had loved Beyon. Tuvaini should have consolidated his position over the men before sending them off to war, but he had no choice: Winter advanced.

In other days he would have found Lapella and been soothed. He gritted his teeth.

Azeem settled into a chair at the scribing table, ready to mark numbers and take names, but Tuvaini would be unpredictable today, changeable. He would show those same traits that had always frustrated him in Beyon. His gaze turned to where Kadeer embraced the floor. "Rise, Potion-master."

Azeem leaned back and placed his quill to the side. Doubtless he found Kadeer, with his twisted beard and stained fingers, to be repellent. Only the cowardly or the unfit would ever seek him out. Tuvaini had been both, in the past, but no longer.

"Kadeer," said Tuvaini, "is there anyone ill in the palace? Anyone asking for a cure?"

Kadeer studied the dais with beady eyes. "Not for some time, Your Majesty. I've had the usual—"

Tuvaini cut him off. "Define the usual."

Kadeer cleared his throat. "Nobody has asked for anything beyond the occasional healing elixir for rheumatism, twisted stomach, sleeplessness—"

"Sleeplessness." One pika seed brought peaceful dreams. Five pika seeds brought convulsions, choking and death. For a moment the sight of Lapella on her bed, distorted and ruined, filled his vision. "Who has asked for sleep ingredients?"

Azeem leaned forwards now, his interest overcoming his repulsion.

"Your Majesty, I feel that—"

Tuvaini snarled, "Don't play with me, Kadeer." He saw the fear in the man's little eyes and felt some comfort, but it was as a drop of water to a parched man.

Kadeer drew in his breath, one last hesitation, before speaking. "The Empire Mother has trouble sleeping at night, Your Magnificence. She frequently asks for relief."

Tuvaini looked past him to the tapestries, to the door, to the corridor beyond. The room felt small and close. The incense made it difficult to breathe.

"Your Majesty?" Azeem's chair screeched against the marble as he stood. "Are you well?"

Tuvaini waved a hand. "I am quite well. Thank you, Kadeer. You may go." He sat in the throne. Kadeer backed away, bowing as he left, leaving ripples in the silk runner. Six slaves rushed forwards to straighten it.

Azeem cleared his throat. "Your Majesty."

"What is it, Azeem?"

"Donato awaits your attention, Magnificence."

Magnificence. He would never hear Lapella call him that. He would never hear her laughter again, nor the little sounds she made when sleeping. Mogyrks, war, Carriers... Lapella had never used those words. He stood. "I shall—" *I shall be the emperor. I shall make war, defeat our enemies, crush the pattern beneath my feet.* "—retire."

Azeem fell to his obeisance. All was quiet. Tuvaini turned and left the room.

CHAPTER THIRTY-THREE

Mesema sat with the women for a lunch of honeyed river-fowl seasoned with yellow pollen. They sat together on the cushions, sharing the food from common platters. The eldest, wives of Beyon's father and grandfather, helped themselves first. They murmured among themselves and paid no heed to Mesema or Beyon's wives. After they had their fill, Atia, the tall, dark First Wife, took her food, followed by Chiassa, Hadassi, and finally Marren. Lana did not take her share until everyone else had served themselves, though she had the status of an Old Wife. She was so small and timid that Mesema wondered how she had survived so long in the palace. But then she remembered Beyon kissing Lana's forehead, and how much straighter Lana had stood in the emperor's presence. Beyon's affection had protected her all these years.

Mesema did not feel that Beyon's attentions would yield her the same benefit. Something had happened in the palace, signalled by the arrival of the High Mage. The women whispered nervously among themselves, but nobody quite knew what to make of things: Beyon had not returned, and Mesema feared that his marks had been discovered. If that were true, then all the women connected to him had instantly lost their status and protection, even if they did not know it yet. She longed to go to Sarmin again and ask him, but she had not found a time to slip away, and perhaps it would not be so easy to walk the palace unattended again. She wished she knew how to open the secret door in the hall.

Atia was gazing at her over a platter of fruit. In the lantern light her brown eyes looked orange, like fire. "So many important thoughts for a horsegirl."

Mesema swallowed. "Blessings, I did not mean to be rude."

"Blessings," echoed Chiassa with a smile.

"You would be rude," said Atia, turning her attention to a plump fig, "if you welcomed Beyon into your room before he has been to each of ours. You are to be last in his attentions, do you understand?"

The Old Wives stopped their murmuring. Lana laid a hand on Mesema's arm. No one reached for a plate or cup.

"Yes," said Mesema, "I understand."

"Atia would have you wait for ever, as we do," said Marren with a wink.

Chiassa gave a high-pitched giggle. Atia's cheeks turned red, but the silence was broken and the women resumed their meal. Mesema looked from one wife to another in confusion. If they wanted Beyon to visit them, if they cared about him, why did they use the resin? Why did they help his mother work against him?

Because they are afraid, as I am.

"I don't wish to offend you. I would like to be friends." Mesema set down her meat and rinsed her fingers in a bowl of rosewater.

"When she's not riding horses with the emperor, anyway," Hadassi muttered.

Mesema sighed to herself. She never should have mentioned Tumble.

"What?" said Atia, nearly choking on her fig. "Riding horses? I won't allow it."

Lana spoke, her voice barely more than a whisper. "Keleb has showered wisdom upon the emperor, heaven bless him. Don't you think that Beyon should decide such things?"

Mesema smiled at that narrow, timid face. She already thought of Lana as an aunt or grandmother. "It's all right, Little Mother," she said, grasping Lana's hand. "Walk with me." She stood and curtsied at the women. "Blessings of the day."

"Blessings," Chiassa said again, though the others just stared. As they walked, the women's whispers fading behind them, Mesema studied the women in the niche-pictures. They were all the same: pretty, docile. She wasn't sure what she'd expected, but she was disappointed: pretty and docile weren't going to help her survive. She needed allies.

"Lana, I'm curious. Does Beyon have no sisters?"

"He does, but their marriages were arranged long before his father's death. They have been gone for many years. Nessaket made sure the contracts were honoured."

Nessaket. The Empire Mother spent most of her time outside the women's wing. Mesema wished that she could do the same. "Lana, have I met everyone in this wing? It's just us, the Old Wives, the young wives, and Nessaket?"

"Yes." Lana almost said more, but fell silent instead.

Picking her way through secrets, again. Before Mesema could ask another question, they turned into the ocean room and she saw her trunk waiting by the bed, its unstained wood and simple brass fittings too plain for its surroundings. She dropped Lana's hand and rushed towards it.

"Your things?"

"Yes." Mesema pushed the trunk open and pulled out the blanket on the top. It was heavy and thick, too warm for the desert, but she placed it on her bed anyway, still folded. Next was her wedding dress, which made a soft jingle as she lifted it. She felt a lump in her throat when she remembered the women stitching around the fire. The women here didn't sew; they only prettied themselves and whispered.

She could see now that the dress wasn't colorful or revealing enough to wear in the palace. She put it aside with a little sigh.

She ran her hands through the rest of her few possessions: Woollen stockings—why had she thought she might need those? Copper hairpins. A necklace made of river-shells. Riding gear. All these things belonged to a girl, not a woman. A flash of blue set her digging and she pulled Eldra's arrow-fletching from the bottom. Her eyes filled with tears.

"What happened?" Lana stepped forwards.

"Nothing. I just—"

But Lana looked behind her and hurried away, leaving Nessaket standing there instead. Mesema buried the feather and closed the trunk before pressing her head to the carpet.

Nessaket wasted no time. "The prince is dead. The emperor is deposed."

Beyon—they found his marks! Mesema sucked in her breath. Sarmin was not really dead, she knew this. Did Nessaket?

So easily she casts off two sons.

"Rise. We will honour our alliance with your father." Meaning there would still be war. "And we will find a place for you."

What? Mesema straightened her skirt as she stood. Her thoughts raced ahead of her, leaving her mind blank. *Where are you, Beyon?* Her finger told her nothing. She pressed it against her skirt.

Nessaket had already turned away and was looking out into the corridor. "Stay in your room until evening."

"May I ask why, Your Majesty?"

She barely glanced back at Mesema. Something else had her attention. "There are assassins and Carriers about. Stay in your room."

Mesema's heart skipped a beat. She'd seen Sarmin's blood and Beyon's marks, but Nessaket's words shocked her, nevertheless. "Yes, Your Majesty."

"No matter what you hear." And she was gone.

No matter what I hear? The Empire Mother was expecting something—was she part of it? *Part of what?*

Mesema sat on the bed and gathered a cushion to her, the one with Sarmin's dagger inside. Her mother had thoughtfully packed needles and threads in her trunk. She could sew the pillow up a little bit, if her hands weren't trembling so. She wanted to run through the halls, out to the courtyard, find the stables, get on Tumble…

If I can find the river, then I can find my people…

And so would the pattern. After a time she rose, walked to the window and peered through the carved wooden screen. The women of the palace could look out upon the soldiers, but none of them could look in. The women belonged to the emperor.

The emperor. So was there no emperor now? The soldiers moved about as if nothing strange had happened. White-hatted men were loading a waggon train. Mesema thought some of their horses looked familiar. *Of course.* Her eyes followed a chestnut mare being led through the courtyard. Those horses belonged to Arigu's men.

Arigu was here, in the palace. He hadn't fled—had he exposed Beyon? Or was it Nessaket? Or someone else?

If Beyon is exposed, then what about me? She pulled the pillow close. Always with the selfish thoughts—she was born under the Scorpion's tail, after all. Sarmin was selfless in comparison.

Male voices murmured in the corridor—not Beyon's, not Arigu's; nobody she recognised. She crept across the room and opened her door a crack to peep out. A soldier stood between two graceful fountains, glancing uninterestedly at the colorful walls. She cringed as his dark eyes slid over her, but she remained unseen. He moved forwards, and eight men came behind him. He turned and whispered orders, pointing at several closed rooms. The men went through the doors.

Mesema watched the leader, hoping for some clue to what was happening. He tapped his finger against his belt, as if tracing a beat to a song. She wondered what it might be. She'd never heard a Cerani song, but now she thought maybe they had drums just like Felting ones. Doors reopened; his fingers stopped moving and he made a fist instead. He closed his eyes.

Hadassi's angry voice pierced the air. "What is the meaning of this? My husband will kill you for entering this wing!"

"You're not allowed in here!" Marren sounded more annoyed than angry.

A third woman screamed, and everything went silent except for the sound of footsteps on carpet. The men returned in twos, each hauling one of Beyon's frightened wives between them. Mesema moved from the door and crouched on the floor close to the wall, her breath suddenly ragged in her throat.

"I demand an explanation," she heard Atia say. "We are the wives of the emperor."

The leader spoke. "The emperor," he said, "is dead."

Mesema knew that was a lie; her finger traced Beyon's movements somewhere on the other side of the palace. But his wives had no way of knowing this. She kept her head low to the floor and peered out again, the dagger-pillow still clutched between her hands. The wives stared at one another until, in a single moment, they all reached the same thought.

"None of us is pregnant," said Chiassa, touching her straw-colored hair. "He had no heirs."

Mesema remembered the green vase. She wondered where Lana might be right now. Had Nessaket warned her as well?

"We're not here to kill you and the unborn," said the leader; "we're to take you downstairs. That's all."

"The assassin will kill us, then." Hadassi tried to jerk her arms away from the soldiers who held her as Chiassa screamed and fainted.

Mesema drew her arms about herself and tried to still her trembling.

The leader sighed. He looked sad, and yet impatient. "Come, now." But Hadassi had finally struggled free and now she ran towards the end of the hall. Mesema wondered if she was making for the secret door. The two soldiers who had held her chased behind, one laughing as if it were a game. He caught Hadassi just as she passed Mesema's room and grabbed her by the hair. "We'll make it quick, then," he grunted, and something warm and dark splattered Mesema's face. *What—?* She wiped it from her eyes as the dark-haired woman lay spasming, face-down on the floor. The soldier moved away. A metallic, salty taste filled Mesema's mouth. *Blood.* The soldier had drawn his dagger over the woman's throat, and the blood…

Mesema screamed, squeezing the pillow between her hands, creating a snow of feathers.

The soldier swung around, astonished at first, and then amused. He held the dagger, still dripping, at his side, not ready to use, but not sheathed either. Mesema kept her eyes on his face.

He prodded her door wider. "It's the savage girl, crawling on the floor with feathers."

"Maybe that's how they say welcome." The soldier's partner arrived at his side, stepping over Hadassi's twitching body. "If you know what I mean."

"Hey—" Another of the soldiers leaned forwards. "Wasn't she with him? The emp— Beyon?"

"I heard she was in his tent." The killer's eyes were dark, almost black.

His partner licked his lips and waved his dagger like a fan. His green eyes darted back and forth as he studied her skin. Banreh had told her the ones with the light-colored eyes were given by their families as payment to the empire. She wondered where he had come from, whether he missed his family.

"What should we do with her?" All eyes turned now to their leader. He studied her a moment, frowning. She already knew what sort of man he was; he wouldn't kill her if he didn't have to.

"We'll take her to the general." He shot a glance around his soldiers. "All of them are wanted alive." He pointed to the man clutching his dripping dagger. "You'll find yourself answering to me for that later, then to the general, and if you live long enough, the emperor's Knife might find you. Spill royal blood and there's a price to pay."

Sarmin stared at the ceiling. Something called to him, a warmth, a resonating mark in the world, and he reached out with his mind, rolled it through his consciousness as he might roll an olive across his tongue, tasting it. He breathed it in. It repelled and yet thrilled, as much as Grada's mind, Mesema's voice or the taking of Tuvaini's dagger. It went down his throat like sweet-wine and set his skin buzzing. *Blood.* When he recognised it he found even more: the after-images of violence and brutality. A sick power ran through him: spilled blood called to the bed he lay on, harm to harm. He could draw lines, if he wished, and create a pattern outside the Master's design. A pattern drawn in blood, as big as the whole palace, might hold the strength to fight back.

No; it was not yet time. He could not draw the Master's attention so early. He would work carefully, slowly, sketching it behind his eyes and keeping it secret until everything was ready. Until enough blood had been shed.

The leader grabbed her, his hand on her arm, and dragged her up and out. She tucked the pillow under her other arm, holding it closed, keeping the dacarba inside, though she knew she couldn't fight them if it came to that. She wished she had grabbed Eldra's blue feather. Two of the men carried Hadassi. Hadassi of the golden skin. Mesema's feet slid in her warm blood. The leader held Mesema's elbow so tightly she felt he would crush it. The soldiers marched all the women down the grand stairs, where it smelled of roses and the banisters gleamed with gold. They turned into a corridor, then another, and another, the corridors all blurring into one. Mesema's stomach twisted in fear. She stumbled, but the soldiers' leader kept her upright.

Arigu waited in an orange room, sitting behind a dark wooden table scattered with parchment and writing implements. She remembered those eyes, hard and all-seeing, and the way his mouth twisted as if he were tasting something unpleasant. He looked at the arrayed women, his eyes lingering over Hadassi's limp form and then Mesema and her bloody clothes. His eyes fell on the torn cushion. Then his gaze returned to the commander.

"There were four wives, Rom, not three plus a horsegirl."

"That one tried to run." The leader gestured towards Hadassi.

"We wanted them alive."

"Regrets, sir."

"I hope for your sake the emperor does not make an issue of it."

"Thank you, sir."

Mesema puzzled over Arigu's words. *The emperor?* Did he speak of Beyon?

"As for young Mesema…'

She met Arigu's eyes. Unlike these other men, Arigu might wonder what she held in her pillow. He would wonder if she knew anything, if she would try to spoil his schemes. She kept perfectly still.

But Arigu's mind was apparently on other matters.

She took a breath. Mesema, once the centrepiece of all Arigu's ambitions, no longer mattered. He must believe the prince dead, and had other plans afoot. *I'm invisible to him now.* She felt free. "Her countryman will deal with her," Arigu said.

The soldiers pulled Mesema forwards and she tripped as the light-eyed soldier opened a door at the back of the room. She tried to turn and look at Beyon's wives, but the soldiers held her too tightly. They traversed another, narrower, corridor that smelled of wet shoes and leather, opened a wooden door and pushed her through.

A lantern illuminated another wooden table, smaller and cleaner than Arigu's. On it lay a single parchment, half-covered in writing. A cold wind blew through a window in the facing wall, moving the parchment like a leaf, but a round red stone kept it from flying away. She knew the stone. She could kiss that stone. Its owner leaned out of the window, his face tilted towards the moon. As the soldiers pushed Mesema forwards he turned, surprise in his eyes.

She ran, dropping her pillow, crying, "Banreh!"

He took her in his arms, his golden hair falling softly against her cheek, and she breathed him in. The soldiers left the room, and closed the door behind them.

"What happened to you?" He drew back and looked at her gown.

"They came to the women's wing and killed one of the emperor's wives."

Her voice sounded weak to her when she said it out loud. "The blood went all over me."

He frowned. "I heard the wives were to be taken, but I never dreamed you'd be involved."

He knew? She let go of him and wrapped her arms around herself instead. "Banreh, how did you get here?"

"Don't you remember? Arigu said that if anything went wrong I should meet his man by the river. And I did."

"But the emperor sent you back with my gifts—"

"Mesema—" The same old tone now, scolding and patient both at once. "—he's not the emperor any more. He had the marks—you know what that means. An heir was found, a new emperor, one who will work with us." Banreh pulled two stools over and eased onto one, wincing as he stretched out his bad leg.

"Us?"

"The Felting."

Mesema settled onto the other stool, folding her hands together in a formal pose. *Careful, now.*

Banreh put a finger against her cheek. "Listen—what worries you? Both brothers are dead, so there is to be no royal marriage. You can go home."

Home. It came back to her in a rush: the fields, the scent of wet wool, the soft voices of the women at their craft; the way she knew what people meant when they looked at her. She could go back across the desert and leave the pattern behind, leave Sarmin on his sickbed, leave Beyon. She would return to her life, work the wool, marry a plainsman. Maybe her father would even let her marry Banreh.

If only it could happen that way… If she fled, the pattern would follow her. It would come after her mother and father and little nephews. The pattern was greedy; she could feel it in her bones. The mage who drove the pattern wanted as much as any man who started a battle, whether it was land, riches, or something else. The difference was that this was a battle most people couldn't fight. She could, though; Sarmin had showed her that. She could stay here and fight.

Banreh moved his finger over her jawline and Mesema shivered. All he ever had to do was touch her and she melted like the spring snow. She couldn't let that muddle her mind.

She cleared her throat. "Banreh, I wouldn't go if they sent me." He smiled, not understanding.

"I'm staying here to fight against the pattern."

"Fight against—?" He chuckled and kissed her forehead. "Have you been drinking too much of that sour Cerani brew? You sound mad."

She blinked and steadied herself. Arguing with Banreh was never easy. "Listen. By staying, I can help the emperor."

"You mean His Majesty Tuvaini?" He used the voice of her teacher, not the voice of her friend.

"I speak of Beyon."

"I see. I know you were with him—you had no choice. He was the emperor. But you must forget about him now and go home. If they ever suspect you might be carrying his child, they'll kill you."

"We didn't—"

"It doesn't matter." Banreh creased his brow at the pillow on the floor. "These people tolerate no heirs but themselves. Do you know what Beyon did when he became the emperor? He killed all his brothers, right out there, in the courtyard. Some of them were just babes."

Mesema swallowed, though her throat felt like stone. Sarmin had told her his brothers had died, but not that Beyon had ordered it. Beyon was Cerani, and the Cerani were brutal; even their palace god was cruel. She had seen the great walls of the city and heard the voices of the thousands who lived within those walls. She had seen the riches of the palace and the beauty of the women inside, and as she held the picture of the empire in her mind, she knew cruelty kept it all safe. She remembered how Beyon had wanted Banreh's head. Perhaps it would have been better for him, and for the empire, if he had taken it. She understood: Herzu's statue stood in the palace not so they could beg for mercy, but because the empire needed Him.

Banreh's fingers tightened around her own, and she rested her forehead on his warm hand. Cruelty did not come without its cost. It had made Sarmin sick, Beyon lonely. What would it make of her?

"Go home," he whispered.

"I—" A twinge drew her eyes westwards: Beyon. It sank through her, skin and bone. He was moving closer.

"What is it?" Banreh looked at the wall. She shrugged and looked away.

"What?"

"I can't see through walls, Banreh."

He narrowed his eyes at her. "I saw that look on your face. What does it mean, Mesema?"

She couldn't show him her finger—she could never show him. Her eyes stung with tears.

"What's wrong with you?"

She gathered the silk of her skirt in her hand, remembering how her body-slaves had transformed her from a horsegirl into a Cerani bride. What was she now?

"It's him," said Banreh, his eyes bright with understanding.

She shook her head no. "Banreh, just kiss me, because I don't know when I'll see you again."

His face went still. "But I thought we—?"

"Banreh." She took his hand in hers, her other hand, the one still unmarked. "You have taught me well—better than you know, perhaps. Let me go now and do my duty."

He put one hand on her shoulder. The other hand still clasped hers.

She sniffed. "Arigu said it was up to you—"

"This isn't about Arigu!" He was angry, at last.

"It isn't about us, either. I wish it were. Oh, how I wish it!" Mesema swallowed. "We are Felt."

Banreh put his forehead against hers. "We carry on."

"We are Felt. We carry on." A chant. A prayer. Their lips met.

She backed away quickly, not wanting to let go, taking in his stained hands, golden hair and green eyes for the last time—

His green eyes that went past her, to the wall, widening with alarm. "Mesema!"

She picked up the cushion and clenched her teeth. It kept her chin from trembling. "I must go."

She took another step backwards and her shoulders met with something hard: a man's chest. A strong man's chest, but not Beyon's; Beyon was too far away. Another hidden door in this palace where no wall could be trusted! Before she could run, a thick arm wrapped around her waist and dragged her through a narrow, dark gap. She smelled fire and spice and damp and rot. Banreh darted forwards, faster than she had thought he could, a sword somehow in his hand, but her captor kicked shut the door and it slammed in his face. Banreh pounded on the wall between them; he shouted for her, and he shouted for Arigu's men. Feathers brushed against Mesema's cheeks as she pulled her knife free and found her captor's flesh. He grunted, but held her hard as he moved through the darkness, her feet barely brushing the floor. The sound of Banreh's pounding grew distant.

The man stopped and for a moment they stood together in the midnight of the hidden passage. His strong arms released Mesema and she blinked, trying to accustom her eyes to the dark. If only she could see her way, she could try to run—but she could not even make out the man who stood before her.

"Careful." The voice came soft, and unexpectedly kind. "There's a drop." She turned to face its owner, careful to keep her balance; the echo told her of vast, empty spaces. A small flame shed light, and their eyes met in the glow. She had seen him before: hair like iron, skin like leather—the servant of Herzu she'd passed in the corridor. Then, violence had risen from his skin like heat from the desert sand. Now his eyes were calm, and he flashed his teeth at her in something close to a smile.

She spoke through the tightness in her throat. "What are you going to do to me?" She calculated how close she'd have to get to stick him; he'd stop her before that.

He looked her over, his eyes lingering briefly on the knife in her hand. "I wasn't planning on doing anything to you." He lifted a lantern from a hook on the wall and placed the small flame inside. As the light grew stronger she could make out stairs, bridges, and black chasms all around her. It was fitting that the palace, with its golden ceilings and bright mosaics, would contain a place so dark and twisting. It would have to.

"Why did you bring me in here?"

"The emperor has requested you."

Mesema's captor did not appear to be in a rush to move on, though she could hear pounding and the yelling of men in the distance. Arigu's soldiers were of little concern to him; surely she, with her pretty little weapon, constituted an even lesser threat. "I want to go back, tell my countryman—"

"That will not be possible." He tore some fabric from his tunic and wrapped it around the wound high on his leg.

She watched the blood seep through the cloth, dark in the lantern light, a warning against the future. Her fingers tightened over the gemmed hilt of Sarmin's dagger. Her vision of standing over the emperor, knife in hand, bloomed in her mind like pain. "I hurt you."

"Not too badly." He tied a knot and smiled again, as if they had reached some agreement. "Follow me. Step where I step—there are rockfalls." He turned, but instead she sank to the floor, where the stone felt cool and solid against her forehead. She did not want to harm anyone. She tried to remember the moment she had thrust that dagger into the man's thigh, but it had slipped away from her; she remembered only that it had felt right. Would it feel right when she killed the emperor? *Mirra!* The prayer broke from her unexpectedly.

"Are you well?" He sounded uncertain, though he didn't seem the uncertain type.

She ignored him and inched forwards. Her elbows met empty space and her head dropped over an abyss. Darkness spun around her, and she could no longer tell whether she looked up or down. She saw nothing, felt nothing when she ran her fingers through the air. *Is this what the pattern feels like?* The void pressed around her. *Is it like this on the inside, with no memories, no fear, no desire?* The idea tempted her. She dangled the dagger over the edge. If she dropped it into the chasm, then she could never use it again.

The old warrior caught her wrist and she started. She hadn't even noticed him moving closer, crouching beside her.

"Tuvaini's dacarba." He made a sound somewhat like laughter and twisted it from her grasp as easily as taking a toy from a baby. "This could come in handy." He put it in his belt and gathered her up.

It was *Sarmin's* knife, but she didn't correct him. "Listen. Don't give that back to me."

He looked down at her. She felt small and warm in his arms, and his fire-and-spice smell brought smoking besna leaves to mind. Some barely remembered spring evening in the longhouse, far away in both distance and time, came back to her, together with the sensation of being cradled in the dark.

"No need to decide that now," he said. "The prince must have given it to you for a reason."

He'd startled her for the second time. "How do you know the prince gave it to me?" The smell of blood on her clothes overcame his scent and her nostalgic moment was lost. She wriggled in his grasp: this was not her father, and this was not the longhouse. This was a strange man, a killer, and she'd been lost in his arms thinking of her childhood. Something in his strength and his stillness had comforted her, something she never would have believed possible when she saw him the first time outside the temple of Herzu.

"I know every weapon in this palace." He put her down and frowned. "Hurry, now; I have other things to do after this. Too many things. Step where I step."

Before long she wished he carried her still. The way was dark, the arched bridges narrow and the stairs crumbling, and on either side of their path lay the chasm. A loose stone slipped under her foot and she counted four seconds before she heard its soft thud below her. At times she wished she could crawl rather than walk, but the man moved so fast that she knew she'd soon lose him, and she didn't want to find herself alone in the darkness. She wished they were going to see Sarmin and not Beyon.

They descended a flight of stairs. There was a wall on her left, and she leaned on it with relief before following him down another flight, and another, until at last they stood on some sort of platform. The man scratched something on the wall and a door swung open. Beyond she saw bright colours, sunlight, and something that looked like a bed.

Her captor produced a length of cloth and wrapped it around his eyes. "Here we are," he said.

CHAPTER THIRTY-FOUR

Eyul watched the horsewoman sleep. Pale, she was. He could see the blue veins running beneath the skin of her throat. He wanted to press his finger there, to feel the life he'd become so expert at cutting away.

Blood crusted her garments, though it was not her own—not yet, though she would suffer soon enough for taking their side. Men died when they lost; women were punished. It would be so easy to pull the blade over that white flesh, to let her bleed out peacefully in the cool light of day. He put a hand on his Knife. The whispers writhed around the hilt, buzzing at his fingertips.

"No."

"No."

"*No.*"

He turned away from her and leaned against the far wall. Since Amalya, he had lost his way. He had killed something in himself where he thought nothing still lived, and with it went all sense of balance, until only the whispers held him now, dead children keeping him true to his oaths.

It smarted where she'd cut him, a long, shallow slice. He hadn't seen her dacarba—she'd surprised him. Something about that reminded him of Amalya.

The sun crept across the floor, lighting Mirra's face in the mosaic of ceramic, stone and glass; Her features came alive in golden hues, a burst of glory before the dark of evening. Eyul grew impatient for Beyon's return, for the time when he could go and hunt Govnan.

The horsewoman stirred and woke, studying the floor a while before sitting up and scanning the room. She looked soft and childlike in sleep, but awake, her face took on angles and edges. At last she looked in his direction and her eyes widened, but she didn't scream.

"I fell asleep?"

He spoke in a low voice, emulating Tuvaini's soothing tone.

"We must keep our voices down. They are looking for us."

"Who is looking for us?"

"Well," he said, letting humour colour his words, "just about everyone." He reached into his robes and she tensed. "Food." He produced the bread and cheese he'd lifted from the soldiers' hall, wrapped in a piece of old linen. He stepped forwards and put it on the floor, a man's length from where she sat.

She slid across the tiles on her knees and reached for the bundle.

"His Magnificence will return soon, heaven bless him," he said, although in fact he didn't know where Beyon was; he'd slipped away before dawn to wander the secret ways. It worried Eyul that Beyon could be cut down by a few Blue Shields while he waited here.

No. Govnan would die first, and then Beyon could be saved. He told himself it was so.

Eyul retreated to listen at the door, wrapping the linen about his eyes before stepping out of the shadow. Soldiers' boots or assassins' slippers would signal the same thing. Then, if she wanted it, he would open that white throat.

The horsewoman consumed everything in the napkin and then picked up the crumbs with her fingers. She wasn't dainty. Eyul could imagine Beyon liking that about her.

"My name is Mesema." She stood, facing him, one hand on the crusted blood of her gown.

"I am Eyul, son of Klemet, Fifty-third Knife-Sworn."

"Knife-Sworn? An assassin?"

"Yes."

Her throat moved as she swallowed: more scared than she looked, then.

"Where are we?"

"This was once the women's wing."

She looked around again. "It's less grand than the one I'm in. *Was in.*" She took a step forwards. "Why did you cover your eyes? Are you injured?"

More than you know. "The light hurts my eyes, that's all."

"Beyon's wives— Did you—? Have they been killed?"

She knew; she saw it in him, that he could have done it—that he *would* have done it, if things were different. Again she reminded him of Amalya. "No. I did not—and only I can kill a royal. They will still be alive." He watched her consider this. This was no naïve young girl, nor any wild savage. She might manage what lay ahead better than he'd thought.

"One of the soldiers killed Hadassi." Mesema watched the floor, as if she could see it there.

"No!" Eyul half-drew his Knife. For an instant he felt foolish, as if murder were a small crime when set against murder by the wrong person. The whispers coiled around his fingers again as the Felting woman turned towards the door.

"He comes."

"He comes."

"*He comes.*"

Mesema's stomach rolled when Beyon crashed into the room; his presence washed over her like music with all the wrong notes, or a room full of men fighting. He was not like Sarmin, and certainly not like Banreh. He walked straight over to her.

"Are you well?"

She nodded, avoiding his eyes. Purple triangles asserted themselves against the honey color of his cheeks and her finger itched, wanting to reach for them, but she dug her nails into her palms instead. It had been days since she'd seen Beyon, but she was always aware of him, aware of his marks and his memories. Beyon embodied everything she feared in the palace, including herself. The vision still pressed against her mind. *Do not forget that you chose to stay, foolish girl.* She looked through the window-screen. Down in the courtyard, white-hatted soldiers were hammering three stakes into bases.

"My lady, you should keep clear of the window." Eyul spoke from where he still knelt on the floor, his head to the tiles.

Mesema didn't realise at first that the old assassin was speaking to her. She stepped back.

"Oh, get up, Eyul." Beyon barely glanced at the man. "I brought you some clean clothes, Zabrina." He held out a swathe of ocean-colored silk. "At least, I believe these tiny scraps to be clothes."

The emperor does not deal with such matters. That's what Lana had said— but then, Beyon wasn't the emperor any longer.

"Thank you." She grabbed the cloth by its corner to avoid touching his hand. His wife's blood still crusted her fingernails. "I'm sorry…'

"Not your fault." Confusion flickered over his features. Mesema gathered the clothes and shifted on her feet.

Beyon snorted, turning to the window. "We stand within an entire wing of the palace. You don't have to change in front of me." He fell silent a moment, watching Arigu's men. "What— What are they doing?"

"I don't know." She held her new clothes against her chest like a doll, or a shield. She thought about Atia, Marren and Chiassa. Three women. Three stakes.

"Come away from the window, Your Majesty, lest you are seen." The assassin again. He stretched his wounded leg, glancing at Mesema.

I stabbed him. Will I stab Beyon next?

Beyon hit a hand against the window-screen. "Eyul." He used a different voice now, lower—colder, the voice he'd used in the tent, looking at Banreh. "They have my wives."

Instead of responding to the emperor, Eyul turned to Mesema. His eyes were still hidden by the cloth and she wondered what he looked at, and what he saw. "You should go and change now," he said in a kind voice that didn't feel kind, a voice that had steel behind it. "In another room."

Mesema nodded. The goddess tiled into the floor stared at her, eyes glowing. She knew it was a goddess because there was no man pictured with her.

Eyul pulled a bit of silk from inside his robes. Then he produced Sarmin's three-sided dagger and wrapped it up like a baby. "Don't forget your knife."

Mesema shook her head at the knife, but he thrust it at her a second time. Beyon stood motionless at the window, his back to her. Resigned, she accepted Eyul's offering. She walked slowly down the corridor and picked a plain white room. This had obviously been the women's wing in a more austere time. A bench spanned the length of three windows. They were not open windows, nor glass, nor screened with wood like the one in the other room: these windows were fitted with a translucent stone that gleamed with yellow light. She had seen jagged bits of the same stone in Sarmin's room. A small word had been carved into the very bottom, but Banreh had never taught her to read or write Cerantic words, or any words, for that matter.

Mesema wondered what Eyul was going to do about Atia, Chiassa and Marren. He put her in mind of her father, somehow, though her father was neither so strong nor so cold. Her father would try to rescue them, but if he couldn't, and they were going to be in pain… She closed her eyes against the light.

The first scream rose from the courtyard.

Nessaket bowed her forehead to the green and white rug when Tuvaini entered. She had centred herself so that the leaf pattern appeared to generate from her emerald-colored skirt. Her spine curved prettily to where her head lay against the silk, a poison flower on a golden stalk.

"Rise and face me, Empire Mother, mother to dead sons." Nessaket sat back on her heels, but kept her eyes cast down, and it angered him. She had always been ready to meet his eye, to speak before spoken to; now she chose to feign humility.

"Speak," he commanded.

"I expected you last night, Your Majesty, but you did not come to me."

"I was occupied with matters of empire." In fact he had watched the shadows glide across his wall, but there was no need to tell her that.

She kept her eyes down, calling back the girl she had been, but she was no longer that girl, and he was no longer the frightened, lonely boy in the shadow of Tahal's robes.

"Did you sleep well without me, Empire Mother Nessaket?" Her shoulders tensed with his words, but she soon found her balance. "I did not, Your Majesty. I have grown accustomed to your arms about me."

He paced around her one way, and then the other. He reminded himself of Beyon. He understood so much more about his cousin now. "We all make sacrifices."

"I know about sacrifice, Your Majesty."

Something in her tone made him turn to face her.

She shifted her knees. A strand of gleaming black hair fell over her chest. "Tahal used to say that the empire does not give itself freely. That those who want it must pay for it."

"In restless nights?"

Her voice grew strong, steely. "I have given more than restless nights, Your Majesty."

The faces of her young boys passed behind his eyes. "You knew the price."

"No price is truly known until it is paid."

Stillness fell over Tuvaini like funereal silk. "And you would teach me this?"

"I have only kept you to your bargain: no wife but myself, no children but mine."

And there it was. Herzu laid a hand upon his shoulder, his claws sinking deep. "Lapella could bear no children!"

"And Sarmin was harmless to you." She spoke in such a quiet voice that if Tuvaini had so much as brushed his slippers against the carpet, he would not have heard it. But he was standing still, and so the words reached him.

Revenge? For Sarmin? He had no idea Nessaket had felt any affection for her second son. Tuvaini knew his madness kept her from visiting him more than once or twice a year. She never spoke of him, with love, or anything else. In Herzu's temple she had agreed to pass him over for the throne, and she must have known what that entailed. She, after all, had seen the last succession, seen the bodies of those boys in the courtyard.

And yet her eyes grew wet and she looked away.

Could Sarmin have been her favorite? That mad, pacing prince who talked to himself for hours? The one who did not himself care whether he lived or died? Tuvaini recalled his wild eyes, the hair dark against his forehead, the lips that curled into a mocking snarl. "Better run, Vizier," Sarmin had said to him.

It is bad luck to kill the mad.

"Rise, Empire Mother, and leave me." Tuvaini settled into his couch. It was much softer than the throne.

She stood with effort, the stiffness of her legs betraying her age. He took no satisfaction in that—indeed, he might yet find some sympathy for her, rediscover his feelings for her in their shared loss and grief. Somewhere inside, he thought he wanted that for them. He held out hope for that. But not today.

She paused, straightening the skirt around her thighs. "Your Majesty, if I may, I have other news."

He waved a hand. "Out with it, then." It struck him once again how much he sounded like Beyon.

"I am with child."

An heir. He had expected to feel joy, but instead his mouth went dry. He rubbed his tongue against his palate before saying, "We shall have to arrange a ceremony, then. A marriage." They had discussed this; it would be a different ceremony from the usual. Normally a priest of Mirra performed a quick joining of hands in the women's quarters, moments before consummation. The emperor and his new wife were the only required witnesses. Tuvaini's wedding would show the court and the empire his new way of doing things: one wife, one heir. It would be large, and public. Already his mind went to the complications, to the concerns of his generals, the disapproval of the priests, the resentment of the nobility in the provinces. Would their wives also expect a new order? Would he cause unrest in every home in the empire?

"I will be queen." Nessaket interrupted his thoughts. She had the steel to remind him, even now.

"Leave me," he repeated, and she left, silent and graceful as a snake. Tuvaini watched the sun glide across the calligraphy on the walls. Sometimes, in the birth of morning or the fall of night, he thought he saw faces there, hidden in the swirls and hooks of ink.

He heard Beyon's wives begin screaming in the courtyard. He didn't care to wonder what method of torture Arigu's men had devised.

Mesema searched her body for new marks. Finding nothing, she scraped the blood from her sandals with Sarmin's dagger. She heard another scream and fell back against the wall as if struck.

After a moment she began her struggle with the silk, forcing the tiny bit of blue-green to cover her as modestly as possible. Her hands shook, making it difficult to fold and tie the slippery fabric.

Chiassa wailed, high-pitched and long, filling the room where Mesema stood as if she were inside it. A cry of fear, not pain, terror, as they approached her. Chiassa, with the golden curls and the funny way of speaking. Mesema sat on the bench and covered her ears. *Why didn't I say yes to Banreh?* If she hadn't moved away from him, if Eyul hadn't been able to grab her, she might be crossing the sands already.

No. The only difference is that Banreh would have fought, and been killed. She was where she belonged. If she were to help Beyon and Sarmin and honour her promise to Eldra, she belonged in the palace, not running away. And she should be with Beyon, not hiding in another room. She rebound her dagger and tucked it into the edge of her skirt before opening the door.

Beyon paced the room, his hands pulling at his black hair.

"Something must be done, Eyul—this is intolerable!"

"That is what they want you to feel, Your Majesty. There are twenty of Arigu's men in that courtyard, ten of them archers. They want to draw us out, kill us both." Eyul leaned against the wall, in shadow, his voice calm.

Another scream pierced the air and Beyon flinched. After a moment Mesema realised that she too was standing with her fists clenched tight.

Eyul's cloth-bound head turned her way and she shivered. The emperor's Knife must not be broken, Sarmin had said. Was Eyul the Knife? She could not imagine breaking that man.

Beyon quickened his pace. "I cannot leave them there to suffer," he said. "That would be the act of a cowardly man—a cowardly *emperor*."

Another scream.

"Eyul!"

"You must keep your voice down, Your Majesty."

Mesema touched Beyon's arm, but he shook her off. "How dare you command me! I am to stand here and watch them die?"

The thought wormed through Mesema's mind, and though she tried to press her tongue down, force her lips closed, it emerged as a whisper. "You could kill them."

Eyul stood straighter from the wall, his bound eyes turning towards hers. Beyon turned to her also. "What?"

From the window came a low moan. Marren's low voice, Marren of the red hair and the jade bracelets. Marren of the sharp eyes.

Mesema swallowed and found her voice. "You—You could kill them. Now. Stop— stop their suffering." Her lips felt numb. Her own words sank through her like sharp needles. It was she who had thought of this and not the emperor. Not the callous, cruel emperor who now turned to the window, regret expressing itself in his mouth, in the set of his shoulders.

"Do it," he said.

Eyul took up position before the window. The sun-dazzled courtyard was a mass of blurs, shapes drawn together in confusion, just as the women's voices joined together in agony. He had known he would not be able to see, not during the day. He drew his Knife and placed it on the sill. Then he retrieved his bow and notched the string on one end.

"Mesema," he said to the woman, the woman who had shown Beyon what Eyul could not, "take the emperor into the secret ways." He braced the tip of the bow against his foot. "Find somewhere to hide."

Beyon's voice rumbled behind him. "I will stay here. It was my decision, and I will take responsibility."

It was the first time Beyon had ever expressed such a sentiment, and though it might have been welcome at some time in the past, it was not welcome today. Eyul bent the wood over his thigh and fitted the string in place. "I do my work alone. It has always been that way."

"Come, Beyon," said Mesema, but the emperor stepped forwards.

"Eyul—"

"It will be painless," Eyul promised. Laughter from the Knife.

"Can you keep that promise, Knife-Sworn?"

"It will be painless," Eyul said again.

"We'll wait in my tomb, then." Beyon allowed the woman to lead him away.

Eyul breathed a sigh of relief as he checked the tension in the bowstring. *His tomb is a strange choice, but wise.* He turned to the Knife again, tapping it with one finger. "There," he murmured. "You've helped me before."

A rustling, and then, "You have to kill them."

"Yes."

"The soldiers are too many and you have little time."

Three women. Three women to add to my list. "I know this." He examined his arrows, chose the first one.

"You are the emperor's Knife."

"I know this also. Where do I point my bow?"

Another voice, younger. "You end both the innocent and the damned, but you are not damned."

"Good. Now tell me where to shoot." He would bring mercy to these women, then find Govnan and kill him. He should have sent Beyon farther away; the tomb was too exposed, too dangerous, but they were not yet ready to move to the desert. The voices were right: there was not enough time. Killing Govnan might buy a little more.

"You bring peace. You send souls to paradise. You give an end both swift and kind. Few in this world have one strong enough to offer mercy in their final moments."

"You mock me."

"Never." A pause. "To your right… down. Down. Now." Eyul let the arrow fly.

"Right through the heart." Satisfaction.

Eyul strung a second arrow. "Again." He could hear shouts below him, white figures running across the diamond pattern.

"Hurry."

"Left, down. No, up. Now!"

Eyul reached for the third and last arrow.

"Be glad you cannot see what the soldiers have done to them, assassin. Be glad that it is not yet time for you to uncover your eyes."

"It will be night soon enough." He heard men running on the floor beneath him, thundering towards the stairs.

"That is not what I meant… Now!"

Eyul released the string and slung the bow across his back. *Do not think about those women. Do not think about Amalya. Keep moving.* He sheathed the Knife and turned for the secret ways.

"An excellent shot. Govnan looks impressed."

Eyul paused, his hand on the hidden door. The soldiers' boots echoed on the stairs, seconds away. "He saw?"

"He watched you from the prince's tower."

Anticipation drew Eyul's breath. At last he would have his moment with

Govnan, to avenge Amalya and to open the way for the hermit to fight the pattern-curse. He slipped into the ways just before the soldiers entered the room behind him.

Eyul uncovered his eyes and ran through the dark, not as quickly as he might have before. The cut made by the horse-woman slowed him down, but he was still fast enough to stay ahead of any would-be pursuers. He knew every drop and chasm in the darkness, and when to take extra care where another man might meet a surprising end. And there were other men; the secret ways had become much less secret of late. He had seen, at various times, Carriers, soldiers, and even Old Wives sneaking along the dark paths to unknown destinations, though they did not see him, or hear him.

Eyul did not pause in his rush towards Govnan, though when he found him, he would wait, he would savour it. But he would find him first.

Halfway there he decided not to enter through the prince's room. The prince, according to Tuvaini, was insane, unpredictable—he might warn Govnan, or interfere in some other way, and Eyul did not relish the idea of killing Beyon's last brother. He would use the door near the tower, at the bottom of the stairs, and wait for Govnan there.

At last he stood unobserved before a wooden door. This one required an arrow shaft. He pushed one in as quietly as he could and gave it a twist, though he needn't have been so careful: the door screeched open on rusty hinges. He kept to the darkness a few minutes longer, waiting to see if anyone was reacting to the sound, but he heard nothing. He wrapped his eyes against the low light and moved out of the hidden ways.

He moved into the shadows behind the curving stairs of the prince's tower. He heard footsteps above him, coming down. The old man was taking the steps carefully, but that didn't mean his elemental would be slow. Eyul looked at the soot-blackened walls, the ash on the floor. Govnan was more dangerous than Amalya had been, but that did not concern him. Govnan would die.

Eyul wished it were night. He wanted to be able to witness the disappointment on Govnan's face when he realised he'd been caught. The fear when the Knife stopped his heart.

"Do you wish to see?"

Eyul fingered the twisted hilt. "Of course I wish to see, but I can't." He kept his voice below a whisper lest the old man hear him.

"But you can. You have clung too long to darkness when the Knife cuts both ways."

Eyul listened for Govnan.

"You are the emperor's Knife."

"You repeat yourself." Somewhere above him, the high mage coughed. Had he heard? Eyul drew the Knife from its hilt.

"You end both the innocent and the damned, but you are not yourself damned."

A child giggled. "I am Pelar, who died at your hand."

"I am Asham, who died at your hand."

"I am Fadil, who died at your hand." The youngest of them all.

Eyul fell back against the wall, tears filling his eyes. Of course they were—he had known that—he *must* have known. "Why do you help me?" He moved his lips more than spoke, but the Knife heard him nevertheless.

"You are the emperor's Knife. Only you can shed royal blood without damnation."

"You said that." *Had they?*

Silence.

Govnan drew closer.

Asham, the eldest, said, "You must see. You are not damned; you are the Knife. You cut both ways and you cut me. But I will help you."

"I will help you," said Pelar.

"I will help you," said Fadil.

"We don't want the Master to use you," said Asham.

Eyul's fingers tensed on the Knife. "Govnan." A thought more than a word.

Silence.

At last Eyul saw the flaw that had been invisible to him before: Govnan was not the enemy. He had accepted what he was told without thinking of another possibility. But he was learning. Amalya's trust had not been misplaced.

"You can see." Pelar's joyous voice.

"You will not be broken," Fadil said.

Eyul reached for his linen wrappings, then hesitated. *Amalya?*

"The Pattern Master took her before you did. She is not with us."

"They are coming." Fadil, serious.

"Very close." Asham.

Eyul freed his eyes and blinked away his tears. He was ready. The sun's dying light trickled through the unseen windows high above him. Standing at the bottom of Sarmin's tower, Eyul was able to pick out every crack, every pebble on the stair, every grain in the ash-cloud that billowed under Govnan's approaching feet. He saw everything, and it caused him no pain. He stepped out into the light.

The high mage came around the last curve and peered down just as heavy boots sounded in the corridor. Eyul motioned to him and mouthed "Carriers." Govnan had burned the tower; he was powerful. Together they could overwhelm the patterned men. But the old man crept back up the stairs and out of sight. *Strange.*

Five Carriers entered and spread out from the base of the stairs to the wall. Though they still wore the clean blue uniforms of the royal guard with burnished pins of rank on their collars, the marks had taken their sense of decorum. Three had discarded their hats; on two they sat askew, the feathers dragging like those of dead birds. The pattern drew parallel lines across their cheeks and noses and marked their chins with triangles of deep blue.

Their faces looked identical now, but they had once been their own men. One, Eyul recalled, had been a joker who spent his free nights playing dice; another had been in love with a kitchen girl, always finding an excuse to stop by the ovens when he should be on patrol. The one in the middle had been a Beyon loyalist. Eyul had told him about the emperor's meeting place in Mirra's garden—but he did not have time to ponder the implications of that right now, because all five had drawn their long hachirahs and were moving forwards. Eyul kept light on his feet, watching their movements, waiting for his opening. The Knife felt warm in his hand.

"Hello," he said, "I bring peace."

They did not react, other than to step towards him again, their eyes blank and unfocused, their weapons ready. *An assassin must be fast and clean. Above all, fast.* He ducked beneath the swinging of two swords, slit the first from hip to shoulder, and cut the second Carrier's hamstring. *Economy of motion, an absence of fear.* These are the first pillars of the Grey Path. He rolled away, ignoring the pain as a blade scraped against his chest, and used his feet to knock the fifth one down. Now the Carriers were between him and Govnan.

One of the Carriers spoke, his voice flat. "Where is the high mage, assassin?"

Eyul smiled. "How would I know?" If Govnan had no defence against the Carriers, then he would protect him: he would do it for Amalya, for Beyon, for the empire. He would do it because that was his purpose. Blood seeped from his wound and over his ribs, soaking his shirt. The wound the horsewoman had given him stung like a hot needle.

Four moved forward as one. The last was dragging his leg behind him, and Eyul made a dervish spin to the far right, slitting that Carrier's throat before he could swing his heavy blade. *Be fast, keep close. Knife-work is intimate.* The fifth was getting up from the floor; barely pausing, Eyul kicked him again, sending him sprawling on his stomach, and dived backwards, out of range of a hachirah. He was dancing to a tune no one else could hear. This was a game he played well. No dead princes, no mage-girl, just Eyul and a sharp edge with death behind it.

They were better fighters now than they had been as guards, but it didn't matter. *Move fast; their boots and heavy blades make them slow.* Before the Carrier could raise his sword to swing again Eyul had launched himself forwards and to the left, landing on the prone man's back and hearing the snap of bone. He ignored his own pain—*getting old; pain is for later.* He leaped clear and turned to face the Carriers again. Two were left on their feet.

The one on Eyul's right charged him, hachirah held high. The other, lame, pulled himself forward with some effort. *Foolish.* Perhaps the person guiding them had grown impatient. Eyul rolled below the slice the first made through the air and got to his feet so close that he could smell the Carrier's stale breath. His head struck the man's chin as he rose to his feet. Teeth snapped together, and part of the Carrier's tongue fell clear. Knife scraped bone as Eyul stabbed him in the heart.

The last Carrier wrapped an arm around Eyul's neck, lost his balance and pulled them both to the floor. Eyul held the Knife firmly as he fell. The twisted metal of the hilt was easy to grip, despite the blood. He lay on top, the Carrier cutting off his breath from behind.

Eyul twisted in the Carrier's grip, found the man's ribs and stabbed down. Immediately he could breathe again. He rolled over to the last, the one with the broken ribs, and slit his throat.

Only then did he notice that the Knife had been silent. He looked over at the stairs and found Govnan looking down at him. "You didn't use your fire," he said, neither accusation nor question.

Govnan smiled. "Prince Sarmin separated me from Ashanagur."

The mad prince? Eyul stood and sheathed his Knife, surprise taking his words.

Govnan descended the last few steps. "Ashanagur was always able to sense flesh," he said, "and though he is gone, it appears he has left that echo of himself with me." He looked out, beyond the archway. "There are more coming."

"Let's get to the ways." Eyul moved to the secret door. He twisted an arrow shaft in the hole to release the catch and together they entered the darkness, tracing their way from memory.

"They are all around," said Govnan in a low voice, "closing in. They think I have the power to get in their way."

"You don't?" Eyul's thoughts turned to Tahal in the church, to Amalya in her tent. Had all hope been lost? Had it all been for nothing? That didn't feel right—it *couldn't* be right.

"I don't." Eyul felt the man's robes brush against his arm and caught the scents of char and sulphur. "But Prince Sarmin does. His magic is older than anything the Tower can access."

So, Tuvaini, you missed something in all your scheming. The mad prince, Tuvaini had called him; useless. He had been wrong. The spark in the line of emperors that had begun with Uthman the Conqueror lived on in his descendants. Would the power that vanquished a continent be enough to defeat the pattern?

Eyul tried to conjure an image of the prince. He remembered Sarmin as a young man, quiet and bookish. Tuvaini had described him very differently.

"The magic in your Knife is similar to his, incorporated in metal." Govnan touched the hilt of the Knife and Eyul jerked away. Another man's hand on the Knife felt like a violation. Could Govnan hear the dead princes? He thought about them and their brother Sarmin.

Govnan led the way up thin, crumbling stairs. "What were you doing there, at the bottom of the burned-out tower?" he asked.

Eyul tested each step before giving it his full weight. "I was going to kill you."

"But you saved me instead." Govnan reached the landing and turned to face him, the darkness of the ways concealing his expression. "You did kill Amalya, though?"

"Not by choice." Eyul felt momentarily dizzy and pressed a hand against his tunic, sticky with blood.

Nothing more was said as they crossed bridges and ascended more stairs; Eyul heard only Govnan's laboured breathing ahead of him and the distant sound of boots. He moved with care. He'd never been to the Tower through the ways and he was unfamiliar with the treacherous twists and narrow bridges in his path. For the first time the smell of rot that rose from the chasm filled him with nausea.

"They can't enter the Tower, can they?" That made sense to Eyul: in all the years of the pattern-curse, not one mage had been marked or killed by a Carrier—not until Amalya left the Tower's protections.

"No. Not yet."

They traversed the blackness in silence. At last the high mage stopped and said, "This is the last stair. Beyond it is one more bridge, then the door to the Tower."

Eyul heard the sound of metal touching metal and caught the stink of lamp-oil. There was a sizzle, then the old man's face was lit in shades of red. In the play of flame and shadow, Eyul remembered Metrishet and felt lightheaded.

Govnan replaced the lamp on the wall. "There are Carriers ahead and behind."

"I will clear your way," Eyul said, steadying himself on his feet.

"They think I am the one who works the old magics." Govnan met Eyul's eyes, and Eyul understood what was left unspoken: *They don't know Prince Sarmin is alive.*

Eyul would keep the secret. He would defend Govnan as if everything depended upon it, as if no one else mattered. He fingered the hilt of his Knife and spoke silently to the young brothers. "I could use your help."

The Knife was silent a moment, and then Eyul heard Asham say, "We will help. It is almost the end."

"The end of what?"

"The end of us."

In the low light Eyul could see a crowd of Carriers, eight of them, standing at the foot of the bridge. Four held hachirahs. Two had daggers, and the others clutched makeshift weapons: a lamp-pole, a sack filled with something heavy—rocks, perhaps. Eyul felt his own blood sticky against his stomach.

Make it good, Knife-Sworn.

Eyul ran at them like a bull, and the first Carriers fell into the dark.

"Good," said Asham.

That's two. Eyul steadied on his feet and gripped his Knife.

Govnan had left for the Tower long before, leaving a burlap bag full of bread, dried meat, and olives. It was Sarmin's first food since Ink and Paper stopped coming, but he was not hungry. The screaming women in the courtyard had brought back the memory of little Kashim, both his cries and the terrible silence that followed. They had brought back his loss and his pain and his futile anger. And just as on that terrible night so many years ago, Eyul the assassin had done the killing. Govnan had called it a mercy, but Sarmin would not hear it. He knew the truth. *It is always wrong.*

He leaned back against the pillows and felt the blood sinking into the courtyard tiles. And there was more: somewhere below him a battle had been fought, and the blood of many pooled into one. *Govnan?* He reached out with his mind, tried to guess who had died, but he could not.

Everywhere blood fell he gathered it to him. There was too much, far too much, and yet not enough to make his own design, to write his own will into blood and pictures and oppose the Master.

An anticipatory silence had fallen over the Carriers. The Master's hand drew their threads taut. He altered his pattern, tightening and twisting the threads until Sarmin felt the breath rush out of him. The spaces and ways he travelled stretched and narrowed; there was nowhere to hide. Sarmin lay trapped, a fish in the Master's net—unless and until he could step out of it and into his own design.

He thought he would lose this game. He had seen the Master's work. He had copied it, passed through it, admired its beauty. But now, when he was so close, and the need so strong, he doubted that he could create such a masterpiece of his own. He needed to learn more about the writing of a red pattern, a blood pattern. Grada's desert journey would help, if enough time remained. Perhaps in that Mogyrk church Grada would find the key.

The pattern writhed around its axis, the centre, where the Master sat spinning his web. They were approaching the endgame. The Master's power was overwhelming; his plan was without fault. Except that he hadn't seen Sarmin. And the emperor's Knife remained unbroken. There was hope. *A hidden piece could spoil the Push.*

Sarmin opened his eyes and searched for the hidden ones in the wall. "Will he find me, Zanasta, before I make my own pattern?" The moonlight slid over the calligraphy, a soft hand silencing any mouths that might respond. "Aherim?"

Silence. They had turned their backs on him. He was friendless in his soft prison.

"Grada?"

Grada followed the road from Gemeth west along the banks of the River Blessing, passing rice fields and reed beds, villages, river ports, and the holiest of temples at the Anwar Quays. She had walked twenty miles on the first day, twenty-five the second. Days passed, and she kept on. The dust coated her legs to the knee and her skin looked almost as pale as Sarmin's. She thought of the prince often as she walked, and when she lay beside the road at night, wrapped in her cloak, she thought of nothing else.

"*Grada?*"

"Sarmin? Are you with me?" She huddled deeper into her cloak and coiled in the sand.

"Always. We are two and one. It is like the Many."

Grada shuddered. "It is not like the Many. The Many was—"

It was rape.

"I'm sorry." Sarmin's thoughts moved behind her eyes.

"The Many… You know when the blowfly bites you and lays its eggs under your skin, and you have to let the maggots grow and crawl around inside you before it's safe to cut them out?"

"No."

"Oh. Well, the Many was like being bitten by a thousand blowflies, but knowing you'll never get the maggots out, no matter how big they get."

Sarmin felt the crawling of blowfly maggots. He had never been bitten, but Grada's memories were there in his head and on his tongue as he lay on his bed fifty miles away in Nooria.

"I'm sorry."

"But this—" Grada shaped the thought in bright colours, "the two of us, together, it's… grapes and honey, flowers, cool water."

"Better." Sarmin put a smile on her lips.

"Better."

Eyul thrust out his leg and sent the fourth Carrier spinning into darkness. Asham's voice murmured, giving warning and advice, a soft and weary comfort in Eyul's bloody work. He could hear Govnan behind him, his breath quick. Eyul ducked under the bag of rocks and rolled to the side, coming to the very edge of the platform, almost losing himself in the chasm. He pushed himself up again, and his Knife sliced the artery it sought.

As he turned to the sixth Carrier, he heard the twang of a bow.

CHAPTER THIRTY-FIVE

Mesema sat with her back against the wall, cradling Beyon's sleeping head in her lap. She tried to move her numb legs, to regain some feeling without waking him. She had passed hungry and passed tired. She had even passed beyond embarrassment when, a few hours ago, Beyon showed her where she could urinate into a chasm in the secret ways by straddling two slender bridges. When she was finished, he did the same.

As they waited for Eyul, Beyon fell into a restless sleep.

Above her reached the scaffold used by the artists who had been working Beyon's face into the vaulted ceiling of his tomb. Either fear or orders had caused them to abandon their trowels and picks and leave the tomb in disarray. Disembodied eyes and the bridge of a nose stared down at her in shades of topaz and amber. Though unfinished, it was a good likeness.

Beyon's coffin lay before her, as big as two horses and worked in gold and silver. It was the twin to the tomb of Satreth I, behind it. Stairs rose beside Satreth's tomb, for the common people to view the body of the Reclaimer. At the foot of Beyon's tomb, workmen had placed the first marble step.

She wanted to leave this place.

Eyul had not returned. Perhaps he had tried to rescue the women. Her idea to kill them had been cruel, but the assassin must have seen the necessity of it. He could not have been so foolish as to risk himself.

She shivered at the trail of her own thoughts. Hours ago Beyon's wives had been laughing and talking—though they were childless and trapped in the women's wing, their lives of no significance to the empire, still they had had meaning to themselves and to their gods. They did not deserve to die like that; it was wrong to let them—

—but so much was already wrong, and she could not change the cruel ways of the palace. Beyon should understand that; he walked those ways himself. Nevertheless, he had been strange with her ever since they left Eyul.

But I can understand if he is afraid of me. I am afraid of me too.

Beyon stirred and sat up. He met her eyes, then turned away.

"Eyul?" he asked, and when she shook her head, he said, "Then we should go to the desert. My men are waiting. I don't know how many…" His voice trailed off. He stood and straightened his robes.

She wondered how many men had stayed faithful after hearing of Beyon's marks. Her father had always had to remain strong; he could never betray any doubt or any hint of illness if he wished to maintain his Riders' respect. She wondered if even Banreh would stay by his side if he showed himself to be weak.

Some of those waiting in the desert could be twice-treacherous, pretending to betray the new emperor, but instead turning upon Beyon. That would be the best way to kill him—to gain his trust, get in close.

Just as she had. The vision reappeared in Mesema's mind, tracing Beyon's lifeless form in sand and blood, putting the knife in her hand. It would come to fruition, and soon. She had the feeling of running downhill, speed overtaking her, compelling her feet to rush headlong. She almost turned her arms in a pinwheel to slow down, but instead, through long practice, she calmed herself by counting stitches. Beyon pulled a pouch from his belt and shook the contents into one hand.

"I have honeyed nuts. I forgot about them until now."

She plucked one from his palm. It was shiny, golden, hard; it barely looked like food. At home, honey kept the consistency of butter, not stone. She popped it into her mouth and rolled it on her tongue, tasting sweet and salt together. She reached for a second, but found herself thinking of Beyon's wives instead, and no longer felt hungry.

"I can see why you keep these in your belt," she said. "They're delicious."

"They're not for me. I usually give them to the slave children."

"You like children?" she asked. The Bright One rose in her mind, though she couldn't see it.

He frowned, studying the floor, where a god Mesema didn't recognise held a hammer aloft. She realised with a pang that Beyon did not wish to discuss children with her now that his wives were dead, now that she had told Eyul to kill them.

But he forgot his own nature. He had threatened to behead Banreh; he had made Sahree, Tarub, and Willa disappear.

"Beyon," she said, wiping salt from her fingers, "listen. What did you do with Sahree and the other body-slaves from the desert?"

"The dungeon." He frowned again. "Probably still there."

"With everything that's happening, will the guards remember they have them?"

"Maybe. Maybe not."

Mesema imagined the kindly old servant starving to death on the cold floor of a stone cell.

He must have seen something in her expression, for he raised his hands in a defensive gesture. "They could have seen your moon-mark. I did it to protect you."

"Exactly," she said, meeting his eyes. "Beyon, listen. I didn't want your wives to die. Cerana brought me here, and Cerana brought the marks to you and me. Cerana has its terrible gods and the prices they demand. The rules of this game were made long before I started playing."

"I know that." He sat down beside her again. "But it's not just Cerana. The rules of Settu are the rules of the world."

She thought about her father, surrounded by the men in his longhouse. He and Banreh huddled together over ink and lambskin, planning war and alliances. There was always blood to pay, always a sacrifice. "I don't know," she said, but she thought she did.

"You think I'm angry at you because my wives died?"

"I thought, maybe." Tears welled in her eyes. "It was a terrible thing."

Atia of the haughty eyes, Chiassa of the golden curls, Hadassi of the pouting mouth and her attention to rank, Marren of the wink and the joke.

He took her hands. "It's true, but not the way you think. If my wives had been kept alive and screaming, I would have gone to save them—not because I loved them; I didn't. They were my mother's creatures; all of them spied on me from the moment they came to the palace. But they were my women, and my responsibility. Tuvaini knows me well. He knows what will draw me out." He drew a breath before continuing, "You were right to protect me from charging in. It's only... When I heard you say the words, I couldn't help but think that the palace had corrupted you—that I had corrupted you—and I was sorry for that."

She looked at their joined hands. "The palace corrupted you as well."

"I was born to it. Sometimes I think that's what the pattern is: the palace's own stink, written on my skin."

"I don't think that."

"You are a good person, Zabrina," he said, kissing her hair. "I've told Eyul to kill many times, and it wasn't always the right thing to do. I thought fear and cruelty were my best tools, but now I see there are other ways to rule. Tuvaini may well be a better emperor."

"I don't believe that. You want to be the emperor."

He laughed. "Of course I *want* to be the emperor, but that doesn't mean I'm a good one. Those are completely different things."

"I like you better now than when you were the emperor." That was true.

"Now, maybe, but we'll see about tomorrow, right?" They both laughed.

"That's about right," she said.

"Mesema," he said, surprising her by using her real name, "it's all slipping away—my throne, my wives—I can barely feel them any more. I can only feel the end coming."

She lifted her head and listened.

"Sometimes I tried so hard to be what an emperor should be, but really all I could think of was having a great tomb, like Satreth. Part of me always just wanted to join my brothers."

I think you will. You will. She pressed her moon-mark to his as she blinked away tears. "Don't slip away just yet. You have a brother who is still alive."

The memories came, happier, but fainter this time: Pelar, running with a red ball. Beyon, cuddled with Sarmin and a book, both boys so small they had room to share on one cushion. His sisters, running after a shaggy dog. Laughter. Sarmin swearing his fealty, Beyon's hand on his head. Mesema on her horse, the wind in her hair.

CHAPTER THIRTY-SIX

Eyul crawled through the secret ways, his blood drawing an invisible path behind him in the dark. He'd taken an arrow below his ribs and a dagger above his knee, but he had overcome the Carriers in the end and Govnan rested safely in the Tower. Now Asham told him to find Prince Sarmin. It hurt. All of it hurt, ever since Amalya; it was right to be wounded, bloodied, to be so damaged. Now he looked the way he felt.

The Knife kept him awake. Whenever blackness appeared before his eyes, or his arms collapsed beneath him, the voices prompted him to keep going. "Only twenty bridges and five hundred steps to go," they said at first, then, "Only thirteen bridges and three hundred steps." Eyul couldn't fathom how they were keeping count; he just crawled on.

He met no other denizens of the secret ways, neither Carriers, nor women, nor aristocrats going about their clandestine business. The Knife guided him, and his path lay clear. At this moment he could see a lantern moving upwards across the chasm: two figures, climbing stairs with ease. A man's voice drifted across the black, but his words eluded Eyul. Could it be Tuvaini with Azeem, perhaps? Herran, with a young assassin? It didn't matter; they wouldn't come to Eyul's side of the way.

Peering at the dark figures made him dizzy and he rested his head against the cool, rough stone.

"Don't stop, Knife. Only eleven bridges and two hundred and thirty-two steps to go. We must see Sarmin." Asham was always serious, determined.

"Sarmin," echoed Fadil, his voice dreamy.

Eyul placed a hand on the next step, and pulled himself up. A corpse-smell filled his nose. Whether it rose from below or from himself, he did not know. "And then what?" he asked, the question released between his teeth.

"He will know what to do with us," Asham said.

"Our brother!" Pelar could not contain his excitement.

"I will die?" The thought occurred to Eyul, but he found he cared little. Silence.

Eyul reached for the next step.

Night fell over the desert, bringing relief from the heat of the sun. Grada moved between the dunes, listening to the song of their whispering sands. The wind played the wastes as a musician would his strings, the tune rising and falling to match her footsteps, up and down, back and forth.

Discordant sounds threw off Grada's rhythm; a distant neigh of a horse caught her ear and then, a second later, the clash of men's voices. She scrambled crosswise on a high dune, then crosswise in the other direction. *Easiest way to get to the top.* There were things she knew, now, that she hadn't known before: Carrier things, though Sarmin had freed her. She balanced on the crest, watching a waggon-train moving north under the moon. Behind them followed soldier upon soldier, ten abreast, the line trailing all the way back to Nooria.

"My Prince. Sarmin." She knew she was always welcome to call on him. She smiled. Just thinking he would join her made the water-pouches feel light across her shoulders.

She must have drawn him from sleep, for he was foggy and slow to form his thoughts. She saw only images: his room, the emperor in his grand robes, and a pretty girl with sand-colored hair. He suppressed the last as he gathered himself.

"Grada."

"An army moves north. Is that your brother?"

Sarmin shuffled through his knowledge, gained from books and scraps of conversation. "Do they wear blue hats?"

"No, white."

"Show me."

She opened herself to him, guided his eyes.

"One of the generals." He reached back through his mother's words. "Arigu just came from the north; perhaps he returns."

Only one rider lacked a white hat, a man with golden hair and pale skin. He wore a loose-fitting, colorful tunic. He turned and looked in Grada's direction as he passed, but his gaze went past her, to the dunes beyond. She could not read it.

She felt the spark of Sarmin's interest. "That one. He reminds me of someone."

The girl. Grada said nothing, but kept her eyes on the blond man. It stung when Sarmin hid his thoughts from her.

"They go north," Sarmin said at last, returning to her with confidence, "to the Wastes. Stay out of their way and they will not bother you." And then, softer, apologetically, "Thank you for showing me."

"Of course, my Prince."

He withdrew, and she continued across the sands. For the first time she felt alone.

Sarmin must have slept, because when he opened his eyes his lamp had burned out and a man was calling his name.

"My Prince."

Sarmin felt under his pillow. The dacarba was still gone.

"Prince Sarmin."

Sarmin opened his eyes. He recognised the man sitting on his bed from his travels in Carrier-dreams. Iron hair, strong arms—but the eyes were different. They were softer than he remembered. He sat up in his bed. "You're the assassin Eyul. You killed my brothers." For an instant Sarmin saw him clearly through the years, through the broken window and across the palace yard, Kashim at his feet with the blood spreading, looking up, returning his stare, unreadable.

Eyul hunched over, one hand on his abdomen, his face drawn and pale.

He said, "I am... the emperor's Knife. I brought them peace."

"And now you bring this peace to me?"

Eyul shook his head. The broken shaft of an arrow protruded between the red fingers on his belly.

Sarmin could sense the blood now, feel it resonating with the courtyard and the soldiers' halls, and with his own blood, drying on his bed. "You're injured." He took no joy in it, and that surprised him.

"Shot through the gut." The assassin grimaced. "Took me... a long while to get here. The Knife wanted to come to you."

"My knife?" But the dagger Eyul drew was of dull metal with a twisted, bloodstained hilt. Sarmin pulled back from it.

"Can... you hear them...? Pelar and Asham—?" Eyul wobbled against the bedpost. He took Sarmin's right hand and pressed the ugly weapon into his palm. "No damnation," he whispered.

In the instant of that first touch Sarmin felt the blood throb in his veins, in the palace, in the ways, the yards, the Maze, all the spilled blood pulsing to his design, ready to flow in new patterns. He felt the wrongness and the rightness of it, like impossible decisions: kill the one for the many, the many for the one.

Sarmin pushed back his covers and stood, the knife in his hand. "There was a time I'd have relished this moment. I'd have slit your throat and still not felt the debt repaid. But you didn't take my brothers from me—neither did my father, not really. You are the emperor's Knife, the sharp edge of his decisions. And the emperor is the empire, the voice of its will...'

Eyul's head lolled, his attention turned inwards, to his blood and pain.

Sarmin frowned. "Lie back. You're hurt." He examined Eyul's wound. "I have no skill in medicine. I can take things apart... making is harder, mending more so, I imagine." Sarmin took Eyul's hand and settled beside him. "I would call Govnan if I could. He might be able to help." The assassin looked old, older even than when he had woken Sarmin just moments before. Age wrinkled around his eyes; a thin string of drool crept from the corner of his mouth. Sarmin held his hand. *It's not good to be alone.* He spoke in a quiet voice, like the old mothers to small children. "It was the empire, you see, the empire that protects us all. There must be sacrifices. On the Settu board you cannot make the Push without losing pieces. The Pattern Master understands this. I understand it now."

Eyul raised his head and smiled. "The Knife," he said.

"Yes, I have it."

"No damnation… but I am sorry, nonetheless." Sarmin felt sure the man was dying. "Grada!"

He found her in her travels, sand between her toes, sun hot on her back. "My Prince."

"There is a man dying here. What should I do?"

She showed him images: her father, her sister, her neighbour. Life in the Maze was fleeting and desperate. If hunger or disease didn't catch you, then likely the violence would. She had sat by many deathbeds, helped dig a dozen holes. He cried for her.

"Hold his hand," she said, "speak of Mirra."

"I would have taken her fishing." Eyul spoke in whispers, his eyes fixed on the ceiling gods, not seeing.

Sarmin pulled him close.

"It's not right—" Eyul's words came with his breath, "—the things they make us do."

And they sat together and Sarmin held the assassin as he once held his brother, and spoke of Mirra.

CHAPTER THIRTY-SEVEN

Mesema dreamed of riding Tumble. She crashed through the tall wheat and took the sharp turns by the riverbed that only her father's best Riders would attempt. She galloped back up the hill and jumped the sheep fence, scaring the animals and the Red Hoof thralls in the pen. She raced along the mountain road, avoiding the mud and waterfalls of spring, until she had a view of the plains stretching beyond her father's lands and into the realms of the traders-who-walked.

The wind blew, raising dust from twenty thousand horses and fifty thousand feet. She saw Windreader, Black Horse, Blue River, Flat Earth, even Red Hoof ribbons raised aloft on spears. The Cerani marched beside them, breastplates bright in the sun, their lines straight, their shoulders proud. The enemy poured down to meet them from the eastern mountains, descending on strange shaggy mounts, so many that she couldn't see the stone beneath their feet. The enemy's cloaks made a pattern of shifting colours and light, unmistakable once recognised, not the Pattern Master's design, but threatening nonetheless. It spread over the grass and reached beneath the feet of her father's men. Mesema tried to shout a warning, but her mouth would not open.

"Mesema." Someone shook her shoulder. "Mesema, dawn approaches."

"I'm awake," she said, sitting up and opening her eyes. Her voice sounded loud, and she realised Beyon had been whispering.

"You had a bad dream." He fiddled with a bundle under his arm. "I got blankets and food."

"You shouldn't have gone. It's dangerous."

"It's dangerous to stay here. In fact, I was thinking we should hide in the tomb until nightfall."

"We are in the tomb."

He motioned behind him. "I meant in the tomb. It has airholes—we can close the lid. That way if anyone comes in here they won't see us."

Mesema looked with horror at the sarcophagus. The lid had been turned diagonally to its base, as if someone had put something inside it, or taken something out. "I think we should go back to the ways, find Sarmin."

"At nightfall." He paused. "The ways are full of Carriers."

"They didn't catch you."

"I know. I can *hear* them."

"How long have you been able to hear them?"

He bit his lip. "For a few hours."

Mesema looked again at Beyon's tomb. She wondered if Carrier voices could influence him, compel him, without his knowing. She shook her head. "How does it make a difference if we find Sarmin by day or by night? We should go now."

"I'm tired," he said, and she wondered if he meant something beyond sleep. "I need to rest."

Mesema wanted Sarmin more than anything in that moment, his soft voice, his kind face. The way he could look at something difficult and give it a name, change it. Mesema glanced at Beyon. She knew he was different from the night before, but she couldn't say how. "All right, we'll rest. And then, if the coast is clear, we'll go straight to Sarmin."

"Good. I'll lift you over." But when Beyon hoisted her above the rim of the gold-and-silver-filigreed tomb, the feeling of wrongness overcame her once again. The silk wrappings meant for his corpse already waited in place. A ceremonial sword made of gold rested on its side, along with an elaborate crown. Beyon would never wear such a crown or such a sword. A strong resin smell rose from it all, a smell of storage chests and funerals.

"No! It's not right—put me down. Put me down!" Fright overwhelmed her caution.

"Shhh." He pushed her over the edge and began his own climb.

She knelt among the rich silks of his shroud. "Listen. I don't like it. I *really* don't like it." *Something terrible is going to happen.*

He settled beside her and rolled open his bundle. "You've always been so brave—I can't believe you're screaming about a tomb." Between the rough material of his stolen blankets Beyon had hidden bread, cheese, dried meats and fruits, and even a skin full of liquid.

Mesema stared at the feast. "I'm very hungry."

"Then eat." He turned his attention to the lid, pushing it in line with the tomb, closing them in.

She could see the weight of it written in the straining of his muscles. She didn't think she could open it alone. She swallowed, and tried to stop her heart from beating so quickly. *The stitches, do the stitches.* She embroidered a garden of flowers in her mind, lily, rose, and thorn. The lid settled into place, and the filigree dappled the morning light, putting Beyon's face half in shadow. His marks looked darker of a sudden.

"I thought you were going to eat." Beyon's eyes flashed towards her.

"I am, I just…" A puff of air escaped her mouth.

Beyon cocked his head, as if listening to something she couldn't hear.

Mesema put a date in her mouth and pressed it with her tongue.

"Mesema." He touched her cheek. "Do not be frightened."

"I'm trying."

He took her chin in a gentle grip. "Now, chew."

She chewed and swallowed. It did help her feel better. She reached for a piece of cheese, and then a piece of bread. She opened the skin and took a swig, only to make a face. "That sour stuff."

"Ale. You should drink it anyway."

She took another swig and reached for some meat. "Aren't you eating?" *Do Carriers eat?*

"I didn't wait; I ate before. Sorry."

She took one more date and rolled the fruit back into its bundle. "I think we should save this." She placed it in the corner and then, after a moment's thought, removed Sarmin's dagger from her belt and put it together with the food. *I can't stab him without a weapon.*

"What do they sound like? The Carriers?" It frightened her to ask, and so she felt she must.

"They're always in the background. It's like standing outside a room full of people. Sometimes you can hear what they're saying, sometimes you can't." Beyon arranged the silks and blankets into a comfortable pallet. He held out an arm to her, and she lay down facing him, watching his eyes. Carrier eyes were blank and dead. His were tired but alive, and they crinkled when he smiled.

"It's still me," he said, tracing her cheekbone with his thumb.

"I know."

"And you're still frightened."

"Not of you."

"Then because you feel trapped in here?"

She spoke without thinking. "I've been trapped since my father decided to send me to Nooria."

Beyon said nothing, only running his finger across her bottom lip.

"What are you doing?"

"If you have to ask, I'm not doing it right."

Mesema thought of Banreh and the touch of his skin. She remembered how his lips sent a shock through her body. She wondered what kissing Sarmin might have felt like. She hadn't given up on her prince just yet.

"You aren't going to kiss me very hard again, are you?"

"No."

She looked down at his chest. "Shouldn't I touch our marks together?"

"No. I'm all right."

"When you were out, did you happen to see the stars?"

He withdrew his hand and pillowed it under his head. "I've been thinking about what we discussed before. About Tuvaini being the emperor."

"Oh?"

"Sarmin would be better."

"What about you?"

Beyon looked down, and Mesema felt her stomach twist. She searched for words. "What about the desert? Just yesterday you said…" When he didn't respond, she kept talking. "Sarmin is… He's not used to people."

"You can help him with that."

"I would be stuck in the women's wing."

"You wouldn't have to be. My mother wasn't. Mesema, promise me you will help him."

Mesema squeezed her eyes shut. Too many promises—to Eldra, then Sarmin, now Beyon—too many to keep, and no way to fulfil them. She thought of Eldra's feather, so far away now, at the bottom of her trunk in the ocean room. She'd meant to have it in her hand the day she stopped the pattern.

She couldn't stop it. She never would.

"Mesema."

"All right." She put a hand over her mouth to keep from crying.

"Thank you," he said, closing his eyes. "I'm just going to rest for a minute now."

He fell silent, and she watched the play of light over his marks. She watched his breath rise and fall in his patterned chest. She had failed him; she never should have agreed to hide in this coffin. Now he would die. She watched him and she waited.

CHAPTER THIRTY-EIGHT

On the fifth day Grada walked another ten miles along the riverbanks, keeping east of the great army. The towns of Colla and Santarch came and went. She watched the dhows, low in the water, burdened with wheat and dates and salt and timber. Merchants passed her in caravans, some a hundred waggons long. None but the drivers so much as noticed her, and even the drivers had nothing but crude jests for a woman in the robes of an Untouchable.

Grada paid them no heed. She carried a prince within her, though he was distracted of late. She wondered about his dying friend.

At the Needle Stone Grada took the mountain road and left the river behind. Only the outpost of Migido lay before her now; beyond that nothing but the vastness of the desert to the west, and to the north, the badlands that would eventually give way to the grass and plains of the Felt.

Travellers were few and far apart on the mountain road. She kept her eyes on the dunes, where the desert lapped against the rocks. The sun beat at her, its brightness almost too fierce to bear, but still she watched the dunes: nomads roamed out there, and bandits, and worse, evil men who preyed on the traffic between one oasis and the next. Cerani patrols kept the mountain road safer than the desert, but it was still not secure.

MAZARKIS WILLIAMS

The heat stifled and dried. The sweat left her without ever making her damp. She arrived at each well as parched as the strips of mutton that sustained her. She filled her stomach until it hurt and filled the skins near to bursting, but it was only ever just enough to reach the next waterhole.

The road became lonely. Travelling by day she saw no one. Sarmin always filled her, though the palace held his attention now—and perhaps the yellow-haired girl, too. She began to hunger for company, and pushed herself harder to reach Migido.

Mesema ran her finger along Beyon's marks as he slept. Her moon-patterned finger picked up whispers and images of those the pattern had taken. A child here, begging for bread; a woman there, opening herself to a lover; a man, whispering secrets to his priest. All these lives had been lost, absorbed by shapes and lines, worked into the obscure plan of the Pattern Master. She riffled through them, a thousand thousand stories, too many for any storyteller to recall. Her throat tightened with sorrow.

"Can you feel them?"

Beyon's voice startled her. She looked into his eyes. Still brown. Still alive. "I can feel them. It's not what you said, it's not sin written here. It's just... people."

"He took them all."

"I know."

"He won't take me."

Mesema felt as if she could breathe at last. "Thank the Hidden God. I thought you'd given up." One less death, one less promise to keep. Beyon would be alive. She smiled and pressed her lips against his in an impulsive kiss. "We'll fight."

But there was something sad about his smile. "We will."

"This is good!" She touched their lips together again, three short happy kisses. Hope. *This is what we've been missing.*

"This is very good," he agreed, kissing her back, long and slow. He drew one hand up her thigh, and her breath caught in her throat, relief transforming into something new. She felt his breath against her cheek, his heart beating under her fingers.

"There's still hope, while we live," she whispered.

CHAPTER THIRTY-NINE

"Beyon remains missing, Your Majesty."
Tuvaini let his gaze slide across the throne room. The royal guards stood motionless at their stations. From the throne the place looked very different this morning: an acre of woven rugs, worked velvet, gold thread, the glitter of gems from statuettes and trinkets in the wall niches, Cerani history stitched on tapestries and stretching back into a faded past. The luxury of Tahal's day had replaced Beyon's ascetic taste, but having it all back, owning it all, pleased him less than he had imagined.

"And has Master Herran no report of Eyul since yesterday?"

"Nothing new, Magnificence."

Eyul had killed Beyon's wives and run into the secret ways. There could be no doubt he turned traitor. He'd kidnapped the horsegirl, too, if Arigu's men were to be believed. Tuvaini could only hope he'd perished somewhere in the darkness, by accident or Carrier, and good riddance. But if Eyul were dead, where were Beyon and the girl? It made him uneasy.

Arigu had marched away. He'd left three days ago, his men forming a long desert train. They would go to the Wastes and organise the horsemen there. The savage chief would have to accept that his daughter had died during the succession, an unfortunate accident. A misunderstanding. The war would begin soon, the fight for a greater empire. It was too late for him to refuse.

"Have you sent to the Islands for my personal guard?" Tuvaini asked.

"I have, Your Majesty."

Tuvaini would breathe easier with the unquestioned loyalty of slave-bred sword-sons around him. With the sword-sons you got what you paid for, and he could pay for a lot.

"Send for Nessaket. I would have her attend me." He liked the sound of that. Let her wait on him and wonder when their marriage might be.

The grand doors opened a crack to admit the herald.

"Astronomer Kleggan has arrived. He seeks audience with Emperor Tuvaini, seventh son of the Reclaimer, Lord of Cerana, Master of the Islands and King across the Sea." The last title represented his claim to Yrkmir.

Tuvaini raised his left hand, and the herald returned to escort the astronomer to the throne. He was both dark and fair in the way of the Westerners, and walked with a conqueror's stride, proud.

"Majesty." The astronomer prostrated himself.

Tuvaini sat back in the throne and opened his hands. "I have sent for you to read my future." He closed his eyes for a moment. He saw Sarmin's face, pale, mad, and at his shoulder, Beyon, honey-gold and fierce, with the look of eagles. Two of the lives he had paid for an uncomfortable throne and Arigu's wars. Something was wrong—there was some piece forgotten, or unlooked-for.

Around the circumference of the throne room lanterns flickered as if a wind had circled the chamber. Tuvaini looked up and studied the room. Something was wrong. Something was coming.

A tremour ran through the palace, vibrating through Tuvaini's soles, through the throne, rattling the jewelled statues in their niches.

The grand doors opened again, and again the herald stepped through. This time he was unsteady, his head bowed.

"A man from the desert seeks audience with Emperor Tuvaini… seventh son of—"

"A commoner from the desert?" Azeem turned in disbelief. "What insolence is this?"

Tuvaini kept his voice calm and low, though ice ran through his veins. "What manner of man?"

For the longest time the herald said nothing, then he started, "Lord—"

The herald coughed, or wept, Tuvaini couldn't tell. Then he raised his face, and across every inch the pattern blazed in blue and red. "Someone old, Majesty. Very old."

The great doors of the throne room swung inwards. The carvings of the gods fell in splinters as if invisible knives pared them away, and in their place was the pattern. The herald fell to one side and a man entered, tall and vital but wrapped about with something ancient, unseen and powerful.

Tuvaini clutched at the armrests of his throne. His voice dried in his throat.

The man wore desert robes, and his long hair fell across it, whiter than the cloth. Where he walked, the weave of the rugs changed as the pattern followed in his wake.

Unchallenged, he reached the middle of the chamber, stopped, and smiled.

Tuvaini found his voice at last. "I know you: you are the hermit, the-man-who-sees. Why have you come here?" His words broke the silence, and the royal guard drew their swords.

"I have come for what is mine," the Pattern Master said.

A dozen threats hurried across Tuvaini's mind, but in the end he asked simply, "And what is that?"

At the doorway more guards were massing, among them the priest of Herzu and the tall figure of General Lurish.

"Why, the throne, of course," the Pattern Master said.

Tuvaini felt his lips twitch. He stood and took a step to the edge of the dais. "And by what right would you stake such a claim?" Better to gain some time, let more soldiers gather, and await the arrival of the Tower mages.

"By the right that you have established for me"—the Pattern Master raised his voice—"*Grandson*. Great-grandson, I should say."

A laugh broke from Tuvaini, but a cold hand rested on his chest. "Any fathers of my grandfathers are dust. My own father was seventy years old when he died."

"Even so," the Pattern Master said, "I am of the line: a second son put aside until the true faith of Mogyrk came and opened doors for everyone."

The High Priests of Mirra and Herzu had shouldered through the guardsmen at the door now, and there were others, summoned from their temples by the commotion. Behind them Tuvaini could see the young wind-sworn mage who had slighted him at the tower.

"You lie!" And if he did not, Tuvaini would make it a lie; he felt no kinship with this desert man.

The Pattern Master spread his hands. "I would not expect my word to put me upon the empire's throne. There are paths to the truth, paths known by the holy and the wise. I am prepared to accept the judgement of your priests and mages, sworn before their gods and their duty to the people of Cerana."

Tuvaini took a step back and felt the hard edge of the throne pressing behind his knees. His plans ran like sand through his fingers. He knew then what Beyon had felt in that moment before he fled. Tuvaini saw his enemy's plan as though it were laid upon a Settu board before him. The Pattern Master had made his Push, and the tiles were falling.

"Have you an objection to their judgement?" the Pattern Master asked. "Perhaps you wish to summon the council once more?"

Tuvaini shook his head. He reached out, touching the air before him, searching for anything, any straw to clutch.

"Your heir," he said. "If it is true, then I am still your heir."

"How fortunate, then, that you have no brothers." The Pattern Master smiled and advanced on the throne.

CHAPTER FORTY

Sarmin had known of the Pattern Master's arrival before word came from Govnan. He knew it by the pricking of his thumbs, and by the ache in his bones. Govnan's voice came on the wind, blowing into the tower room. The Tower had tested the Pattern Master's blood and found his story to be true.

Sarmin shivered. This was a violation. Four lifetimes ago, the Pattern Master had paced this same room. He had been named Helmar then, second son of the Reclaimer's heir, spared the Knife by the Tower because of his latent talents and secured—*preserved*—against an uncertain future.

Sarmin had wasted away for fifteen years; young Helmar had spent only his childhood here, for in Yrkmir's final incursion the palace had been sacked and the boy prince taken. Records of his existence had been lost to all but the mages. Until now.

Sarmin wondered what had become of the men who took Helmar. He wondered what had passed from them to the stolen prince. *What did they make of you, Helmar? What did you learn in the cold mountain lands to bring back to the desert? How are you not yet dead?*

"He is like me." Sarmin didn't want to speak aloud, but the words needed space. He didn't want to talk to an empty room, or to Eyul's unconscious

319

form. When you speak to no one, madness comes tapping at your door. "He is me—a me who was given a chance. A me who crossed the threshold and went outside once more."

He reached under his pillow for the dacarba, the knife he'd taken from Tuvaini. It felt so long ago that he had set his hand upon the hilt and pulled it free. His fingers found only silk and for a panicked moment he scrabbled to find the knife, then he relaxed. Mesema had it. He had given it to her when she left him.

When she left him. She was Beyon's now. And Grada was gone, too, picking her way along the edges of the desert. He had sent her away. Now he was alone. Not even the angels and demons spoke to him.

"When did you find the pattern, Helmar?" Sarmin lay back and rested his head on the coolness of a pillow. "When did you begin the Many? What number of lives have you sewn into your plans?"

Sarmin thought of the pattern, marked across his brother's chest, spreading like a cancer, consuming him. He thought of the child who had spent so many empty days in this very room. *Did you watch the Sayakarva window, and imagine what you would see if it ever opened?*

"I should be angry, too," he said. "I should want to make them all my toys, to play with, and to break. You have a right, Helmar." He thought of Pelar and his ball, of his brothers, almost blurred together now as memories frayed with time. "You have a right."

Beyon whispered in her ear.

Mesema stirred against the silks, noticing his arm no longer cradled her head. Her legs were twisted together, instead of between his. No matter; she was hungry and tired and she wanted to dream about her mother's spiced lamb in a pot. She curled up, but Beyon would not stop whispering, gripping her shoulder tight and pulling her from her mother's longhouse.

"—can't keep him out. He is here—"

"What?" Through her eyelids she could sense the light of day. She didn't hear anyone else in the room. Her bladder felt heavy. She stirred some more, remembering the night past, feeling heat rise in her cheeks. Dirini had told her much of what to expect of men, but she hadn't expected Beyon. She had been advised that her first time would be unpleasant, but Beyon had been patient and considerate. She would not have guessed that of him when they had first met in the desert.

He continued to speak. She pulled silk over her nakedness as she listened. His voice sounded strained, as if part of him didn't want to talk any more. "—the Pattern Master. I can hear him talking to me—"

Something cold slithered in Mesema's stomach and she fell still, barely breathing. She didn't want to open her eyes.

"I won't make it to Sarmin, Zabrina."

We should have gone yesterday. Last night.

"The Pattern Master is strong; I can feel him. Find Sarmin—I can tell they don't know about him—"

"But we were all going to fight together." She could still taste the salt of his skin, feel the wetness between her legs where he had been inside her. "You're the emperor." *Perhaps the father of my child.*

"Not any more." He released her shoulder. "In the secret ways, go straight until you reach the double bridge. Then climb the stairs, turn right and cross two more bridges. Use your dagger to open the door."

"Listen. You said that your men wait in the desert, in the hidden spot where the zabrina flowers. We can go—"

"Repeat the path to Sarmin's room to me."

She let a sob escape, then repeated his directions. "Straight to the double bridge, all the way up, right, two bridges. Use the dagger."

"Good." She felt his lips on her forehead, warm and soft. Alive. "I'm glad I met you, Mesema Windreader."

Silence.

"Beyon?" She kept her eyes shut tight. "Your Majesty?"

Now she opened them, and watched the sunlight play on Beyon's half-carved face upon the ceiling. He had turned the lid again, opened it so that she could get out and leave him behind. "Beyon. Listen. *Listen.*"

She heard a liquid sound that did not belong in this place of stone and silk.

"*Beyon.*" She did not want to look, but she had to.

Beyon lay at the other end of the tomb, one hand covering the gash in his throat. Blood pulsed over his robes and soaked into the silk that lay across their marble bed. The ruby-hilted dagger dropped from his other hand. He tried to wave her off, but it was as if his arm had grown too heavy. As their eyes met, his lost their focus and grew dark: Carrier eyes. Dead eyes.

"Beyon!" Tears wet her cheeks. There was so much blood, more blood than had come from Jakar or Eldra. It ran through the valleys in the silk and pooled around her knees. Even knowing it was too late to save him, she put her hands to his throat, pressing down, trying to keep the blood from leaving him. The pattern spiraled around her skin, climbing to her elbows, purple, red and blue—

She fell into it.

A roar filled her ears, grand and terrifying, like the sound of a flood coming down the mountain.

The Tower— Govnan— Find another way— Kitchens and hot bread— It hurts too much, so much— I was pretty, I had a lover— No way in, continue digging, always— The Tower— Beyon is gone— Find another way— My little girl ran there, among the— So much blood— The horsegirl—

Mesema reached out for a way back to Beyon's tomb, to find some thread to pull herself from the river of voices, but the current took her, careless of her strength, dragging her under and through the darkness, passing her from eye to eye, body to body, seeing corridor, desert, river, alley, and church. She tossed through a cascade of lives, searching for a set of words or images she could put together into a pattern that made sense. And then she heard a cool, amused voice, rising above the incoherence to address her.

"You have lost control, visitor. With Beyon's sacrifice my power has become too much for you at last. Come to me now and show yourself."

She drifted, gathering the bits of herself together as the images paraded past her eyes.

The speaker became angry. "You can no longer hide from me, Govnan. My Carriers will find a way into your Tower. They will tear it down from the inside."

He is guessing! He does not know who I—

"Not Govnan, then?"

Mesema was shocked into silence, afraid to think lest the Master hear her.

"It matters not." The Master affected boredom, but she sensed something wrong in him—something had not gone to his plan. She did not allow her mind to reflect on what that might be. "Your self will soon disappear within us. You will take your form and your place as the design requires."

"No," she said, surprising herself, "I do not belong in your pattern."

"A girl!" The Master laughed.

"What did you mean, Beyon's sacrifice?" she asked. "How did you make Beyon climb in his tomb and kill himself?"

"I didn't. He did that because it had to happen, because the pattern required it."

"But the pattern is yours."

A pause. The Master's attention was briefly elsewhere. "I wanted a girl-mage, but she was taken from me. One more hides in the Tower. But you are not that one, I think."

"I am not a mage."

"Tell me, girl-not-a-mage, how do you plan to defy me?"

Talking with the Pattern Master allowed her to filter the other voices from her mind. Now she concentrated on finding her way out. *The hare's path.* So long ago, as she stood on the fence of her father's sheep-pen, the Hidden God had shown her the path through the Many. It began with an arc and two intersecting circles. The pattern's shapes, so terribly familiar to her eyes, could not be seen here, but she felt them brush against her mind like spiderwebs.

"I will defy you by living." She felt her way along the strings, finding the form she sought. Like a path in a maze, it might not lead where she wished; she might have to search again, and again. But each one came with an image, the view from the Carrier who held it. She discarded all the unfamiliar scenes, hoping Carriers in a specific area were somehow linked. *Alley. Sewer... No. Corridor.* Yes. She felt out, hoping for two parallel lines. And then, quickly, as she would ride Tumble through the Hair Streams, knowing her way, gaining speed, she turned at a circle, nearly done, and directly through a diamond, sensing that Carrier's surprise, seeing the memories that rose in his mind, unbidden. *I had a son. He was—* That man stood in the secret ways. *Yes.* And then she released the strings, disappearing into the web as the hare had hidden itself in the grass. This was the hardest part, letting go. *Believing.*

She had the sensation of falling, and once again she looked up at Beyon's half-finished face set in the vaulted ceiling. She felt his blood against her back, cold and sticky. *How long have I been lost?* She wiggled her fingers.

"You have betrayed yourself," said the Master, bringing back the conversation she had almost forgotten, "by speaking of our late, great emperor. I know where you are." She felt him leave her, a rough, scraping sensation, like a knife withdrawing from a wound.

She jumped up and gathered a sheet around her nakedness. The markings still covered her skin from fingertips to elbows. Beyon lay before her, his skin grey, his head tilted back, and all around him glistened the pattern—half-moon, crescent, triangle, star, two lines, circle—all in shades of red, shimmering in the unstained silk and lighting the rubies of Sarmin's dagger. She grabbed the blade, found the bundle of food and drink, and stood over him. "Goodbye, Beyon." A fierce memory of him, golden, vital, clutched her, but Beyon had gone beyond blood and broken flesh. Nothing held her to his remains.

She climbed over the side to where the pattern spread across the tiles and ran for the secret ways.

Sarmin felt it, the spilling of blood, the rushing loss of life, the death of his last brother. "Beyon!" he cried, rousing the assassin from his deathlike sleep.

"He is gone, then, the emperor." Eyul's voice creaked. He did not open his eyes.

"My brother!" Sarmin tore at his hair, hit his forehead against the wall.

Eyul spoke again. "You are the emperor now. The Knife... evil. You must find the centre..." Eyul, near-dead, trailed off. He was as still as everything else in Sarmin's room.

"Do not speak to me of evil! I know what evil is!" *Where is Mesema? Is she hurt?* "My friend needs help—the empire needs help, and I am stuck in this room."

Eyul didn't answer.

Grada is just one person. The Master commands a multitude. He could feel the pattern closing around him, suffocating him. It would not be long before the Master found him. With a groan he fled from the Master, from his tower room, from Eyul's pain and Beyon's death, from his failings and inabilities... He ran, and he found Grada.

Grada saw the vultures late on the sixth day of her journey: a distant spiral-ling of birds, black dots against the wideness of the sky. She watched them as she drew closer. So many. How many were dead, to summon such a host? The vultures circled and descended, and more flew in to take their place in the air. *Circle first, once, twice, then descend in a third loop.* A pattern.

The watchtowers of Migido came into view, black against the red eye of the setting sun. Grada walked on, her feet sore, her mouth dry, and an acid weight in her stomach.

No smoke. Sarmin had joined her, though his mind darkened with grief. Who had died? He did not say.

There should always be smoke, for cooking, for firing clay, for all the things a town needs. The shadows of Migido reached towards her, but no smoke rose from its chimneys, no lights shone from the windows. There were no beggars, no children, no dogs. Those were the outer layers of any town…

Grada reached the first house. It was dark, the door ajar.

"Hello?" Her voice sounded thin.

Don't go in. Her thought, and Sarmin's.

She walked on, along the deserted street. A soft wind rustled the leaves of fig trees as she passed. Her feet shuffled in the sand that rippled here and there over the cobbles.

The twilight thickened. The heat of the day ran from her as the sun's glow died in the west.

Silence.

"You should go around," Sarmin said. *No more pain, I can't—*

"I don't want to see." The horror of it crawled on Grada's cooling skin. She didn't want to see what the vultures were feasting upon, but she had to.

She moved towards the main square, the rough stone catching at her robes as she edged along the side of a building.

"I came through Migido when I was a little girl—my mother and I were on our way to Nooria. I remember a festival, and dancing. An old lady was kind to me." She approached the building's corner slowly, one hand brushing over the stonework.

"You should go around…" Sarmin wavered. They both treasured kindnesses. They both held a store of such precious moments, and returned to them, time and again. *Please, you should go around.*

"I—" Grada spoke out loud, not meaning to, and a dark explosion burst before her in a great rushing and screeching. Grada screamed too—

Vultures. They are just vultures.

Somewhere in his distant room, Sarmin had shouted in terror.

Grada stepped around the corner, and more vultures launched themselves skywards, squawking their annoyance. They would return at first light.

The gloom hid all detail. Grada could see the town square, clear of stalls. One camel pulled at the tether holding him to a post, but no people. It looked for a moment as though a caravan had been unloaded with the sacks laid carelessly here and there.

"No." Sarmin took it in through her eyes, and his dread and grief fell on her so hard that her legs sagged beneath her. She felt him try to turn away. "There is—" His voice broke. "There is a pattern to it."

And Grada saw it: the pattern to the bodies. The vultures had disturbed it a little, leaving a spill of entrails here, an arm yanked out there. A small child had been dragged from her position, and half a baby had been left in the open, where the birds had been clustered.

Half a baby? She felt Sarmin choking; he had seen death only twice before now. Once it had been at a distance, and the other had been a Carrier-dream.

All of a sudden the stench hit Grada, and she bent double, retching. It was as if she'd forgotten to breathe before now.

So many?

She wiped her mouth and straightened, looking around. She couldn't leave them and she feared to walk among them.

"Why?" she asked aloud. Twice a hundred corpses lay before her, arranged in a tiled pattern of square and triangle that spread out to form a circle, a mandala, like a stylised flower from a mosaic.

"The Grand Pattern needed it." Across a hundred miles she could feel the tears roll down his face.

"I don't understand!"

Sarmin showed her the Pattern Master's design, how it pierced the world, how it spanned years and miles.

"It needs to be anchored." His voice was slow now, like a litany. "The pattern needs to be anchored in the world if it is to stand; for it to endure things must be done, acts undertaken, moments that must fall just so. The patterns on the Carriers' skin are part of it, and so is this.

"And there is more." Other deaths, other patterns on sand, on grass, in blood. Even Sarmin's brothers, the last one falling just today—the source of his great sadness—all to anchor the Grand Pattern, all to give it foundation. All so a lost prince could return in triumph.

Sarmin's anger rose, and the hairs on Grada's neck stood on end. She felt it grow, a quiet storm at first, within him, within her, and the beating of her heart became a drum, a pounding on the walls of her chest.

"Oh *Helmar*!" She backed away from the square, a snarl on her lips. "Oh Helmar."

This cannot stand. Her thought, and Sarmin's.

"How can it be stopped?"

"A magic of many parts."

"Tell me," Grada said, as she turned and fled from the square.

She reached the road and began her trek through the encroaching sands, circling around the dead town. "Tell me, Sarmin."

"A magic of many parts," he repeated, and his thoughts filled her, golden and complex. "Blood against blood. I've been gathering the pieces, and you've shown me nearly everything I need."

"How can—? It isn't possible."

"I will try—and you, Grada, you must find the Mogyrk church." He sent images, vague directions based on what others had told him. "That is the source of his power. I need to see it."

"Then I shall go." A new determination rose within her and she returned to the town. She made her way to the camel. The memories she carried would show her how to ride it.

Sarmin listened: there it was again, a scraping on the other side of the secret door. He remembered when he heard the noise for the first time, so many weeks ago, when Tuvaini came through, bringing with him the promise and horror of the outside world. Then Beyon came. He felt Beyon's loss as a physical pain. He squeezed shut his eyes and gritted his teeth.

And then Mesema. *And what happened to Mesema?* The idea that she might be somewhere in the palace, afraid and alone, drove him close to madness. He was stuck here, and she...

He stood and passed Eyul's crumpled form on the bed. He'd put some wine into the man's mouth a little while ago, but he wasn't sure if it had been swallowed. He crossed the soft carpet to the hidden door and tapped, as a servant might.

"Hello? Is someone there?" He thought it safe to speak; an assassin wouldn't be fumbling with the switch.

Someone whispered, and he put his ear against the stone.

"Sarmin! It's me!"

Joy bloomed in him. "Mesema!" *My bride!* "There's a catch—Tuvaini told me once. You have to put a dagger in it, or a dacarba, right up to the hilt."

"I have your knife." After a minute something clicked and the wall swung wide. It amazed Sarmin, every time. Mesema ran in, looking wild as a legend, with a silken sheet wrapped around her, her hair hanging in tangles, and blood streaked across her cheeks. She held his dacarba in her right hand.

"Beyon's dead."

"I know."

"He took his own life to keep from joining the pattern."

Sarmin sat on his bed. He hadn't expected that—an assassin, he'd thought, or maybe some Carriers—but to take his own life, as a final act of bravery… He felt the tears come once again and wiped them away. "But it can't be. After he died, the pattern was stronger."

"Yes." The way Mesema thrust out her chin told him that she hadn't changed her mind about fighting. "His blood raised a pattern all around him. The Pattern Master—" Her bravery was short-lived. She looked past him to the assassin and gave a little cry.

Sarmin watched her face, how the lines grew longer when she was worried. "I've been giving him wine," he told her. "Do you have any healing?"

"A little." She crossed to the bed, and as she pulled up Eyul's shirt Sarmin's gaze fell with shock upon her arms. Red and blue pattern-marks spiralled from her wrist to her elbow, each shape part of the Master's plan, each line drawing them closer to the endgame. She raised a hand over the assassin's wound, but hesitated to touch it. "This will kill him."

"I think so."

"You were hurt—who healed you?"

"Govnan, but I have no way to call him." He felt it a lack in himself that he could not call on the mages, that he must wait and hope that they called to him upon the wind. And he felt a lack in himself that he could not reassure her.

Mesema took a breath and leaned over the assassin, reaching out to stroke his hair. "Poor man. Lucky he's not conscious, he can't feel the pain."

Sarmin wasn't so sure of that, but he didn't say so. Her marks drew his eye and he wanted to touch them, study them, even now. "He killed my brothers."

"Yes." She looked away, her face troubled. "I know."

"It's good to see you."

"Is it?" She fell against him then, and he felt her tears against his skin. "It's good to see you, too." They stood that way for some time, lit by the evening sun burning through the broken window, her breath tickling his neck, his hands feeling the warmth of her skin beneath the thin sheet. In all the years in this room only Grada had come this close, and that had been in a killing embrace. "The Carriers almost found me," she said. "I crouched in the dark and watched them run into the tomb to kill me."

"But you got to me," he said.

"I did."

She stepped away from him, and immediately he wanted her back again. "Sarmin, if I carried Beyon's child, would you still like me?"

A child! Someone else to love. He thought of Beyon's eyes, the way he had laughed, his strong and powerful voice. He remembered trailing behind Beyon in the halls, his brothers around him, a laughing huddle, but always behind, struggling to keep close enough to see Beyon disappear around the next corner or beyond a door. *Don't leave me,* he would always think. *Don't leave me.* "Yes," he breathed, "oh, yes." He paused. There would be no secrets from his bride. "But I love Grada, too."

She looked up at him. "That's all right. I love Banreh." He smiled and took her hand.

CHAPTER FORTY-ONE

Tuvaini tied his robes and stepped into his silken slippers. It was the fourth day of the rule of Helmar the Restorer. Azeem waited before him, as he always had, not yet marked, though the guards at the door showed stripes across the backs of their hands. He could not speak of anything with them there.

Tuvaini was now Prince Tuvaini, the descendant of the Son of Heaven, the heir to the throne. He was not entirely sure why Helmar had allowed that, or why he'd left him unmarked, so far at least. He wished for company, perhaps. He had left Nessaket free of the pattern as well, and Tuvaini was glad of it, for the sake of the child—if there really was a child. He could never be sure with Nessaket.

He slipped on his rings and bracelets, thinking of the sea. The sea came to his mind often now. With Lapella gone, all connection to his homeland had been lost. He had also lost the throne, and that was truly gone. Even if he did inherit after Helmar, this was not the city he loved, the empire he loved: thousands were already dead, and the rest were marked and silent. This was the centre of a doomed empire. It had begun its slow decline with Beyon, but Helmar's work was quicker.

He felt a lump rising in his throat, but feigned a cough instead. "Let us go to the temple." Helmar had no interest in Cerani gods, so Herzu's temple might be safe from Carrier eyes.

Azeem led the way. Travelling the corridors no longer held any pleasure for Tuvaini. It had begun with Lapella's death, a vague distaste for the mosaics and tapestries that showed the way from one grand room to another, but with Helmar's ascendance distaste had solidified to aversion, and now Tuvaini longed for the simple whitewashed walls and the natural flower gardens of his old home. He approached the temple of Herzu with relief, for the dark and ugliness felt more true.

Nessaket waited on a bench, her hair shining and straight as ever, shoulders stiff. He took his place beside her and gazed up at the golden effigy of their patron god. Azeem settled further back, near the corridor, ready to alert them should anyone else enter.

"I wait for you every day," Nessaket said.

"I have been quite busy, as you might expect."

"The last time a new emperor took the throne, the wives of the old emperor died."

"Ah, but you are not yet my wife."

She fell silent, fiddling with the sapphire charm around her neck. "We should be grateful."

"Should we?"

"Let me be frank. When one considers our treachery, this is one of the best possible outcomes. You are still an heir, and we are both unmarked."

"I see your point." He did not feel grateful.

"I want to come to the throne room today."

"Your best plan is to stay unnoticed."

She tugged at her necklace. "I am no ordinary woman, to wait in a gilded room!"

"He is no ordinary man—you think to charm him, to dazzle him with your beauty? I would guess him immune to such tactics. This is no game."

"As you said, I am not your wife yet, and you cannot command me."

"Your life is yours to waste, but our child—" *Truly, the last thing I have to lose.*

"Our child's life depends on what we are able to do next, and that depends on knowing everything we can know about him—including whether he can be swayed by a woman!"

She thinks to betray me. She will marry the hermit if she can. Tuvaini looked once more at the god-statue towering over them in the dark. "Do as you will. I care not." The lie felt sour on his lips as he left the temple and made his way to the throne room.

Mesema crept along the kitchen corridors. Wearing a coarse sack and with her hair pulled back, she could pass for a toilet-keeper or offal-bearer. She left the marks on her arms exposed—all the servants bore marks now, and she would look suspicious without them. She held in her hand a bucket full of water. Cheese, bread, and dried fruits were hidden inside her rough clothes, secured within a filthy linen sash.

The disguise had been Sarmin's idea; he had told her how Grada had sneaked out of the palace after he freed her, dressed in clothes from the Maze and carrying a bucket of slops, so when the last of Govnan's food had been eaten, she had ripped a hole in the bag and pulled it over her head.

Now Mesema moved quickly, acting as if her filthy business couldn't wait. A soldier approached, his eyes blank and unfocused, and she bent her head, hiding her own eyes, her heart racing. She nearly screamed when his arm brushed her shoulder, but then he moved on, turning into another corridor. Even in the Pattern Master's new order, the ones who dealt in blood and shit were not fit to be acknowledged.

She was frightened, but thirst and hunger were driving her even more. Govnan sent word on the air that he could not leave the Tower, surrounded as it was by Carriers. Sarmin could not leave his room, though he would not tell her why. Eyul, the expert at sneaking, could not move at all. And so it fell to her to find food and water. She climbed a staircase and paused, sending her senses out for a moment. She hadn't yet learned to stop search-ing for Beyon with her moon-mark. Then she continued on, up the tower stairs, to her prince. At the door she rapped twice, quickly, then paused, then gave a third rap.

Sarmin opened the door and smiled. "That was fast."

She laid the food out on his pattern-carved table, then rushed over to Eyul. His lips were peeling and his tongue was thrust out between his front teeth. She dipped a ladle in the bucket and dribbled some water in his mouth.

Sarmin chewed on a piece of bread. "I have to join Grada now."

Mesema nodded, though his times with Grada unsettled her. He stared at nothing, and sometimes talked out loud, even of intimate things. She picked up some food and started nibbling some cheese.

Sarmin sat on the bed and went into his trance. When he joined Grada, a peaceful look came over his face.

Mesema looked at Eyul instead. She couldn't understand what held him here—he should be dead with those injuries, but instead he still suffered. He was rarely lucid; when they were open, his fever-bright eyes watched Sarmin. But now he looked at her and his cracked lips moved.

She moved in closer, to hear his whisper.

"How is evil destroyed?" Broken ghosts of words from an over-dry tongue. The stench of his suppurating wound stung her eyes.

He spoke again. "Only with the emperor's Knife." He took one deep, rattling breath, then fell quiet. She put a hand lightly on his chest, but just when she thought he had stopped, he took another ragged breath. This was the end. She sat on the bed and held his hand, remembering a lullaby her mother used to sing to her. She found the notes, putting into it her own grief, her own hope, and her own love. His mouth curled into something close to a smile, and she thought he was comforted.

Grada stopped on the leeward side of the dune and clambered from her camel. The trip had gone well, overall. She'd seen no bandits, nor Carriers. She'd found all the waterholes as she followed the common path—it made sense to stay on that road, since others who went from waterhole to waterhole had also seen the church.

And she saw it now. "My Prince," she called. She climbed to the top of the dune and lay down just behind the crest. The church rose high on the other side; if anyone was standing in that tall white point they would see her. No one shouted a warning or came after her, so she raised her head to take a better look.

All lay quiet, save for the wind blowing sand across the white stone. She could see nothing through the narrow windows, and the door was shut tight.

"Grada." Sarmin filled her mind. She could hear a woman singing. Strange.

"Should I go in, my Prince?"

I don't want you to go in. Sarmin's thought. "I think you should." Grada took a deep breath and stood.

"His pattern has more than one centre, but this is an important one, a centre of his faith, of his vision. The tomb where my brother died—that's another centre. When he joins them, when his bridge is complete, his power in the palace will be total."

"How do I break it?" As Grada skittered down the dune, sand spilled under her sandals.

"I'm not sure. We need to look inside."

The door was taller than it had looked from a distance. It rose to twice her height and came to a sharp point at the top. She smelled myrrh and candles. She'd been to a temple of Mirra once and it had been filled with the same scent. The hasp lifted without resistance, and she pushed the door open.

A long, vaulted hall lay before her, picked out in harsh relief of light and shadow. Everywhere lay the pieces of men and women, nomads from the look of their clothes. Here was a leg; there, a red-stained hand. She gagged, but the resin-smell of the incense helped her keep her stomach. A blood-writ pattern covered the floor and the walls, gleaming where the sun found it, and in the centre, an old man pulled himself up from a chair and straightened his legs beneath him, waiting to greet her. She crossed the hall, stepping over limbs, trying not to meet the glassy stares of the severed heads. Fear made her hands tremble, but no terrors seized her, only sorrow for the dead. She knew the Pattern Master, as he knew her: he had written his story across her and through her in his own hand.

The sweat ran cold between her breasts and the scar across her back ached as if Govnan had never worked his magic there. She stopped when she came close enough to speak.

The man's white hair fell in greasy locks to his shoulders. A milky film clouded his eyes, and his head made little jerks, turning to the side every few seconds as if slapped. But his mouth curled in a snarl, and he spoke as a younger man would: "You are marked, but no longer one of mine."

This can't be, thought Sarmin. *He's supposed to be in the palace.*

Grada answered the old man. "I'm not a Carrier any more."

"Interesting. What are you doing here?"

"I'm curious about the pattern."

"More interesting." The old man snorted. "Lucky for you I don't need another body for my church." He reached for her, and in a flash of red she felt her pattern-marks writhe upon her skin, like fire ants crawling, attempting to rearrange themselves, to undo what Sarmin had done for her and more. Just as quickly she felt Sarmin changing them back, keeping her to herself, holding himself within her.

The old man gave a grunt of exasperation. "Who freed you?" Grada drew her knife and tried to slash at him, but her arm did not reach far enough. She stepped closer, but it was still the same: she could not reach him, no matter how close he appeared.

But whatever barrier had stood between them dissolved when he grabbed her knife-arm with icy fingers. He twisted and her hand went numb, the blade dropping to the stone floor. He ignored her cries and pressed a finger to one of her marks, a red triangle suspended over blue, and instantly she felt him inside her, rifling through her past as a thief would a drawer. She felt the gorge rising in her throat and could not stop it. She heaved, and vomit trickled down her lips and chin. She saw herself enter Sarmin's chamber, his brief fight, and the dagger going into his chest. Then she saw him play with her marks, fixing her. The Master watched, and as he dug his fingernails into her arm his mouth was open and drooling.

"*This* is what I missed," he hissed. "Prince Sarmin is alive." He pressed his finger on another mark. "No matter. We will kill him again."

No! Sarmin's thought, or hers? It didn't matter. She kicked out at his weak legs and was satisfied when he lost his balance and released her. She dived for her knife.

The Master laughed, rolling on the floor with the dead. "You can't kill me."

I am faster than he is, and his body is old. She backed away. "Maybe not, but I can wreck your design." She stepped over a severed arm and kicked it to the side. He did not laugh this time. Rage twisted his wet mouth as she reached down and grabbed the severed head of a woman with long, dark hair. She tossed it behind her.

"Stop that!"

"Why are there no Carriers here? Did you believe we would not think to come?" Sarmin's words were carried from the palace and over the desert to her mouth.

"There are no Carriers here because I don't need them." He found his legs once again and stood tall.

Grada saw a hand and kicked it away. She rubbed her sandal over the blood-design beneath. "You are old and weak."

"This body is old, but I am not weak. But maybe it's time for a switch. Perhaps I won't kill Prince Sarmin; maybe I should take his body instead."

Rage made her strong. She lifted a dripping torso and heaved it across the room. He had taken her body, forced her to do things… She screamed, a mindless, bloody shout, remembering the soldiers she had thrown into the chasm; remembering lying over Sarmin, pressing the knife between his ribs. She would not let the Pattern Master take Sarmin's body; she would not let him make Sarmin do those things. She ran at him, her dagger held in front of her, taking him off guard, and the blade found a home between his ribs as his legs collapsed beneath him for a second time. He fell, laughter bubbling with the blood in his mouth.

"Good girl," he said, "But you can't kill me. I am Carried." And as his blood hit the stone floor, the pattern around him glowed with new life.

CHAPTER FORTY-TWO

"No!" Sarmin leaped to his feet. Mesema looked up from where she sat on the bed with Eyul's hand cradled in her own.

"I can't beat him! I thought a pattern in blood... but that's *his* path. I can't do those things—we would just drown each other in gore! His pattern is too strong, and we've only made it stronger!" From tomb to church, Helmar to Beyon, the Grand Pattern had found its final anchor.

"Eyul is dead," she said, her voice quiet.

Sarmin looked at the old assassin. "I think he would be glad for it." Some sad note echoed inside him.

With Eyul dead, the last flaw in the pattern was removed. The design was both terrible and perfect; Sarmin could see it without closing his eyes. He felt himself drawn to its beauty, even knowing it meant the end. "The Pattern Master will use my body," he said.

Mesema drew the dacarba from her sash and folded Eyul's hands about the ruby-hilt. "Wherever the assassin has gone, let him go armed." She fell silent for a time, thinking or praying.

Sarmin looked at the assassin and wondered if he had joined Mirra or Herzu, or gone somewhere else entirely. His eyes scanned the walls, wishing that the hidden ones would show themselves again.

Mesema stirred. "We should leave this room. We have waited here too long as it is, and they will find us."

"I can't leave this room." It hurt to say it.

"So we will stay here with Eyul?" Her voice lowered, perhaps out of politeness to the corpse. "It is very hot."

"I can't leave," he said again.

"Why is that? You never told me why."

He hesitated. *Will she believe me? Will she know I am mad?* But he knew he had to tell her: *Only the truth for my princess.* "You see the gods in the ceiling, but there are also angels. And demons, on the wall."

Her head turned towards the wall, blue eyes searching.

"They prophesy for me. They told me you were coming. They told me all about you. They warn me about things, too, but of late, they are quiet."

Mesema walked to the wall, drew her hand across it. "That's why you don't leave? Because they are your family?"

He marvelled at her insight. "No—I mean, yes, but it's really because they prophesied that I would never leave. They told me I would die in this room. And when I tried to leave, tried to get to you, I… couldn't."

She stood back and squinted at the wall, her hands on her hips. "There is a pattern here."

"Yes. Can you see them? It is easier as the sun sets, when—"

Mesema picked up a chair, the one Tuvaini had sat in during his last visit. It was a narrow piece, with roses carved into the back and along the legs. Sarmin had never found it comfortable, which was why he'd made Tuvaini sit in it. She raised it over her head and crashed it against the wall. Paper split and plaster crumbled. *Zanasta!* Half his face vanished into a puff of white powder. Mesema stumbled back and picked up the chair again, hitting Aherim. The room filled with a fog of plaster dust. *Again.*

Sarmin started coughing.

Mesema could barely lift the chair now; she gripped it firmly and took runs at the wall instead. And she killed them all, angels and demons alike, and the dust settled over Eyul like a shroud.

Sarmin looked at the devastation. The faces were gone, their patterns, gone—not because of a magical working, not because of bloodshed, but because of a chair.

"Let's go," Mesema said, throwing the chair aside.

"They told me I would die here." Sarmin shook his head, dust falling from it.

Mesema shrugged. "Maybe you will. But nobody said you had to wait here to find out." She held up Eyul's Knife. "How is evil destroyed? With the emperor's Knife."

This was what Eyul had tried to tell him. He took the twisted hilt in his hand. This was his gift from Eyul and from his father. This was all he had, now. This, Grada, and Mesema. As he followed her he thought he heard his brothers cheering.

"I am very disappointed," said the Pattern Master.

Tuvaini held his sigh and fingered his empty dacarba-sheath. He still wore it, to remind himself of everything he had given up. "What has disappointed you, Your Majesty?"

The Pattern Master appeared to have gained something in the last few minutes; he looked stronger and younger. He had about him what Tuvaini's mother called "the glow of children." He leaned forwards now in his throne, glaring. "Prince Sarmin is alive."

"Impossible!" On the other side of the throne, Nessaket nearly jumped.

"I was assured of his death before I arrived here—and yet it appears you failed."

"Govnan said—" Too late, Tuvaini realised his mistake. *Govnan.* Of course. The old man had protected his precious mage-born. Tuvaini spoke with bitterness. "He is most likely taking refuge at the Tower with the High Mage."

"I think not." The Pattern Master stood and paced to the edge of the dais. He was so like Beyon that Tuvaini caught his breath. "There is enough in the prince's old room to keep him there."

Tuvaini found that ridiculous. He had spoken to the prince—he knew that the prince wanted nothing more than to leave that soft prison. But he remained silent.

Five Carriers entered the room and silently approached the throne. They always came in groups of five. They stood near Helmar, still saying nothing. It unnerved Tuvaini that they did not require speech to communicate. It made it difficult to spy; he felt crippled, robbed of a sense.

One of the Carriers handed Helmar a bundle the size of a loaf of bread. Helmar held it to his forehead in concentration. Then he threw it down and cursed in his Yrkman way, "Devil's hells! That's not the one." Tuvaini felt a thrill of pleasure at the Master's frustration.

The Master kicked the bundle over to Tuvaini. "The assassin is dead. They say this belongs to you. You didn't happen to kill Eyul and take his Knife?"

"No." Tuvaini unwrapped his gift. Inside the dirty linen lay his own dacarba, its bejewelled settings now crusted with blood. *Eyul.* He had been Tuvaini's faithful companion for many years, and despite his betrayal he still missed the man, his direct way of talking, his quiet observations. Now he would never see him again. "Where did you find this?" he asked.

"In Sarmin's room." Helmar tapped his chin absently.

"Sarmin is dead." *And nothing has changed.*

"No."

Tuvaini sheathed his dacarba, feeling a burst of excitement. His weapon felt good on his hip. Sarmin might be alive, and the Knife was missing; he didn't know why that made Helmar angry, but it was enough that it did. He glanced at Nessaket, who stared ahead, shaking. Helmar had not objected to her presence, but her behaviour now was strange. She would make it difficult for Tuvaini to decide what to do next.

I want to protect her—why do I want to protect her, even now? Tuvaini's gaze flickered out over the assembled court: nobles, servants, soldiers, and slaves all bearing colourful marks, all of them eerily silent in their courtly poses. Several reclined stiffly on cushions, belying their relaxed positions. Others stood with goblets held to their mouths, though they never sipped their wine. One held, motionless, in the pose of a court dancer. Helmar had placed them all like dolls and he, like a child, played king before them.

All of a sudden, as if pulled by some hidden string, the Carriers turned as one to the ruined doors, a communal question in the tilt of their heads. The doors swung inwards.

Nessaket rose from her chair and stumbled forwards as Prince Sarmin entered the room, trailed by a yellow-haired woman.

Sarmin stopped just inside the throne room. It hadn't changed at all since his father's time, since before he'd been put in his tower. It was strange to think that nothing had changed, that courtiers sat on the same pillows he had jumped on as a child, that one of them might sip from the same dented goblet he'd dropped when he sat in his father's lap. Even his mother stood by the throne, just as she always had, with Tuvaini on the other side.

But the resemblance was only skin-deep. The courtiers all showed marks now, and the faces they turned to him were blank. No scheming or negotiation happened here, only obedience.

And his mother hadn't ever cried like that in Tahal's time. He wondered what had upset her so. He gave her a small bow.

The Pattern Master paced on the dais. He both looked and did not look like the old man Grada had killed. That had truly been Helmar; the ancient body he wore from his days trapped in the prison that became Sarmin's. He wore a new body now; perhaps the body of a relative, for he had the same hair, the same copper eyes. He was younger and stronger—had the Master sacrificed his own son or grandson to the Pattern?

He smiled now at Sarmin. "You've brought yourself, and the mage-girl, too. I thank you for sparing me the trouble."

Carriers crowded behind them. Mesema clung to his side. Two moved forwards as one.

Helmar's eyes fell upon Mesema, and a cold rage rose within Sarmin. He spoke, trying to draw the man's attention. "You are like me, Helmar."

That surprised the Pattern Master.

I must keep him talking, keep him distracted.

"How so?"

"We were both trapped in that tower. We were both lonely. Now we want things. We're greedy."

"I don't need to want," said the Pattern Master. "Everything already belongs to me."

"Not me. Not her." They had crossed half the distance now. Sarmin didn't reach for Eyul's Knife, not yet. "Tell me, Helmar, did you leave that room? Did you step out, or were you dragged?"

The Master's open mouth quivered, but no words came.

"Were you taken?" Sarmin asked, "ripped from it? Did you leave something there—some of you? Something precious? The thing that made you whole?"

The glow of rubies drew Sarmin's eyes to the dacarba at Tuvaini's hip. Tuvaini inclined his head. His eyes sent a message, but what message, Sarmin could not tell. He kept walking, Mesema quiet at his side.

"I will wear your body, and she will bear my child." Helmar had gathered himself, but his voice lacked its old conviction. His eyes flicked over his captive audience. Tuvaini for his part turned to Helmar and frowned. *Ah, so you didn't expect him to make his own heir.* Tuvaini was his heir only until a better one came along. Sarmin knew what that felt like.

Sarmin had crossed three-quarters of the way from the doors to the throne. Mesema straightened her shoulders and let go of his arm, as they had planned. He'd felt her trembling: he knew how frightened she was, and his pride in her courage chased his own fear away as she stepped forwards, head held high. "I will bear your child, Master, if you let Sarmin go free."

Helmar laughed. "This is not your father's longhouse, girl. We do not make deals with wombs and weapons. I am the emperor, and the Master of this land. I will have both of you as I desire."

"I am marked," Mesema said, showing him her arms. "Perhaps you don't want me."

"You'll do." He was easy now, relaxing into his game.

He can't sense Beyon's child. Helmar was not all-powerful. Sarmin stepped forwards, using Mesema's body as cover as he put a hand on the hilt of Eyul's Knife. Tuvaini took a step forwards and Sarmin froze, but the vizier did not betray him. Instead he turned his head away, affecting the Master's boredom.

An ally, then. That gave Sarmin strength. Mesema took another step, and Sarmin followed behind her. As she dropped into an obeisance, Sarmin gripped the Knife-hilt harder and stepped around her. Someone whispered to him, a familiar, boyish voice: "Sarmin, we'll show you where his heart lies."

At last Helmar turned away from his audience and focused on Sarmin, a curious expression on his face. "What—?"

At that moment Tuvaini drew his dacarba and plunged it hilt-deep between Helmar's shoulders. Sarmin's mother screamed and ran from the dais.

Sarmin felt the Carriers behind him surge forwards, reaching for him, as the Master turned and wrapped a hand around Tuvaini's neck. Shapes traced themselves along the vizier's cheeks and neck, flashing in jewelled shades of blue and red, and then faded. Both men dropped to their knees. Tuvaini was limp, Helmar wheezing—then Helmar collapsed.

The Carriers stopped as one. Sarmin felt their fingers slip from his shoulders and as he edged away from them, Tuvaini sat up and examined his hands. *No, not Tuvaini. Tuvaini is dead.* The vizier's eyes turned to him, and his face looked stronger and more handsome than before. "You cannot kill me. I am Carried."

The Pattern Master got up and looked after Nessaket. Then he looked at Mesema, still prone on the floor. "This one is younger." He glanced at his own dead body. "But which body do I want? Shall I keep this one?" He laid a hand on Tuvaini's robes. "It's healthier than yours, Prince. But you are prettier."

Mesema stood quickly and moved in front of Sarmin again, hiding the Knife. He loved her then more than ever. She moved with sure, quick steps, turning one way then the other, holding the Pattern Master's eye, shielding the Knife. Sarmin caught an edge of her thoughts—*the hare, the hare, follow the hare's path*—and it puzzled him.

"Does that please you, Helmar?" he asked, "to play dress-up with others' bodies? To lose your way in strangers' flesh?"

"It pleases me to use and discard Cerani as they used and discarded me."

Such a narrow view. Again Sarmin felt disappointment in Helmar's lack of imagination. "You'll be alone once we're all dead."

"I have always been alone."

Sarmin blinked. He heard the same sad note that had sounded for Eyul, for all the men the empire had used and broken and cast aside. Mesema didn't hear it; she rushed forwards, distracting the Master, the hare still in her mind—he glimpsed an image of it racing through the pattern in wind-blown grass. Mesema knelt before Helmar and clung to his knees. "Oh please, Master, *please*!" she shouted. A sharp terror ran through Sarmin: she was touching Helmar, skin to skin, and the Master could pass into her body if he wished it. She would die, and Beyon's child with her.

But the Master's face stretched in disgust and he kicked her away, and in that moment Sarmin set pity aside and finally leaped forwards with Eyul's Knife. The whispers guided him as promised, their words shaping his muscles, driving the blade. "Raise your arm. Aim to the left. Angle it up. Just so. *Strike!*" And the dagger plunged into Helmar's chest with a flash of light. Sarmin's arm vibrated, a buzzing that shook his entire body, took his legs from under him and set his teeth to chattering. Tuvaini's corpse fell backwards against the throne, but they remained linked, the Knife in Tuvaini's chest and Sarmin's hand on the Knife. Sarmin could hear Mesema talking, shouting, far away, yet he was unable to move. The light flowed into him, and with it voices, images, desires, regrets, memories—*lives*. Every life Helmar had taken flowed into Sarmin, filling his mind with so much pain and noise that he thrashed on the dais, screaming. And still the Knife held Helmar, anchoring him to Tuvaini's dying flesh.

Darkness.

Sarmin floated, watching the thin, wasted prince convulse on the dais, and the pretty horsewoman kneel over him. Tuvaini was dead, the Knife still in his heart. The Carriers had fallen like Settu pieces after the Push, no motion left in them. He floated over the Cerani in their throne room: a useless empire for a useless people. The chatter rose in his mind like a river after the rains, and in the midst of it all, a single voice found him. "Sarmin." His father's voice. The Old Emperor, Tahal.

"Prince Sarmin is only within me. I am the Many."

"You are Sarmin."

That did not feel right, but he listened to the old man anyway.

"These lives are not yours. You must put them back."

"I am the Many. These lives belong to Us. With them we can level this city, form an ocean, travel to the stars."

"What for, Sarmin? What for? Below you lies the empire—my empire. You were saved for this moment. You must do the right thing."

"The empire is naught but blood and cruelty, sacrifice and pain. An ocean is good. A mountain is good."

"Think of all who will die."

"They will join Us."

"And the horsegirl?"

He looked down at the blonde woman and searched the Many for her name. He found the One who knew it and held that life in his mind as he spoke. "Mesema." And then he saw that the mouth of the young prince moved, and the woman gave a cry of joy and kissed his brow.

"You have put yourself back. Now for the others."

Put them back. A magic of many parts. A puzzle of many pieces.

He could feel her lips and arms, soft, nice. He remembered another woman, too. Her name was Grada. He reached out to where she trekked through the desert on camelback, the sun hot on her back, her mouth dry with thirst.

"Grada."

"My Prince!"

"The Master is dead."

Grada said nothing, only smiled in her mind and quickened her camel's pace. The other voices began to stir. The lives, the disembodied souls that he held within him began to pull apart, distinguish themselves against the Whole. The Many began to disintegrate.

He touched against them, found their pattern-places. He matched mind to body and built them again. He could not replace them all; some had been too long apart and were too broken, but he mended hundreds—a child's game of fitting shapes to holes. The men and women in the throne room stood and looked at one another in wonder. He reached out beyond that room, to the city, and then beyond to the desert, rivers and ocean. He mended thousands. Citizens returned to themselves throughout the empire. The joy rose from them and made his heart sing.

When he was finished, a piece of the Many remained in him: the ones Helmar had killed. Their lives' power persisted, their memories and regrets confused and muddled together.

"I'm sorry," he said to them. "I can't do anything for you." They did not hear him; they were dead. Helmar had stolen their lives, and now Sarmin held only an echo of what they had been. He kept their ghosts, the book of their lives written out beneath his skin, but he promised to use them wisely. They deserved no less.

"You have done well, my son." His father sounded proud. Sarmin smiled in Mesema's arms. "Now you must leave the Knife and join yourself."

"I'm in the Knife?"

"You put yourself there today, as you put me there another day, when Eyul came into the sand-city. You don't know your power, but you will, in the years ahead..." Tahal's voice grew indistinct. Sarmin heard other voices and smelled incense and wine. He opened his eyes and looked up at Mesema's face. He touched her cheek, and she smiled through her tears.

"I didn't know if you would open your eyes again," she said. Sarmin sat up and looked around the room. He'd erased the marks from his court-iers—perhaps he had erased all the marks? He would know soon enough. He stood, feeling the power of those extra lives running through his veins and in his mind. He looked at the man at the bottom of the dais,

someone he hadn't noticed before. "What is your name?"

"Azeem, Your Majesty."

"Azeem, send for Govnan in the Tower. There is much to discuss. And bring my mother to attend me."

Azeem bowed and withdrew.

And Sarmin settled into his throne.

✝

ACKNOWLEDGEMENTS

I would like to thank my agent, Ian Drury, for believing in this book, and Jo Fletcher, for taking a chance on it.

I'm thrilled Night Shade Books is my U.S. publisher and grateful for Ross Lockhart's patient support. Thanks to Allan Kausch for his careful eye, Amy Popovich for her beautiful work, and David Senior for his remarkable map.

Thanks to everyone at Quercus, Jo Fletcher Books, and Night Shade Books who completed tasks both small and large to get *The Emperor's Knife* ready for publication.

THE STORY OF SARMIN AND MESEMA
CONTINUES IN

KNIFE-SWORN

BOOK TWO OF TOWER AND KNIFE